Today's bestselling authors take you . . .

Out of This World

"INTERLUDE IN DEATH"
BY *NEW YORK TIMES* BESTSELLING AUTHOR J. D. ROBB

At a police conference off-planet, Lieutenant Eve Dallas is forced to forsake duty to take down a rogue ex-cop—and save the man she loves. . . .

"KINSMAN"
BY SUSAN KRINARD, *USA TODAY* BESTSELLING AUTHOR OF
ONCE A WOLF

Searching the universe for a missing ship, two telepaths lose themselves in each other—mind, body, and soul. . . .

"IMMORTALITY"
BY MAGGIE SHAYNE, *USA TODAY* BESTSELLING AUTHOR OF *DESTINY*

On an island in the Caribbean, a man pulls a drowning woman out of the sea, a centuries-old witch with one last wish to share with him—and one last hope. . . .

"MAGIC LIKE HEAT ACROSS MY SKIN"
BY *NEW YORK TIMES* BESTSELLING AUTHOR LAURELL K. HAMILTON

A preview of Laurell K. Hamilton's new hardcover, *Narcissus in Chains!*

It's been six months since vampire hunter Anita Blake has seen the two men in her life. Now a kidnapping brings them together—closer than a woman, a vampire, and a werewolf have ever been before. . . .

Out of This World

J. D. ROBB
LAURELL K. HAMILTON
SUSAN KRINARD
and
MAGGIE SHAYNE

JOVE BOOKS, NEW YORK

This is a work of fiction. Names, characters, places, and incidents are either the product of the author's imagination or are used fictitiously, and any resemblance to actual persons, living or dead, business establishments, events, or locales is entirely coincidental.

OUT OF THIS WORLD

A Jove Book / published by arrangement with the authors

PRINTING HISTORY
Jove edition / August 2001

All rights reserved.
Copyright © 2001 by Penguin Putnam Inc.
"Interlude in Death" copyright © 2001 by Nora Roberts.
"Kinsman" copyright © 2001 by Susan Krinard.
Excerpt from *Secret of the Wolf* copyright © 2001 by Susan Krinard.
"Immortality" copyright © 2001 by Margaret Benson.
Excerpt from *The Gingerbread Man* copyright © 2001 by Margaret Benson.
"Magic Like Heat Across My Skin" (from *Narcissus in Chains*) copyright © 2001 by Laurell K. Hamilton.

This book, or parts thereof, may not be reproduced in any form without permission. For information address: The Berkley Publishing Group, a division of Penguin Putnam Inc., 375 Hudson Street, New York, New York 10014.

Visit our website at
www.penguinputnam.com

ISBN: 0-515-13109-1

A JOVE BOOK®
Jove Books are published by The Berkley Publishing Group, a division of Penguin Putnam Inc., 375 Hudson Street, New York, New York 10014. JOVE and the "J" design are trademarks belonging to Penguin Putnam Inc.

PRINTED IN THE UNITED STATES OF AMERICA

10 9 8 7 6 5 4 3 2 1

Contents

Interlude in Death

J. D. Robb

Learning is not child's play;
we cannot learn without pain.
                    —ARISTOTLE

Happy is the child whose father
goes to the devil.
     —SIXTEENTH-CENTURY PROVERB

1

The faces of murder were varied and complex. Some were as old as time and the furrows scoring them filled with the blood spilled by Cain. One brother's keeper was another's executioner.

Of course, it had been rather elementary to close that particular case. The list of suspects had been, after all, pretty limited.

But time had populated the earth until by the early spring of 2059 it so crawled with people that they spilled out from their native planet to jam man-made worlds and satellites. The skill and ability to create their own worlds, the sheer nerve to consider doing so, hadn't stopped them from killing their brothers.

The method was sometimes more subtle, often more vicious, but people being people could, just as easily, fall back on ramming a sharpened stick through another's heart over a nice patch of lettuce.

The centuries, and man's nature, had developed more than alternative ways to kill and a variety of victims and motives. They had created the need and the means to punish the guilty.

The punishing of the guilty and the demand for justice for the innocent became—perhaps had been since that first extreme case of sibling rivalry—an art and a science.

These days, murder got you more than a short trip to the Land of Nod. It shut you up in a steel and concrete cage where you'd have plenty of time to think about where you went wrong.

But getting the sinner where justice deemed he belonged was the trick. It required a system. And the system demanded its rules, techniques, manpower, organizations, and loopholes.

And the occasional seminar to educate and inform.

As far as Lieutenant Eve Dallas was concerned, she'd rather face a horde of torked-out chemi-heads than conduct a seminar on murder. At least the chemi-heads wouldn't embarrass you to death.

And as if it wasn't bad enough that she'd been drafted to attend the Interplanetary Law Enforcement and Security Conference, as if it wasn't horrifying enough that her own commander had ordered her to give a seminar, the whole ball of goddamn wax had to take shape off-planet.

Couldn't hold the sucker in New York, Eve thought as she lay facedown on the hotel bed. Just couldn't find one spot on the whole fucking planet that could suit up. Nope, just had to send a bunch of cops and techs out into space.

God, she hated space travel.

And of all the places in the known universe, the site-selection committee had to dump them on the Olympus Resort. Not only was she a cop out of her element, but she was a cop out of her element giving a seminar in one of the conference rooms in one of the ridiculously plush hotels owned by her husband.

It was mortifying.

Sneaky son of a bitch, she thought, and wondered if any of the muscles and bones in her body that had dissolved during landing on Olympus had regenerated. He'd planned it, he'd worked it. And now she was paying for it.

She had to socialize, attend meetings. She had to—dear Christ—give a speech. And in less than a week, she would have to get back on that fancy flying death trap of Roarke's and face the journey home.

Since the idea of that made her stomach turn over, she considered the benefits of living out the rest of her life on Olympus.

How bad could it be?

The place had hotels and casinos and homes, bars, shops. Which meant it had people. When you had people, bless their mercenary hearts, you had crime. You had crime, you needed cops. She could trade in her New York Police and Security badge for an Interplanetary Law Enforcement shield.

"I could work for ILE," she muttered into the bedspread.

"Certainly." On the other side of the room, Roarke finished studying a report on one of his other properties. "After a while, you wouldn't think twice about zipping from planet to space station to satellite. And you'd look charming in one of those blue-and-white uniforms and knee-high boots."

Her little fantasy fizzed. Interplanetary meant, after all, interplanetary. "Kiss my ass."

"All right." He walked over, bent down and laid his lips on her butt. Then began working his way up her back.

Unlike his wife, he was energized by space travel.

"If you think you're getting sex, pal, think again."

"I'm doing a lot of thinking." He indulged himself with the long, lean length of her. When he reached the nape of her neck, he rubbed his lips just below the ends of her short, disordered cap of hair. And feeling her quick shiver, grinned as he flipped her over.

Then he frowned a little, skimming a finger along the shallow dent in her chin. "You're a bit pale yet, aren't you?"

Her deep-golden-brown eyes stared sulkily into his. Her mouth, wide, mobile, twisted into a sneer. "When I'm on my feet again, I'm going to punch you in that pretty face of yours."

"I look forward to it. Meanwhile." He reached down, began unbuttoning her shirt.

"Pervert."

"Thank you, Lieutenant." Because she was his, and it continuously delighted him, he brushed a kiss over her torso, then tugged off her boots, stripped off her trousers. "And I hope we'll get to the perversion part of our program shortly. But for now." He picked her up and carried her out of the bedroom. "I think we'll try a little postflight restorative."

"Why do I have to be naked?"

"I like you naked."

He stepped into a bathroom. No, not a bathroom, Eve

mused. That was too ordinary a word for this oasis of sensual indulgence.

The tub was a lake, deep blue and fed by gleaming silver tubes twined together in flower shapes. Rose trees heavy with saucer-size white blooms flanked the marble stairs that led into a shower area where a waterfall already streamed gently down gleaming walls. The tall cylinders of mood and drying tubes were surrounded by spills of flowers and foliage, and she imagined that anyone using one of them would look like a statue in a garden.

A wall of glass offered a view of cloudless sky turned to gold by the tint of the privacy screen.

He set her down on the soft cushions of a sleep chair and walked to one of the curved counters that flowed around the walls. He slid open a panel in the tiles and set a program on the control pad hidden behind it.

Water began to spill into the tub, the lights dimmed, and music, softly sobbing strings, slid into the air.

"I'm taking a bath?" she asked him.

"Eventually. Relax. Close your eyes."

But she didn't close her eyes. It was too tempting just to watch him as he moved around the room, adding something frothy to the bath, pouring some pale gold liquid into a glass.

He was tall and had an innate sort of grace. Like a cat did, she thought. A big, dangerous cat that only pretended to be tame when it suited his mood. His hair was black and thick and longer than her own. It spilled nearly to his shoulders and provided a perfect frame for a face that made her think of dark angels and doomed poets and ruthless warriors all at once.

When he looked at her with those hot and wildly blue eyes, the love inside her could spread so fast and strong, it hurt her heart to hold it.

He was hers, she thought. Ireland's former bad boy who had made his life, his fortune, his place by hook or—well— by crook.

"Drink this."

He liked to tend her, she mused as she took the glass he offered. She, lost child, hard-ass cop, could never figure out if it irritated or thrilled her. Mostly, she supposed, it just baffled her.

"What is it?"

"Good." He took it back from her, sipped himself to prove it.

When she sampled it, she found that he was right, as usual. He walked behind the chair, the amusement on his face plain when he tipped her back and her gaze narrowed with suspicion. "Close your eyes," he repeated and slipped goggles over her face. "One minute," he added.

Lights bled in front of her closed lids. Deep blues, warm reds in slow, melting patterns. She felt his hands, slicked with something cool and fragrant, knead her shoulders, the knotted muscles of her neck.

Her system, jangled from the flight, began to settle. "Well, this doesn't suck," she murmured, and let herself drift.

He took the glass from her hand as her body slipped into the ten-minute restorative program he'd selected. He'd told her one minute.

He'd lied.

When she was relaxed, he bent to kiss the top of her head, then draped a silk sheet over her. Nerves, he knew, had worn her out. Added to them the stress and fatigue of coming off a difficult case and being shot directly into an off-planet assignment that she detested, and it was no wonder her system was unsettled.

He left her sleeping and went out to see to a few minor details for the evening event. He'd just stepped back in when the timer of the program beeped softly and she stirred.

"Wow." She blinked, scooped at her hair when he set the goggles aside.

"Feel better?"

"Feel great."

"A little travel distress is easy enough to fix. The bath should finish it off."

She glanced over, saw that the tub was full, heaped with bubbles that swayed gently in the current of the jets. "I just bet it will." Smiling, she got up, crossed the room to step down into the sunken pool. And lowering herself neck-deep, she let out a long sigh.

"Can I have that wine or whatever the hell it is?"

"Sure." Obliging, he carried it over, set it on the wide lip behind her head.

"Thanks. I've gotta say, this is some . . ." She trailed off, pressed her fingers to her temple.

"Eve? Headache?" He reached out, concerned, and found himself flipping into the water with her.

When he surfaced, she was grinning, and her hand was cupped possessively between his legs. "Sucker," she said.

"Pervert."

"Oh, yeah. Let me show you how I finish off this little restorative program, ace."

Restored, and smug, she took a quick spin in the drying tube. If she was going to live only a few more days before crashing into a stray meteor and being burned to a cinder by exploding rocket fuel on the flight back home, she might as well make the best of it.

She snagged a robe, wrapped herself in it, and strolled back into the bedroom.

Roarke, already wearing trousers, was scanning what looked like encoded symbols as they scrolled across the screen of the bedroom tele-link. Her dress, at least she assumed it was a dress, was laid out on the bed.

She frowned at the sheer flow of bronze, walked over to finger the material. "Did I pack this?"

"No." He didn't bother to glance back, he could see her suspicious scowl clearly enough in his mind. "You packed several days' worth of shirts and trousers. Summerset made some adjustments in your conference wardrobe."

"Summerset." The name hissed like a snake between her lips. Roarke's major domo was a major pain in her ass. "You let him paw through my clothes? Now I have to burn them."

Though he'd made considerable adjustments to her wardrobe in the past year, there were, in his opinion, several items left that deserved burning. "He rarely paws. We're running a little behind," he added. "The cocktail reception started ten minutes ago."

"Just an excuse for a bunch of cops to get shit-faced. Don't see why I have to get dressed up for it."

"Image, darling Eve. You're a featured speaker and one of the event's VIPs."

"I hate that part. It's bad enough when I have to go to your deals."

"You shouldn't be nervous about your seminar."

"Who said I'm nervous?" She snatched up the dress. "Can you see through this thing?"

His lips quirked. "Not quite."

"Not quite" was accurate, she decided. The getup felt thin as a cloud, and that was good for comfort. The flimsy layers of it barely shielded the essentials. Still, as her fashion sense could be etched on a microchip with room to spare, she had to figure Roarke knew what he was doing.

At the sound of the mixed voices rolling out of the ballroom as they approached, Eve shook her head. "I bet half of them are already in the bag. You're serving prime stuff in there, aren't you?"

"Only the best for our hardworking civil servants." Knowing his woman, Roarke took her hand and pulled her through the open doorway.

The ballroom was huge, and packed. They'd come from all over the planet, and its satellites. Police officials, technicians, expert consultants. The brains and the brawn of law enforcement.

"Doesn't it make you nervous to be in the same room with, what, about four thousand cops?" she asked him.

"On the contrary, Lieutenant," he said laughingly. "I feel very safe."

"Some of these guys probably tried to put you away once upon a time."

"So did you." Now he took her hand and, before she could stop him, kissed it. "Look where it got you."

"Dallas!" Officer Delia Peabody, decked out in a short red dress instead of her standard starched uniform, rushed up. Her dark bowl of hair had been fluffed and curled. And, Eve noted, the tall glass in her hand was already half empty.

"Peabody. Looks like you got here."

"The transport was on time, no problem. Roarke, this place is seriously iced. I can't believe I'm here. I really appreciate you getting me in, Dallas."

She hadn't arranged it as a favor, exactly. If she was going

to suffer through a seminar, Eve had figured her aide should
suffer, too. But from the look of things Peabody seemed to
be bearing up.

"I came in with Feeney and his wife," Peabody went on.
"And Dr. Mira and her husband. Morris and Dickhead and
Silas from Security, Leward from Anti-Crime—they're all
around somewhere. Some of the other guys from Central and
the precincts. NYPSD is really well represented."

"Great." She could expect to get ragged on about her
speech for weeks.

"We're going to have a little reunion later in the Moon-
scape Lounge."

"Reunion? We just saw each other yesterday."

"On-planet." Peabody's lips, slicked deep red, threatened
to pout. "This is different."

Eve scowled at her aide's fancy party dress. "You're telling me."

"Why don't I get you ladies a drink? Wine, Eve? And
Peabody?"

"I'm having an Awesome Orgasm. The drink, I mean, not,
you know, personally."

Amused, Roarke brushed a hand over her shoulder. "I'll
take care of it."

"Boy, could he ever," Peabody muttered as he walked
away.

"Button it." Eve scanned the room, separating cops from
spouses, from techs, from consultants. She focused in on a
large group gathered in the southeast corner of the ballroom.
"What's the deal there?"

"That's the big wheel. Former Commander Douglas R.
Skinner." Peabody gestured with her glass, then took a long
drink. "You ever meet him?"

"No. Heard about him plenty, though."

"He's a legend. I haven't gotten a look yet because there's
been about a hundred people around him since I got here.
I've read most of his books. The way he came through the
Urban Wars, kept his own turf secure. He was wounded during the Atlanta Siege, but held the line. He's a real hero."

"Cops aren't heroes, Peabody. We just do the job."

2

Eve wasn't interested in legends or heroes or retired cops who raked in enormous fees playing the lecture circuit or consulting. She was interested in finishing her one drink, putting in an appearance at the reception—and only because her own commander had ordered her to do so—then making herself scarce.

Tomorrow, she thought, was soon enough to get down to work. From the noise level of the crowd, everyone else thought so, too.

But it appeared the legend was interested in her.

She barely had the wineglass in her hand, was just calculating the least annoying route around the room, when someone tapped on her shoulder.

"Lieutenant Dallas." A thin man with dark hair cut so short it looked like sandpaper glued to his scalp, nodded at her. "Bryson Hayes, Commander Skinner's personal adjutant. The commander would very much like to meet you. If you'd come with me."

"The commander," she returned even as Hayes started to turn away, "looks pretty occupied at the moment. I'll be around all week."

After one slow blink, Hayes simply stared at her. "The commander would like to meet you now, Lieutenant. His schedule through the conference is very demanding."

"Go on." Peabody whispered it as she nudged Eve with her elbow. "Go on, Dallas."

"We'd be delighted to meet with Commander Skinner." Roarke solved the problem by setting his own drink aside, then taking both Eve's and Peabody's arms. It earned him an adoring-puppy look from Peabody and a narrow scowl from his wife.

Before Hayes could object or adjust, Roarke led both women across the ballroom.

"You're just doing this to piss me off," Eve commented.

"Not entirely, but I did enjoy pissing Hayes off. Just a bit of politics, Lieutenant." He gave her arm a friendly squeeze. "It never hurts to play them."

He slipped through the crowd smoothly, and only smiled when Hayes, a muscle working in his jaw, caught up in time to break a path through the last knot of people.

Skinner was short. His reputation was so large, it surprised Eve to note that he barely reached her shoulders. She knew him to be seventy, but he'd kept himself in shape. His face was lined, but it didn't sag. Nor did his body. He'd allowed his hair to gray, but not to thin, and he wore it militarily trim. His eyes, under straight silver brows, were a hard marble blue.

He held a short glass, the amber liquid inside neat. The heavy gold of his fifty-year ring gleamed on his finger.

She took his measure in a matter of seconds as, she noted, he took hers.

"Lieutenant Dallas."

"Commander Skinner." She accepted the hand he held out, found it cool, dry and more frail than she'd expected. "My aide, Officer Peabody."

His gaze stayed on Eve's face an extra beat, then shifted to Peabody. His lips curved. "Officer, always a pleasure to meet one of our men or women in uniform."

"Thank you, sir. It's an honor to meet you, Commander. You're one of the reasons I joined the force."

"I'm sure the NYPSD is lucky to have you. Lieutenant, I'd—"

"My husband," Eve interrupted. "Roarke."

Skinner's expression didn't waver, but it chilled. "Yes, I

recognized Roarke. I spent some of my last decade on the job studying you."

"I'm flattered. I believe this is your wife." Roarke turned his attention to the woman beside Skinner. "It's a pleasure to meet you."

"Thank you." Her voice was the soft cream of the southern United States. "Your Olympus is a spectacular accomplishment. I'm looking forward to seeing more of it while we're here."

"I'd be happy to arrange a tour, transportation."

"You're too kind." She brushed a hand lightly over her husband's arm.

She was a striking woman. She had to be close to her husband in age, Eve thought, as their long marriage was part of Skinner's pristine rep. But either superior DNA or an excellent face-and-body team had kept her beauty youthful. Her hair was richly black, and the gorgeous tone of her skin indicated mixed race. She wore a sleek silver gown and starry diamonds as if she'd been born to such things.

When she looked at Eve it was with polite interest. "My husband admires your work, Lieutenant Dallas, and he's very exacting in his admiration. Roarke, why don't we give these two cops a little time to talk shop?"

"Thank you, Belle. Excuse us, won't you, Officer?" Skinner gestured toward a table guarded by a trio of black-suited men. "Lieutenant? Indulge me." When they sat, the men moved one step back.

"Bodyguards at a cop convention?"

"Habit. I wager you have your weapon and shield in your evening bag."

She acknowledged this with a little nod. She would have preferred to wear them, but the dress didn't allow for her choice of accessories. "What's this about, Commander?"

"Belle was right. I admire your work. I was intrigued to find us on the same program. You don't generally accept speaking engagements."

"No. I like the streets."

"So did I. It's like a virus in the blood." He leaned back, nursed his drink. The faint tremor in his hand surprised her. "But working the streets doesn't mean being on them, necessarily. Someone has to command—from a desk, an office, a war room. A good cop, a smart cop, moves up the ranks. As you have, Lieutenant."

"A good cop, a smart cop, closes cases and locks up the bad guys."

He gave one short laugh. "You think that's enough for captain's bars, for a command star? No, the word 'naive' never came up in any of the reports I've read on you."

"Why should you read reports on me?"

"I may be retired from active duty, but I'm still a consultant. I still have my finger in the pie." He leaned forward again. "You've managed to work and close some very high-profile cases in the murder book, Lieutenant. While I don't always approve of your methods, the results are unarguable. It's rare for me to judge a female officer worthy of command."

"Excuse me. Back up. Female?"

He lifted his hand in a gesture that told her he'd had this discussion before and was vaguely weary of it. "I believe men and women have different primary functions. Man is the warrior, the provider, the defender. Woman is the procreator, the nurturer. There are numerous scientific theories that agree, and certainly social and religious weight to add."

"Is that so?" Eve said softly.

"Frankly, I've never approved of women on the force, or in certain areas of the civilian workplace. They're often a distraction and rarely fully committed to the job. Marriage and family soon—as they should for women—take priority."

"Commander Skinner, under the circumstances, the most courteous thing I can think of to say is you're full of shit."

He laughed, loud and long. "You live up to your reputation, Lieutenant. Your data also indicate that you're smart and that your badge isn't something you just pick up off the dresser every morning. It's what you are. Or were, in any case. We have that in common. For fifty years I made a difference, and my house was clean. I did what had to be done, then I did what came next. I was full commander at the age of forty-four. Would you like to be able to say the same?"

She knew when she was being played, and kept her face and tone neutral. "I haven't thought about it."

"If that's true, you disappoint me. If that's true, start thinking. Do you know, Lieutenant, how much closer you would be right now to a captaincy if you hadn't made some ill-advised personal decisions?"

"Really?" Something began to burn inside her gut. "And how would you know the promotion potential of a homicide cop in New York?"

"I've made it my business to know." His free hand balled into a fist, tapped lightly, rhythmically on the tabletop. "I have one regret, one piece of unfinished business from my active duty. One target I could never keep in my sights long enough to bring down. Between us, we could. I'll get you those captain bars, Lieutenant. You get me Roarke."

She looked down at her wine, slowly ran a fingertip around the rim. "Commander, you gave half a century of your life to the job. You shed blood for it. That's the single reason I'm not going to punch you in the face for that insult."

"Think carefully," he said as Eve got to her feet. "Sentiment over duty is never a smart choice. I intend to bring him down. I won't hesitate to break you to do it."

Riding on fury, she leaned down very close, and whispered in his ear. "Try it. You'll find out I'm no fucking nurturer."

She stepped away, only to have one of the bodyguards move into her path. "The commander," he said, "isn't finished speaking with you."

"I'm finished speaking with the commander."

His gaze shifted from her face briefly, and he gave the faintest nod before he edged closer, clamped a hand on her arm. "You'll want to sit down, Lieutenant, and wait until you've been dismissed."

"Move your hand. Move it now, or I'm going to hurt you."

He only tightened his grip. "Take your seat and wait for leave to go. Or you're going to be hurt."

She glanced back at Skinner, then into the guard's face. "Guess again." She used a short-arm jab to break his nose, then a quick snap kick to knock back the guard beside him as he surged forward.

By the time she'd spun around, planted, she had her hand in her bag and on her weapon. "Keep your dogs on a leash," she said to Skinner.

She scanned the faces of cops who'd turned, who'd moved forward, to see if there was trouble coming from another direction. Deciding against it, she turned away and walked through the buzzing crowd.

She was nearly at the door when Roarke fell in step beside her, draped an arm around her shoulders. "You got blood on your dress, darling."

"Yeah?" Still steaming, she glanced down at the small splatter. "It's not mine."

"I noticed."

"I need to talk to you."

"Um-hmm. Why don't we go upstairs, see what the valet can do about that bloodstain? You can talk before we come down to have a drink with your friends from Central."

"Why the hell didn't you tell me you knew Skinner?"

Roarke keyed in the code for the private elevator to the owner's suite. "I don't know him."

"He sure as hell knows you."

"So I gathered." He waited until they were inside the car before he pressed a kiss to her temple. "Eve, over the course of things, I've had a great many cops looking in my direction."

"He's still looking."

"He's welcome to. I'm a legitimate businessman. Practically a pillar. Redeemed by the love of a good woman."

"Don't make me hit you, too." She strode out of the elevator, across the sumptuous living area of the suite, and directly outside onto the terrace so she could finish steaming in fresh air. "The son of a bitch. The son of a bitch wants me to help him bring you down."

"Rather rude," Roarke said mildly. "To broach the subject on such a short acquaintance, and at a cocktail reception. Why did he think you'd agree?"

"He dangled a captaincy in my face. Tells me he can get it for me, otherwise I'm in the back of the line because of my poor personal choices."

"Meaning me." Amusement fled. "Is that true? Are your chances for promotion bogged down because of us?"

"How the hell do I know?" Still flying on the insult, she rounded on him. "Do you think I care about that? You think making rank drives me?"

"No." He walked to her, ran his hands up and down her arms. "I know what drives you. The dead drive you." He leaned forward, rested his lips on her brow. "He miscalculated."

"It was a stupid and senseless thing for him to do. He barely bothered to circle around much before he hit me with it. Bad strategy," she continued. "Poor approach. He wants your ass, Roarke, and bad enough to risk censure for attempted bribery if I report the conversation—and anyone believes it. Why is that?"

"I don't know." And what you didn't know, he thought, was always dangerous. "I'll look into it. In any case, you certainly livened up the reception."

"Normally I'd've been more subtle, just kneed that jerk in the balls for getting in my way. But Skinner had gone into this tango about how women shouldn't be on the job because they're nurturers. Tagging the balls just seemed too girly at the time."

He laughed, drew her closer. "I love you, Eve."

"Yeah, yeah." But she was smiling again when she wrapped her arms around him.

$\mathcal{A}$s a rule, being crowded ass to ass at a table in a club where the entertainment included music that threatened the eardrums wasn't Eve's idea of a good time.

But when she was working off a good mad, it paid to have friends around.

The table was jammed with New York's finest. Her butt was squeezed between Roarke's and Feeney's, the Electronic Detective Division captain. Feeney's usually hangdog face was slack with amazement as he stared up at the stage.

On the other side of Roarke, Dr. Mira, elegant despite the surroundings, sipped a Brandy Alexander and watched the entertainment—a three-piece combo whose costumes were red-white-and-blue body paint doing wild, trash-rock riffs on American folk songs. Rounding out the table were Morris, the medical examiner, and Peabody.

"Wife shouldn't've gone to bed." Feeney shook his head. "You have to see it to believe it."

"Hell of a show," Morris agreed. His long, dark braid was threaded through with silver rope, and the lapels of his calf-length jacket sparkled with the same sheen.

For a dead doctor, Eve thought, he was a very snappy dresser.

"But Dallas here"—Morris winked at her—"was quite some warm-up act."

"Har har," Eve replied.

Morris smiled serenely. "Hotshot lieutenant decks legend of police lore's bodyguards at law enforcement convention on luxury off-planet resort. You've got to play that all the way out."

"Nice left jab," Feeney commented. "Good follow-through on the kick. Skinner's an asshole."

"Why do you say that, Feeney?" Peabody demanded. "He's an icon."

"Who said icons can't be assholes?" he tossed back. "Likes to make out like he put down the Urban Wars single-handed. Goes around talking about them like it was all about duty and romance and patriotism. What it was, was about survival. And it was ugly."

"It's typical for some who've been through combat to romanticize it," Mira put in.

"Nothing romantic about slitting throats or seeing Fifth Avenue littered with body parts."

"Well, that's cheerful." Morris pushed Feeney's fresh glass in front of him. "Have another beer, Captain."

"Cops don't crow about doing the job." Feeney glugged down his beer. "They just do it. I'da been closer, Dallas, I'da helped you take down those spine crackers of his."

Because the wine and his mood made her sentimental, she jabbed him affectionately with her elbow. "You bet your ass. We can go find them and beat them brainless. You know, round out the evening's entertainment."

Roarke laid a hand on her back as one of his security people came to the table and leaned down to whisper in his ear. Humor vanished from his face as he nodded.

"Someone beat you to it," he announced. "We have what's left of a body on the stairway between the eighteenth and nineteenth floors."

3

Eve stood at the top of the stairwell. The once pristine white walls were splattered with blood and gray matter. A nasty trail of both smeared the stairs. The body was sprawled on them, faceup.

There was enough of his face and hair left for her to identify him as the man whose nose she'd broken a few hours before.

"Looks like somebody was a lot more pissed off than I was. Your man got any Seal-It?" she asked Roarke.

When Roarke passed her the small can of sealant, she coated her hands, her shoes. "I could use a recorder. Peabody, help hotel security keep the stairwells blocked off. Morris." She tossed him the can. "With me."

Roarke gave her his security guard's lapel recorder. Stepped forward. Eve simply put a hand on his chest. "No civilians—whether they own the hotel or not. Just wait. Why don't you clear Feeney to confiscate the security disks for this sector of the hotel? It'll save time."

She didn't wait for an answer, but headed down the steps to the body. Crouched. "Didn't do this with fists." She examined his face. One side was nearly caved in, the other largely untouched. "Left arm's crushed. Guy was left-

handed. I made that at the reception. They probably went for
the left side first. Disabled him."

"Agreed. Dallas?" Morris jerked his head in the direction
of the seventeenth floor. A thick metal bat coated with gore
rested on a tread farther down the stairs. "That would've
done the trick. I can consult with the local ME on the autopsy, but prelim eyeballing tells me that's the weapon. Do
you want me to dig up some evidence bags, a couple of field
kits?"

She started to speak, then hissed out a breath. The smell
of death was in her nostrils, and it was too familiar. "Not
our territory. We've got to go through station police. Goddamn it."

"There are ways to get around that, with your man owning
the place."

"Maybe." She poked a sealed finger in a blood pool,
nudged something metal and silver. And she recognized the
star worn on the epaulets of hotel security.

"Who would be stupid enough to beat a man to death in
a hotel full of cops?" Morris wondered.

She shook her head, got to her feet. "Let's get the ball
rolling on this." When she reached the top of the steps, she
scanned the hallway. If she'd been in New York, she would
now give the body a thorough examination, establish time of
death, gather data and trace evidence from the scene. She'd
call her crime scene unit, the sweepers, and send out a team
to do door-to-doors.

But she wasn't in New York.

"Has your security notified station police?" she asked
Roarke.

"They're on their way."

"Good. Fine. We'll keep the area secure and offer any and
all assistance." Deliberately, she switched off her recorder.
"I don't have any authority here. Technically, I shouldn't
have entered the crime scene area. I had a previous altercation with the victim, and that makes it stickier."

"I own this hotel, and I hold primary interest in this station.
I can request the assistance of any law enforcement agent."

"Yeah, so we've got that clear." She looked at him. "One
of your security uniforms is missing a star. It's down there,
covered with body fluid."

"If one of my people is responsible, you'll have my full cooperation in identifying and apprehending him."

She nodded again. "So we've got that clear, too. What's your security setup for this sector?"

"Full-range cameras—corridors, elevators, and stairwells. Full soundproofing. Feeney's getting the disks."

"He'll have to hand them to station police. When it's homicide, they have a maximum of seventy-two hours before they're obliged to turn the investigation over to ILE. Since ILE has people on-site, they'd be wise to turn it over now."

"Is that what you want?"

"It's not a matter of what I want. Look, it's not my case."

He took a handkerchief out of his pocket and wiped the blood smear from her hand. "Isn't it?"

Then he turned as the chief of police stepped off the elevator.

Eve hadn't been expecting a statuesque brunette in a tiny black dress with enough hair to stuff a mattress. As she clipped down the hall on towering high heels, Eve heard Morris's reverent opinion.

"Hubba-hubba."

"Jeez, try for dignity," Eve scolded.

The brunette stopped, took a quick scan. "Roarke," she said in a voice that evoked images of hot desert nights.

"Chief. Lieutenant Dallas, NYPSD. Dr. Morris, NYC Medical Examiner."

"Yes. Darcia Angelo. Chief of Olympus Police. Excuse my appearance. I was at one of the welcome events. I'm told we have a possible homicide."

"Verified homicide," Eve told her. "Victim's male, Caucasian, thirty-five to forty. Bludgeoned. The weapon, a metal bat, was left on scene. Preliminary visual exam indicates he's been dead under two hours."

"There's been a prelim exam?" Darcia asked. Coldly.

"Yes."

"Well, we won't quibble about that. I'll verify personally before my team gets here."

"Messy down there." Coolly, Eve handed over the can of Seal-It.

"Thanks." Darcia stepped out of her evening shoes. Eve couldn't fault her for it. She did the same thing herself, when

she remembered. When she'd finished, she handed the can
back to Eve. Darcia took a small recorder out of her purse,
clipped it where the fabric of her dress dipped to hug her
breasts.

Morris let out a long sigh as she walked into the stairwell.
"Where do you find them?" he asked Roarke. "And how can
I get one of my very own?"

Before Eve could snarl at him, Feeney hurried down the
hall. "Got a snag with the disks," he announced. "Stairway
cams were overridden for a fifty-minute period. You got
nothing but static there, and static for two sixty-second in-
tervals on the twentieth-floor corridor. Somebody knew what
they were doing," he added. "It's a complex system, with a
fail-safe backup plan. It took a pro—with access."

"With that time frame there had to be at least two people
involved," Eve stated. "Premeditated, not impulse, not crime
of passion."

"You got an ID on the victim? I can run a background
check."

"Police chief's on scene," Eve said flatly.

For a moment Feeney looked blank. "Oh, right. Forgot we
weren't home, sweet home. The locals going to squeeze us
out?"

"You weren't," Darcia said as she came out of the stairwell, "ever—in an official capacity—in."

"On the contrary," Roarke told her. "I requested the assistance of the lieutenant and her team."

Irritation flickered across Darcia's face, but she controlled
it quickly. "As is your privilege. Lieutenant, may I have a
moment of your time?" Without waiting for an answer, Darcia walked down the corridor.

"Arrogant, territorial, pushy." Eve glared at Roarke. "You
sure can pick them."

He only smiled as his wife's retreating back. "Yes, I certainly can."

"Look, Angelo, you want to bust my balls over doing a
visual, you're wasting your time and mine." Eve tugged her
lapel recorder free, held it out. "I verified a homicide, at the
request of the property owner. Then I stepped back. I don't
want your job, and I don't want your case. I get my fill of
walking through blood in New York."

Darcia flipped her mane of glossy black hair. "Four months ago I was busting illegal dealers in Colombia, risking my life on a daily basis and still barely able to pay the rent on a stinking little two-room apartment. In the current climate, cops are not appreciated in my country. I like my new job."

She opened her purse, dropped Eve's recorder inside. "Is that job in jeopardy if I refuse to hand over this case to my employer's wife?"

"Roarke doesn't fight my battles, and he doesn't fire people because they might not agree with me."

"Good." Darcia nodded. "I worked illegals, bunko, robbery. Twelve years. I'm a good cop. Homicide, however, is not my specialty. I don't enjoy sharing, but I'd appreciate any help you and your associates are willing to give in this matter."

"Fine. So what was this dance about?"

"Simply? So you and I would both be aware it *is* my case."

"You need to be aware that earlier tonight I punched the dead man in the face."

"Why?" Darcia asked suspiciously.

"He got in my way."

"I see. It'll be interesting to find out if you and I can close this matter without getting in each other's way."

Two hours later, for convenience's sake, the two arms of the investigation gathered in Roarke's on-site office.

"The victim is identified as Reginald Weeks, thirty-eight. Current residence is Atlanta, Georgia, Earth. Married, no children. Current employer, Douglas R. Skinner, Incorporated. Function personal security." Darcia finished, inclined her head at Eve.

"Crime scene examination of body shows massive trauma." Eve picked up the narrative. "Cause of death, most likely, fractured skull. The left side of the head and body were severely traumatized. Victim was left-handed, and this method of attack indicates foreknowledge. Security for the stairwell and the twentieth floor were tampered with prior to and during the act. A metal bat has been taken into evidence and is presumed to be the murder weapon. Also taken into evidence a silver-plated star stud, identified as part of the hotel security team's uniform. Chief Angelo?"

"Background data so far retrieved on Weeks show no criminal activity. He had held his current employment for two years. Prior that, he was employed by Right Arm, a firm that handles personal security and security consults for members of the Conservative Party. Prior to that he was in the military, Border Patrol, for six years."

"This tells us he knows how to follow orders," Eve continued. "He stepped up in my face tonight because Skinner, or one of Skinner's arms, signaled him to do so. He laid hands on me for the same reason. He's trained, and if he was good enough to last six years in the Border Patrol and land a job in Right Arm, he's not the type of guy who would go into a soundproof stairwell with a stranger, even under duress. If he'd been attacked in the corridor, there'd be a sign of it. If they took him on the twentieth floor, what the hell was he doing on the twentieth floor? His room, his security briefing room, and Skinner's suite are all on twenty-six."

"Could've been meeting a woman." Feeney stretched out his legs. "Conventionitis."

"That's a point," Eve allowed. "All evidence points to this being a planned attack, but a woman could have been used as a lure. We need to verify or eliminate that. You want to track it down, Feeney?"

"Captain Feeney may assist my officers in that area of investigation." Darcia merely lifted her eyebrows when Eve turned to her. "If he is agreeable. As I hope he will be to continuing to work with the hotel security team."

"We're a real agreeable group," Eve said with a wide, wide smile.

"Excellent. Then you have no problem accompanying me to twenty-six to inform the victim's employer of his death."

"Not a one. Peabody. My aide goes with me," Eve said before Darcia could speak. "Non-negotiable. Peabody," Eve said again, gesturing as she walked out of the room and left Darcia assigning her officers to different tasks. "I want your recorder on when we talk to Skinner."

"Yes, sir."

"If I get hung up, I need you to wheedle an update out of the local ME. If you can't open him up, tag Morris and have him use the good buddy, same field approach."

"Yes, sir."

"I want to find the uniform that star came from. We need to check recyclers, the valet, outside cleaning sources. Get chummy with the home team. I want to know the minute the sweepers and crime scene units reports are in. I'm betting there's going to be traces of Seal-It on that bat, and nobody's blood but the victim's on the scene. Fucking ambush," she grumbled, and turned as Darcia came out.

Darcia said nothing until she'd called for the elevator and stepped inside. "Do you have a history with Douglas Skinner, Lieutenant?"

"No. Not until tonight."

"My information is that he specifically called you to his table to speak with you privately. You, apparently, had words of disagreement, and when the victim attempted to prevent you from leaving the table, you struck him. Would this be accurate?"

"It would."

"What were those words of disagreement between you and Douglas Skinner?"

"Am I a suspect in this case or a consultant?"

"You're a consultant, and as such I would appreciate any and all data."

"I'll think about it." Eve stepped out on twenty-six.

"If you have nothing to hide."

"I'm a cop," Eve reminded her. "That line doesn't work on me." She rang the bell, waited. She watched the security light blink to green, kept her face blank while she and her companions were scanned. Moments later, Skinner opened the door himself.

"Lieutenant. It's a bit late for paying calls."

"It's never too late for official calls. Chief Angelo, Douglas Skinner."

"Pardon the intrusion, Commander Skinner." Darcia's voice was low and respectful, her face quietly sober. "We have some unfortunate news. May we come in?"

"Of course." He stepped back. He was dressed in the long white robe provided by the hotel, and his face looked pale against it. The large living area was dimly lit and fragrant from the bouquets of roses. He ordered the lights up 10 percent, and gestured toward the sofa.

"Please, ladies, sit. Can I get you anything? Coffee, perhaps?"

"We're not here to chat. Where were you between twenty-two hundred and midnight?"

"I don't like your tone, Lieutenant."

"Please, excuse us." Darcia stepped in smoothly. "It's been a difficult night. If I could ask you to verify your whereabouts, as a formality?"

"My wife and I came up to our suite a bit after ten. We retired early, as I have a long, busy day scheduled tomorrow. What's happened?"

"Weeks got his brains bashed in," Eve said.

"Weeks? Reggie?" Skinner stared at Eve. Those hard blue eyes widened, darkened, and seemed to draw a cast of gray over his skin as shock shifted into fury. "Dead? The boy is dead? Have you determined Roarke's *whereabouts*? Or would you go so far as to cover up murder to protect him? She attacked Weeks only hours ago." He pointed at Eve. "An unprovoked and vicious assault on one of mine because I questioned her about her alliance with a criminal. You're a disgrace to your badge."

"One of us is," Eve agreed as Skinner sank into a chair.

"Commander." Darcia stepped forward. "I know this is a shock for you. I want to assure you that the Olympus PD is actively pursuing all avenues of investigation."

For a moment he said nothing, and the only sound was his quick, labored breathing. "I don't know you, Chief Angelo, but I know who pays you. I have no confidence in your investigation as long as it's bankrolled by Roarke. Now, excuse me. I have nothing more to say at this time. I need to contact Reggie's wife and tell her she's a widow."

4

"*Well, that went well.*" Eve rolled her shoulders as she headed back to the elevator.

"If one doesn't mind being accused of being a fool or a dirty cop."

Eve punched the elevator button. "Ever hear the one about sticks and stones in Colombia?"

"I don't like that one." Obviously stewing, Darcia strode onto the elevator. "And I don't like your Commander Skinner."

"Hey, he's not mine."

"He implies Roarke is my puppet master. Why does he assume that, and why does he believe Roarke is responsible for Weeks's death?"

The quiet, respectful woman was gone, and in her place was a tough-eyed cop with steel in her voice. Eve began to see how Darcia Angelo had risen through twelve years in Colombia.

"One reason is Weeks annoyed me, and since I'm just a procreating, nurturing female, it would be up to my warrior, defender, penis-owning husband to follow through."

"Ah." Darcia sucked in her cheeks. "This is an attitude I recognize. Still, splattering a man's brains is considerable overcompensation for such a minor infraction. A very large leap of conclusion for the commander to make. There's more."

"Might be. I haven't worked it out yet. Meanwhile, Skinner seemed awfully alert for someone who'd already gone to bed. And while the lights in the living area were on low when we walked in, they were full on in the bedroom off to the right. He didn't close the door all the way when he came out."

"Yes, I noticed that."

"Suite's set up along the same basic floor plan as the one I'm in. Second bedroom off to the left. There was a light on in there, too. His wife had that door open a crack. She was listening."

"I didn't catch that," Darcia mused, then glanced back when Peabody muttered.

"She missed it, too," Eve said. "She hates that. And if Belle Skinner was eavesdropping from the second bedroom, she wasn't snuggled up with the commander in the master, was she? No connubial bliss, which is interesting. And no alibi."

"What motive would Skinner have for killing one of his own bodyguards?"

"Something to think about. I want to check some things out." She stopped the elevator so both Darcia and Peabody could exit. "I'll get back to you."

Being willing to fall into step with Darcia Angelo didn't mean she couldn't make some lateral moves of her own. If she was going to wade into a murder investigation off her own turf, without her usual system and when her badge was little more than a fashion accessory, she was going to make use of whatever tools were available.

There was one particular tool she knew to be very versatile and flexible.

She was married to him.

She found Roarke, as she'd expected to, at work on the bedroom computer. He'd removed his dinner jacket, rolled up his sleeves. There was a pot of coffee beside him.

"What have you got?" She picked up his cup, gulped down half his coffee.

"Nothing that links me or any of my business dealings with Skinner. I have some interests in Atlanta, naturally."

"Naturally."

"Communications, electronics, entertainment. Real estate, of course." He took the cup back from her, idly rubbed her ass with his free hand. "And during one lovely interlude previous to my association with you, a nicely profitable smuggling enterprise. Federal infractions—"

"Infractions," she repeated.

"One could say. Nothing that bumped up against state or local authorities."

"Then you're missing something, because it's personal with him. It doesn't make any sense otherwise. You're not a major bad guy."

"Now you've hurt my feelings."

"Why does he latch on to you?" she demanded, ignoring him. "Fifty years a cop, he'd have seen it all. And he'd have lost plenty. There are stone killers out there, pedophiles, sexual predators, cannibals, for Christ's sake. So why are you stuck in his craw? He's been retired from active, what, six years, and—"

"Seven."

"Seven, then. Seven years. And he approaches me with what could be considered a bribe or blackmail, depending on your point of view, to pressure me into rolling over on you. It was arrogant and ill-conceived."

She thought it through as she paced. "I don't think he expected it to work. I think he expected me to tell him to fuck off. That way he could roll us into a ball together and shoot two for one."

"He can't touch you—or me, for that matter."

"He can make things hot by implicating us in a homicide. And he's laying the groundwork. He pushes my buttons in a public venue, then gets one of his monkeys to get in my face. Altercation ensues. A couple hours later, monkey has his brains splattered all over the stairway of a Roarke Enterprises hotel—and what's this! Why it's a clue, Sherlock, and a dandy one, too. A star stud from one of Roarke Securities uniforms, floating in the victim's blood."

"Not particularly subtle."

"He doesn't have time to be subtle. He's in a hurry," she continued. "I don't know why, but he's rushing things. Shove circumstantial evidence down the throat of the local authorities and they've got to pursue the possibility that the irritated husband and suspected interplanetary hoodlum ordered one of his own monkeys to teach Skinner's a lesson."

"You touched my wife, now I have to kill you?" Roarke's shrug was elegant and careless. "Overdramatic, over-romanticized. Particularly since you punched him in the face before I could ride to the rescue."

"In his narrow little world, men are the hunters, the defenders. It plays when you look at it through his window. It's another miscalculation though, because it's not your style. You want the hell beat out of someone, you do it yourself."

He smiled at her fondly. "I like watching you do it even more, darling."

She spared him a look. "Standard testing on you, any profile would kick the theory out of the park. You're just not hardwired to pay somebody to kill, or to get your dick in a twist because somebody hassles me. We could have Mira run you through a Level One testing just to push that aside."

"No, thank you, darling. More coffee?"

She grunted, paced a bit more while he rose to go to the mini AutoChef for a fresh pot and cups. "It's a sloppy frame. Thing is, Skinner believes you're capable, and that if he dumps enough on the ILE if and when they take over he'll push you into an investigative process that will mess you up—and me by association."

"Lieutenant, the ILE has investigated me in the past. They don't worry me. What does is that if it goes that far, your reputation and career could take some bruises. I won't tolerate that. I think the commander and I should have a chat."

"And what do you think he's counting on?" she demanded.

"Why disappoint him?" Coffee cup in hand, he sat on the arm of his chair. "I've compiled personal and professional data on Skinner. Nothing seems particularly relevant to this, but I haven't studied his case files in depth. Yet."

Eve set down the coffee he'd just poured her with a little snap of china on wood. "Case files? You hacked into his case files? Are you a lunatic? He gets wind of that, you're up on charges and in lockup before your fancy lawyers can knot their fancy ties."

"He won't get wind of it."

"CompuGuard—" She broke off, scowled at the bedroom unit. CompuGuard monitored all e-transmissions and programming on-planet or off. Though she was aware Roarke had unregistered equipment at home, the hotel system was a different matter. "Are you telling me this unit's unregistered?"

"Absolutely not." His expression was innocent as a choirboy's. "It's duly registered and meets all legal requirements. Or did until a couple of hours ago."

"You can't filter out CompuGuard in a few hours."

Roarke sighed heavily, shook his head. "First you hurt my feelings, now you insult me. I don't know why I put up with this abuse."

Then he moved fast, grabbing her up, hauling her against him and crushing her mouth with a kiss so hot she wondered if her lips were smoking.

"Oh, yes." He released her, picked up his coffee again. "That's why."

"If that was supposed to distract me from the fact that you've illegally blocked CompuGuard and broken into official data, it was a damn good try. But the joke's on you. I was going to ask you to dig up the data."

"Were you really, Lieutenant? You never fail to surprise me."

"They beat him until his bones were dust." Her tone was flat, dull. All cop. "They erased half his face. And left the other half clean so I'd know as soon as I saw him. The minute he stepped in front of me tonight, he was dead. I was the goddamn murder weapon." She looked back at the computer. "So. Let's get to work."

They culled out cases during Skinner's last decade of active duty and cross-referenced with anything relating to them during the seven years of his retirement. It overlapped the time before Roarke had come to America from Ireland, but it seemed a logical place to start.

As the caseload was enormous, they split it. Eve worked on the bedroom unit, and Roarke set up in the second bedroom.

By three, Eve's temples were throbbing, her stomach raw

from caffeine intake. And she'd developed a new and reluctant admiration for Commander Skinner.

"Damn good cop," she acknowledged. Thorough, focused,
and up until his retirement, he had apparently dedicated himself, body and soul, to the job.

How had it felt to step away from all that? she wondered.
It had been his choice, after all. At sixty-four, retirement was
an option, not a requirement. He could have easily put in
another ten years on active. He might have risen to commis-
sioner.

Instead, he'd put in his fifty and then used that as a spring-
board in a run for Congress. And had fallen hard on his face.
A half century of public service hadn't been enough to offset
views so narrow even the most dug-in of the Conservative
Party had balked. Added to that, his platform had swung
unevenly from side to side.

He was an unwavering supporter of the Gun Ban, something the Conservatives tried to overturn at every opportunity. Yet he beat the drum to reinstate the death penalty,
which alienated the Liberals from mid-road to far left.

He wanted to dissolve legal and regulated prostitution and
strike out all legal and tax benefits for cohabiting couples.
He preached about the sanctity of marriage, as long as it was
heterosexual, but disavowed the government stipend for professional mothers.

Motherhood, the gospel according to Skinner stated, was
a God-given duty, and payment in its own right.

His mixed-voice and muddled campaign had gone down
in flames. However much he'd rebounded financially via lec-
tures, books, and consults, Eve imagined he still bore the
burns of that failure.

Still, she couldn't see how Roarke tied into it.

Rubbing her forehead, she pushed away and got up to
work out the kinks. Maybe she was overreacting. Did she
want it to be personal for Skinner because he'd made it personal for her? Maybe Roarke was no more than a symbol
for Skinner. Someone who had slipped and slid around the
system that Skinner himself had dedicated his life to.

She checked her wrist unit. Maybe she'd catch some sleep,
go back to it fresh in the morning. She would juggle the data
first, though, so that when she looked at it again it would be

in a new pattern. Whatever she was missing—and her gut still told her she was missing something—might float to the top.

"Computer, extrapolate any and all references to Roarke . . ." She yawned hugely, shook her head to clear it. "In any and all files, personal and professional, under Skinner, Commander Douglas."

Working . . .

"List references chronologically, first to last, um . . . give me official police records first, followed by personal files."

Understood. Working. . . . No reference to Roarke under Skinner, Commander Douglas police records. Reference under Skinner, Captain Douglas only. . . . Extrapolating personal files . . .

"Yeah, well, you keep saying that, but . . ." Eve whirled around, stared at the monitor. "Computer, stop. List any and all reference to Roarke under Skinner, Douglas, any rank."

Working . . . first listed reference in Skinner, Captain Douglas, case file C-439014, to Roarke, Patrick a/k/a O'Hara, Sean, a/k/a MacNeil, Thomas, date stamped March, twelve, twenty-thirty-six. Subject Roarke suspect in illegal weapons running, illegal entry into United States, grand theft auto and conspiracy to murder of police officers. Subject believed to have fled Atlanta area, and subsequently the country. Last known residence, Dublin, Ireland. Case file complete, investigative data available. Do you wish full case file?

"Yes. In hard copy."

Working . . .

Eve sat down again, slowly as the computer hummed. 2036, she thought. Twenty-three years ago. Roarke would have been what, twelve, thirteen?

It wasn't Roarke that was at the root of Skinner's obsession.

It was Roarke's father.

$\mathcal{A}$t *his own unit, Roarke ran through layers of Skinner's* financials. Among the most clear-cut motives for murder were greed, revenge, jealousy, sex, fear of disgrace, and profit. So he'd follow the money first.

There was a possibility, he'd decided, that Skinner had invested in one of his companies—or a competitor's. Perhaps he'd lost a substantial amount of money. Men had hated men for less.

And financially Skinner had taken a beating during his run for Congress. It had left him nearly broke as well as humiliated.

"Roarke."

"Hmm." He held up a finger to hold Eve off as she came into the room. "Communications," he said. "I have an interest in the Atlanta media sources, and they were very unkind to Skinner during his congressional attempt. This would have weighed heavily against his chances of winning. Media Network Link is mine outright, and they were downright vicious. Accurate, but vicious. Added to that, he's invested fairly heavily in Corday Electronics, based in Atlanta. My own company has eroded their profits and customer base steadily for the last four years. I really should finish them off with a takeover," he added as an afterthought.

"Roarke."

"Yes?" He reached around absently to take her hand as he continued to scroll data.

"It goes deeper than politics and stock options. Twenty-three years ago illegal arms dealers set up a base in Atlanta, and Skinner headed up the special unit formed to take them down. They had a weasel on the inside, and solid information. But when they moved in, it was a trap. Weasels turn both ways, and we all know it."

She took a deep breath, hoping she was telling it the way it should be told. Love twisted her up as often, maybe more often, than it smoothed things out for her.

"Thirteen cops were killed," she continued, "six more wounded. They were outgunned, but despite it, Skinner broke the cartel's back. The cartel lost twenty-two men, mostly soldiers. And he bagged two of the top line that night. That led to two more arrests in the next twelve months. But he lost one. He was never able to get his hands on one."

"Darling, I might've been precocious, but at twelve I'd yet to run arms, unless you're counting a few hand-helds or homemade boomers sold in alleyways. And I hadn't ventured beyond Dublin City. As for weaseling, that's something I've never stooped to."

"No." She kept staring at his face. "Not you."

And watched his eyes change, darken and chill as it fell into place for him. "Well, then," he said, very softly. "Son of a bitch."

5

As a boy, Roarke had been the favored recipient of his father's fists and boots. He'd usually seen them coming, and had avoided them when possible, lived with them when it wasn't.

To his knowledge, this was the first time the old man had sucker punched him from the grave.

Still, he sat calmly enough, reading the hard copy of the reports Eve had brought him. He was a long way from the skinny, battered boy who had run the Dublin alleyways. Though he didn't care much for having to remind himself of it now.

"This double cross went down a couple of months before my father ended up in the gutter with a knife in his throat. Apparently someone beat Skinner to him. He has that particular unsolved murder noted in his file here. Perhaps he arranged it."

"I don't think so." She wasn't quite sure how to approach Roarke on the subject of his father and his boyhood. He tended to walk away from his past, whereas she—well, she tended to walk into the wall of her own past no matter how often, how deliberately, she changed directions.

"Why do you say that? Look, Eve, it isn't the same for me as it is for you. You needn't be careful. He doesn't haunt me. Tell me why if my father slipped through Skinner's fingers in Atlanta, Skinner wouldn't arrange to have his throat slit in Dublin City."

"First, he was a cop, not an assassin. There's no record in the file that he'd located his target in Dublin. There's correspondence with Interpol, with local Irish authorities. He was working on extradition procedures should his target show up on Irish soil, and would likely have gotten the paperwork and the warrant. That's what he'd have wanted," she continued, and rose to prowl the room. "He'd want the bastard back on his own turf, back where it went down and his men were killed. He'd want that face-to-face. He didn't get it."

She turned back. "If he'd gotten it, he could've closed the book, moved on. And he wouldn't be compelled to go after you. You're what's left of the single biggest personal and professional failure of his life. He lost his men, and the person responsible for their loss got away from him."

"Dead wouldn't be enough, without arrest, trial, and sentencing."

"No, it wouldn't. And here you are, rich, successful, famous—and married, for Christ's sake—to a cop. I don't need Mira to draw me a profile on this one. Skinner believes that perpetrators of certain crimes, including any crime that results in the death of a police official, should pay with their life. After due process. Your father skipped out on that one. You're here, you pay."

"Then he's doomed to disappointment. For a number of reasons. One, I'm a great deal smarter than my father was." He rose, went to her, skimmed a finger down the dent in her chin. "And my cop is better than Skinner ever hoped to be."

"I have to take him down. I have to fuck over fifty years of duty, and take him down."

"I know." And would suffer for it, Roarke thought, as Skinner never would. As Skinner could never understand. "We need to sleep," he said and pressed his lips to her brow.

She dreamed of Dallas, and the frigid, filthy room in Texas where her father had kept her. She dreamed of cold and hunger and unspeakable fear. The red light from the sex club across the street flashed into the room, over her face. And over his face as he struck her.

She dreamed of pain when she dreamed of her father. The tearing of her young flesh as he forced himself into her. The snapping of bone, her own high, thin scream when he broke her arm.

She dreamed of blood.

Like Roarke's, her father had died by a knife. But the one that had killed him had been gripped in her own eight-year-old hand.

In the big, soft bed in the plush suite, she whimpered like a child. Beside her, Roarke gathered her close and held her until the dream died.

She was up and dressed by six. *The snappy jacket that* had ended up in her suitcase fit well over her harness and weapon. The weight of them made her feel more at home.

She used the bedroom 'link to contact Peabody. At least she assumed the lump under the heap of covers was Peabody.

"Whaa?"

"Wake up," Eve ordered. "I want your report in fifteen minutes."

"Who?"

"Jesus, Peabody. Get up, get dressed. Get here."

"Why don't I order up some breakfast?" Roarke suggested when she broke transmission.

"Fine, make it for a crowd. I'm going to spread a little sunshine and wake everybody up." She hesitated. "I trust my people, Roarke, and I know how much I can tell them. I don't know Angelo."

He continued to read the morning stock reports on-screen. "She works for me."

"So, one way or the other, does every third person in the known universe. That tells me nothing."

"What was your impression of her?"

"Sharp, smart, solid. And ambitious."

"So was mine," he said easily. "Or she wouldn't be chief of police on Olympus. Tell her what she needs to know. My father's unfortunate history doesn't trouble me."

"Will you talk to Mira?" She kept her gaze level as he

rose, turned toward her. "I want to call her in, I want a consult. Will you talk to her?"

"I don't need a therapist, Eve. I'm not the one with nightmares." He cursed softly, ran a hand through his hair when her face went blank and still. "Sorry. Bloody hell. But my point is we each handle things as we handle them."

"And you can push and nudge and find ways to smooth it over for me. But I can't do that for you."

The temper in her voice alleviated a large slice of his guilt over mentioning her nightmare. "Screen off," he ordered and crossed to her. Took her face in his hands. "Let me tell you what I once told Mira—not in a consult, not in a session. You saved me, Eve." He watched her blink in absolute shock. "What you are, what I feel for you, what we are together saved me." He kept his eyes on hers as he kissed her. "Call your people. I'll contact Darcia."

He was nearly out of the room before she found her voice. "Roarke?" She never seemed to find the words as he did, but these came easy. "We saved each other."

There was no way she could make the huge, elegant parlor feel like one of the conference rooms in Cop Central. Especially when her team was gorging on cream pastries, strawberries the size of golf balls, and a couple of pigs' worth of real bacon.

It just served to remind her how much she hated being off her own turf.

"Peabody, update."

Peabody had to jerk herself out of the image of the good angel on her shoulder, sitting with her hands properly folded, and the bad angel, who was stuffing another cream bun in her greedy mouth. "Ah, sir. Autopsy was completed last night. They let Morris assist. Cause of death multiple trauma, most specifically the skull fracture. A lot of the injuries were postmortem. He's booked on a panel this morning, and has some sort of dead doctors' seminar later today, but Morris will finesse copies of the reports for you. Early word is the tox screen was clear."

"Sweepers?" Eve demanded.

"Sweepers' reports weren't complete as of oh-six-hundred.

However, what I dug up confirmed your beliefs. Seal-It traces on the bat, no blood or bodily fluid but the victim's found on scene. No uniform missing an epaulet star has been found to date. Angelo's team's doing the run on recylers, valets, outside cleaning companies. My information is the uniforms are coded with the individual's ID number. When we find the uniform, we'll be able to trace the owner."

"I want that uniform," Eve stated, and when she turned to Feeney, the bad angel won. Peabody took another pastry.

"Had to be an inside job on the security cameras," he said. "Nobody gets access to Control without retina and palm scans and code clearance. The bypass was complicated, and it was done slick. Twelve people were in the control sector during the prime period last night. I'm running them."

"All right. We look for any connection to Skinner, any work-related reprimands, any sudden financial increase. Look twice if any of them were on the job before going into private security." She took a disk off the table, passed it to Feeney. "Run them with the names on here."

"No problem, but I work better when I know why I'm working."

"Those are the names of cops who went down in the line of duty in Atlanta twenty-three years ago. It was Skinner's operation." She took a deep breath. "Roarke's father was his weasel, and he turned a double cross."

When Feeney only nodded, Eve let out a breath. "One of the names on there is Thomas Weeks, father to Reginald Weeks, our victim. My guess is if Skinner had one of his slain officer's kids on his payroll, he's got others."

"Follows if one was used to build a frame around Roarke, another would be," Feeney added.

She checked her wrist unit when the door buzzer sounded. "That'll be Angelo. I want you running those names, Feeney, so I'm not giving them to her. Yet. But I'm going to tell her, and you, the rest of it."

While Eve was opening the door for Darcia, Skinner opened his to Roarke.

"A moment of your time, Commander."

"I have little to spare."

"Then we won't waste it." Roarke stepped inside, lifted a brow at Hayes. The man stood just behind and to the right of Skinner, and had his hand inside his suit jacket. "If you thought I was a threat, you should've had your man answer the door."

"You're no threat to me."

"Then why don't we have that moment in private?"

"Anything you say to me can be said in front of my personal assistant."

"Very well. It would've been tidier, and certainly more efficient, if you'd come after me directly instead of using Lieutenant Dallas and sacrificing one of your own men."

"So you admit you had him killed."

"I don't order death. We're alone, Skinner, and I'm sure you've had these rooms secured against recording devices and surveillance cameras. You want to take me on, then do it. But have the balls to leave my family out of it."

Skinner's lips peeled back over his teeth. "Your father was a dickless coward and a pathetic drunk."

"Duly noted." Roarke walked to a chair, sat. "There, you see. We already have a point of agreement on that particular matter. First let me clarify that by 'family,' I meant my wife. Second, I must tell you you're being too kind regarding Patrick Roarke. He was a vicious, small-minded bully and a petty criminal with delusions of grandeur. I hated him with every breath I took. So you see, I resent, quite strongly resent, being expected to pay for his many sins. I've plenty of my own, so if you want to try to put my head on a platter, just pick one. We'll work from there."

"Do you think because you wear a ten-thousand-dollar suit I can't smell the gutter on you?" Color began to flood Skinner's face, but when Hayes stepped forward, Skinner gestured him back with one sharp cut of the hand. "You're the same as he was. Worse, because he didn't pretend to be anything other than the useless piece of garbage he was. Blood tells."

"It may have once."

"You've made a joke out of the law, and now you hide behind a woman and a badge she's shamed."

Slowly now, Roarke got to his feet. "You know nothing of her. She's a miracle that I can't, and wouldn't, explain to the likes of you. But I can promise you, I hide behind nothing. You stand there, with fresh blood on your hands, behind your shield of blind righteousness and your memories of old glory. Your mistake, Skinner, was in trusting a man like my father to hold a bargain. And mine, it seems, was thinking you'd deal with me. So here's a warning for you."

He broke off as Hayes shifted. Fast as a rattler, Roarke drew a hand laser out of his pocket. "Take your bloody hand out of your coat while you still have one."

"You've no right, no authority to carry and draw a weapon."

Roarke stared at Skinner's furious face, then grinned. "What weapon? On your belly, Hayes, hands behind your head. Do it!" he ordered when Hayes shot Skinner a look. "Even on low these things give a nasty little jolt." He lowered the sight to crotch level. "Especially when they hit certain sensitive areas of the anatomy."

Though his breathing was now labored, Skinner gestured toward Hayes.

"To the warning. You step back from my wife. Step well and cleanly back, or you'll find the taste of me isn't to your liking."

"Will you have me beat to death in a stairwell?"

"You're a tedious man, Skinner," Roarke said with a sigh as he backed to the door. "Flaming tedious. I'd tell your men to have a care how they strut around and finger their weapons. This is my place."

Despite its size, Eve found the living area of the suite as stifling as a closed box. If she were on a case like this in New York, she would be on the streets, cursing at traffic as she fought her way to the lab to harass the techs, letting her mind shuffle possibilities as she warred with Rapid Cabs on the way to the morgue or back into Central.

The sweepers would tremble when she called demanding a final report. And the asses she would kick on her way through the investigation would be familiar.

This time around Darcia Angelo got to have all the fun.

"Peabody, go down and record Skinner's keynote, since he's playing the show must go on and giving it on schedule."

"Yes, sir."

The morose tone had Eve asking, "What?"

"I know why you're leaning toward him for this, Dallas. I can see the angles, but I just can't adjust the pattern for them. He's a legend. Some cops go wrong because the pressure breaks them inside, or because of the temptations or just because they were bent that way to begin with. He never went wrong. It's an awful big leap to see him tossing aside everything he's stood for and killing one of his own to frame Roarke for something that happened when Roarke was a kid."

"Come up with a different theory, I'll listen. If you can't do the job, Peabody, tell me now. You're on your own time here."

"I can do the job." Her voice was as stiff as her shoulders as she started for the door. "I haven't been on my own time since I met you."

Eve set her teeth as the door slammed, and was already formulating the dressing-down as she marched across the room. Mira stopped her with a word.

"Eve. Let her go. You have to appreciate her position. It's difficult being caught between two of her heroes."

"Oh, for Christ's sake."

"Sit, before you wear a rut in this lovely floor. You're in a difficult position as well. The man you love, the job that defines you, and another man who you believe has crossed an indelible line."

"I need you to tell me if he could have crossed that line. I know what my gut tells me, what the pattern of evidence indicates. It's not enough. I have data on him. Most of it's public domain, but not all." She waited a beat while Mira simply continued to study her, calm as a lake. "I'm not going to tell you how I accessed it."

"I'm not going to ask you. I already know quite a bit about Douglas Skinner. He is a man devoted to justice—his own vision of it, one who has dedicated his life to what the badge stands for, one who has risked his life to serve and protect. Very much like you."

"That doesn't feel like much of a compliment right now."

"There is a parting of the ways between you, a very elemental one. He's compelled, has always been compelled, to spread his vision of justice like some are compelled to spread their vision of faith. You, Eve, at your core, stand for the victim. He stands for his vision. Over time, that vision has narrowed. Some can become victims of their own image until they become the image."

"He's lost the cop inside the hype."

"Cleanly said. Peabody's view of him is held by a great many people, a great many in law enforcement. It's not such a leap, psychologically speaking, for me to see him as becoming so obsessed by a mistake—and the mistake was his own—that cost the lives of men in his command that that failure becomes the hungry monkey on his back."

"The man who's dead wasn't street scum. He was a young employee, one with a clean record, with a wife. The son of one of Skinner's dead. That's the leap I'm having trouble with, Dr. Mira. Was the monkey so hungry that Skinner could order the death of an innocent man just to feed it?"

"If he could justify it in his mind, yes. Ends and means. How worried are you about Roarke?"

"He doesn't want me to worry about him," Eve answered.

"I imagine he's much more comfortable when he can worry about you. His father was abusive to him."

"Yeah. He's told me pieces of it. The old man knocked hell out of him, drunk or sober." Eve dragged a hand through her hair, walked back toward the window. There was barely a hint of sky traffic.

How, she wondered, did people stand the quiet, the stillness?

"He had Roarke running cons, picking pockets, then he'd slap him around if he didn't bring home enough. I take it his father wasn't much good at the rackets because they lived in a slum."

"His mother?"

"I don't know. He says he doesn't know either. It doesn't seem to matter to him." She turned back, sat down across from Mira. "Can that be? Can it really not matter to him what his father did to him, or that his mother left him to that?"

"He knows his father started him on the path of, let's say circumventing the law. That he has a predisposition for violence. He learned how to channel it, as you did. He had a goal—to get out, to have means and power. He accomplished that. Then he found you. He understands where he came from, and I imagine it's part of his pride that he became the kind of man a woman like you would love. And, knowing his . . . profile," Mira said with a smile. "I imagine he's determined to protect you and your career in this matter, every bit as much as you're determined to protect him and his reputation."

"I don't see how . . ." Realization hit, and Eve was just getting to her feet when Roarke walked in the door.

"Goddamn it. Goddamn it, Roarke. You went after Skinner."

6

"*Good morning, Dr. Mira.*" Roarke closed the door behind him, then walked over to take Mira's hand. The move was as smooth as his voice, and his voice smooth as cream. "Can I get you some more tea?"

"No." Her lips twitched as she struggled to control a chuckle. "Thanks, but I really have to be going. I'm leading a seminar right after the keynote session."

"Don't think you can use her as a shield. I told you to stay away from Skinner."

"That's the second time someone's accused me of hiding behind a woman today." Though his voice remained mild, Eve knew the edge was there. "It's getting annoying."

"You want annoying?" Eve began.

"You'll have to forgive her," Roarke said to Mira as he walked her to the door. "Eve tends to become overexcited when I disobey."

"She's worried about you," Mira said under her breath.

"Well, she'll have to get over it. Have a good session." He nudged Mira out the door, closed it. Locked it. Turned. The edge was visible now. "I don't need a fucking shield."

"That was a figure of speech, and don't change the subject. You went at Skinner after I told you to stay clear of him."

"I don't take orders from you, Eve. I'm not a lapdog."

"You're a civilian," she shot back.

"And you're a consultant on someone else's case, and your authority here, in my bloody world, is a courtesy."

She opened her mouth, closed it. Hissed. Then she turned on her heel, strode out through the terrace doors, and kicked the railing several times.

"Feel better now?"

"Yes. Because I imagined it was your stupid, rock-hard head." She didn't look back, but braced her hands on the railing and looked out over what was indeed one of Roarke's worlds.

It was lavish and extravagant. The slick spears of other hotels, the tempting spreads of casinos, theaters, the glitter of restaurants were all perfectly placed. There were fountains, the silver ribbons of people glides, and the lush spread of parks where trees and flowers grew in sumptuous profusion.

She heard the click of his lighter, caught the scent of his obscenely expensive tobacco. He rarely smoked these days, she thought.

"If you'd told me it was important for you to have a face-to-face with Skinner, I'd have gone with you."

"I'm aware of that."

"Oh, Christ. Men. Look, you don't need to hide behind me or anybody. You're a tough, badass son of a bitch with a really big penis and balls of titanium steel. Okay?"

He cocked his head. "One minute. I'm imagining throwing you off the balcony. Yes." He nodded, took a long drag on the cigarette. "That's indeed better."

"If Skinner took a couple of pops at your ego, it's because he knew it was a good target. That's what cops do. Why don't you just tell me what happened?"

"He made it clear, while Hayes stood there with a hand inside his coat and on his weapon, that my father was garbage and by association so am I. And that it was long past time for my comeuppance, so to speak."

"Did he say anything that led to him ordering Weeks killed?"

"On the contrary, he twice pointed the finger at me. Full of barely restrained fury and seething emotion. You could almost believe he meant it. I don't think he's well," Roarke continued and crushed out his cigarette. "Temper put a very unhealthy color in his face, strained his breathing. I'll have to take a pass through his medical records."

"I want to take a pass at his wife. Angelo agreed, after some minor complaints, to set it up so we can double-team her later this afternoon. Meanwhile, Peabody's on Skinner, between us we'll track down the uniform, and Feeney's running names. Somebody on your security staff worked that bypass. We find out who, we link them back to Skinner and get them into interview, we change the complexion of this. Maybe put it away before ILE comes in."

She glanced back toward the suite as the 'link beeped. "Are we okay now?"

"We seem to be."

"Good. Maybe that's Angelo with the setup for Belle Skinner." She moved past Roarke to the 'link. Rather than Darcia's exotic face, Feeney's droopy one blipped on screen.

"Might have something for you here. Zita Vinter, hotel security. She was in Control between twenty-one-thirty and twenty-three hundred last night. Crossed her with your list. Popped to Vinter, Detective Carl, Atlanta cop under Skinner. Line of duty during the botched bust. Vinter's wife was pregnant with their second kid—a son, Marshall, born two months after his death. Older kid was five. Daughter, Zita."

"Bull's-eye. What sector is she in now?"

"She didn't come in today. Didn't call in either, according to her supervisor. Got her home address. Want me to ride with you?"

She started to agree, then looked back at Roarke. "No, I got it. See what else you can find on her, okay? Maybe you can tag Peabody when the keynote crap's over. She's good at digging background details. Owe you one, Feeney. Let me have the address."

After she'd ended transmission, Eve hooked her thumbs in her front pockets and looked at Roarke. "You wouldn't know where 22 Athena Boulevard might be, would you?"

"I might be able to find it, yes."

"I bet." She picked up her palm-link from the desk, stuck it in her pocket. "I'm not riding in a limo to go interview a suspect. It's unprofessional. Bad enough I'm taking some civilian wearing a fancy suit with me."

"Then I'll just have to come up with some alternate transportation."

"While you're at it, dig up your file on Zita Vinter, security sector."

He drew out his palm PC as they started out. "Always a pleasure to work with you, Lieutena___ ""

"Yeah, yeah." She stepped into the ___ ate elevator while he ordered something called a GF2000 brought to a garage slot. "Technically, I should contact Angelo and update her."

"No reason you can't. Once we're on the way."

"No reason. Saves time this way."

"That's your story, darling, and we'll stick to it. Vinter, Zita," he began as she scowled at him. "Twenty-eight. Two years with Atlanta PSD, then into private security. She worked for one of my organizations in Atlanta. Clean work record. Promoted to A Level over two years ago. She put in for the position here six months ago. She's single, lives alone. Lists her mother as next of kin. Her employment jacket's clean."

"When did you contract for this convention deal?"

"Just over six months ago," he said as they stepped off into the garage. "It was one of the incentives to have several of the facilities complete."

"How much do you want to bet Skinner's kept in close contact with his dead detective's daughter over the years? Angelo finesses a warrant for Vinter's 'link records, we're going to find transmissions to and from Atlanta. And not just to her mother."

When he stopped, put his PC away, she stared. "What the hell is this?"

Roarke ran a hand over the sleek chrome tube of the jet-bike. "Alternate transportation."

It looked fast and it looked mean, a powerful silver bullet on two silver wheels. She continued to stare as Roarke offered her a crash helmet.

"Safety first."

"Get a grip on yourself. With all your toys I know damn well you've got something around here with four wheels and doors."

"This is more fun." He dropped the helmet onto her head.

"And I'm forced to remind you that part of this little interlude was meant to be a bit of a holiday for us."

He took a second helmet, put it on. Then tidily fastened hers. "This way you can be my biker bitch." When she showed her teeth, he only laughed and swung a leg nimbly over the tube. "And I mean that in the most flattering way possible."

"Why don't I pilot, and you can be my biker bitch?"

"Maybe later."

Swearing, she slid onto the bike behind him. He glanced back at her as she adjusted her seat, cupped her hands loosely at his hips. "Hang on," he told her.

He shot like a rocket out of the garage, and her arms latched like chains around his waist. "Lunatic!" she shouted as he blasted into traffic. Her heart flipped into her throat and stayed there while he swerved, threaded, streaked.

It wasn't that she minded speed. She liked to go fast, when she was manning the controls. There was a blur of color as they careened around an island of exotic wildflowers. A stream of motion when they rushed by a people glide loaded with vacationers. Grimly determined to face her death without blinking, she stared at the snag of vehicular traffic dead ahead.

Felt the boost of thrusters between her legs. "Don't you—"

She could only yip and try not to choke on her own tongue as he took the jet-bike into a sharp climb. Wind screamed by her ears as they punched through the air.

"Shortcut," he shouted back to her, and there was laughter in his voice as he brought the bike down to the road again, smooth as icing on cake.

He braked in front of a blindingly white building, shut off all engines. "Well, then, it doesn't come up to sex, but it's definitely in the top ten in the grand scheme."

He swung off, removed his helmet.

"Do you know how many traffic violations you racked up in the last four minutes?"

"Who's counting?" He pulled off her helmet, then leaned down to bite her bottom lip.

"Eighteen," she informed him, pulling out her palm 'link to contact Darcia Angelo. She scanned the building as she relayed a message to Darcia's voice mail. Clean, almost brutally clean. Well constructed, from the look of it, tasteful and likely expensive.

"What do you pay your security people?"

"A Level?" They crossed the wide sidewalk to the building's front entrance. "About twice what a New York police lieutenant brings in annually, with a full benefit package, of course."

"What a racket." She waited while they were scanned at the door and Roarke coded in his master. The requisite computer voice welcomed him and wished him a safe and healthy day.

The lobby was tidy and quiet, really an extended foyer with straight lines and no fuss. At the visitors' panel, Eve identified herself and requested Zita Vinter.

I'm sorry, Dallas, Lieutenant Eve, Ms. Vinter does not respond. Would you care to leave a message at this time?

"No, I don't care to leave a message at this time. This is police business. Clear me into Apartment Six-B."

I'm sorry, Dallas, Lieutenant Eve, your credentials are not recognized on this station and do not allow this system to bypass standard privacy and security regulations.

"How would you like me to bypass your circuits and stuff your motherboard up your—"

Warning! Verbal threats toward this system may result in arrest, prosecution, and monetary fines up to five thousand credits.

Before Eve could spit out a response, Roarke clamped a hand on her shoulder. "This is Roarke." He laid his hand on the palm plate. "ID 151, Level A. You're ordered to clear me and Lieutenant Dallas to all areas of this compound."

Identification verified. Roarke and companion, Dallas, Eve, are cleared.

"Lieutenant," Eve said between her teeth as Roarke pulled her toward an elevator.

"Don't take it personally. Level six," he ordered.

"Damn machine treated me like a civilian." The insult of it was almost beyond her comprehension. "A *civilian.*"

"Irritating, isn't it?" He strolled off onto the sixth floor.

"You enjoyed that, didn't you? That 'Roarke and companion' shit."

"I did, yes. Immensely." He gestured. "Six–B." When she said nothing, he rang the buzzer himself.

"She didn't answer before, she's not going to answer now."

"No." He dipped his hands lightly in his pockets. "Technically . . . I suppose you need to ask Chief Angelo to request a warrant for entry."

"Technically," Eve agreed.

"I am, however, the owner of this building, and the woman's employer."

"Doesn't give you any right to enter her apartment without legal authority or permission."

He simply stood, smiled, waited.

"Do it," Eve told him.

"Welcome to my world." Roarke keyed in his master code, then hummed when the lock light above the door remained red. "Well, well, she appears to have added a few touches of her own, blocked the master code. I'm afraid that's a violation of her lease agreement."

Eve felt the little twist in her gut and slipped her hand under her jacket to her weapon. "Get in."

Neither questioned that whatever methods had been taken, he could get around them. Through them. He took a small case of tools out of his pocket and removed the anti-intruder panel on the scanner and identification plate.

"Clever girl. She's added a number of tricky little paths here. This will take a minute."

Eve took out her 'link and called Peabody. "Track down Angelo," she ordered. "We're at 22 Athena Boulevard. Six-B. She needs to get over here. I want you with her."

"Yes, sir. What should I tell her?"

"To get here." She dropped the 'link back in her pocket, stepped back to Roarke just as the lock lights went green. "Move aside," she ordered and drew her weapon.

"I've been through a door with you before, Lieutenant." He took the hand laser out of his pocket, and ignored her snarl when she spotted it. "You prefer low, as I recall."

Since there wasn't any point in biting her tongue or slapping at him for carrying, she did neither. "On my count." She put a hand on the door, prepared to shove it open.

"Wait!" He caught the faint hum, and the sound sent his

heart racing. The panel lights flashed red as he yanked Eve away from the door. They went down in a heap, his body covering hers.

She had that one breathless second to understand before the explosion blasted the door outward. A line of flame shot into the air, roaring across the hall where they'd been standing seconds before. Alarms screamed, and she felt the floor beneath her tremble at a second explosion, felt the blast of vicious heat all over her.

"Jesus! Jesus!" She struggled under him, slapped violently at the smoldering shoulder of his jacket with her bare hands. "You're on fire here."

Water spewed out of the ceiling as he sat up, stripped off the jacket. "Are you hurt?"

"No." She shook her head, shoved the hair soaked with the flood of the safety sprinklers out of her face. "Ears are ringing some. Where are you burned?" Her hands were racing over him as she pushed up to her knees.

"I'm not. The suit's fucked is all. Here, now. We're fine." He glanced back at the scarred and smoldering hole that had been the doorway. "But I'm afraid I'm going to have to evict Six-B."

Though she doubted it was necessary, Eve kept her weapon out as she picked her way over still smoking chunks of wall and door. Smoke and wet clogged the air in the hall, in the apartment, but she could see at one glance that the explosion had been smaller than she'd assumed. And very contained.

"A little paint and you're back in business."

"The explosion was set to blow the door, and whoever was outside it." There were bits of broken crockery on the floor, and a vase of flowers had fallen over, spilling water into the rivers already formed by the sprinkler system.

The furniture was sodden, the walls smeared with streaks from smoke and soot. The hallway walls were a dead loss, but otherwise, the room was relatively undamaged.

Ignoring the shouts and voices from outside the apartment, he moved through it with Eve.

Zita was in bed, her arms crossed serenely across her chest. Holstering her weapon, Eve walked to the bed, used two fingers to check for the pulse in the woman's throat.

"She's dead."

7

"*Your definition of cooperation and teamwork apparently* differs from mine, Lieutenant."

Wet, filthy, and riding on a vicious headache, Eve strained while Darcia completed her examination of the body. "I updated you."

"No, you left a terse message on my voice mail." Darcia straightened. With her sealed hands, she lifted the bottle of pills on the nightstand, bagged them. "When you were, apparently, at the point of illegally entering this unit."

"Property owner or his representative has the right to enter a private home if there is reasonable cause to believe a life or lives may be in danger, or that said property is threatened."

"Don't quote your regulations at me," Darcia snapped. "You cut me out."

Eve opened her mouth, then blew out a long breath. "Okay, I wouldn't say I cut you out, but I did an end run around you. In your place, I'd be just as pissed off. I'm used to being able to pursue a line on an investigation in my own way, on my own time."

"You are not primary on this case. I want this body bagged and removed," Darcia ordered the uniforms flanking the bedroom doors. "Probable cause of death, voluntary self-termination."

"Wait a minute, wait a minute. Wait!" Eve ordered, throwing out a hand to warn the uniforms back. "This isn't self-termination."

"I see an unmarked body, reclining in bed. Hair neatly brushed, cosmetic enhancements unblemished. I see on the bedside table a glass of white wine and a bottle of pills prescribed for use in painless, gentle self-termination. I have here," she continued, holding up another evidence bag containing a single sheet of paper, "a note clearly stating the subject's intention to end her own life due to her guilt about her part in the death of Reginald Weeks. A death she states was ordered by Roarke and for which she was paid fifty thousand, in cash. I see a satchel containing that precise amount of cash on the dresser."

"Roarke didn't order anyone's murder."

"Perhaps not. But I am accustomed to pursuing a line on an investigation in my own way. On my own time." She tossed Eve's words back at her. "Commander Skinner has lodged a complaint claiming that Roarke threatened him this morning, with words and a weapon. Security disks at the hotel verify that Roarke entered the commander's suite and remained there for seven minutes, forty-three seconds. This incident is corroborated by one Bryson Hayes, Skinner's personal assistant, who was present at the time."

There was no point in kicking something again and pretending it was Roarke's head. "Skinner's in this up to his armpits, and if you let him deflect your focus onto Roarke, you're not as smart as I thought. First things first. You're standing over a homicide, Chief Angelo. The second one Skinner's responsible for."

Darcia ordered her men away by pointing her finger. "Explain to me how this is homicide, and why I shouldn't have you taken to the first transport and removed from this station. Why I should not, on the evidence at hand, take Roarke in for interview as a suspect in the murder of Reginald Weeks." Temper pumped into her voice now, hot and sharp. "And let me make this clear: Your husband's money pays my salary. It doesn't buy me."

Eve kept her focus on Darcia. "Peabody!" As she waited for her aide to come to the room, Eve struggled with her own temper.

"Sir?"

"What do you see?"

"Ah. Sir. Female, late twenties, medium build. No sign of struggle or distress." She broke off as Eve took an evidence bag from Darcia, passed it over. "Standard barb, commonly used in self-termination. Prescription calls for four units. All are missing. Date on the bottle is two weeks ago, prescribed and filled in Atlanta, Georgia."

Eve nodded when she saw the flicker in Darcia's eyes, then handed Peabody the note.

"Apparently suicide note, with signature. Computer-generated. The statement therein is contradictory to other evidence."

"Very good, Peabody. Tell Chief Angelo how it contradicts."

"Well, Lieutenant, most people don't have self-termination drugs tucked in their med cabinets. Unless you're suffering from an incurable and painful illness, it takes several tests and legalities to access the drug."

Darcia held up a hand. "All the more reason to have them around."

"No, sir."

"Ma'am," Darcia corrected with a smirk at Eve. "In my country a female superior is addressed as 'ma'am.'"

"Yes, ma'am. It may be different in your country as to the process of accessing this sort of drug. In the States, you have to register. If you haven't—that is, if you're still alive within thirty days of filling the prescription, you're on auto-recall. The drugs are confiscated and you're required to submit to psychiatric testing and evaluation. But besides that, it doesn't play."

"Keep going, Peabody," Eve told her.

"The note claims she decided to off herself because she was guilty over events that took place last night. But she already had the drug in her possession. Why? And how? You established time of death at oh-four-hundred this morning, so she got her payoff and the guilts awful close, then the means to self-terminate just happen to be in her possession. It's way pat, if you follow me."

She paused, and when Darcia nodded a go-ahead, pulled in a breath and kept going. "Added to that, it doesn't follow that she would rig her apartment door to an explosive, or set another in the surveillance area to destroy the security disks of the building. Added to that," Peabody continued, obviously enjoying herself now, "Roarke's profile is directly opposed to hiring out hits, especially since Dallas popped the guy, which is one of the things he admires about her. So when you add that all up, it makes that note bogus, and this unattended death becomes a probable homicide."

"Peabody." Eve dabbed an imaginary tear from her eye. "You do me proud."

Darcia looked from one to the other. Her temper was still on the raw side, which she could admit colored her logic. Or had. "Perhaps, Officer Peabody, you could now explain how person or persons unknown gained access to this unit and persuaded this trained security expert to take termination drugs without her struggling."

"Well . . ."

"I'll take over now." Eve patted her shoulder. "You don't want to blow your streak. Person or persons unknown were admitted to the unit by the victim. Most likely to pay her off or to give her the next stage of instructions. The termination drugs were probably mixed into the wine. Person or persons unknown waited for her to slip into the first stage of the coma, at which time she was carried in here, laid out nice and pretty. The note was generated, the stage set. When it was determined that victim was dead, the explosives were rigged, and person or persons unknown went on their merry way."

"She sort of sees it," Peabody added helpfully. "Not like a psychic or anything. She just walks it through with the killer. Really mag."

"Okay, Peabody. She was a tool," Eve continued. "No more, no less. The same as Weeks was a tool. She probably joined the force to honor her father, and he used that, just as he's using Roarke's father to get to him. They don't mean anything to him as people, as flesh and blood. They're just steps and stages in his twenty-three-year war."

"Maybe not tools, then," Darcia countered, "but soldiers. To some generals they are just as dispensable. Excuse us, Officer Peabody, if you please."

"Yes, ma'am. Sir."

"I want an apology." She saw Eve wince, and smiled. "Yes, I know it'll hurt, so I want one. Not for pursuing a line of investigation, and so on. For not trusting me."

"I've known you less than twenty-four hours," Eve began, then winced again. "All right, shit. I apologize for not trusting you. And I'll go one better. For not respecting your authority."

"Accepted. I'm going to have the body taken to the ME, as a probable homicide. Your aide is very well trained."

"She's good," Eve agreed, since Peabody wasn't around to hear and get bigheaded about it. "And getting better."

"I missed the date, the significance, and I shouldn't have. I believe I would have seen these things once my annoyance with you had ebbed a bit, but that's beside the point. Now, I need to question Roarke regarding his conversation with the commander this morning, and regarding his association with Zita Vinter. To keep my official records clean, you are not included in this interview. I would appreciate it, however, if you'd remain and lead my team through the examination of the crime scene."

"No problem."

"I'll keep this as brief as I can, as I imagine both you and Roarke would like to go back and get out of those damp, dirty clothes." She tugged the sleeve of Eve's jacket as she passed. "That used to be very attractive."

"*She was easier on me than I'd've been on her,*" Eve admitted as she rolled the stiffness out of her shoulders. She'd hit the floor under Roarke harder than she'd realized and figured she should take a look at the bruises.

After a long, hot shower.

Since Roarke's response to her statement was little more than a grunt as they rode up to their suite, she took his measure. He could use some cleaning up himself, she thought. He'd ditched the ruined jacket, and the shirt beneath it had taken a beating.

She wondered if her face was as dirty as his.

"As soon as we clean up," she began as she stepped out of the elevator and into the parlor. And that was as far as she got before she was pressed up against the elevator doors with his mouth ravaging hers.

Half her brain seemed to slide out through her ears. "Whoa. What?"

"Another few seconds." With his hands gripping her shoulders and his eyes hot he looked down at her. "We wouldn't be here."

"We are here."

"That's right." He jerked the jacket halfway down her arms, savaged her neck. "That's damn right. Now let's prove it." He stripped the jacket away, ripped her shirt at the shoulder. "I want my hands on you. Yours on me."

They already were. She tugged and tore at his ruined shirt, and because her hands were busy, used her teeth on him.

Less than a foot inside the room, they dragged each other to the floor. She rolled with him, fighting with the rest of his clothes, then arching like a bridge when his mouth clamped over her breast.

Need, deep and primal, gushed through her until she moaned his name. It was always his name. She wanted more. More to give, more to take. Her fingers dug into him—hard muscle, damp flesh. The scent of smoke and death smothered under the scent of him so that it filled her with the fevered mix of love and lust that he brought to her.

He couldn't get enough. It seemed he never could, or would. All of the hungers, the appetites and desires he'd known paled to nothing against the need he had for her—for everything she was. The strength of her, physical and that uniquely tensile morality, enraptured him. Challenged him.

To feel that strength tremble under him, open for him, merge with him, was the wonder of his life.

Her breathing was short, shallow, and he heard it catch, release on a strangled gasp when he drove her over the first peak. His own blood raged as he crushed his mouth to hers again, and plunged inside her.

All heat and speed and desperation. The sound of flesh slapping, sliding against flesh mixed with the sound of ragged breathing.

She heard him murmuring something—the language of his youth, so rarely used, slid exotically around her name. The pressure of pleasure built outrageously inside her, a glorious burn in the blood as he drove her past reason with deep, hard thrusts.

She clung, clung to the edge of it. Then his eyes were locked on hers, wild and blue. Love all but swamped her.

"Come with me." His voice was thick with Ireland. "Come with me now."

She held on, and on, watching those glorious eyes go blind. Held on, and on while his body plunged in hers. Then she let go, and went with him.

Sex, Eve had discovered, could, when it was done right, benefit body, mind, and spirit. She hardly bitched at all about having to dress up to meet with Belle Skinner at a ladies' tea. Her body felt loose and limber, and while the dress Roarke handed her didn't fit her image of cop, the weapon she snugged on under the long, fluid jacket made up for it.

"Are you intending to blast some of the other women over the watercress sandwiches and petit fours?" he asked.

"You never know." She looked at the gold earrings he held out, shrugged, then put them on. "While I'm swilling tea and browbeating Belle Skinner, you can follow up on a hunch for me. Do some digging, see if Hayes was connected to any of the downed cops under Skinner's command during the botched bust. Something there too close for employer/employee relations."

"All right. Shoes."

She stared at the needle-thin heels and flimsy straps. "Is that what you call them? How come guys don't have to wear death traps like those?"

"I ask myself that same question every day." He took a long scan after she'd put them on. "Lieutenant, you look amazing."

"Feel like an idiot. How am I supposed to intimidate anyone dressed in this gear?"

"I'm sure you'll manage."

"Ladies' tea," she grumbled on the way out. "I don't know why Angelo can't just haul the woman in to her cop shop and deal."

"Don't forget your rubber hose and mini-stunner."

She smirked over her shoulder as she stepped onto the elevator. "Bite me."

"Already did."

The tea was already under way when Eve walked in. Women in flowy dresses, and some—Jesus—in hats, milled about and gathered under arbors of pink roses or spilled out onto a terrace where a harpist plucked strings and sang in a quavery voice that instantly irritated Eve's nerves.

Tiny crustless sandwiches and pink frosted cakes were arranged on clear glass platters. Shining silver pots steamed with tea that smelled, to Eve, entirely too much like the roses.

At such times she wondered how women weren't mortified to be women.

She tracked down Peabody first and was more than slightly amazed to see her stalwart aide decked out in a swirly flowered dress and a broad-brimmed straw hat with trailing ribbons.

"Jeez, Peabody, you look like a—what is it—milkmaid or something."

"Thanks, Dallas. Great shoes."

"Shut up. Run down Mira. I want her take on Skinner's wife. The two of you hang close while Angelo and I talk to her."

"Mrs. Skinner's out on the terrace. Angelo just walked in. Wow, she's got some great DNA."

Eve glanced back, nodded to Angelo. The chief had chosen to wear cool white, but rather than flowing, the dress clung to every curve.

"On the terrace," Eve told her. "How do you want to play it?"

"Subtly, Lieutenant. Subtle's my style."

Eve lifted her brows. "I don't think so."

"Interview style," Darcia said and breezed onto the terrace. She stopped, poured tea, then strolled to the table where Belle was holding court. "Lovely party, Mrs. Skinner. I know we all want to thank you for hosting this event. Such a nice break from the seminars and panels."

"It's important to remember that we're women, not just wives, mothers, career professionals."

"Absolutely. I wonder if Lieutenant Dallas and I might have a private word with you? We won't take up much of your time."

She laid a hand on the shoulder of one of the women seated at the table. Subtle, Eve thought. And effective, as the woman rose to give Darcia her chair.

"I must tell you how much I enjoyed the commander's keynote this morning," Darcia began. "So inspiring. It must be very difficult for him, and you, to deal with the convention after your tragic loss."

"Douglas and I both believe strongly in fulfilling our duties and responsibilities, whatever our personal troubles. Poor Reggie." She pressed her lips together. "It's horrible. Even being a cop's wife for half a century . . . you never get used to the shock of violent death."

"How well did you know Weeks?" Eve asked.

"Loss and shock and sorrow aren't connected only to personal knowledge, Lieutenant." Belle's voice went cool. "But I knew him quite well, actually. Douglas and I believe in forming strong and caring relationships with our employees."

Likes Angelo, Eve thought. Hates me. Okay, then. "I guess being full of shock and sorrow is the reason you eavesdropped from your bedroom instead of coming out when we notified Commander Skinner that one of his security team had been murdered."

Belle's face went very blank and still. "I don't know what you're intimating."

"I'm not intimating, I'm saying it straight out. You were in the spare room—not the master with the commander. I know you were awake, because your light was on. You heard us relay the information, but despite this close, personal relationship, you didn't come out to express your shock and loss. Why is that, Mrs. Skinner?"

"Dallas, I'm sure Mrs. Skinner has her reasons." Darcia put a light sting of censure in her voice, then turned a sympathetic smile to Belle. "I'm sorry, Mrs. Skinner. The lieutenant is, quite naturally, on edge just now."

"There's no need for you to apologize, Chief Angelo. I understand, and sympathize—to an extent—Lieutenant Dallas's desire to defend and protect her husband."

"Is that what you're doing?" Eve tossed back. "How far

would you go? How many close, personal relationships are you willing to sacrifice? Or didn't you have one with Zita Vinter?"

"Zita?" Belle's shoulders jerked, as if from a blow. "What does Zita have to do with any of this?"

"You knew her?"

"She's our godchild, of course I . . . Knew?" Every ounce of color drained out of the lovely face so that the expertly applied enhancements stood out like paint on a doll. "What's happened?"

"She's dead," Eve said flatly. "Murdered early this morning, a few hours after Weeks."

"Dead? *Dead?*" Belle got shakily to her feet, upending her teacup as she floundered for balance. "I can't—I can't talk to you now."

"Want to go after her?" Darcia asked when Belle rushed from the terrace.

"No. Let's give her time to stew. She's scared now. Over what she knows and what she doesn't know." She looked back at Darcia. "We had a pretty good rhythm going there."

"I thought so. But I imagine playing the insensitive, argumentative cop comes naturally to you."

"Just like breathing. Let's blow this tea party and go get a drink." Eve signaled to Peabody and Mira. "Just us girls."

8

In the bar, in a wide, plush booth, Eve brooded over a fizzy water. She'd have preferred the good, hard kick of a Zombie, but she wanted a clear head more than the jolt.

"You've got a smooth, sympathetic style," she said to Darcia. "I think she'll talk to you if you stay in that channel."

"So do I."

"Dr. Mira here, she's got the same deal. You'd be able to double-team her." Eve glanced toward Mira, who was sipping white wine.

"She was shocked and shaken," Mira began. "First, she'll verify the information about the death of her godchild. When she does, grief will tangle with the shock."

"So, she'll be even more vulnerable to the right questions presented in the right style."

"You're a cold one, Dallas," Darcia said. "I like that about you. I'd be very agreeable to interviewing Belle Skinner with Dr. Mira, if that suits the doctor."

"I'm happy to help. I imagine you intend to talk to Skinner again, Eve."

"With the chief's permission."

"Don't start being polite now," Darcia told her. "You'll ruin your image. He won't want to talk to you," she went on. "Whatever his feelings toward you were before, my impression is—after his keynote—he's wrapped you and Roarke together. He hates you both."

"He brought us up at his keynote?"

"Not by name, but by intimation. His inspiring, rather cheerleader-type speech took a turn at the midway point. He went into a tangent on cops who go bad, who forget their primary duties in favor of personal comforts and gains. Gestures, body language . . ." Darcia shrugged. "It was clear he was talking about this place—luxury palaces built on blood and greed, I believe he said—and you. Bedfellows of the wicked. He got very worked up about it, almost evangelical. While there were some who appeared enthusiastic and supportive of that particular line of thought, it seemed to me the bulk of the attendees were uncomfortable—embarrassed or angry."

"He wants to use his keynote to take slaps at me and Roarke, it doesn't worry me." But Eve noticed Peabody staring down into her glass. "Peabody?"

"I think he's sick." She spoke quietly, finally lifted her gaze. "Physically, mentally. I don't think he's real stable. It was hard to watch it happen this morning. He started out sort of, well, eloquent, then it just deteriorated into this rant. I've admired him all my life. It was hard to watch," she repeated. "A lot of the cops who were there stiffened up. You could almost feel layers of respect peeling away. He talked about the murder some, how a young, promising man had become a victim of petty and soulless revenge. How a killer could hide behind a badge instead of being brought to justice by one."

"Pretty pointed," Eve decided.

"A lot of the terrestrial cops walked out then."

"So he's probably a little shaky now himself. I'll take him," Eve said. "Peabody, you track down Feeney, see what other details you can dig out on the two victims and anyone else on-site who's connected with the bust in Atlanta. That fly with you, Chief Angelo?"

Darcia polished off her wine. "It does."

Eve detoured back to the suite first. She wanted a few more details before questioning Skinner again. She never doubted Roarke had already found them.

He was on the 'link when she got there, talking to his head of hotel security. Restless, Eve wandered out onto the terrace and let her mind shuffle the facts, the evidence, the lines of possibilities.

Two dead. Both victims' fathers martyred cops. And those connected to Roarke's father and to Skinner. Murdered in a world of Roarke's making, on a site filled with police officials. It was so neat, it was almost poetic.

A setup from the beginning? It wasn't a crime of impulse but something craftily, coldly planned. Weeks and Vinter had both been sacrifices, pawns placed and disgarded for the greater game. A chess game, all right, she decided. Black king against white, and her gut told her Skinner wouldn't be satisfied with a checkmate.

He wanted blood.

She turned as Roarke stepped out. "In the end, destroying you won't be enough. He's setting you up, step by step, for execution. A lot of weapons on this site. He keeps the pressure on, piles up the circumstantial so there's enough appearance that you might have ordered these hits. All he needs is one soldier willing to take the fall. I'm betting Hayes for that one. Skinner doesn't have much time to pull it off."

"No, he doesn't," Roarke agreed. "I got into his medical records. A year ago he was diagnosed with a rare disorder. It's complicated, but the best I can interpret, it sort of nibbles away at the brain."

"Treatment?"

"Yes, there are some procedures. He's had two—quietly, at a private facility in Zurich. It slowed the process, but in his case . . . He's had complications. A strain on the heart and lungs. Another attempt at correction would kill him. He was given a year. He has, perhaps, three months of that left. And of that three months, two at the outside where he'll continue to be mobile and lucid. He's made arrangements for self-termination."

"That's rough." Eve slipped her hands into her pockets. There was more—she could see it in Roarke's eyes. Something about the way he watched her now. "It plays into the rest. This one event's been stuck in his gut for decades. He wants to clear his books before he checks out. Whatever's eating at his brain has probably made him more unstable, more fanatic and less worried about the niceties. He needs to see you go down before he does. What else? What is it?"

"I went down several more layers in his case file on the bust. His follow-ups, his notes. He believed he'd tracked my father before he'd slipped out of the country again. Skinner used some connections. It was believed that my father headed west and spent a few days among some nefarious associates. In Texas. In Dallas, Eve."

Her stomach clenched, and her heart tripped for several beats. "It's a big place. It doesn't mean . . ."

"The timing's right." He walked to her, ran his hands up and down her arms as if to warm them. "Your father and mine, petty criminals searching for the big score. You were found in that Dallas alley only a few days after Skinner lost my father's trail again."

"You're saying they knew each other, your father and mine."

"I'm saying the circle's too tidy to ignore. I nearly didn't tell you," he added, resting his forehead on hers.

"Give me a minute." She stepped away from him, leaned out on the rail, stared out over the resort. But she was seeing that cold, dirty room, and herself huddled in the corner like an animal. Blood on her hands.

"He had a deal going," she said quietly. "Some deal or other, I think. He wasn't drinking as much—and it was worse for me when he wasn't good and drunk when he came back. And he had some money. Well." She took a deep breath. "Well. It plays out. Do you know what I think?"

"Tell me."

"I think sometimes fate cuts you a break. Like it says, okay, you've had enough of that crap, so it's time you fell into something nice. See what you make out of it." She turned back to him then. "We're making something out of it. Whatever they were to us, or to each other, it's what we are now that counts."

"Darling Eve. I adore you."

"Then you'll do me a favor. Keep yourself scarce for the next couple of hours. I don't want to give Skinner any opportunities. I need to talk to him, and he won't talk if you're with me."

"Agreed, with one condition. You go wired." He took a

small jeweled pin from his pocket, attached it to her lapel. "I'll monitor from here."

"It's illegal to record without all parties' knowledge and permission unless you have proper authorization."

"Is it really?" He kissed her. "That's what you get for bedding down with bad companions."

"Heard about that, did you?"

"Just as I heard that a large portion of your fellow cops walked out of the speech. Your reputation stands, Lieutenant. I imagine your seminar tomorrow will be packed."

"My . . . Shit! I forgot. I'm not thinking about it," she muttered on the way out. "Not thinking about it."

She slipped into the conference room where Skinner was leading a seminar on tactics. It was some relief to realize she'd missed the lecture and had come in during the question-and-answer period. There were a lot of long looks in her direction as she walked down the side of the room and found a seat halfway from the back.

She scoped out the setup. Skinner on stage at the podium, Hayes standing to his back and his right, at attention. Two other personal security types on his other side.

Excessive, she thought, and obviously so. The message was that the location, the situation, posed personal jeopardy for Skinner; but he was taking precautions and doing his job.

Very neat.

She raised her hand, and was ignored. Five questions passed until she simply got to her feet and addressed him. And as she rose, she noted Hayes slide a hand inside his jacket.

She knew every cop in the room caught the gesture. The room went dead quiet.

"Commander Skinner, a position of command regularly requires you to send men into situations where loss of life, civilian and departmental, is a primary risk. In such cases, do you find it more beneficial to the operation to set personal feelings for your men aside, or to use those feelings to select the team?"

"Every man who picks up a badge does so acknowledging he will give his life if need be to serve and protect. Every commander must respect that acknowledgment. Personal feelings must be weighed, in order to select the right man for the right situation. This is a matter of experience and the accumulation, through years and that experience, of recognizing the best dynamic for each given op. But personal feelings—i.e., emotional attachments, private connections, friendships, or animosities—must never color the decision."

"So, as commander, you'd have no problem sacrificing a close personal friend or connection to the success of the op?"

His color came up. And the tremor she had noticed in his hand became more pronounced. " 'Sacrificing,' Lieutenant Dallas? A poor choice of words. Cops aren't lambs being sent to slaughter. Not passive sacrifices to the greater good, but active, dedicated soldiers in the fight for justice."

"Soldiers are sacrificed in battle. Acceptable losses."

"No loss is acceptable." His bunched fist pounded the podium. "Necessary, but not acceptable. Every man who has fallen under my command weighs on me. Every child left without a father is my responsibility. Command requires this, and that the commander be strong enough to bear the burdon."

"And does command, in your opinion, require restitution for those losses?"

"It does, Lieutenant. There is no justice without payment."

"For the children of the fallen? And for the children of those who escaped the hand of justice? In your opinion."

"Blood speaks to blood." His voice began to rise, and to tremble. "If you were more concerned with justice than with your own personal choices, you wouldn't need to ask the question."

"Justice is my concern, Commander. It appears we have different definitions of the term. Do you think your goddaughter was the best choice for this operation? Does her death weigh on you now, or does it balance the other losses?"

"You're not fit to speak her name. You've whored your badge. You're a disgrace. Don't think your husband's money or threats will stop me from using all my influence to have that badge taken from you."

"I don't stand behind Roarke any more than he stands behind me." She kept talking as Hayes stepped forward and laid a hand on Skinner's shoulder. "I don't stand on yesterday's business. Two people are dead here and now. That's my priority, Commander. Justice for them is my concern."

Hayes stepped in front of Skinner. "The seminar is over. Commander Skinner thanks you for attending and regrets Lieutenant Dallas's disruption of the question-and-answer period."

People shuffled, rose. Eve saw Skinner leaving, flanked by the two guards.

"Ask me," someone commented near her, "these seminars could use more fucking disruptions."

She made her way toward the front and came up toe to toe with Hayes.

"I've got two more questions for the commander."

"I said the seminar's over. And so's your little show."

She felt the crowd milling around them, some edging close enough to hear. "You see, that's funny. I thought I came in on the show. Does he run it, Hayes, or do you?"

"Commander Skinner is a great man. Great men often need protection from whores."

A cop moved in, poked Hayes on the shoulder. "You're gonna want to watch the name-calling, man."

"Thanks." Eve acknowledged him with a nod. "I've got it."

"Don't like play cops calling a badge a whore." He stepped back, but he hovered.

"While you're protecting the great man," Eve continued, "you might want to remember that two of his front-line soldiers are in the morgue."

"Is that a threat, Lieutenant?"

"Hell, no. It's a fact, Hayes. Just like it's a fact that both of them had fathers who died under Skinner's command. What about your father?"

Furious color slashed across his cheekbones. "You know nothing of my father, and you have no right to speak of him."

"Just giving you something to think about. For some reason I get the feeling that I'm more interested in finding out who put those bodies in the morgue than you or your great man. And because I am, I will find out—before this show breaks down and moves on. That one's a promise."

9

If she couldn't get to Skinner, Eve thought, she'd get to Skinner's wife. And if Angelo and Peabody hadn't softened and soothed enough, that was too fucking bad. Damned if she was going to tiptoe around weepy women and dying men, then have to turn the case over to the interplanetary boys.

It was her case, and she meant to close it.

She knew that part of her anger and urgency stemmed from the information Roarke had given her. His father, hers, Skinner, and a team of dead cops. Skinner was right about one thing, she thought as she headed for his suite. Blood spoke to blood.

The blood of the dead had always spoken to her.

Her father and Roarke's had both met a violent end. That was all the justice she could offer to the badges lost so many years before. But there were two bodies in cold boxes. For those, whatever they'd done, she would stand.

She knocked, waited impatiently. It was Darcia who opened the door and sent Eve an apologetic little wince.

"She's a mess," Darcia whispered. "Mira's patting her hand, letting her cry over her goddaughter. It's a good foundation, but we haven't been able to build on it yet."

"Any objections to me giving the foundation a shake?"

Darcia studied her, pursed her lips. "We can try it that way, but I wouldn't shake too hard. She shatters, we're back to square one with her."

With a nod, Eve stepped in. Mira was on the sofa with Belle, and was indeed holding her hand. A teapot, cups, and countless tissues littered the table in front of them. Belle was weeping softly into a fresh one.

"Mrs. Skinner, I'm sorry for your loss." Eve sat in a chair by the sofa, leaned into the intimacy. She kept her voice quiet, sympathetic, and waited until Belle lifted swollen, red-rimmed eyes to hers.

"How can you speak of her? Your husband's responsible."

"My husband and I were nearly blown to bits by an explosive device on Zita Vinter's apartment door. A device set by her killer. Follow the dots."

"Who else had cause to kill Zita?"

"That's what we want to find out. She sabotaged the security cameras the night Weeks was murdered."

"I don't believe that." Belle balled the tissue into her fist. "Zita would never be a party to murder. She was a lovely young woman. Caring and capable."

"And devoted to your husband."

"Why shouldn't she be?" Belle's voice rose as she got to her feet. "He stepped in when her father died. Gave her his time and attention, helped with her education. He'd have done anything for her."

"And she for him?"

Belle's lips quivered, and she sat again, as if her legs quivered as well. "She would never be a party to murder. He would never ask it of her."

"Maybe she didn't know. Maybe she was just asked to deal with the cameras and nothing else. Mrs. Skinner, your husband's dying." Eve saw Belle jerk, shudder. "He doesn't have much time left, and the loss of his men is preying on him as he prepares for death. Can you sit there and tell me his behavior over the last several months has been rational?"

"I won't discuss my husband's condition with you."

"Mrs. Skinner, do you believe Roarke's responsible for something his father did? Something this man did when Roarke was a child, three thousand miles away?"

She watched tears swim into Belle's eyes again, and

leaned in. Pressed. "The man used to beat Roarke half to death for sport. Do you know what it feels like to be hit with fists, or a stick, or whatever the hell's handy—and by the person who's supposed to take care of you? By law, by simple morality. Do you know what it's like to be bloody and bruised and helpless to fight back?"

"No." The tears spilled over. "No."

"Does that child have to pay for the viciousness of the man?"

"The sins of the fathers," Belle began, then stopped. "No." Wearily, she wiped her wet cheeks. "No, Lieutenant, I don't believe that. But I know what it has cost my husband, what happened before, what was lost. I know how it's haunted him—this good, good man, this honorable man who has dedicated his life to his badge and everything it stands for."

"He can't exorcise his ghosts by destroying the son of the man who made them. You know that, too."

"He would never harm Zita, or Reggie. He loved them as if they were his own. But . . ." She turned to Mira again, gripped her hands fiercely. "He's so ill—in body, mind, spirit. I don't know how to help him. I don't know how long I can stand watching him die in stages. I'm prepared to let him go because the pain—sometimes it's so horrible. And he won't let me in. He won't share the bed with me, or his thoughts, his fears. It's as if he's divorcing me, bit by bit. I can't stop it."

"For some, death is a solitary act," Mira said gently. "Intimate and private. It's hard to love someone and stand aside while they take those steps alone."

"He agreed to apply for self-termination for me." Belle sighed. "He doesn't believe in it. He believes a man should stand up to whatever he's handed and see it through. I'm afraid he's not thinking clearly any longer. There are moments . . ."

She steadied her breathing and looked back at Eve. "There are rages, swings of mood. The medication may be partially responsible. He's never shared the job with me to any great extent. But I know that for months now, perhaps longer, Roarke has been a kind of obsession to him. As have you. You chose the devil over duty."

She closed her eyes a moment. "I'm a cop's wife, Lieutenant. I believe in that duty, and I see it all over you. He would see it, too, if he weren't so ill. I swear to you he didn't kill Reggie or Zita. But they may have been killed for him."

"Belle." Mira offered her another tissue. "You want to help your husband, to ease his pain. Tell Lieutenant Dallas and Chief Angelo what you know, what you feel. No one knows your husband's heart and mind the way you do."

"It'll shatter him. If he has to face this, it'll destroy him. Fathers and sons," she said softly, then buried her face in the tissue. "Oh, dear God."

"Hayes." It clicked for Eve like a link on a chain. "Hayes didn't lose a father during the bust. He's Commander Skinner's son."

"A single indiscretion." Tears choked Belle's voice when she lifted her head again. "During a bump in a young marriage. And so much of it my fault. My fault," she repeated, turning her pleading gaze to Mira. "I was impatient, and angry, that so much of his time, his energies went into his work. I'd married a cop, but I hadn't been willing to accept all that that meant—all it meant to a man like Douglas."

"It isn't easy to share a marriage with duty." Mira poured more tea. "Particularly when duty is what defines the partner. You were young."

"Yes." Gratitude spilled into Belle's voice as she lifted her cup. "Young and selfish, and I've done everything in my power to make up for it since. I loved him terribly, and wanted all of him. I couldn't have that, so I pushed and prodded, then I stepped away from him. All or nothing. Well. He's a proud man, and I was stubborn. We separated for six months, and during that time he turned to someone else. I can't blame him for it."

"And she got pregnant," Eve prompted.

"Yes. He never kept it from me. He never lied or tried to hide it from me. He's an honorable man." Her tone turned fierce when she looked at Eve.

"Does Hayes know?"

"Of course. Of course he knows. Douglas would never shirk his responsibilities. He provided financial support. We worked out an arrangement with the woman, and she agreed to raise the child and keep his paternity private. There was no point, no point at all in making the matter public and complicating Douglas's career, shadowing his reputation."

"So you paid for his . . . indiscretion."

"You're a hard woman, aren't you, Lieutenant? No mistakes in your life? No regrets?"

"Plenty of them. But a child—a man—might have some problem being considered a mistake. A regret."

"Douglas has been nothing but kind and generous and responsible with Bryson. He's given him everything."

Everything except his name, Eve thought. How much would that matter? "Did he give him orders to kill, Mrs. Skinner? Orders to frame Roarke for murder?"

"Absolutely not. Absolutely not. But Bryson is . . . perhaps he's overly devoted to Douglas. In the past several months, Douglas has turned to him too often, and perhaps, when Bryson was growing up, Douglas set standards that were too high, too harsh for a young boy."

"Hayes would need to prove himself to his father."

"Yes. Bryson's hard, Lieutenant. Hard and cold-blooded. You'd understand that, I think. Douglas—he's ill. And his moods, his obsession with what happened all those years ago is eating at him as viciously as his illness does. I've heard him rage, as if there's something else inside him. And during the rage he said something had to be done, some payment made, whatever the cost. That there were times the law had to make room for blood justice. Death for death. I heard him talking with Bryson, months ago, about this place. That Roarke had built it on the bones of martyred cops. That he would never rest until it, and Roarke, were destroyed. That if he died before he could avenge those who were lost, his legacy to his son was that duty."

"Pick him up." Eve swung to Darcia. "Have your people pick Hayes up."

"Already on it," Darcia answered as she switched on her communicator.

"He doesn't know." Belle got slowly to her feet. "Or he's not allowing himself to know. Douglas is convinced that Roarke's responsible for what's happened here. Convinced himself that you're part of it, Lieutenant. His mind isn't what it was. He's dying by inches. This will finish him. Have pity."

She thought of the dead, and thought of the dying. "Ask

yourself what he would have done, Mrs. Skinner, if he were standing in my place now. Dr. Mira will stay with you."

She headed out with Darcia, waited until they were well down the hall. "There should be a way to separate him from Skinner before we bag him. Take him quietly."

Darcia called for the elevator. "You're some ruthless hard-ass, aren't you, Dallas?"

"If Skinner didn't give him a direct order, there's no point in smearing him with Hayes, or making the arrest while he's around. Christ, he's a dead man already," she snapped when Darcia said nothing. "What's the fucking point of dragging him into it and destroying half a century of service?"

"None."

"I can request another interview with Skinner, draw him away far enough for you to make the collar."

"You're giving up the collar?" Darcia asked in a shocked voice as they stepped onto the elevator.

"It was never mine."

"The hell it wasn't. But I'll take it," Darcia added cheerfully. "How'd you click to the relationship between Skinner and Hayes?"

"Fathers. The case is lousy with them. You got one?"

"A father? Doesn't everyone?"

"Depends on your point of view." She stepped off the car on the main lobby level. "I'm going to round up Peabody, give you a chance to coordinate your team." She checked her wrist unit. "Fifteen minutes ought to . . . Well, well. Look who's holding court in the lobby lounge."

Darcia tracked, studied the group crowded at two tables. "Skinner looks to have recovered his composure."

"The man likes an audience. It probably pumps him up more than his meds. We could play it this way. We go over, and I apologize for disrupting the seminar. Distract Skinner, get him talking. You tell Hayes you'd like to have a word with him about Weeks. Don't want to disturb Skinner with routine questions and blah, blah. Can you take him on your own?"

Darcia gave her a bland stare. "Could you?"

"Okay, then. Let's do it. Quick and quiet."

They were halfway across the lobby when Hayes spotted them. Two beats later, he was running.

"Goddamn it, goddamn it. He's got cop instincts. Circle that way," Eve ordered, then charged the crowd. She vaulted the smooth gold rail that separated the lounge from the lobby. People shouted, spilled back. Glassware crashed as a table overturned. She caught a glimpse of Hayes as he swung through a door behind the bar.

She leaped the bar, ignoring the curses of the servers and patrons. Bottles smashed, and there was a sudden, heady scent of top-grade liquor. Her weapon was in her hand when she hit the door with her shoulder.

The bar kitchen was full of noise. A cook droid was sprawled on the floor in the narrow aisle, its head jerking from the damage done by the fall. She stumbled over it, and the blast from Hayes's laser sang over her head.

Rather than right herself, she rolled and came up behind a stainless-steel cabinet.

"Give it up, Hayes. Where are you going to go? There are innocent people in here. Drop your weapon."

"Nobody's innocent." He fired again, and the line of heat scored across the floor and finished off the droid.

"This isn't what your father wants. He doesn't want more dead piling up at his feet."

"There's no price too high for duty." A shelf of dinnerware exploded beside her, showering her with shards.

"Screw this." She sent a line of fire over her head, rolled to the left. She came up weapon first and cursed again as she lost the target around a corner.

Someone was screaming. Someone else was crying. Keeping low, she set off in pursuit. She turned toward the sound of another blast and saw a fire erupt in a pile of linens.

"Somebody take care of that!" she shouted and turned the next corner. Saw the exit door. "Shit!"

He'd blasted the locks, effectively sealing it. In frustration she rammed it, gave it a couple of solid kicks, and didn't budge it an inch.

Holstering her weapon, she made her way back out the mess and smoke. Without much hope, she ran through the lobby, out the main doors to scan the streets. By the time she'd made it to the corner, Darcia was heading back.

"Lost him. Son of a bitch. He had a block and a half on me." Darcia jammed her own weapon home. "I'd never have caught him on foot in these damn shoes. I've got an APB out. We'll net the bastard."

"Fucker smelled the collar." Furious with herself, Eve spun in a circle. "I didn't give him enough credit. He knocked some people around in the bar kitchen. Offed a droid, started a fire. He's fast and smart and slick. And he's goddamn mean on top of it."

"We'll net him," Darcia repeated.

"Damn right we will."

10

"*Lieutenant.*"

Eve winced, turned and watched Roarke walk toward her. "Guess you heard we had a little incident."

"I believe I'll just see to some damage control." Humor cut through the anger on Darcia's face. "Excuse me."

"Are you hurt?" Roarke asked Eve.

"No. But you've got a dead droid in the bar kitchen. I didn't kill it, in case you're wondering. There was a little fire, too. But I didn't start it. The ceiling damage, that's on me. And some of the, you know, breakage and stuff."

"I see." He studied the elegant facade of the hotel. "I'm sure the guests and the staff found it all very exciting. The ones who don't sue me should enjoy telling the story to their friends and relations for quite some time. Since I'll be contacting my attorneys to alert them to a number of civil suits heading our way, perhaps you'd take a moment to fill me in on why I have a dead droid, a number of hysterical guests, screaming staff, and a little fire in the bar kitchen."

"Sure. Why don't we round up Peabody and Feeney, then I can just run through it once?"

"No, I think I'd like to know now. Let's just have a bit of a walk." He took her arm.

"I don't have time to——"

"Make it."

He led her around the hotel, through the side gardens, the patio cafe, wound through one of the pool areas and into a private elevator while he listened to her report.

"So your intentions were to spare Skinner's feelings and reputation."

"Didn't work out, but, yeah, to a point. Hayes made us first glance." The minute she was in the suite, she popped open a bottle of water, glugged. Until that moment she hadn't realized the smoke had turned her throat into a raw desert of thirst. "Should've figured it. Now he's in the wind, and that's on me, too."

"He won't get off the station."

"No, he won't get off. But he might take it in mind to do some damage while he's loose. I'll need to look at the maps and plats for the resort. We'll do a computer analysis, earmark the spots he'd be most likely to go to ground."

"I'll take care of that. I can do it faster," he said before she could object. "You need a shower. You smell of smoke."

She lifted her arm, sniffed it. "Yeah, I guess I do. Since you're being so helpful, tag Peabody and Feeney, will you? I want this manhunt coordinated."

"*Too many places for him to hide.*" An hour later, Eve scowled at the wall screens and the locations the computer had selected. "I'm wondering, too, if he had some sort of backup transpo in case this turned on him, someone he's bribed to smuggle him off-site. If he gets off this station, he could go any fucking where."

"I can work with Angelo on running that angle down," Feeney said. "And some e-maneuvering can bog down anything scheduled to leave the site for a good twenty-four hours."

"Good thinking. Keep in touch, okay?"

"Will do." He headed out, rattling a bag of almonds.

"Roarke knows the site best. He'll take me around to the specified locations. We'll split them up with Angelo's team."

"Do I coordinate from here?" Peabody asked.

"Not exactly. I need you to work with Mira. Make sure

Skinner and his wife stay put and report if Hayes contacts them. Then there's this other thing."

"Yes, sir." Peabody looked up from her memo book.

"If we don't bag him tonight, you'll have to cover for me in the morning."

"Cover for you?"

"I've got the notes and whatever in here." Eve tossed her ppc into Peabody's lap.

"Notes?" Peabody stared at the little unit in horror. "Your seminar? Oh, no, sir. Uh-uh. Dallas, I'm not giving your seminar."

"Just think of yourself as backup," Eve suggested. "Roarke?" She walked to the door and through it, leaving Peabody sputtering.

"Just how much don't you want to give that seminar tomorrow?" Roarke wondered.

"I don't have to answer that until I've been given the revised Miranda warning." Eve rolled her shoulders and would have sworn she felt weight spilling off them. "Sometimes things just work out perfect, don't they?"

"Ask Peabody that in the morning."

With a laugh, she stepped into the elevator. "Let's go hunting."

They hit every location, even overlapping into Angelo's portion. It was a long, tedious, and exacting process. Later she would think that the operation had given her a more complete view of the scope of Roarke's pet project. The hotels, casinos, theaters, restaurants, the shops and businesses. The houses and buildings, the beaches and parks. The sheer sweep of the world he'd created was more than she'd imagined.

While impressive, it made the job at hand next to impossible.

It was after three in the morning when she gave it up for the night and stumbled to bed. "We'll find him tomorrow. His face is on every screen on-site. The minute he tries to buy any supplies, we'll tag him. He has to sleep, he has to eat."

"So do you." In bed, Roarke drew her against him. "Turn it off, Lieutenant. Tomorrow's soon enough."

"He won't go far." Her voice thickened with sleep. "He needs to finish it and get his father's praises. Legacies. Bloody legacies. I spent my life running from mine."

"I know." Roarke brushed the top of her head with his lips as she fell into sleep. "So have I."

This time it was he who dreamed, as he rarely did, of the alleyways of Dublin. Of himself, a young boy, too thin, with sharp eyes, nimble fingers, and fast feet. A belly too often empty.

The smell of garbage gone over, and whiskey gone stale, and the cold of the rain that gleefully seeped into bone.

He saw himself in one of those alleyways, staring down at his father, who lay with that garbage gone over, and smelled of that whiskey gone stale. And smelled, too, of death—the blood and the shit that spewed out of a man at his last moments. The knife had still been in his throat, and his eyes—filmed-over blue—were open and staring back at the boy he'd made.

He remembered, quite clearly, speaking.

Well now, you bastard, someone's done for ya. And here I thought it would be me one day who had the pleasure of that.

Without a qualm, he'd crouched and searched through the pockets for any coin or items that might be pawned or traded. There'd been nothing, but then again, there never had been much. He'd considered, briefly, taking the knife. But he'd liked the idea of it where it was too much to bother.

He'd stood then, at the age of twelve, with bruises still fresh and aching from the last beating those dead hands had given him.

And he'd spat. And he'd run.

*H*e was up before she was, as usual. Eve studied him as she grabbed her first cup of coffee. It was barely seven A.M. "You look tired."

He continued to study the stock reports on one screen and the computer analysis of potential locations on another. "Do I? I suppose I could've slept better."

When she crouched in front of him, laid a hand on his thigh, he looked at her. And sighed. She could read him well enough, he thought, his cop.

Just as he could read her, and her worry for him.

"I wonder," he began, "and I don't care to, who did me the favor of sticking that knife in him. Someone, I think, who was part of the cartel. He'd have been paid, you see, and there was nothing in his pockets. Not a fucking punt or pence on him, nor in the garbage hole we lived in. So they'd have taken it, whatever he hadn't already whored or drank or simply pissed away."

"Does it matter who?"

"Not so very much, no. But it makes me wonder." He nearly didn't say the rest, but simply having her listen soothed him. "He had my face. I forget that most times, remember that I've made myself, myself. But Christ, I have the look of him."

She slid into his lap, brushed her hands through his hair. "I don't think so." And kissed him.

"We've made each other in the end, haven't we, Darling Eve? Two lost souls into one steady unit."

"Guess we have. It's good."

He stroked his cheek against hers, and felt the fatigue wash away. "Very good."

She held on another minute, then drew back. "That's enough sloppy stuff. I've got work to do."

"When it's done, why don't we get really sloppy, you and I?"

"I can get behind that." She rose to contact Darcia and get an update on the manhunt.

"Not a sign of him anywhere," Eve told Roarke, then began to pace. "Feeney took care of transpo. Nothing's left the station. We've got him boxed in, but it's a big box with lots of angles. I need Skinner. Nobody's going to know him as well as Skinner."

"Hayes is his son," Roarke reminded her. "Do you think he'd help you?"

"Depends on how much cop is left in him. Come with me," she said. "He needs to see us both. He needs to deal with it."

*   *   *

He looked haggard, Eve thought. His skin was gray and pasty. How much was grief, how much illness, she didn't know. The combination of the two, she imagined, would finish him.

But, she noted, he'd put on a suit, and he wore his precinct pin in the lapel.

He brushed aside, with some impatience, his wife's attempt to block Eve.

"Stop fussing, Belle. Lieutenant." His gaze skimmed over Roarke, but he couldn't make himself address the man. "I want you to know I've contacted my attorneys on Hayes's behalf. I believe you and Chief Angelo have made a serious error in judgment."

"No, you don't, Commander. You've been a cop too long. I appreciate the difficulty of your position, but Hayes is the prime suspect in two murders, in sabotage, in a conspiracy to implicate Roarke in those murders. He injured bystanders while fleeing and caused considerable property damage. He also fired his weapon at a police officer. He's currently evading arrest."

"There's an explanation."

"Yes, I believe there is. He's picked up his father's banner, Commander, and he's carrying it where I don't think you intended it to go. You told me yesterday no losses are acceptable. Did you mean it?"

"The pursuit of justice often . . . In the course of duty, we . . ." He looked helplessly at his wife. "Belle, I never meant—Reggie, Zita. Have I killed them?"

"No, no." She went to him quickly, wrapped her arms around him. And he seemed to shrink into her. "It's not your fault. It's not your doing."

"If you want justice for them, Commander, help me. Where would he go? What would he do next?"

"I don't know. Do you think I haven't agonized over it through the night?"

"He hasn't slept," Belle told her. "He won't take his pain medication. He needs to rest."

"I confided in him," Skinner continued. "I shared my thoughts, my beliefs, my anger. I wanted him to carry on my mission. Not this way." Skinner sank into a chair. "Not this way, but I beat the path. I can't deny that. Your father killed for sport, for money, for the hell of it," he said to Roarke. "He didn't even know the names of the people he murdered. I look at you and see him. You grew out of him."

"I did." Roarke nodded. "And everything I've done since has been in spite of him. You can't hate him as much as I can, Commander. No matter how hard you try, you'll never reach my measure of it. But I can't live on that hate. And I'm damned if I'll die on it. Will you?"

"I've used it to keep me alive these past months." Skinner looked down at his hands. "It's ruined me. My son is a thorough man. He'll have a back door. Someone inside who'll help him gain access to the hotel. He'll need it to finish what he started."

"Assassinate Roarke?"

"No, Lieutenant. Payment would be dearer than that. It's you he'll aim for." He lifted a hand to a face that had gone clammy. "To take away what his target cherishes most."

When he hissed in pain, Eve stepped forward. "You need medical attention, Commander. You need to be in the hospital."

"No hospitals. No health centers. Try to take him alive, Dallas. I want him to get the help he needs."

"You have to go." Belle stepped in. "He can't take any more of this."

"I'll send Dr. Mira." Even as Eve spoke, Skinner slumped in the chair.

"He's unconscious." Roarke instinctively loosened Skinner's tie. "His breathing's very shallow."

"Don't touch him! Let me—" Belle jerked back as her eyes met Roarke's. She took a long, deep breath. "I'm sorry. Could you help me, please? Take him into his bedroom. If you'd call for Dr. Mira, Lieutenant Dallas, I'd be grateful."

His body's wearing down," Eve said once Skinner was settled in the bedroom with Mira in attendance. "Maybe it's better all around if he goes before we take Hayes."

"His body was already worn down," Roarke corrected. "But he's let go of his reason to live."

"There's nothing to do but leave him to Mira. The computer didn't think Hayes would come back to the hotel. Skinner does. I'm going with Skinner. Hayes wants me, and he knows Skinner's on borrowed time so he has to move fast." She checked her wrist unit. "Looks like I'm going to give that damn seminar after all."

"And make yourself a target?"

"With plenty of shield. We'll coordinate your security people and Angelo's and pluck him like a goose if he tries for a hit here." She started out, pulling a borrowed communicator out of her pocket.

Then drew her weapon as she saw Hayes step out of the stairway door at the end of the corridor.

"Stop!" She pounded after him when he ducked back into the stairwell. "Get to security!" Eve shouted at Roarke. "Track him!"

Roarke shoved through the door ahead of her. The weapon in his hand was illegal. "No. You track him."

Since cursing was a waste of time, she raced down the stairs with him. "Subject sighted," she called through the communicator as they streaked down the stairs. "Heading down southeast stairwell, now between floors twenty-one and twenty. Moving fast. Consider subject armed and dangerous."

She clicked the communicator off before she spoke to Roarke. "Don't kill him. Don't fire that thing unless there's no choice."

A blast hit the landing seconds before their feet. "Such as now?" Roarke commented.

But it was Eve who fired, leaning over the railing and turning the steps below into rubble. Caught in midstride, Hayes tried to swing back, bolt for the door, but his momentum skewed his balance.

He went down hard on the smoking, broken steps.

And Angelo shoved through the door, weapon gripped in both hands.

"Trying to take my collar, Dallas?"

"All yours." Eve stepped down, onto the weapon that had flown out of Hayes's hand. "Two people dead. For what?" she asked Hayes. "Was it worth it?"

His mouth and his leg were bleeding. He swiped at the

blood on his chin while his eyes burned into hers. "No. I should've been more direct. I should've just blown you to hell right away and watched the bastard you fuck bleed over you. That would've been worth everything, knowing he'd live with the kind of pain his father caused. The commander could've died at peace knowing I'd found his justice. I wanted to give him more."

"Did you give Weeks or Vinter a choice?" Eve demanded. "Did you tell them they were going to die for the cause?"

"Command isn't required to explain. They honored their fathers, as I honor mine. There's no other choice."

"You signaled Weeks to move in on me, and he didn't have a clue what it was going to cost him. You had Vinter sabotage the cameras, and when she realized why, you killed her."

"They were necessary losses. Justice requires payment. You were going to be my last gift to him. You in a cage," he said to Roarke. "You in a coffin." He smiled at Eve when he said it. "Why aren't you giving your seminar, Lieutenant? Why the hell aren't you where you're scheduled to be?"

"I had a conflict of . . ." She shot to her feet. "Oh, God. Peabody."

She charged through the door and out into the corridor. "What floor? What floor?"

"This way." Roarke grabbed her hand, pulled her toward the elevator. "Down to four," he said. "We'll head left. Second door on the right takes us behind the stage area."

"Explosives. He likes explosives." She dragged out her communicator again as she willed the elevator to hurry. "She's turned hers off. Son of a bitch! Any officer, any officer, clear Conference Room D immediately. Clear the area of all personnel. Possible explosive device. Alert Explosive Division. Clear that area now!"

She was through the door and streaking to the left.

I sent her there, was all she could think. And I smirked about it.

Oh, God, please.

There was a roaring in her ears that was either her own rush of blood, the noise of the audience, or the shouted orders to clear.

But she spotted Peabody standing behind the podium and

leaped the three steps on the side of the stage. Leaped again
the minute her feet hit the ground and, hitting her aide mid-
body, shot them both into the air and into a bruised and
tangled heap on the floor.

She sucked in her breath, then lost it again as Roarke
landed on top of her.

The explosion rang in her ears, sent the floor under her
shaking. She felt the mean heat of it spew over her like a
wave that sent the three of them rolling in one ball toward
the far edge of the stage.

Debris rained over them, some of it flaming. Dimly she
heard running feet, shouts, and the sizzling hiss of a fire.

For the second time in two days, she was drenched with
the spray of overhead sprinklers.

"Are you all right?" Roarke said in her ear.

"Yeah, yeah. Peabody." Coughing, eyes stinging with
smoke, Eve eased back, saw her aide's pale face, glassy eyes.
"You okay?"

"Think so." She blinked. " 'Cept you've got two heads,
Dallas, and one of them's Roarke's. It's the prettiest. And I
think you've really gained some weight." She smiled vaguely
and passed out.

"Got herself a nice concussion," Eve decided, then turned
her head so her nose bumped Roarke's. "You are pretty,
though. Now get the hell off me. This is seriously undigni-
fied."

"Absolutely, Lieutenant."

While the med-techs tended to Peabody, and the Explosives Division cordoned off the scene, Eve sat outside the
conference room and drank the coffee some unnamed and
beloved soul had handed her.

She was soaked to the skin, filthy, had a few cuts, a medley
of bruises. She figured her ears might stop ringing by Christ-
mas.

But all in all, she felt just fine.

"You're going to have a few repairs on this dump of
yours," she told Roarke.

"Just can't take you anywhere, can I?"

She smiled, then got to her feet as Darcia approached.
"Hayes is in custody. He's waived his right to attorney. My
opinion, he'll end up in a facility for violent offenders, men-

tal defectives. He's not going to serve time in a standard cage. He's warped. If it's any consolation, he was very disappointed to hear you aren't splattered all over what's left of that stage in there."

"Can't always get what you want."

"Hell of a way to skate out of giving a workshop, though. Have to hand it to you."

"Whatever works."

Sobering, Darcia turned. "We beat interplanetary deadline. Thanks."

"I won't say anytime."

"I'll have a full report for your files by the end of the day," she said to Roarke. "I hope your next visit is less . . . complicated," she added.

"It was an experience watching you in action, Chief Angelo. I'm confident Olympus is in good hands."

"Count on it. You know, Dallas, you look like you could use a nice resort vacation." She shot out that brilliant smile. "See you around."

"She's got a smart mouth. I've got to admire that. I'm going to check on Peabody," she began, then stopped when she saw Mira coming toward her.

"He's gone," Mira said simply. "He had time to say good-bye to his wife, and to ask me to tell you that he was wrong. Blood doesn't always tell. I witnessed the termination. He left life with courage and dignity. He asked me if you would stand in the way of his departmental service and burial."

"What did you tell him?"

"I told him that blood doesn't always tell. Character does. I'm going back to his wife now."

"Tell her I'm sorry for her loss, and that law enforcement has lost one of its great heroes today."

Mira leaned over to kiss Eve's cheek, smiling when Eve squirmed. "You have a good heart."

"And clear vision," Roarke added when Mira walked away.

"Clear vision?"

"To see through the dreck and the shadows to the core of the man."

"Nobody gets through life without fucking up. He gave fifty years to the badge. It wasn't all what it should've been, but it was fifty years. Anyway." She shook off sentiment. "I've got to check on Peabody."

Roarke took her hand, kissed it. "We'll go check on Peabody. Then we'll talk about that nice resort vacation."

In a pig's eye, she thought. She was going home as soon as humanly possible. The streets of New York were resort enough for her.

Look for *Eve* and *Roarke* to return in

SEDUCTION IN DEATH

coming in September from Berkley Books!

Kinsman

Susan Krinard

1

Jonas Kane VelArhan strode toward Persephone Station's docking bay with little thought to the people who moved quickly out of his way, or the glances they cast after him, full of hostility and fear.

He was a Kinsman. Kinsmen had been objects of envy and resentment in human space for nearly a century, ever since explorer and telepath Eeva Kane initiated a lasting peace between humanity and the alien shaauri.

Kinsman. For Jonas the name was a source of pride. He and those like him, Eeva's descendants and recruits, were the adopted kin of the shaauri—the only humans allowed to enter and cross the alien space that separated the two clusters of human worlds. They were a breed apart.

A Kinsman telepath on a human trade ship guaranteed its safe passage. Even those Kinsmen born without the telepathic gift held vital roles in the maintenance and administration of Kinsman stations and ships. Kinsmen held control of most interstellar commerce within the Concordat. They alone kept the fragile peace. They were privileged, rich . . . and sometimes hated.

Jonas was accustomed to the distrust of ordinary humans. But he hadn't expected the obstacles his own people had thrown up in his face when he made the simple request to return to Persephone, the world to which this station belonged. After seven years among the shaauri, he'd expected a warmer welcome.

Oh, the obstacles weren't obvious, never broached directly. It seemed the Directors at Kinsman Prime wished to "debrief" him before he returned to duty. That in itself wasn't surprising. But he kept remembering the behavior of the nontelepathic bureaucrats in the Station's Kinsman precinct office, the way they'd avoided his gaze. As if they had something to hide.

Or was it him? Were his perceptions so changed?

His steps slowed, and he paused beside a viewport looking out on Persephone, a jeweled sphere far below, streaked with emerald and purple. It had been so long since he'd followed in his father's footsteps as Kinsman liaison for the ruling Challinor family on Persephone. So long since the accident that had killed his wife and taken the lives of Calypso and Georg Challinor, leaving him the sole survivor.

He'd been within his rights to resign his duties temporarily and concentrate on healing from his injuries. Within his rights to return when he felt ready. But he'd spent more time with his adopted shaauri family than any other adult Kinsman in the past century, and naturally the Directors would wish to know what he had learned.

He had learned how to do without reliable use of the telepathic powers he'd been born with. He had learned to understand the complex shaauri language by immersing himself in the alien culture instead of depending upon his mind to read the subtle nuances that most humans missed. He was familiar with the slightest shifts in their body language. He had given himself up to the ministrations of shaauri doctors, who had adapted his ears to hear the high pitches and subvocal sounds that shaauri made, and who had altered his vocal cords to produce those same sounds.

Now he was almost as mentally blind as the nontelepathic Kinsmen who never dealt with the shaauri. Perhaps this sense of wrongness was simply the vast gulf he felt between him and his people. Paranoia. Looking for something that wasn't there, just because he had come to suspect that the accident had not been an accident at all.

But he did suspect. He had to learn the truth. On Persephone he could request an audience with Thetis Challinor, the ruler, or "Archon," of the planet. She hated the shaauri, but it was a place to start. If she had similar suspicions about the mission that had ended in the death of her son and heir . . .

"I beg your pardon."

He emerged from his reverie at the sound of the young woman's voice and the touch of her fingers on his sleeve. His first reaction was to shake her off and be on his way, but a glance at her face made him pause.

She was a stranger to him. Small, compact, with a shapely figure and a piquant face framed by straight blond hair. Pretty, under the garish face decorations that Persephoneans favored, and dressed in knee-length tunic and pants that fit more snugly than had been the fashion when he had left human space.

"What do you want?" he asked.

She dropped her gaze. Her eyes were pale, matching the hair. "I am sorry . . . sir. I recognized you by your uniform. I need the help of a Kinsman . . ." She trailed off, losing her nerve under his stare.

Of course—just another worldbound human who knew nothing of Kinsmen but legends and was ignorant of the proprieties. She clearly didn't realize that one who wished to hire a Kinsman didn't accost him in a public corridor but made formal application at the nearest Kinsman precinct office. What would such a girl—no trader or corporate employee or wealthy traveler, by his educated guess—want with a Kinsman in any case?

She looked up, and he saw the determination in her eyes. He let his gaze stray to her small, straight nose, the pointed chin, the surprisingly full lips.

Lush lips. He had not been with a human woman, Kinsman or otherwise, in nearly seven years. The last woman had been his wife. He'd been celibate since the accident. The shaauri were not fond of celibacy, but he had been alone among them.

His groin tightened into instant arousal. To lie with one of his own again . . .

But she wasn't his own. He moved to walk away. "If you wish to hire a Kinsman, go to the office in sector nine."

Her feet tapped out a firm rhythm behind him. "I've been

there," she said. "They won't even listen. Please—I need your help."

He came to a stop. Something flickered in his mind—a spark where a flame had dwelled, alerting him into utter stillness. He could almost, *almost* shape it, nurse it along to the old brightness. He tried, and failed. All it gave him was the hint of warning, of depths untapped, of secrets.

All hidden in this woman.

He turned to her again and flowed into the receptive state that he had taught himself during his alien pilgrimage. His senses focused on the woman, noting every tiny change in her posture, every twitch of her skin, every shift of her gaze. Humans were not nearly so difficult to read as shaauri.

Yes, she was hiding something. But she was also telling the truth. She needed help, and badly. He thought that she particularly felt alone.

As he did.

"Who are you?" he asked.

A smile crossed her lips, and faded. "My name is Téa. Galatéa Dianthe, of Eldoris Province on Persephone. My brother was a member of the crew of the Royal trade ship *Eurydice.* It left on a trade run to the Nine Worlds three weeks ago. It never returned, and I know that the only people who could look for it are—"

He held up his hand. "I know nothing of this *Eurydice,* or of lost ships. I've been out of human space for seven years."

"Mr.—"

"Kane VelArhan."

Her eyes widened. "The last part of the name, VelArhan—it comes from your shaauri family, the one that adopted you?"

"If you know that much about Kinsmen, you know we do not take assignments directly from the client. I will direct you to—"

"Kane VelArhan," she said breathlessly, heedless of the discourtesy of interrupting him. "Kane was the human surname of the Kinsman who worked for our royal family many years ago. Even in the provinces, we knew of him."

"My father," he said. *And I, for too brief a time.*

"Then you are exactly who I need. The other Kinsmen won't even see me. But your family served the Challinors.

You would care what became of them—" She clasped her hands at her waist. "You would care if the second heir to the throne had disappeared in shaauri space. Wouldn't you?"

His attention was caught by a single sentence: *"You would care if the second heir to the throne had disappeared."*

The *second* heir. Lord Hector Challinor was heir apparent, first grandson of Thetis Challinor. Unless much had changed during his self-imposed exile, the next in line was Miklos Challinor, a young man Jonas remembered as something of a likable hothead. He had a sister as well, who'd been serving in the Concordat's Navy during Jonas's brief tenure at the palace.

Hector, Miklos, and Kori, Thetis's grandchildren, left orphaned by the accident. Téa was right. He did care what became of them, because he had been pilot of the ship in which their parents lost their lives.

He held Téa still with his gaze. "This lost ship *Eurydice* carried a Persephonean heir?"

"Yes." Her eyes grew bright, all naive courage. "My brother was a member of the crew. It was a new ship, very fast, and my brother was so proud to serve—" She swallowed. "It hasn't come back, and it never reached the Nine Worlds."

Jonas had no doubt that she was telling the truth. All he need do was check the latest Persephonean newscasts. But why would such a disaster be ignored by Kinsmen, especially those on this station? If a ship was lost, so was the Kinsman or Kinsmen on board. No stone would be left unturned to find them.

And Persephone would be in an uproar.

He thought back to the faces of his fellow Kinsmen. They'd been tense, too void of expression. Perhaps they thought he already knew. But they hadn't wanted him down on Persephone.

"A ship can't simply disappear in shaauri space, not with a Kinsman on board—"

"There was no Kinsman on board."

Shaauri did not laugh, not as humans did. The sound Jonas made was more of a snarl. "You said the ship went into the shaauri zone."

"Yes."

"No human ship enters shaauri territory without a Kinsman."

"This one did." She lifted her chin to meet his stare. "It hasn't been announced on the newscasts. The royal family must know, but they're keeping it secret. My brother—Acteon—told me before he left and swore me to silence. He promised to send me word when they reached the Nine Worlds. I know something's gone wrong."

Jonas caught her by the arm and pulled her after him toward the observation deck. He sat her down on a bench overlooking the rows of small ships in their berths, his sleek shaauri craft among them.

"I have been away for seven years," he said, "but seven years doesn't change the nature of the universe." Even though he stood over her, menacing and grim, she showed no sign of fear. After a long moment he sat beside her. "Start from the beginning. Tell me how a human ship dared to enter shaauri space without a Kinsman, and how it has gone unnoticed."

A frown settled between her brows. "Lord Miklos—the heir presumptive—captains the Royal trade flagship, *Eurydice*. Acteon told me that he decided to cross space without a Kinsman. He picked a special crew of volunteers. Acteon considered it a great challenge."

"A challenge." *Suicide.* "Why?"

"I don't entirely understand. Something about . . . problems with other Persephonean ships. Problems with—I'm sorry—with Kinsmen delaying important trade to the Nine Worlds, upsetting schedules. Rumors. We'd all heard them. But my brother knew more. He said that Lord Miklos was angry and planned to make a stand—to prove that humans were ready to deal directly with shaauri instead of relying on Kinsmen. Acteon believed that Lord Miklos could get them across." She twisted her fingers in her lap. "People don't know Lord Miklos is missing. He's supposed to be on a diplomatic trade mission to Hanuman. But I'm afraid something happened to the ship. The shaauri—" She broke off, her eyes pleading. "The other Kinsmen won't help. They act like they don't know, but they have to, don't they? Could a ship cross shaauri space without Kinsmen learning of it?"

She reached out, almost touched him. "I need to know if my brother is dead or alive."

Jonas felt an upwelling of nausea tighten his chest. The implications of Téa's words would have been stunning . . . if not for what had happened seven years ago.

Kinsmen delaying trade. Why? Persephone was one of their major clients, with the highest percentage of trade ships crossing to and from the Nine Worlds. Persephone, like other worlds in the Concordat, relied on the raw materials of the frontier to feed their populations and to provide fuel, and the Nine required the Concordat's expertise and advanced technology. Their dependence upon each other was the reason that Kinsmen were necessary.

Miklos Challinor was a high-spirited young man, but it would take some great provocation to make him attempt something so flagrantly dangerous. Defying a century of custom, tradition, the very rules that made human-alien peace possible. Would Thetis Challinor have known of this, and approved, even at the risk of provoking the shaauri into a second war?

And why wasn't the Kinsman grapevine ringing with news of this outrage? Kinsmen had to know about it, had to have caught the transgressors at one of the many stations scattered at every wormhole that led into shaauri territory. Shaauri wouldn't have been left to deal with the intruders.

But if Kinsmen had caught the ship, and no one else knew . . .

Either his people had lost the *Eurydice,* or something else had happened. And Kinsmen didn't want that something else known.

"I recognize," Téa said into his silence, "that what my brother did was foolhardy. Wrong, by our treaty with the shaauri."

His attention snapped back to her. "Do you know why my people must accompany every human ship that makes use of shaauri wormholes?"

"Because of the war. Because you are telepaths."

"Because my ancestors were the first to understand the shaauri. Humans were freely crossing shaauri space when the shaauri reclaimed it after a long absence. Shaauri territorial instincts are powerful. Warnings were exchanged. Ordinary humans misinterpreted shaauri communications, because they were incapable of hearing a third of the shaauri vocalizations, or of understanding their complex body language. The humans who encountered shaauri in their space managed to insult the shaauri beyond mending."

"And that led to war," Téa said softly.

"Yes. It lasted for years, until Eeva Kane used her telepathy to 'read' the shaauri and established the first real communications with them. One of the leading shaauri Lines adopted her as one of their own—Line Arhan. My Line. And they did the same with her family and a few others in her party. They became shaauri in all but blood and were given permission to cross the shaauri zone unmolested."

Téa regarded him earnestly. "And all Eeva's descendants, and those of the telepaths she recruited, had the same privileges. I heard that as children, Kinsmen even live with their shaauri families."

"Yes." He thought of Lashii, and Hraan, and the other members of his Line-bond. They were more family to him now than any human could be, and yet he was alone. "Because we are as shaauri, we grant a temporary Line adoption to the crew of human trade ships, which protects them as we are protected. Any ship that attempts to cross without one of us is out-Line, alien. And the shaauri are not merciful with intruders."

Staring out at the ranked ships, Téa shuddered.

Inexplicably, he was moved to comfort her. She was very near, and the warmth of her body felt completely different from that of the shaauri with their glossy red fur. Again he was reminded that she was a woman. A human woman. Lovely, and in need.

But there were things he could not tell her, things that wouldn't give her peace even if he did. Persephone had been in secret negotiations with a faction of progressive shaauri for years, long before that fateful explosion that had killed the original Challinor heir.

Jonas's father had been Kinsman-Challinor liaison when the catalyst for those negotiations came about. Thorfinn Kane VelArhan was the only Kinsman involved, though he would have informed the Kinsman Directors of his work and progress.

It was likely that other Kinsmen learned of the negotiations. Had those negotiations succeeded, trade might be carried out independently of the Kinsmen and their monopoly.

Some—many—Kinsmen wouldn't wish to see that happen. But Jonas would never have believed that any Kinsman would stoop to outright treachery and assaults against the royal family—if not for the "accident."

And now this.

Were those secret and threatening negotiations behind the loss of two ships seven years apart? If so, the negotiations must have continued. They must be close to succeeding. Which made Lord Miklos's provocative act rash indeed.

If he could speak with Thetis Challinor, he might know more. But if he approached her now, he would call attention to himself and the things he needed to learn. The things he *must* learn.

The alternative could be death, war, destruction. The dissolution of the alliances that humans like the Challinors had worked so hard to build from the ashes of the original colonies.

And he, Jonas Kane VelArhan, perhaps least human of all Kinsmen, was the one who had to find answers.

A light touch settled on the back of his hand. Fingertips. Slightly calloused, as with manual labor, but gentle. Unafraid.

"You will help me," she said, as if he'd already agreed.

He met her clear gaze. "What do you want of me?"

"To take me into shaauri space. To discover what happened. To find out if my brother is still alive."

She didn't know what she asked. She treated him as if he were a free agent, able to do as he liked. He hadn't yet reported for his debriefing, but he was still of the Kinsmen. Loyal to his people. As she was loyal to hers.

Such a woman would be a burden to him. Except that he knew she told the truth about her brother and the *Eurydice,* he had no reason to trust her. No reason to do more than collect all the information she had and then dismiss her.

His touch-starved body gave him reason enough.

"I know you doubt me," she said. Her hand tightened over his, surprisingly strong. "I do have something to give you in exchange for your help."

His imagination conjured up an image of the two of them on his ship, in his bed, entangled on the *min*-silk sheets. Her slender legs curled round him, pulling him inside her. She gasped and cried out as he entered, thrust, remembered what it was to be human.

Such bargains could be made. But he had not yet sunk so low.

"There is nothing you can give me," he said roughly, pulling free.

"You're wrong. Among your people, telepaths are only a little more common than they are among ordinary humans. No one has ever found a way to genetically manipulate humans to produce the trait, or even test for it before puberty. But you need more telepaths. They are the ones who guide human ships. You need to find all the telepaths you can from all over the Concordat and recruit them, so that you can have telepathic children."

His mouth went dry at her words. She was not so ignorant as she pretended. He and Jennara . . . might have had such children, if she'd survived. Every telepathic Kinsman was expected to produce children until one was born with the talent.

"What are you saying?" he whispered.

"I am a telepath," she said calmly, as if such a pronouncement was as unimportant as a casual jest. "I can give you children. And I will, if you help me find my brother."

2

The shock was plain on his face, though he was quick to smooth his expression. Kori Galatéa Challinor breathed a prayer of gratitude that he hadn't recognized her for what she was from the first moment of their meeting.

He would hardly have reason to remember the child she'd been—a child he had met rarely, only when his father had attended formal functions at the palace. Her disguise was carefully assembled, but there was always the risk that his telepathic skills would uncover her true identity in spite of her mental shields.

Obviously there were still a few things she had to learn about Kinsmen. This one in particular.

Jonas Kane VelArhan. Kinsman, adopted of the shaauri Arhan Line. He wore the deep red uniform of his people— the same red as shaauri fur—barred with telepath black at the shoulders. At his back he carried the curved shaauri knife, presented to each Kinsman child upon his or her formal adoption into a shaauri Line. His hair was dark, his body tall and well formed, his features handsome, like his father's.

Jonas Kane VelArhan. He was the very one she'd waited so long to find. The one her operatives in Royal Intelligence had finally located after so many years, the one who might know what lay behind the "accident" that had killed her parents. Who might be willing to help her.

Help not the third heir in line for the Persephonean throne, Thetis Challinor's granddaughter, but the sister of a simple crewman serving on the *Eurydice*. And a telepath, possessing the one bargaining chip no Kinsman could pass up.

She felt the full weight of his stare. It was enough to intimidate any ordinary human, quite without the addition of his telepathic powers. As a girl, she'd been fascinated by Kinsmen and their alien ways, dreamed young-girl dreams of roaming the space lanes as one of them.

But that was before her parents died, and she became an officer of Royal Intelligence. Before she came to believe that Kinsmen could betray their own species. Before she learned how lonely it could be as a telepath among nontelepaths, unable to share her gift, further set apart from her fellow Persephoneans by her rank and her profession.

Maybe that was why she was all too aware of Jonas as a man as well as a Kinsman. A man who was attracted to the woman she pretended to be. She didn't need her training or telepathy to recognize that much. Or the way he was trying to hide it.

"You claim to be a telepath?" he said, his deep voice skeptical.

Let him underestimate her; she would need every advantage she could get if he proved to be enemy rather than ally. "Can't one telepath recognize another?" she countered. He didn't answer. His gray eyes were shielded—would his mind be shielded as well?

Her thoughts flashed to a possible future, one in which she was his contracted mate. Sharing his bed, lying beneath him, feeling him move inside her. She was no virgin, but . . . a Kinsman for a lover—this man, with his alien ways and arrogance and ability to share her thoughts? Unexpectedly, it excited her and woke a powerful yearning she finally recognized for what it was. The need to belong. To be wanted. To be loved.

She forced the yearnings from her mind. There would be no need to share his bed. Persephonean technology could easily enable her to donate eggs from her body to be nurtured in artificial wombs. Not that she had any intention of going so far. She had no compunction about deceiving one Kinsman in order to save Persephone, perhaps humanity itself.

"There are many such temporary contracts on Persephone," she said. "I would sign one to give you children. Is that useful to you?"

With a smooth, supple motion he got to his feet and paced away. "Do you know what you're offering?"

"Yes. My brother is all the family I have left."

His back was a field of black-barred maroon, turned firmly against her. He didn't quite believe her. Was afraid to believe her.

"You need more proof," she said. She gathered herself, closed her eyes, and reached into his mind. There was resistance, but not on the surface. That was easy enough to skim.

What startled her was the profound sense of isolation that surrounded him. Isolation not only from ordinary humanity but from his own people as well. Isolation even from the shaauri among whom he had lived. It was as if he was neither human, nor alien, nor Kinsman.

And beyond that . . . a barrier so strong she couldn't hope to penetrate it.

"You've been living among the shaauri for the past seven years," she said, sifting through what she'd discovered. "You have a shaauri friend named Hra . . . *Hraan.*" She pronounced the alien name as he did in his mind, with a roll on the *r* and a slight break between the two vowels. "Your ship is a shaauri vessel, a gift from your alien family. You care about what happens to the Challinors. Your first name is Jonas. And you want what I offer."

She hardly had time to brace herself before he spun around and all but leaped at her, his fingers curled centimeters from her shoulders. It was not the reaction of a human.

"Never," he said harshly, "*never* enter another telepath's mind without permission."

Kori was not the type who flinched at danger; in her line of work, you didn't let others see your weaknesses or lose your nerve easily. Jonas Kane VelArhan almost made her slip.

"I'm sorry. I . . . haven't been around many telepaths." That, at least, was the truth.

He straightened and looked at her through half-lidded

eyes. "Among Kinsman, no man or woman reads a fellow Kinsman's thoughts unless invited. It is an unthinkable breach of conduct."

That, then, might explain why he hadn't known who and what she was. Still didn't know. Honor among Kinsmen.

"You read shaauri thoughts," she said.

"Shaauri are not true telepaths, but they form bonds that are not dissimilar. We touch only the thoughts connected with the words they speak, to help us interpret."

"And non-Kinsman humans?" she said, suddenly rebellious. "Do you grant them the same courtesy?"

He let out a slow breath, well in hand again. "Three-quarters of my people are not telepaths," he said. "We do not invade the thoughts of others. It's the worst kind of violation, a rape of the mind. And we value truth, as the shaauri do. They don't lie in the way of humans. We follow their example."

Kori was careful not to let her eyes reveal the slightest skepticism. *You're wrong, Jonas. You're lying right now— to yourself. If I'm right, your people are more than capable of deception.*

"I am not lying," she said. "Surely you can see that much?"

His stare took on an eerie distance, as if he had retreated into some alien persona. "You offer yourself—your children—to the Kinsmen."

"To you."

"You would sign a contract to give me at least one telepathic child. It might take years—"

"I know."

He backed away and walked to the wide viewport that overlooked the docks. His hands clenched on the smooth metal railing.

If he didn't agree, if she could find no other way to win his cooperation, she would lose the best means she had to uncover a potentially deadly Kinsman plot.

She rose and went to stand behind him. Carefully she laid her palm against his back. The alien cloth was warm and smooth under her skin. His breathing caught and released.

Abdera's moons. Touching him like this was almost like

reading his mind. He needed a human touch. He needed *her,* and she couldn't afford to give herself.

But he wouldn't come out of this unrewarded.

"Please," she whispered. "I wouldn't regret . . . such a bargain."

Muscles tensed and shifted beneath her palm. She thought he was about to fling her off, refuse. He didn't so much as turn his head.

"Very well," he said. "In exchange for my help in locating the *Eurydice,* you give me one telepathic child and surrender all parental rights to him or her. We can negotiate about any other children produced before. The contract will continue until the birth of the telepathic child, or for five years, on the condition that you are prepared to produce one child a year."

It was cold, so cold. "That will be no difficulty," she said stiffly, withdrawing her hand. "It's not as if I'll be bearing the children myself. I will donate one ovum a year, and give you guardianship of any telepathic child. But the non-telepathic children must be mine, to raise as I wish."

He turned to face her, a strange light in his eyes. "You labor under a misapprehension," he said. "Kinsmen do not use artificial-birth technology. To shaauri, family is life. No shaauri female would consider letting her children be taken from her body. If you sign the contract, you will return to Kinsman Prime as my mate, and the children we make together will be carried in your womb."

This time it was her turn to hide her shock. None of her carefully gathered intelligence had revealed this little facet of Kinsman life. Now it was clear why he had reacted so strongly to her offer.

He expected her to sacrifice five years of her life, to live among strangers, bear as many as five children, and possibly give at least one of them up forever.

Of course it would never happen. She was third in line to the throne, a member of the royal family. There were others who could assume the throne if she and both her brothers died—Persephone was no longer an absolute monarchy—but tradition would not allow such an unorthodox union.

She had to make Jonas believe that Téa Dianthe *would.* The fate of all humans and shaauri might depend upon him.

That, and the life of her brother and his ship's crew. If they were not already lost.

Heat surged back into her face. "I . . . see."

His smile held a bitter edge. "Have you changed your mind?"

"No." All her tension and anger flowed into her hands. She clenched them and let them relax. "I haven't changed my mind. For my brother's sake."

"Then we will sign a personal contract aboard my ship, and register it when we return."

"We'll leave right away?"

"When I've learned all I can at this station, and you've told me everything you know about the *Eurydice* and its captain's intentions. They should have filed a flight plan here, if they left from Persephone. But if they went without a Kinsman—"

"My brother gave me their flight plan," she said. "You're going to ask the other Kinsmen here what they know about the *Eurydice*?"

"I may have more success than you did." His voice grew rough. "Did you attempt to enter their minds?"

"I couldn't sense anything concrete."

He frowned. "All Kinsmen can block, but they seldom feel the need." His gaze turned inward. "While I'm gone, you're to wait at my ship. I'll take you there now."

So quickly, then. She'd met him a mere half hour ago and already she was committed. Just not quite in the way Jonas Kane VelArhan assumed.

He led her from the observation deck and into one of the piers strung with docked starships, some like pretty silver jewels, others gaudy with paint and decoration.

His ship was the strangest of all. It wasn't so much that the shaauri vessel appeared vastly different from a human ship, but there was a certain alienness to it that couldn't be ignored. Kinsmen used some shaauri technology, but she guessed that this one was unique.

"Afraid?" he said behind her as she hesitated at the end of the ramp. The airlock hatch slid open.

In answer she stepped into the ship. The main cabin was utilitarian but not uncomfortable, with room enough for six passengers. Jonas ducked into the cockpit and the air circulators hummed to life, releasing a faint, unusual scent. Shaauri, perhaps. Only Kinsmen ever got close enough to smell them.

"Make yourself comfortable," Jonas said. "I'll be back within a few hours. There are provisions in the galley, aft. It's not luxurious, but it should suffice."

She nodded her thanks. He paused at the hatch to stare at her, dark brows drawn, as if he would say something more personal. As if he might actually speak to her as his future mate and mother of his children.

With a slight shake of his head, he stepped out of the ship.

Kori settled into one of the seats nearest the cockpit and rested her chin on steepled fingers. It was too risky to contact her operatives on the station or Persephone; she had no idea what sorts of sensors or alarms this ship carried. From now on, she was on her own.

And she had plenty of thinking to do.

He returned, as promised, after a few hours. Kori had paced from one end of the ship to the other, studying it carefully, debating all the while how much she ought to reveal to her uncertain ally. At least she needn't fear that he would violate her thoughts; he'd been clear on that score, almost to the point of irrationality.

"You were right about the Kinsmen on this station," he said, leaning on the inner hatch of the airlock. Kori noticed that casual grace, hinting at ease and yet promising instant readiness for action. She forced her gaze away from his lean, muscular thighs, his narrow waist and broad chest, focusing on his face.

"They wouldn't talk to you?" she asked.

"They were . . . less than forthcoming." His expression seemed to say that he wondered the same of her. She looked back with innocent concern. "Most of them are low-level clerks and bureaucrats, and probably don't know much more than we do. If they know anything at all."

Cautiously she brushed the outer layer of his thoughts. He was discouraged—more than discouraged—by the behavior of his people. He was beginning to think he couldn't quite trust them, and that possibility cut him deeply. Better to make excuses for them than admit that Kinsman honor was no longer sacrosanct.

But he was just as committed to learning the truth as she. "What do we do next?" she asked.

He shook off his melancholy. "You said you know the *Eurydice*'s flight plan. It wasn't registered here at Persephone station, so we'll have to rely on the information your brother gave you and hope it's correct." He moved to a console on the port side of the ship, opposite the seats, and called up star charts from the ship's computer. "Can you show me, here?"

The charts were no different than those used by Royal Intelligence. With the slight hesitation befitting one who didn't have such easy access to starflight technology, she marked out Miklos's route.

"He departed into shaauri space from the most underutilized wormhole in the Concordat," Jonas said. "The Vishnu system is too out of the way for most traders to bother with. Lord Miklos chose as wisely as he could, for a man behaving like a crazed *hylpup*."

"Hylpup?"

"That's the closest most humans can come to pronouncing the actual shaauri word. It's a beast of the shaauri homeworld. They were so easy to hunt that the shaauri nearly wiped them out, and put the remaining few thousand of them under protection. They are singularly stupid animals."

Kori swallowed her annoyance. "But you said the shaauri don't hunt them anymore. Maybe they aren't so stupid after all."

He gave her a narrow sideways glance. "You'll sit with me in the cockpit and tell me whatever else you know while we travel. We'll set out for Vishnu immediately. I've already cleared my flight plan with Persephone Station Control." He took her arm and steered her through the cockpit hatch. "I registered my route through shaauri space with the Kinsman office. It's necessary, to regulate traffic and keep it flowing smoothly."

"And to make sure everyone obeys the rules," Kori muttered.

"There are always some who do not." He settled in his seat and began to run a systems check.

"They don't know we're looking for the *Eurydice*?"

His jaw set. "I told them that I'd recruited a telepathic female for our people and was taking her back to Kinsman Prime for evaluation. That supersedes my debriefing." Station Control gave him clearance to depart, and he disengaged the docking clamps. "They have no reason to question me, even though I'm taking a very indirect route."

That was something to be grateful for. Maybe the Kinsmen on this station really didn't know much about the lost ship. But others were sure to—in shaauri territory.

As for Jonas . . . he had not quite lied to his fellow Kinsman, but he had deceived them. Even without so much as brushing his thoughts, she felt his agitation and shame. He wouldn't last two days in Royal Intelligence.

She almost found herself wondering if there was something admirable in that.

The ship, which Jonas called *A'amia*—named for a sort of predatory bird on the shaauri homeworld—slipped free of station traffic and began the hours-long flight to the Concordat wormhole that would take them to Vishnu. After the autopilot was engaged, there was little for Jonas to do, and less for Kori.

She didn't intend to let the time go to waste.

"There's so much I don't know about the Kinsmen," she said, when Jonas leaned back in his seat. "It would help me to understand what I'm . . . getting into."

His gray eyes flickered with interest and what might have been amusement. "Second thoughts, Mes Dianthe?"

"Téa," she said. "There isn't much point in being formal, if we're going to—" She broke off, feigning embarrassment. "Is it all right if I call you Jonas?"

"It's acceptable," he said. "You're not yet family, but you will be."

Did she imagine that entirely different glint in his eyes? She shifted in her seat and pretended a sudden fascination with the ship's console. "Could we go somewhere more comfortable to talk?"

"Are these quarters too close for you, Téa? You'll have to get used to them."

"I'm sure you don't do everything in this little space."

"No. Not everything." He rose and left the cockpit, not

looking back to see if she followed. He led her past the main cabin and into the small galley in the stern of the ship, rigged with a table and two seats.

"Would you like *kaffé*?" he offered, stopping at the food station, "or do you prefer to begin learning more about the shaauri?"

"Does that mean shaauri don't drink *kaffé*?"

"The shaauri sense of taste is a thousand times more sensitive than a human's, as is their hearing," he said. "Kinsmen prefer a shaauri beverage." His fingers moved deftly over the galley console, and in a few moments he held a steaming cup of golden liquid in his hands. "It's an acquired taste. Do you care to try?"

It was a dare, as if he were testing her commitment to this venture by such simple means. She reached for the cup, and he placed it in her hands.

The smell was slightly spicy and altogether alien. She took a seat at the table, gingerly lifting the cup to her lips.

Her first sip of the beverage was startling. It was unlike anything she'd had before. Deliberately she took another taste.

"Do you find it strange, Téa?" Jonas asked.

"No. I like it."

He settled opposite her and drank from his own cup with obvious pleasure. "Don't lie. You're not very good at it."

How little he knew. "Neither are Kinsmen, according to what you said. Or they shouldn't be."

He went on alert, his brief cordiality fading. "You said you wanted to learn about my people," he said. "But I'm sure you already share the opinions of most Worldbound." Before she could respond, he stopped her with a gesture. "You never told me your theory about the *Eurydice*'s disappearance."

She curled her fingers around the cup to savor the heat, though she hardly needed it in the climate-controlled ship. "I don't have a theory. I don't know much about anything, really. My brother was the ambitious one. I stayed at home in Eldoris Province on the family farm . . . until I came to the station."

"And what was home like?"

"Nothing that would interest a Kinsman. I was just your typical Worldbound, after all."

"Then this is your first trip off-planet?"

"Yes."

"I admire your courage. You've tackled a great deal for your maiden voyage."

She listened for mockery in his words and heard none. "Thank you."

"And you know more about Kinsmen than I thought most Worldbound did." He caught her gaze and held it. "Enough to think that Kinsmen have something to do with the *Eurydice*'s disappearance?"

He wasn't reading her mind, and she was fairly certain she hadn't said anything so blunt. "I . . . was thinking more about the shaauri," she said. "Wouldn't they be the real danger?"

"If their territory is invaded, yes."

As if she'd lost her taste for the alien drink, Kori pushed her cup away. "It's said that they look like giant cats."

"A great oversimplification, because humans don't have a better frame of reference." He took her cup and put it into the recycler. "They are bipedal, furbearing, highly intelligent beings. I can show you holovids, if you feel up to it."

"I want to be prepared, in case we meet any."

"Very well." He left the galley for the computer console and called up a holovid of a single shaaurin. In spite of Kori's pretended ignorance, she knew very well what the aliens looked like. The image was still startling.

This one, she guessed, was male, with dark red, black-barred fur covering his body. He wore a loose, pocketed vest and trousers, and his feet and hands were bare. To call him a cat on two legs was, indeed, a gross oversimplification. The face was full of alert intelligence, bewhiskered and mobile, with pointed ears set slightly to the sides of his head. The whiskers ran in two curved parallel rows in an arch from the cheekbones to the middle of his forehead, like parentheses.

"It isn't only their appearance and language that make them different from humans," he said, leaning close to her. She could smell the masculine scent of him, clean and just slightly exotic, like the ship. "Shaauri, for instance, don't lie . . . not as we use the word. They have their own subtle forms of deception, but lying as we know it is alien to their thinking."

"And that's why Kinsmen aren't supposed to lie, either."

"We have acquired many shaauri tastes and customs."

"Which is one reason people don't trust you. Why they're afraid."

"Humans always fear what's different."

"You're still human, Jonas." She looked up at him, daring him to move away. "I'm not afraid of you."

Unexpectedly he cupped her chin in his hand. There was no doubt at all, she thought, that he was human. Her mouth went dry.

"I wouldn't want you to be afraid," he said with surprising gentleness. "I want you to . . ." He stopped, let her go, and returned to the original subject. "Humans resent us because we control the shipping lanes through the shaauri zone, and we ask payment for our services. Therefore, their trade profits are reduced."

She was grateful for the chance to be honestly annoyed. "Some say you ask too much. Persephoneans were the first in the Concordat to rediscover starflight. If it weren't for our scientists, all the colonies would be gone by now, and not even Kinsmen would be in space." She took in a deep breath. "People still remember the war. And they believe you prefer shaauri to your own kind. Do you?"

It came out as a challenge. His mouth curled in a genuine smile. "Not always."

The brush of his lips on hers was as ephemeral and sweet as a waterfall in the Cerberan desert.

3

All at once the ship seemed to lose its gravity. Kori floated a few centimeters off the deck and touched down again only when he drew back and let her go.

He walked away, giving her a chance to collect herself. This wasn't supposed to happen. She was on assignment, one that might prove to be very dangerous. She had to keep her head—and her feet firmly planted on solid ground.

This . . . reaction . . . was only because he was different, a telepath like her. And because sometimes she let herself remember how lonely she was.

Jonas leaned casually against one of the passenger seats as if he had felt nothing. Let him see, then, how little *she* was disturbed.

"Tell me about shaauri mating customs," she said.

He lifted a brow. "A complicated question." He strode back to the computer and called up another image, this one a two-dimensional chart of alien names. "To understand that, you have to understand that shaauri clans are made up of families, Lines, with very complex relationships among themselves. A clan is like a human nation, but the Line is everything. A shaaurin's first loyalty is to his Line, and then his clan."

"Or hers?"

"Or hers. Shaauri males and females are equals."

"You said that shaauri females bear their own young."

"Yes. But both shaauri males and females are encouraged to leave home upon first reaching adulthood, even though any shaaurin is vulnerable outside the Line-bond. Shaauri Lines are very close-knit; only young shaauri can tolerate being alone for any length of time. The nearest human equivalent for their period of wandering would be our word 'walkabout.' It's the risk they take to win higher status in the Line, and perhaps mate to bring in new blood." His lashes dropped to shade his eyes. "Shaauri youths are expected to experiment sexually, but shaauri females are fertile only four times a year. If a female becomes pregnant and has not established a new Line of her own, she returns to her original Line to give birth. The child belongs to that Line, and its genetic history is carefully recorded."

"What about the father?"

"He has nothing to do with the child unless he becomes the female's lifemate, or the two of them attract enough affiliates to form their own Line."

Kori sat down in the nearest chair. "Lifemate?"

"Lifemating has great significance to shaauri. It is the foundation of every Line, and it cannot be broken by anything but death. Many shaauri never find a lifemate. Once there was only one lifemated couple per Line. Now there can be more, but it is still a sacred, unbreakable trust between two shaauri. The children of such matings are considered particularly blessed."

"But if it's so uncommon, how does a shaaurin find a lifemate?"

"I told you that shaauri are not true telepaths, but they possess abilities not unlike telepathy. A female shaaurin drawn to a male for the purpose of lifemating must convince her chosen one to give up every other female for her. Often the female takes the initiative, but males are by nature . . . reluctant to surrender their sexual freedom. In the opposite case, a male also must convince the female to accept him as father of all her children. Ritualized personal combat is not uncommon in such instances. There's also kidnap-formating, when a shaaurin needs more leverage to win his or her chosen one—though it can be risky, since the Line is entitled to kill the kidnapper if they catch him or her. That's a kind of courageous deception that shaauri admire—being able to enter a rival's territory and escape alive."

"It sounds barbaric."

"No more barbaric than the human willingness to change mates even after sacred oaths are taken, or their propensity to make war among themselves. The shaauri gave that up long ago; conflict even between Lines or clans is almost always resolved through personal challenge. Line concerns are dealt with on Line level and are not allowed to spread beyond. Shaauri do not condone mass slaughter."

Kori jerked up in her seat. "Neither do we. The Concordat is at peace—"

"Not so long ago, the colony worlds of the Concordat were little more than barbaric enclaves fighting for supremacy."

"Until my great—" She stopped herself. She'd been about to reveal her identity by telling him that her own great-great-grandfather had been the one to establish lasting peace among human worlds. "Until Priam Challinor created the Concordat."

"Yes. He had great charisma. But even he couldn't stop war with the shaauri. And that's why you need us."

You. Us. Ordinary humans and Kinsmen. Did he mean to remind her of the gulf between them? Put her in her place?

"My Line, Arhan, specializes in dealing with humans," he said. "They have a powerful curiosity about us. When I lived among them, I was treated almost exactly as a shaaurin. But . . ." He looked down at the top of the seat and ran his finger along the upholstery. "I learned that it is not possible for a human to become a shaaurin."

The sadness in his voice startled her. He went from arrogant to vulnerable in an instant, and she didn't know which was the real Jonas. Or why he should choose to let her see anything of his inner heart.

"Did you want to be?" she asked gently.

"When my wife was killed, I thought I did."

It was necessary to feign surprise, but she found that she had no need to pretend sympathy. She reached up to cover his hand with her own.

"I'm sorry. I didn't realize—"

He gazed at her hand. "Our ship was damaged in space.

An explosion due to engine malfunction. I survived."

The accident. Would he let slip what had happened, what he must believe Téa Dianthe ignorant of . . . that *he'd* been the Kinsman pilot on the ship bearing the Challinor heir on a supposedly secret diplomatic mission to shaauri space?

But that much he wasn't prepared to share. "It was a long time ago."

"Seven years?" she said, making it sound like a guess. "That's why you went to live among the shaauri. All that time away from humans . . ."

He turned his hand to clasp hers. "The shaauri love life. They taught me to want to live."

Once again she was surprised and almost moved by his desire to confide in her. The woman he must think she was.

Because he thought she was *his* woman. He wasn't speaking now of cold contracts and parental rights. His thumb stroked over her knuckles so lightly that the touch sent shivers sweeping up her arm.

"Your wife was a telepath, too?" she asked.

"She was."

"That must have given you . . . a special bond. Like the shaauri lifemates."

His fingers stilled. She could feel a wall slam down between them, stronger than any mere mental block. Then, without warning, he caught her shoulders in his hands and took her mouth.

This kiss was anything but gentle. It wasn't quite violent, not quite angry, but she knew he was trying to make a point: that he didn't have to have any kind of bond with a woman to enjoy her. And perhaps that she shouldn't expect anything to develop between them just because she was a telepath.

She didn't care. She returned his kiss with equal fervor, losing herself in the moment. Her hands kneaded the hard muscle of his waist while his tongue explored her lips and mouth. Let him see that she could give as good as she took. Let him see just what a non-Kinsman could do.

Jonas made a movement with his knee, and the seat on which she was half-kneeling began to recline. He eased her down, until she found herself lying on her back, and he knelt beside her seat-turned-couch.

Her thoughts were becoming dangerously clouded, but it

wasn't because of anything Jonas did with his mind. His hands ran lightly over the shape of her body, surprisingly expert for a man who hadn't been among humans for such a long time. He kissed the angle of her jaw, the soft skin beneath, the pulse at the base of her neck. He cupped her breasts in his palms, teasing her nipples into peaks through the curve-hugging fabric of her tunic.

It occurred to her that he was well on his way to consummating the contract between them here and now, and she wasn't going to stop him. *Abdera's moons* . . . she wanted him. And he would only trust her more if she let him make love to her. The act was completely justifiable in the context of her mission.

But she had to stay in control. She had to know what was going on in his mind. He would never be more off his guard than when his body needed so urgently.

As she'd learned to do long ago, she separated her consciousness, letting one part of herself respond to his caresses and guiding the other to probe his thoughts. Carefully, so carefully, testing the barrier he'd put between them.

Hunger was all she felt at first. His wanting. Physical, yes, but also the powerful yearning to join with another human being. He would feel the same about any woman.

No, not any. *She* was what he desired. Not merely the outward trappings of her altered hair and eyes and provincial cosmetics, but what he had touched of her mind and heart.

She felt a yielding in his mind, almost an embrace. The wall shuddered. Behind it she glimpsed a vision, like the blinding light of a supernova—a vision of unity with another soul such as she'd never known, far beyond any mere joining of two bodies.

Was this what two telepaths could feel when they shared everything? Could humans, like shaauri, lifemate for all eternity? The light pulled at her, seductive, demanding . . .

Too much. This wasn't what she'd bargained for. Her body tensed against him; her mind became clumsy in its exploration. Behind the light was a vast gulf of darkness, a wasted region of nothingness lodged in his mind, a blackened wound.

His defenses closed up, thrusting her out. She felt as though she'd been hurled across the room.

The ship's computer chimed a warning.

Jonas pulled himself off her and stumbled back, uncharacteristically awkward. He wiped his hand across his mouth. His gray eyes were glazed, more with shock than passion. Abruptly he turned on his heel and strode to the cockpit.

Kori lay still, remembering to breathe. The sensation of violent rejection was mental only; her body ached, but not from any wound. She pushed herself up on her elbows and shook her head to clear it.

Following Jonas into the cockpit did not seem like a very good idea. One thing was for certain . . . she'd better be ready to handle him more professionally next time.

If there was a next time.

Jonas concentrated on guiding the A'amia through the Vishnu system to the mouth of the outbound wormhole, ignoring the searing pain in his head and the shock of nearly losing himself in Téa Dianthe.

Losing himself not only in her body but in her mind.

He leaned back in his seat and rubbed his temples. The mere fact that he had shared a mental link with Téa was something of a miracle. The telepathic centers of his brain had been injured in the explosion, and flickered to life only rarely, like the burned-out drive of a derelict ship.

Téa didn't know that. She thought he was a fully functional telepath. She'd tried to read his mind again and triggered a chain reaction that set his brain alight.

He had come close to such an experience, once, with Jennara. Even they hadn't been able to forge a complete link, when both were in the prime of their telepathic powers. Such a link was rarer for Kinsmen than lifemates were among the shaauri.

It had almost happened with a stranger, and not merely because he wanted her. Wanting wasn't enough.

A mere few hours had passed since they'd left Persephone Station, moving at one-tenth the speed of light. It felt like eons. The trip through the Concordat wormhole to Vishnu had been brief as the blink of an eye—and now they were nearly at the mouth of the wormhole into shaauri space.

After that, their search for the *Eurydice* would begin in

earnest. No more time for dalliance. He couldn't guess the extent or nature of the danger they were facing.

Apart from that posed by Téa Dianthe. He wasn't even sure what he feared. Caring for her? Finding that he wanted more from her than a contract mate and a telepathic child? Daring to trust enough to admit how damaged and uncertain he was?

The computer prompted him to pay attention. The signal buoy at the mouth of the wormhole transmitted clearance, and he piloted the ship in. The familiar curving, flickering walls closed about him. A journey of a hundred light-years took only a handful of hours.

Téa didn't appear at the cockpit hatch until the *A'amia* exited the wormhole and was in shaauri space.

He was hypersensitive to the sound of her breathing, her scent, her slightest shift in posture behind him. He wanted very badly to know what she was thinking. Feeling.

"Where are we?" she asked, her voice slightly strained.

"Approaching KS13, the Kinsman border station in this precinct of shaauri space."

"Shaauri space," she repeated. She sat down beside him, gazing out the canopy.

"Yes. If the *Eurydice* came this way, the station will have records. The ship couldn't have passed undetected."

"Nothing ever gets past a Kinsman."

The words were dry but not hostile. He chose to ignore any double meanings. "Patrolling the shaauri wormholes is part of our function."

"Then why didn't the Kinsmen here catch the *Eurydice*? Why didn't anyone at Persephone Station know about it?"

"That's what we're here to find out."

He pushed his awareness of her to the back of his thoughts and transmitted his approach to the station. They would know he was coming, of course, from his filed flight plan. They wouldn't know *why* he was here.

How would they react when they learned?

The Kinsman station was of standard design, its docks nearly empty save for a few smallish trade vessels that used this less-traveled route to the Nine Worlds. The station transmitted docking instructions to his ship's computer, and he finished the maneuver manually, slipping into his assigned berth.

"This shouldn't take too long," he said, rising from the console. "I have full access to all station records."

"Why don't you just retrieve them from the ship?"

"It's better if I go in person. I have nothing to hide, do I? I'll speak to the Station Administrator and take any other steps that seem necessary. In the meantime, I suggest you get some sleep."

She stood up to block his path. "You're not going alone."

"Don't be foolish. This is a Kinsman station, and you'll only get in the way."

"But you told your fellow Kinsmen that I was your recruit. Wouldn't it be natural for me to get a sense of my new home?"

As little as he wanted her near him, she had a valid point. Her presence wouldn't be questioned under the circumstances.

"Very well. But let me do the talking. Being Worldbound, you'll undoubtedly find plenty to hold your interest without interfering."

She dipped a curtsy. "Shall I stand and gape openmouthed in awe at Kinsman splendor, and breathe a few prayers of gratitude for my good fortune?"

He looked at her sharply. Her attitude seemed less and less like that of the young provincial who had first approached him at Persephone Station. Her body language was too challenging, too confident. Again he was struck with the knowledge that she was keeping secrets.

And he didn't have the means to read her thoughts, even if he would.

"They'll expect you to be intimidated," he said. "This is Kinsman territory."

4

The corridors of the Kinsman station were nearly empty compared to the bustling crowds at Persephone's. The few people Jonas and Téa passed wore Kinsman maroon, very few barred with black. Most were clerks and supervisory personnel, non-telepaths involved in the day-to-day operation of the station. They nodded to Jonas in recognition of his status and dismissed Téa with a glance.

"Persephoneans think Kinsmen live in luxury," Téa commented. "You are wealthy, but it doesn't show here."

"This is a working station," he said. "We, like the shaauri, save our luxuries for our private lives."

She accepted this without comment, hurrying to match his long strides. Reluctantly he slowed down to accommodate her.

"We're almost to the records office. It should take no more than a few minutes to search the station's database for any mention of the *Eurydice* or other unauthorized vessels passing this way. You'll have to wait outside; non-Kinsmen aren't permitted."

This time she didn't argue. He left her just outside the office, pausing at the entrance to have his DNA scanned. The clerk in charge glanced up from his desk with obvious curiosity, undoubtedly aware from Jonas's profile that he'd been living among the shaauri.

"Welcome back, sir," he said. "The station is at your disposal."

Jonas gave him a nod and moved to the nearest terminal.

Fifteen minutes later, he had what he wanted. The data were inexplicably buried in deactivated buffers, and anyone running a cursory search might not have found their formation at all.

An unauthorized ship, unusually fast, had passed through this system three weeks ago without acknowledging Kinsman hails or docking for inspection. A Kinsman vessel was sent in pursuit, following the unauthorized ship into the wormhole leading deeper into the shaauri zone, while a coded warning was sent ahead to the Kinsman station at the other end.

There were no further records. No indication as to whether or not the ship had been caught, or what happened on the other side. Such an open-ended report was far from normal, especially in the case of a flagrant challenge to Kinsman authority. The ship could not possibly have disappeared.

But the *Eurydice* had come this way. Someone knew more about the situation than he or she was willing to commit to the records.

Jonas ended his inquiry and left the terminal. Téa was right to be concerned about her brother. And he was right to wonder exactly what was going on.

"Did you find what you needed, sir?" the clerk asked with a pleasant smile.

"In part." He braced his hands on the clerk's desk. "I'll need to speak to the Administrator."

"That can be arranged, of course. I can page her personal assistant and request an appointment." He consulted his screen. "I'm certain that the Administrator will be able to see you tomorrow."

"Not tomorrow. Today."

The clerk shifted uneasily and glanced at Jonas's bars of rank. "I'll see what I can do. May I tell her assistant the nature of your appointment?"

"It's of a private nature."

"Of course." There was a delay of several minutes while

he contacted the assistant and explained his request, and then he turned back to Jonas.

"It's done, sir. The Administrator will see you immediately, if it is convenient." He called up station schematics on his screen, indicating the location of the Administrator's office. "Would you like a download?"

"I'll find it." He remembered to smile. "Thank you for your help."

He nearly tripped over Téa as he walked out the door.

"Well?" she said. "Did you learn anything?"

"Enough to know that your brother's ship did come this way. There are no records as to its ultimate fate."

"Where are we going now?"

"To the Administrator's office. She's the final authority on this station. She'll know what isn't in the official records."

"Then they are hiding something."

They. She meant Kinsmen. And he was afraid she was right.

"I'll have to ask you to stay outside once more," he said. "This could be a delicate interview."

"You don't think I'm up to it?"

"I think you don't know my people nearly well enough," he said. The Téa who had recently emerged—defiant, cocky, confident as any star voyager—was very likely to do something rash.

Her jaw set stubbornly, but she agreed to wait in the lounge outside the Administrator's office. Jonas left her absorbed in an entertainment holovid, one she wasn't apt to find in non-Kinsman space.

The Administrator was waiting for him in her large, utilitarian office, her stiff posture outlined against the viewport with its framed panorama of a nearby world. She wore Kinsman red, bearing insignia of rank rather than the black bars of a telepath.

"Jonas Kane VelArhan," she said, inclining her head. "It's an honor to welcome you to our station, especially after your long absence."

"Thank you."

"I am Ardath Faust KeVelRasi. Please, sit down."

Jonas sat in one of the comfortable chairs facing her desk. "I don't wish to take up any more of your time than necessary," he said. "I'm inquiring into the whereabouts of a certain Persephonean trade vessel, the *Eurydice,* which apparently failed to return to home space some weeks ago. Station records are not complete. I was hoping that you might have further information."

KeVelRasi was not surprised by his question. She consulted her desk screen and tapped her chin.

"Ah, yes. Such a vessel did pass through our jurisdiction . . . an unauthorized ship with no Kinsman on board. She refused to answer our hails. We pursued and sent an alert to the next inbound station."

"So I gathered from your records. But there doesn't seem to be anything further about this ship after it left your jurisdiction. Surely it would have been detained somewhere along its route."

The administrator pursed her lips and gazed at him. "Yes. I see. May I ask why this interests you?"

"Before I went on leave, I was liaison for Persephone. I hope to be reassigned to that office. Naturally I must know everything of importance that has occurred in Persephonean trade and Kinsman relations during my absence."

"And how did you happen to learn of this ship?"

Her posture broadcast extreme unease, and a tic pulsed at the corner of her mouth. She was stalling, trying to think of some way of deflecting his questions.

Stalling, because she knew more than she was willing to tell.

"A relative of one of her crew members approached me on Persephone station," he said with absolute truthfulness. "Oddly enough, the ship's disappearance is not common knowledge on Persephone, though the entire situation is unprecedented since the end of the war."

Her gaze slid away from his. "Yes. I . . . may be able to obtain some additional information for you by tomorrow. I'd be happy to make our finest guest accommodations available tonight."

So that she would have time to find a safe answer for him.

He could press the issue; he outranked her, and the longer he waited the more likely that she—and whoever else wanted to keep this matter quiet—would be able to elude his questions. But he had no real excuse for appearing to be anxious, not without putting her even more on her guard.

"Very well," he said, rising. "I trust that more information will be forthcoming."

"I'll do what I—" KeVelRasi cast a glance behind him, frowning. "This is a private meeting. If you wish to make an appointment—"

"Jonas?"

He turned. Téa stood in the doorway, arms folded across her chest, face wary. "I thought that I . . ." She trailed off as if in confusion.

She was anything but confused. Jonas strode to her, caught her arm and pulled her forward to face the Administrator.

"Your pardon, Cousin. This is Téa Dianthe, a Persephonean telepath I'm taking to Kinsman Prime for testing."

The Administrator looked Téa up and down with barely concealed contempt. "I presume you haven't had time, Cousin Kane VelArhan, to teach her telepathic protocols. She just attempted to enter my mind."

Jonas tightened his grip on Téa's arm. "She has much to learn. She also has considerable ability. If the Directors find her acceptable, her talent will qualify her for high rank among us." He smiled. "She may be mother to children who will keep our people strong."

He stared pointedly at KeVelRasi's insignia of rank, trusting that she understood his message. The Administrator might feel contempt for Téa now, but not when she became his contracted mate and bore him a telepathic child. Let KeVelRasi not forget to whom she spoke.

She chose not to provoke him further. "I'll arrange guest quarters for you and your recruit immediately, Cousin Kane VelArhan. Please wait for my assistant. You may place a meal order on the room's computer, and it will be brought to you at your convenience."

"Your words have a pleasant sound," he said in formal Shaaurii. She blinked, inclined her head, and returned to her screen.

Jonas led Téa from the room.

"I asked you to remain outside," he said.

"The woman was lying. I thought that—"

"I wouldn't realize it? Is that why you came in uninvited? To scan her thoughts?"

"I knew *you* wouldn't. And she wasn't expecting me."

That was true enough. He glanced around for listeners. It had come to this, that he trusted a Worldbound outsider more than his own people. "You could have made things much worse," he said. "Fortunately, I had an excuse for your behavior. But even Kinsmen non-telepaths are trained to block mental intrusions, and to recognize when they occur." He drew her to a corner of the lounge. "What did you learn?"

"That she's afraid, and she knows more than she would ever admit to you."

"Then you took an unnecessary risk. I'd already ascertained that much."

Their conversation was cut short by the Administrator's assistant, who offered to escort them to the guest quarters.

They were, as promised, quite sumptuous. There was a single large bed, covered with a shaauri tapestry worth many thousands of Concordat credits. Other weavings hung on the wall. Scattered about the room were human and shaauri objets d'art. The colors were the earth tones favored by shaauri, dominated by reds and yellows.

Jonas made a quick inspection of the room, not sure what he was looking for. Shaauri didn't plant listening devices in the quarters of their rivals or enemies, and neither did Kinsmen. Until now, no Kinsman had enemies among his own.

There was a first time for everything.

Téa sat on the edge of the bed, regarding him watchfully. He drew cups of *kaffé* and *arao* from the galley's dispenser and handed her the human beverage.

"Thank you," she said. She didn't drink. "Something really is going on, isn't it? Whatever happened to the *Eurydice,* it wasn't ordinary."

Nothing about this is ordinary, Jonas thought. He found himself staring at Téa, noticing too keenly the expanse of bed behind her, and thinking how easy it would be to join her on it. How much he wanted to lose himself in her very human embrace.

She noticed his look and returned it boldly. "Tell me what you're thinking."

He wrenched his thoughts back to business. "I believe," he said, "that the Administrator wishes to delay us at this station." He shook his head, amazed at his acceptance of

what would have been unthinkable to him seven years ago.
"If she's worried, then she must be feeling pressure from
someone of higher rank and authority. She holds the highest
non-telepath rank among us. And that means that what happened to the *Eurydice* is more complicated than we guessed."

"Because Kinsman telepaths are involved?"

He considered how much to tell her. She didn't know
about the secret Persephonean negotiations with the shaauri,
and how their success could threaten Kinsman dominance of
the shaauri trade routes. Until he had more proof, he wasn't
prepared to brand any of his people as traitors and murderers.

Better to give her the other possibility, grim as it was. "I
don't know. If this were routine, either the *Eurydice* would
have been caught and slapped with severe fines and penalties
for flouting Kinsman authority, or there'd be some indication—" He hesitated and knelt before Téa. "If Kinsmen
didn't catch the *Eurydice* and it never reached the Nine
Worlds, it may have fallen into shaauri hands."

"I was always afraid . . ." She waged a short battle for
composure. "What would that mean?"

"It would mean that Kinsmen didn't do what the shaauri
expect them to—keep other humans under control." *If the
Directors knew that the* Eurydice *had fallen to shaauri, they
wouldn't broadcast it. They might even go to great lengths
to hide it. Kinsmen are supposed to be infallible.* "A non-
Kinsman human ship entering shaauri space would be a
shame upon Kinsmen, but a direct violation to shaauri. A
threat."

"Would . . . they be killed?"

He didn't try to evade her pleading gaze. "It is possible.
It would depend on which Line or clan caught the ship. If
they chose to deal with the intrusion personally, or—since it
involved humans—take the matter to the triennial clan as-
sembly."

"Kinsmen wouldn't try to save them? They're supposed to
be the go-betweens, aren't they?"

*But they might choose not to jeopardize our alliance by
challenging the shaauri over an incident that casts us in such
a bad light.*

"I don't know," he said honestly.

"We can go farther into shaauri territory and find out."

"Not until we're sure that we can't get the information within Kinsman jurisdiction." *And if shaauri aren't involved, we don't want to bring them into it.*

Téa closed her eyes and looked more shaken than she had at any time since they'd been together. "I always knew my brother might be dead, killed by shaauri. But realizing that it might be true . . ."

"There's no reason to give hope up yet."

She sighed deeply and opened her eyes. They glittered with moisture. "There's something else, Jonas. No matter what we discover, you may have to decide . . . whether to keep helping me, or stand against your own people."

She wasn't so ignorant that she couldn't see all the repercussions of the situation. He set his cooling *arao* down on the bedside table, untasted. "I know," he said. "I'll keep my side of our bargain."

She touched his cheek. Her fingers were warm and soft. "Thank you," she said. Slowly she leaned forward, bringing her mouth level with his. "I also know how to keep my bargains."

And she kissed him. Full on the mouth, with deliberate purpose. Jonas needed no telepathy to understand her unspoken message.

She gripped his shoulders to pull him up, and they tumbled onto the bed. The shaauri tapestry was as sensuous as it was beautiful. Jonas had little thought for it, however, and eyes only for the woman beneath him.

Whatever hesitation she'd had in the past was gone. She wanted him. The body didn't lie, no more than one's deepest inner thoughts. Jonas didn't know if her ardor was the age-old need for closeness in the face of adversity, or simple desire. Either way, it was real.

Last time he'd been the one to pull away, because he was afraid. He'd felt her come close to touching his mind as few had ever done—his burned-out, crippled mind—and reaching his very soul. Hadn't he rejected her as forcefully as one telepath could reject another? Hadn't he vowed to hold himself apart until their bargain must be sealed?

Yet she offered herself again, gladly. And he found he could not refuse.

Joy such as he hadn't known in many years caught him

unaware. He kissed Téa soundly. Her hands searched for the seals on his uniform, slipped into the opening at his neck and stroked down his chest. The seals of her tunic yielded at his touch, and the fabric peeled from her body like a second skin.

He gazed in wonder at what lay revealed. Perhaps she was not so extraordinary among women: she was neither tall nor full-breasted nor remarkable in any way. But she was beautiful to him. He thought he would have felt the same even had she not been the first woman he'd lain with in seven years.

Téa. He brushed her nipple with his fingertip. She arched her back and gave a soft cry. He stroked the palms of his hands over her arms, breasts, and ribs. With the wonder of rediscovering something nearly forgotten, he explored what she offered.

Her breasts were sweet to his tongue, her little gasps like the most exquisite shaauria melody. But she didn't merely lie passively beneath him. She pushed him away long enough to strip the upper part of his uniform from his shoulders and chest, removing his adoption-knife from its sheath at his waist. She paused when she found the scars across his torso.

"These scars," she murmured. "The accident—"

"Yes," he said.

"You could have had them erased." Her gaze met his, soft and gentle. "But you wanted to remember her. Your wife." She traced the scars first with her finger and then with her tongue, a healing caress filled with unconditional acceptance.

He shuddered. She skimmed her hand down to his belly. With one accord they removed the remainder of their clothing and lay side by side.

Flesh on flesh. Jonas breathed in the human, female scent of her body. He acquainted himself with the curves and angles that belonged uniquely to Téa Dianthe. He kissed her belly and her thighs. He tasted the moisture pooled between them. He parted her legs, and she stroked him intimately as she guided him home.

He plunged inside. She moaned. The rhythm came back to him easily, sweetly. Each time he left her, he couldn't wait to bury himself in her body once more.

Téa. He couldn't tell if he spoke the word aloud, or in his mind. Her legs locked about his hips. Her hands ran unceasingly up and down his back. The sounds she made told him that she was coming very close to completion. And he . . .

He stood at the very edge of some new galaxy, ablaze with a million stars to explore, a billion worlds untouched by man or shaauri. He could reach out and hold them in his hands.

They danced about him, whirling faster and faster. One of them filled his vision, became as vivid as a human soul. Téa. And then, just as he tumbled free into the vastness of space, it happened again.

She exploded into his mind. Their minds locked, linked. His body and hers convulsed in perfect synchronicity.

The galaxy shrank down to the size of a room, a bed, and two people. Téa sat up, her eyes glazed. Jonas rolled away and stumbled out of the bed. His mind had been seared from the inside out, but one thing he could see with utter clarity.

"You aren't Téa Dianthe," he whispered hoarsely. "Who are you?"

5

K*ori had known this moment would arrive sooner or* later. But she'd never expected it to come like this.

Her body throbbed, but her thoughts spun like a neutron star. She had shared Jonas's mind. Totally, miraculously, wonderfully. It had lasted just an instant, long enough for every one of her barriers to be shattered. For him to realize she had deceived him.

And for her to realize that, before the sharing, he hadn't been *able* to read her mind.

She calmed the trembling in her hands. That mental union, even incomplete, had seemed too much to bear in the ship. She had borne it this time, but everything had changed. A part of Jonas was inside her. And she was in Jonas.

She knew what it was like to be so close to another person that you forgot where you ended and he began. God help her.

"Who are you?" he repeated, his face as hard as Thoran granite.

She drew the coverlet up to her shoulders. It hurt to see him like this, regarding her as he would an enemy. It hurt to have to hurt him.

Unprofessional. Hopelessly unprofessional.

"My name is Kori Galatéa Challinor," she said.

He snatched up his uniform and pulled it on with sharp jerks. "Challinor," he said. "Daughter of Calypso and Georg. The sister of—"

"Miklos Challinor. Who disappeared aboard the *Eurydice,* just as I told you."

He shook his head and went to stand as far away from her as the room would allow. "You lied to me."

He said "lied" in the way another man might speak of murder, with loathing and something like horror.

Kori found herself looking at the coverlet between her fingers rather than his angry eyes.

"Yes," she said. "But I never knew for sure that you wouldn't recognize me immediately. I couldn't trust your Kinsman scruples about reading non-Kinsman minds, or that you . . ." She hesitated, preparing herself for more of his anger. "I didn't realize that you had lost the ability to do so."

If his physical reaction was anything to go on, that wasn't something he would ever have admitted—certainly not to her.

"I . . . assume that happened in the accident," she continued. "You can't fully use your telepathy. That part of your mind is damaged somehow."

"Yes. By shrapnel from the explosion."

"I'm sorry." She imagined herself in his position, and shuddered. To lose such a gift . . . "It must be very difficult."

"I've learned to live with it."

Had he? She wanted to go to him, put her arms around his rigid body. Instead she got out of bed and dressed quickly. "And I owe you an explanation. I work in Royal Intelligence. I knew who you were when I came to find you at Persephone Station. I thought it was expedient under the circumstances to conceal my identity—until I knew whose side you were really on."

"Expedient."

"I've learned caution, especially where Kinsmen are concerned. I had my people watching for your return from shaauri space. You were Kinsman liaison for my world for a brief time. You were also the pilot of the ship on which my parents, and your wife, lost their lives. An accident I have come to believe . . . was no accident. I think that you believe the same."

"Did you get that from my thoughts?"

"Only partly. You've been troubled by what little we've learned of the *Eurydice*'s disappearance. You're afraid that your own people are somehow involved, that they're hiding something. Deceiving not only the Concordat but other Kinsmen. When I came to you with my story about the *Eurydice*, you knew it might be tied in. As I did."

"But you didn't trust me enough to tell me this from the beginning."

"What if you'd been in on the conspiracy that took the life of my parents? What if your escape from the accident wasn't just luck?"

He balled his fists. "You think I'd be a part of murdering my own wife?"

"I couldn't be sure. I've . . . long since come to know that wouldn't be possible."

"My thanks, Lady Kori." He executed a bitterly mocking bow. "So now I know that all this"—he waved a hand at the bed—"is merely political."

"I still want to find my brother. But there's more at stake— the peace we've held for a nearly a century." She sighed. "Seven years ago, you were taking my parents to a secret negotiation with certain influential shaauri. It was unprecedented in shaauri-human relations. You must know how it started . . ."

"Your father, Lord Georg Challinor, saved a small band of young and reckless shaauri who entered human space illegally, at a time when anti-shaauri feelings ran high in the Concordat. They would have been murdered if your father hadn't interceded."

"Yes. It helped that my father was a telepath—a weak one, but able to communicate with shaauri better than most humans. And when those young shaauri grew to adulthood and earned places of prominence in their society, they were willing to open trade negotiations with my family, apart from the Kinsman." She rose and paced away from the bed, keeping her distance from Jonas. "If they'd succeeded, it would have meant an end to Kinsman control of the wormholes. And even though my parents were killed, my grandmother has honored my father's memory and continued those negotiations . . . until recently. Until the *Eurydice* disappeared."

Jonas was silent for a time, flexing his fists. He struck the back of a chair with restrained violence.

"Why?" he demanded. "Why would your brother risk everything by taking an unescorted human ship into the shaauri zone at such a critical juncture?"

"Miklos didn't know about the negotiations, unlike me and my elder brother. I learned what he'd done only after the *Eurydice* left human space." She turned and forced herself to meet Jonas's accusing gaze. "I know that there are Kinsmen who'd do anything to stop negotiations that would limit their power in any way. I've already gathered evidence that Kinsmen high in your ranks, possibly Directors, are deliberately impeding trade from Persephone to the Nine Worlds, slowing things down to the point that it's beginning to hurt our economy and raise questions. It's their way of punishing us for the negotiations, warning us to stop, without openly admitting that they oppose them."

Jonas shook his head. "I knew nothing of this—"

"How could you? I kept that information secret from everyone but my grandmother, my elder brother, and Intelligence. Somehow Miklos found out. I decrypted his private log, in which he said that he was tired of playing games with the shaauri—that he was going to force the issue once and for all by challenging the Kinsman monopoly. If Kinsmen tried to stop him, he would create an incident no one could ignore. And if shaauri caught him . . . he would do what our father had done and communicate with them directly. He was willing to bet his life on that one possibility."

"He was a fool," Jonas said. "He doesn't know the shaauri or what they're capable of—"

"That was—*is*—like Miklos, to act rashly. That's why I kept things from him. But I didn't completely succeed. And now he's vanished, and I don't know who has him. I still need your help." She took a step forward and held out her hand. "You and I have to learn if Kinsmen were responsible for the deaths of my parents and your wife, and my brother's disappearance. We must expose whoever did it."

"You trust me?"

"Yes. After what happened—"

"You think you know me."

"I know enough. And . . ." She balanced between pride,

cool sense, and irrational emotion. "I care about you, Jonas. This has hurt you, too."

If she'd expected a similar declaration from him, she was to be disappointed. The muscles in his jaw tightened and released. Though she made no attempt to read his thoughts, she felt the renewed barrier he had wedged in place between them.

"I have just as much a stake in this as you do," he admitted. "How can you help me?"

"I'm not without experience. I've done off-world work before, and I've studied Kinsmen. There's also the small fact that I have a way to help us locate my brother's ship if we pass anywhere near her."

"If the *Eurydice* still exists."

She swallowed. He was right . . . it could be destroyed, blown into atoms by whoever captured it, no proof left behind. But she had to hope otherwise.

"My grandmother rules Persephone, and she's always hated the shaauri. She remembers the war, and blames them for her son's death. And now my brother . . . if she believes that they've killed him, she'll use her influence in the Concordat to break off all relations with Kinsmen and shaauri. She gave me a deadline to get to the bottom of this. If I don't, and soon, we may be facing another war. Do you think the shaauri want that?"

"They have no love for war such as we wage it. I can speak for them—but not for my own people. They're insane if they think a return to war will help them keep power."

Her heart went out to him, to his obvious pain and despair. Keeping professional distance, and control, was simply no longer possible. "Whoever is behind this must have some plan. Maybe all they wanted to do was disrupt the negotiations by making Thetis Challinor withdraw from them. If they thought it would be that simple, they were very much mistaken."

"Kinsman arrogance," Jonas said. "Stupid pride." He looked up at her, all fierce alien intensity. "Not all Kinsmen would believe as they do. Some of us cherish peace—"

"I know. You're proof enough of that."

His shoulders relaxed, and a little of his guard dropped with them. "Kori Challinor," he said, looking at her as if for the first time. "I saw you as a child, before you went into the Persephonean Academy. You've changed. You had dark hair, eyes."

She fingered her hair. "This is temporary. I'll keep it for now—to throw potential enemies off guard." She smiled. "I remember seeing you at the palace many times, with your father. But I was away when you became liaison. I never got to know you."

"And what does the granddaughter of the ruler of Persephone think of Jonas Kane VelArhan?" he asked. "Do you regret . . ."

"No. I wish it had happened under better circumstances. But for now—" She held out her hand again. He hesitated, then took it in a warm, firm grip.

"For now," he finished, "we have hunting to do."

She was just on the point of losing herself in his touch and his gaze when she was distracted by a light flashing in the corner of her vision. Jonas followed her glance to the comm unit on the wall.

"A message," he said, activating the comm. "From the Administrator."

The message began to play out in the Administrator's steady contralto, devoid of visual accompaniment.

"Jonas Kane VelArhan. I hope that you find your quarters satisfactory. I regret to tell you that urgent business has called me away from the station, and I will be unable to pursue your inquiry for several days. I hope you'll make yourself comfortable in the meantime; the station is at your disposal.

"I can share one additional piece of information. The unauthorized ship fired upon our vessels when we pursued. This was naturally unexpected, and accounts for our failure to detain the ship. I hope to have more data upon my return."

The message ended. Jonas leaned back in his chair, frowning. Kori slammed her palm on the console.

"She's lying. My brother wouldn't have fired on anyone. I doubt the ship was even armed, though I know it was modified for maximum speed and maneuverability."

"It's obvious that the Administrator is avoiding us. We won't learn anything more here."

"Then we go on to follow my brother's route."

He looked up at her. "Yes. Until we reach the end."

They found the Royal Persephonean ship Eurydice *far* more easily than Jonas had had any right to hope.

A hour after receiving the Administrator's message, Jonas and Lady Kori—Jonas was more than willing to make use of that formality—were back on the *A'amia* and tracking the *Eurydice*'s route deeper into shaauri space. The way led through another wormhole, one of three in the proximity of the station, and exited near a Kinsman station on the outskirts of a double-star system.

But this time they acknowledged the station's routine hails without stopping. As soon as they reentered normal space, Lady Kori produced a data card bearing an encrypted signal. The signal was disguised to blend in with the radio static of space and would trigger a response from the *Eurydice,* should she be anywhere in the vicinity. With Jonas's assistance, Kori patched the signal through the *A'amia*'s comm for wide dispersal throughout the star system.

The chance of receiving a response was slim; the *Eurydice* might be far from this region of space. But Lady Kori went at it with her now familiar tenacity, and when no return signal was received, they moved on to another wormhole and another system to try again. Kori located her brother's ship on the third attempt.

The *Eurydice* lay derelict in the midst of an asteroid belt, one more bit of flotsam orbiting the nearby sun. The signal she sent back to the *A'amia* was her only sign of life.

Kori gazed into the main monitor, her posture too rigid for the composure she pretended.

"It is the *Eurydice*," she said. "I never expected to find her so quickly."

Jonas rubbed his jaw and studied the ship. At a kilometer away from the ship, the *A'amia*'s sensors told him that it was abandoned, or at least unmanned. And it had suffered considerable damage.

The big questions were how, and why.

"It doesn't make sense," Kori said. "The Kinsmen must have known about this. And if they did—"

"The Administrator of KS13 was indeed lying to us."

They looked at each other. Jonas hid the turmoil that had gripped him ever since her revelation.

No, before that. Since their lovemaking, when she'd burst into his mind like a solar flare, exposing him, laying him bare, and . . .

Changing him. For the first time in seven years he felt a flicker of real life in the part of his brain that had died. A sense that, if he tried, he could enter her mind and see exactly what she was thinking and feeling.

Was such healing possible? He was afraid to hope. He had almost become adjusted, resigned to being forever crippled among his own people.

Oh, he was still a Kinsman, and useful because of his affinity with the shaauri. But he was stripped of an ability he'd taken for granted as much as sight and hearing, one that no non-telepath could comprehend. And he knew he wasn't worthy of the high status accorded Kinsman telepaths. When he told them of his loss, they would regard him as no longer truly one of them.

Now . . . now that fate was in question. But if the awakening in his mind proved to be merely a phantom perception, all hope was indeed lost. Just as he'd lost the brief comfort of intimacy with a woman who didn't exist.

Lady Kori Galatéa Challinor had lied to him, and he had been blind enough—crippled enough—to fall for her deception. She'd twisted him around her finger and penetrated his deepest defenses. She had even claimed to care for him.

By the shaauri gods, he still wanted her. That hadn't changed. But he'd shielded himself and his mind against her. And no matter what identity she chose to go by, royal family or not, she'd made a bargain, and he intended to hold her to her word.

As he would keep his.

Kori shifted and looked away. "Someone took a great deal of trouble to hide the *Eurydice*. Who, why, and what did they do with my brother and his crew?"

"If Kinsmen are behind this, it must be a renegade group. Such actions would never be sanctioned by the Directors."

"Wouldn't they?"

He resisted the urge to counter with a biting comment

about Worldbound prejudice. She wasn't ordinary World-bound by any stretch of the imagination.

"If there are traitors," he said tightly, "they're working against all Kinsmen and shaauri as well as your people. We will stop them."

"Just the two of us?"

"Yes. If it comes to that."

She fell silent and stepped back to lean against the bulkhead, her body supple and deceptively slight in a plain gray shipsuit. He found it all too easy to become distracted by her beauty, and the natural courage and spirit that she wore in any guise. Distraction was the last thing he could allow himself.

"They . . . whoever *they* are . . . could very well know that we're looking for the *Eurydice*," she said.

That thought had occurred to him as well. Despite what he'd said to Kori, there was no telling how far this conspiracy, if conspiracy it was, had spread among the Kinsmen. There'd been no whisper of it in shaauri territory.

Let it be only a few warped individuals. Let some honor remain in being a Kinsman.

"That's a risk we'll have to take," he said, "unless you prefer to give up now."

She pushed away from the bulkhead. "Not for all the moons of Croesus."

"Then we'll need to board the ship and look around."

"Yes. And if I know my brother, he's left a private log for any Persephonean who finds the ship—in a place his enemies wouldn't look for it. Maybe we'll get our answers there."

As she turned toward the hatch to the main cabin, he touched her arm. The spark of her innermost essence filled his mind. Confusion, anger, fear for her brother, all the emotions she was so adept at hiding—including an attraction to him that was very real.

His mind *was* healing, and she was the cause. He snapped his mental shields back into place.

"You know what we might find."

"Yes. They may all be dead on that ship."

"You won't be alone, Lady Kori," he said. It was scant

comfort, but she smiled, and his heart clenched at her quiet gratitude.

"Kori," she said. "It's Kori." She caught his hand, squeezed it, and left the cockpit.

He let her go ahead to don one of the ship's two space suits while he maneuvered the ship through the asteroid belt, close to the *Eurydice*. From this vantage the damage was even more apparent.

Jonas set the *A'amia*'s computer to warn him if another vessel approached their position. He took additional precautions, hoping they wouldn't prove necessary.

Hoping that he and Kori would find the right answers.

The Eurydice *was as dead and silent within as it* appeared from outside, every system off-line and not a living soul on board.

Protected by streamlined shaauri space suits adapted to human form, Jonas and Kori moved between the two ships with small handheld thrusters and entered an airlock nearest the flight deck. Life support and gravity were disabled, every trace of atmosphere had been blown out, and the interior was space-cold.

Jonas saw at once that the *Eurydice* was no ordinary vessel. She was designed to hold a crew of perhaps twenty, with ample cargo space. But her shape was that of a cruiser rather than a cargo ship. The command deck had a number of innovations he hadn't seen on standard Persephonean vessels, and he suspected that the engines were also enhanced. Kori had hinted as much.

Kori immediately began to search for her brother's secret log while Jonas inspected the damage that penetrated the outer hull. It resembled the results of a shaauri attack, but everything looked too neat. Staged. And the *Eurydice* wasn't armed, in spite of the Administrator's claims.

Jonas made his way to engineering, gliding weightless down the companionways to the heart of the ship. His practiced eye told him that the ship could be made spaceworthy again with a few days of hard work. In fact, she was of substantial value, not a piece of junk to be abandoned.

Her crew had been either spaced or captured, unless this

had truly been an accident. Jonas no more believed that than he believed his own accident was a simple matter of bad luck or engine failure.

"Jonas?"

He flipped on the comm link in his helmet. "Here."

"I located my brother's log. You'd better come up."

He found Kori anchored to the command chair by a rigid grip, her face set and pale. "It's partially damaged, but there's enough here to make everything clear." She held up a thumb-size capsule. "Listen."

A man's baritone voice sounded from the capsule. *"This is Miklos Challinor, commander of the* Eurydice. *To whoever finds this message: please see that it reaches Persephonean Royal Intelligence or Lady Kori Challinor.*

"If you are Kinsmen. I beg you to consider the good of all humankind and prevent the likelihood of renewed conflict and war between human and shaauri.

"On 2.15.150, the Eurydice, *attempting to cross shaauri space without benefit of Kinsman escort, was pursued and attacked by a Kinsman vessel. The* Eurydice *was forced to surrender. It immediately became obvious that these Kinsmen were not interested in holding and fining the* Eurydice; *the crew has been taken prisoner and is to be transported to some unknown location.*

"These Kinsmen intend to use me and my crew for some political purpose of their own, one they are keeping hidden from the rest of their people. They have damaged the Eurydice *to simulate an attack by shaauri to cover the effect of their weapons. They may intend to hold us hostage, or use our disappearance or deaths to generate suspicion and hostility between human and shaauri. I can only speculate.*

"I do not know if shaauri are involved, but I am convinced that these Kinsmen will go to any lengths to maintain their status and prevent any easing of shaauri-human relations.

"Get word to Lady Kori Challinor. These renegade Kinsmen must be stopped, for the sake of us all."

Kori stopped the recording. Jonas could see the bleakness of her eyes through the visor of her helmet.

"It's what we feared," she said. "There is a conspiracy, and Kinsmen are out to stop the negotiations by any means possible."

"*Some* Kinsmen," Jonas said. His stomach was clenched in misery, knowing what his people had done. How low they'd fallen. "This can't be widely known—"

"It obviously involved the Administrator on KS13, possibly even the staff on Persephone Station. Why else did they make it so hard for you to get information on the *Eurydice*?"

"I don't know. But we're going to find out."

"There are only two ways to do that. We either confront your leaders directly and force them to admit that a conspiracy exists or we go on as we have been—penetrate the enemy's defenses, find my brother, and expose them ourselves." She slipped the capsule into her suit pocket. "Which do you think is less risky?"

"It's no longer your problem. I'm taking you back to Persephone. These are my people, and I'll deal with them."

She let go of the command chair and floated toward him. "Out of the question. This involves my world and the entire Concordat—"

"These traitors already have a member of your royal family. I don't know what they think they have to gain by any of this, but they're obviously desperate enough to act rashly, even lethally. If they get you as well, there's no telling what they'll do. I won't allow it."

"*You* won't—"

An alarm sounded in his helmet comm link. He listened to the *A'amia*'s message and cursed himself for an idiot.

"No more time," he said. "My ship has just informed me that another vessel is approaching at high speed. We have to get back to the *A'amia*."

6

*K*ori was no fool. She followed him back to the airlock
and to his ship, concentrating on moving quickly and efficiently. Jonas ran to the cockpit while she stripped out of her
suit.

The approaching ship was a Kinsman vessel, a cruiser of
unfamiliar design. It was also armed to the teeth. It hailed
the *A'amia* with none of the usual courteous preliminaries.

*"Attention. Your vessel has been found in violation of
Treaty regulation five-oh-six. Prepare to be boarded."*

Jonas knew that regulation. It was the same one they
would have used on the *Eurydice*—if they'd been interested
in legalities—but it didn't apply to him.

"This is Jonas Kane VelArhan of the shaauri-registered
vessel *A'amia*. Identify yourself."

The Kinsman ship didn't respond. Instead, her gunports
opened and made a very adequate display of her weaponry.

Kori joined him in the cockpit. "These must be our enemies."

Jonas nodded. "We can't outrun them. We'll have to let
ourselves be boarded, and play innocent."

"You know that won't work. And I'm not sure you'll be
much good at lying."

He smiled grimly. "I'm inclined to agree—but you have

great skill at lying, even to telepaths. A rare ability."

She ignored his sarcasm. "They took hostages; we can do the same thing. It'll give us some leverage. You do have weapons aboard this ship?"

"A few."

"I've devised a telepathic technique that's been useful in my work for Intelligence. Under certain circumstances, I can . . . disappear."

Jonas guessed her meaning. "You mean that you can cloud the minds of others, so that you appear not to be there. They don't see you."

"That's right." One corner of her mouth tilted up. "Not something you'd have tried, given your dislike for deception. But it works. Back on the station, I managed to stay invisible to the Administrator—and you—for a good five minutes while I listened to your conversation from the doorway."

"She wasn't a telepath."

"But you are, and it worked on you. It's the best chance we've got. I'll arm myself and stay as far out of the way as possible, absolutely still. You pretend to surrender. Keep them occupied any way you can, but distract them. When the time is right, I'll grab as many of our friends as I—"

"I'm no longer a telepath, as you discovered on KS13," he said harshly. "I get occasional flashes of the old ability, but for the most part, I'm mentally blind. Or was, until—" He broke off. "It wouldn't have been difficult to deceive me."

She paced a tight circle and stopped directly in front of him. "I don't believe it's all gone. For one thing, you knew I was a fraud after we were . . . together."

So he had. And soon he would have to test his mental abilities once more. But he couldn't risk Kori.

"It doesn't matter," he said. "What you propose is extremely dangerous and would take tremendous skill and power. Your chances of success—"

"—may not be great, but you don't have a better plan." She touched his arm. "You're still too tied up in being a Kinsman, facing Kinsmen who aren't behaving the way they're supposed to. Trust me. I'm better at this than you are."

He had no choice but to trust her. "Very well." He strode to the weapons locker beside the hatch and pulled out a heavy-duty disruptor. "This is the best I have."

She weighed the gun in her hand. "It'll do."

The ship rang with the sound of grappling hooks from the Kinsman ship locking on to the *A'amia.*

"This is it," Kori said. She stepped out into the main cabin and took up a position slightly behind a projecting bulkhead. She went very still. Jonas paused to slip a smaller weapon into his shipsuit pocket and waited for the boarding party.

The airlock cycled and the first of the boarders stepped out into the cabin. He wore Kinsman red, his shoulders single-barred for the lowest telepath rank, and carried a disruptor. He was followed by a woman, also a telepath, and two non-telepaths, all armed like the first.

"Jonas Kane VelArhan," the first man said, standing at his ease.

Jonas recognized him at once, and concealed his dismay. "Artur Constano VelRauthi," he said. "I didn't expect to meet you again under these circumstances."

"It has been a long time, hasn't it, brother-in-law?" He nodded to his compatriots, who spread out to either side of him, all seeming as relaxed as he was. Not one of them looked toward Kori. "I won't do you the disservice of assuming you don't know why we're here."

"I have an idea. You had the *Eurydice* bugged to warn you if anyone approached her."

"We didn't expect the ship to be found." Constano smiled faintly. "It seems you've shown an inordinate curiosity about the *Eurydice*'s fate. Our ally on KS13 says that you've asked a lot of questions."

"Reasonable ones, considering the lack of information," Jonas said. "The ship's disappearance isn't yet known on Persephone. Given the rank of her commander, you didn't expect the *Eurydice*'s fate to remain unexamined for long—"

"No. We were assuming it wouldn't. You just moved up the timetable. Presently I'll ask you why you became involved in this the minute you got back from shaauri space, and what you've learned." He glanced around the cabin. "I understand you had a passenger, a female candidate from Persephone. Does she have something to do with your presence here?"

"She . . . suggested certain things to me, and I chose to investigate."

"Interesting. Where is she?"

"I left her on the *Eurydice* when I was alerted of your approach."

"Indeed." Constano arched a brow. "I doubt it. I have a suspicion that she may be of more importance than you pretend." He advanced farther into the cabin, sweeping it with his gaze. His first exploration took him toward the cockpit, away from Kori, but abruptly he turned and started in her direction. He hadn't seen her, not yet. But it was only a matter of time.

Jonas drew his disruptor from his pocket. Four weapons trained on him. He ignored them.

"You're right," he said. "She is rather remarkable." And he aimed his gun directly at Lady Kori Challinor.

Jonas had betrayed her.

The shock was sufficient that Kori simply stood and stared at him as Constano VelRauthi's henchwoman approached her and snatched the disruptor from her hand.

"Remarkable, indeed," Constano said. He looked her over with a sardonic half-smile. "A very gifted telepath to be able to hide in plain sight." His expression grew more intense, and Kori felt as if someone were prying open her skull. She slammed down her defenses.

"Ah," Constano said. "I thought you bore some resemblance to your brother . . . Lady Kori Challinor."

"She's my gift to you, Artur," Jonas said. "The third in line to the throne of Persephone."

Kori stared at Jonas and reached instinctively for his thoughts. He, too, was blocking any intrusion. There was no reassurance from him that this was not the betrayal it seemed.

How could it be? He'd been capable of hiding his mental handicap from her until their intimacy. But this kind of falsehood wasn't in him.

Constano glanced at Jonas. "Yes, we have Miklos Challinor and his crew. Now I understand how you came to know about the *Eurydice*'s disappearance when Thetis Challinor was keeping it so quiet. Lady Kori *is* an officer in Royal

Intelligence . . . though her position is supposed to be more honorary than real."

"What have you done with Lord Miklos?" Kori demanded.

"In good time, my lady." He gestured to one of his men, who stepped into the cockpit. "It's very generous," he said to Jonas, "for you to offer the lady to us. But I must wonder why you've suddenly decided to support our cause."

"You never bothered to ask me if I was interested."

"You weren't around to ask. But it didn't occur to us that you would take our side, given your loyalty to the Challinors."

"My loyalty," Jonas said, "is to Kinsmen, and whatever will preserve our way of life."

Constano's nonchalant attitude vanished. "And our cause," he said, "is to do exactly that—"

"By making sure that the Challinors don't succeed in their independent negotiations with the shaauri."

Constano showed no surprise. He held out his hand, and Jonas passed him the small disruptor. Constano gave it to one of his men. "You do seem to be very well informed. As I assume Lady Kori is, or she wouldn't be here. Did she hire you, or did you take this upon yourself?" He shrugged. "It doesn't matter. But given your dogged pursuit of the *Eurydice* since leaving Persephone Station—yes, we have people there, as well as on every Kinsman station in the shaauri zone—I'm forced to wonder why you chose this moment to surrender the lady and yourself."

Jonas met Constano's gaze steadily. "She approached me shortly after I returned to human space, because my father and I both served as liaisons to Persephone. But I'd already learned that a faction of Kinsmen was operating independently, and clandestinely, to sabotage the Challinor negotiations and any chance of more open human-shaauri interaction. You haven't been as careful as you should have been in choosing whom to involve in your conspiracies." He tapped his temple. "It wasn't difficult to learn the essence of your plans."

He was clearly implying that he had read other Kinsman minds to gather such information. Kori knew that shouldn't be possible.

Either he was trying some desperate new plan to gain an

advantage for both of them, or all her carefully trained judgment was worthless. Her judgment . . . and her emotions.

"The Jonas I knew," Constano said, "would never have
entered another mind without permission. He stood by every
Kinsman law with absolute dedication." He tilted his head.
"When did you learn of this, Jonas—before or after the 'accident' that killed my sister and Lady Kori's parents?" He
shook his head. "Of course it wasn't an accident. We had to
stop Georg Challinor."

Jonas didn't show Constano any change of expression. "I
learned about the plan to eliminate the heir and his wife after
Jennara and I had piloted the diplomatic courier ship far into
shaauri territory. My wife was part of your conspiracy, and
had kept it from me very successfully until then." He smiled
coldly. "She was surprisingly good at hiding her plans, even
from me. She told me that she was supposed to trigger the
bomb that would kill the Challinors, and get us both off
the ship safely. She also convinced me, quite eloquently, of
the rightness of your cause. But at the last minute she had a
change of heart. She planned to betray you."

"Yes. We were always watching her. I'd hoped she would
remain loyal to me, and our purpose." He shrugged. "A pity
she had to die. You, however, escaped—and fled to the
shaauri."

"I was injured. I had much to consider after the incident,
to decide where my loyalties lay."

"And now you decide they lie with us?" He gave a disbelieving snort. "You know that we were responsible for Jennara's death. You and your father lived and worked with the
Challinors. Why should you help us now? Why not go to the
authorities?"

"Jennara and I . . . ceased being close long before the accident. She must have told you that much. During my years
of living among the shaauri, I came to realize that her death,
and my injury, were unfortunate but tolerable by-products of
a necessary action to preserve our way of life. Ordinary humans cannot be trusted with the alliances we've worked so
hard and long to build. They are inferior, incapable of understanding."

"And so you would join us—lie, even kill—to stop Thetis
Challinor and all others like her?"

"Yes."

Kori swallowed, battered by the resonance of truth in his voice. His thoughts were still closed to her. But she found that the deepest part of her being—the part he had touched when they'd made love—believed in his loyalty. Believed in *him*. It wasn't a matter of rationally weighing the possibilities, as she had done throughout her career in Intelligence. Her certainty came out of something more powerful.

Love.

If not for years of discipline, that blinding revelation might have undone her completely. Instead, she filed it away for future examination. Later she would *feel* what it meant. Later, when she and Jonas were free again.

She was going to make damned sure they both had that chance.

"We will give you an opportunity to prove your sincerity," Constano said. It took Kori a moment to realize he was speaking to Jonas, not to her. "My subordinates here will escort you and Lady Kori to our station, while I and the rest of my people remain to finish repairing the *Eurydice*. We have important plans for the ship."

Jonas glanced at Kori with lifeless eyes. "What do you intend to do with her and the other hostages?"

"Let's just say that it's fortunate you have no personal affection for the lady." He gestured to his followers, who closed in on Kori and Jonas and herded them toward the airlock. As if by accident, Jonas brushed Kori's arm. The contact set waves of sensation spiraling through her body. And it told her everything she needed to know.

Something had happened to Jonas's mind. It was alive and awake again. He knew exactly what he was doing.

Whatever happened from now on, she wouldn't be alone.

The conspirators' base was a day's journey by wormhole and sublight speed into a part of shaauri space even less traveled than the route Miklos had chosen for the *Eurydice*. A small space station, formerly abandoned, circled the dead planet of a white dwarf. Revived for the unlawful purposes of the rebels, the station bristled with Kinsman vessels, several of them armed, as well as a shaauri ship.

Now the *A'amia* joined them.

The station's brig lay at the Stratton's most protected heart, well guarded by Kinsman security. Hard faces watched Constano's lieutenants march Jonas and Kori down corridor after featureless corridor; Kori didn't dare open her mind enough to search for her brother's presence, but she knew he was here. He, and all his crew.

She had little hope of being reunited with Miklos immediately, and Constano's people didn't surprise her. They sent Jonas away in the custody of two guards, and without ceremony or explanation pushed her through the door of a high-security cell.

She spent the next two days in the cell with no outside contact other than the guard who brought her meals. Any mind that passed within her reach remained inaccessible. She quieted her worry over her brother and Jonas by practicing breathing and meditation exercises, preparing herself for the next challenge.

On the third day, the guards came for her again and took her to another cell, identical to the first . . .

Except that it was already occupied.

Two young men and a woman surged up from the low bench built into the wall of the cell, their expressions caught in wary surprise. The man in the middle was Miklos. His appearance was haggard, but healthy enough under the circumstances. He stared at Kori, and his face blanched in distress.

"Kori?" he said hoarsely. "No. You can't be here."

"I'm afraid I am." She stepped forward to embrace him, feeling his violently mixed emotions. Typical of Miklos. He didn't do anything by half measures. That was why the people of Persephone loved him—and why both of them were in this dangerous situation.

"Are they listening?" she whispered into his ear.

"Don't know," he answered in the same low tones. "But some of them are telepaths. Better assume they are."

She pulled free of his hold and gripped his shoulders. "I wish I could say I'm glad to see you," she said. "At least you're alive."

"And you came after me, didn't you? Kori, Kori—"

"What did you expect? It's my business to know anything

that affects Royal security. You couldn't expect to go running off on this kind of harebrained scheme without my learning of it. I knew there was something wrong when you didn't return in a reasonable time, given what you were trying to do. So did Grandmother. I came out to find your ship."

"You found us." His shoulders slumped for a moment, and then he straightened again. "I'm sorry, Kori. I wanted to prove that we—non-Kinsmen—were ready to cross shaauri space and deal with the shaauri ourselves. But I never guessed that there was a real conspiracy against us, against Persephone, by the Kinsmen—"

"Some Kinsmen, in any case," Kori said. She nodded to Miklos's crew members and sat down on the bench. "How do you think I found you? A Kinsman helped me locate the *Eurydice*. I thought he was trustworthy—until he turned me over to Constano." She allowed bitterness to show on her face. "You knew that Kinsmen were impeding Persephonean trade with the Nine Worlds, but you didn't know why. Have *they* told you why they attacked you and took you prisoner?"

"Why should they bother to hide it? We can't escape. We've tried." He sat down beside her, his normally mobile face taut with anger and frustration. "Negotiations between Persephone and certain influential shaauri, which I didn't even know about." He laughed. "I've condemned my own crew—"

Kori shook him gently. "Where are the rest?"

"In other cells. After the first escape attempt, they were careful to separate us."

"Then you must have made them worry." She squeezed his arm. "If Grandmother and I had confided in you about the negotiations, you never would have done this. You would have waited. It's as much my fault as anyone's."

"No. You had reason not to trust my judgment. You're not taking this off my shoulders." He gave her a wry smile. "You were always the responsible one, Kori, even more than Hector. The one with the real brains, like Grandmother. If we get out of this, you'll find me a changed man."

"That'll be something to see." She returned his smile and deliberately let it fade. "These same conspirators were behind our parents' deaths." She nodded grimly at Miklos's curse. "Mother and Father were on their way to begin the negotiations with the shaauri when their ship was sabotaged. The Kinsman liaison—Kane VelArhan—who survived the supposed accident was the man I approached to help me find you. I made the mistake of believing he was our ally."

"Kane VelArhan—Jonas? I remember him." His eyes narrowed. "So he survived to betray us."

"His loyalty is to his fellow Kinsmen. I learned that to my cost." She returned his comforting grip. "Look, I don't know how much time we have. Tell me everything you know—what they plan for you and the *Eurydice*." She glanced up at the bare white walls. "It hardly matters if they hear—I have a feeling that Constano would tell us sooner or later, just so he could gloat."

"I've noticed that about him," Miklos said dryly. "He's one of the chiefs in this operation. And there are shaauri on their side, Kori. A few of them are here now."

"Shaauri who want to keep the treaty the way it is, for reasons of their own," Kori guessed. "But I'm willing to bet the shaauri in general don't know any more about this than we did—or than Kinsman Prime does."

"You think any Kinsmen can be trusted?"

"I don't think all of them are ready to start a war. And that's what this is leading to, no matter what Constano and his cohorts believe. Now, tell me what you've learned."

Miklos dropped his elbows onto his knees. "Now that I know they killed our parents, it all makes sense. I understand that they were already planning to disrupt these negotiations by setting up some sort of conflict between Persephone and the shaauri—create new suspicions and hostility—and I gave them the perfect opportunity when I showed up with the *Eurydice*." He ran his hand through his hair. "I almost outran them. She's a damned fine ship."

"But they caught you."

"Yes. And they've been working on a scheme to use the *Eurydice* and the crew to make it appear that rogue shaauri attacked and destroyed us without sufficient provocation."

"I was on the ship. The damage appeared to be from shaauri weapons."

"Exactly. They went to some pains to fix that up. And that's only the start. They're putting together a false captain's log, using simulations of my voice, to pin the supposed attack on one shaaurin in particular—the son of some shaauri elder who's important in the negotiations."

Kori whistled silently. "And they would arrange for someone from Persephone to find the wreckage . . . and a few bodies, and the log—"

"And report to Grandmother, who already hates the shaauri—"

"And who only continued these negotiations for the sake of our father and his memory. If Grandmother thought shaauri had killed you, she wouldn't forgive them, even if some considered your unauthorized travel across shaauri space to be sufficient provocation. She would not only break off the negotiations, but she'd likely accuse the shaauri's chief negotiator of murder." She shook her head. "Do these people have any idea what they're starting?"

"We know exactly what we're starting," a voice said from the open doorway. Constano waved a pair of Kinsman guards ahead of him into the cell. Miklos's crew members closed in around the Challinors protectively, but they were separated and hustled out of the room.

"How pleasant to see you again, Lady Kori. I hope you haven't found our accommodations too primitive." He glanced at Miklos. "Since your brother has already told you half the story, I'll be happy to complete it," Constano said. "You'll be an important new addition to our operation." Another pair of guards, with minimal courtesy and weapons at the ready, urged the Challinors to follow Constano into the corridor.

The room to which they were led was an office adapted to serve as a meeting room, with a large table at the center and as many as thirty chairs crowded around it. A number of the chairs were occupied: by twelve of Constano's ranking compatriots, Jonas, and four shaauri.

Shaauri. Miklos had warned her, but it was still something of a shock to see them so close. No alien had ever visited Persephone, and even Kori, in her varied travels on behalf of Royal Intelligence, hadn't met one. They kept rigidly apart from humans.

Except Kinsmen. And these shaauri were likely traitors to their own kind.

The shaauri, dressed in loose vests and trousers, seemed

ill at ease in the human-shaped chairs, though Kori couldn't be sure what emotions passed behind those exotic features. Tilted red-gold eyes regarded her and Miklos steadily. Triangular ears, lined with rows of sensitive hairs, twitched and angled forward and back. The whiskers, which appeared almost comical in vids, were anything but amusing on the living beings. One shaaurin laid his hand on the table, revealing intricately painted nails that resembled claws.

Symbolism. For the shaauri, the smallest movements held great meaning. It was almost impossible for most humans to learn all the variations, which was why telepathy was so useful in communication. The fact that shaauri vocal cords produced sounds far beyond the threshold of human hearing didn't make matters any easier.

The guards pushed Kori and Miklos into chairs across the table from Jonas and the aliens. Jonas was as expressionless as the shaauri. He sat a single chair's width from the nearest shaaurin, the red of his uniform nearly matching the fur of the aliens.

"You wanted to know our plans, Lady Kori," Constano said, sitting down at the head of the table. "We've been discussing you at some length, and we think we've found an excellent way of exploiting your presence here." He nodded to Miklos. "Your brother enhanced our program with his fortuitous arrival, and you've done the same. It seems that you not only found the *Eurydice,* damaged in an unprovoked attack by a shaauri youth, but you vowed to seek revenge."

Kori leaned back in her chair. "Did I? That doesn't seem very likely."

"I think you'll find that it makes perfect sense. And since you'd convinced a certain Kinsman to help you, you also found yourself in possession of a ship with the capability to hunt down your brother's murderer in his own space."

"The *A'amia.*"

"Indeed. With your many skills, you managed to take the ship from Kane VelArhan, who bore you some misplaced loyalty because he'd once worked with your family. You left him in a life pod and went in pursuit of the young shaaurin and his small crew, whose own ship had been damaged in the conflict. You found him in the process of repairing his vessel, and brought the *A'amia*'s shaauri weapons to bear.

His crew-kin were wiped out, but he disabled your ship and boarded while you were otherwise engaged. You and he fought and killed each other." He sighed. "Very tragic—and the end of any hope of closer ties between Persephone and the shaauri."

7

*K*ori laughed. *She laughed long enough that four pairs of* shaauri eyes widened and eight fringed ears flattened sideways, while the Kinsmen glanced at each other in consternation.

"You seem to have it all worked out," she said at last. "But you're assuming a great deal of stupidity on the part of the shaauri, as well as myself. Shaauri might attack my brother's ship for trespass and treaty violation, but they'd be just as likely to call in the Kinsmen to deal with it. What you're describing is a very risky and dangerous act. Just who is the shaaurin who would behave so rashly?"

"You know something of the shaauri, Lady Kori, but you obviously aren't aware that shaauri youths can be quite wild. In their walkabout years apart from clan and Line, they have few inhibitions, and some are said to go temporarily mad. Add to this a personal resentment of humans—" He shrugged. "The young shaaurin responsible for your death is the offspring of one of the elders negotiating with Thetis Challinor. This youth is known among his peers to resent the prospect of closer ties with humans. The *Eurydice* proved too much of a temptation when it intruded upon shaauri territory."

Kori steepled her hands beneath her chin. "Let me guess.

You'll arrange to have someone from my world find all three derelict ships and enough intact debris to provide sufficient proof of what happened. Thetis Challinor will find herself minus two grandchildren and royal heirs, all because of the hostile act of an offspring of the very shaaurin she's supposed to be negotiating with in good faith. But since her granddaughter attacked and killed a shaaurin of an influential Line, the shaauri aren't likely to offer much sympathy."

"Very good, Lady Kori."

She stood up. "I understand that you're on the verge of starting a new war—one that's as likely to hurt you and all Kinsmen as it is the rest of us."

"A war? I don't think so. Thetis Challinor isn't so stupid, whatever her personal feelings. But it will set back these negotiations, possibly halt them for years, and by the time that lost ground is recovered we'll have a better, more permanent plan in place."

"Unless the Concordat and the shaauri learn how they've been manipulated."

"They won't." He glanced at his shaauri allies. "We have our own shaauri, who—"

"Have learned to lie like humans? Deceive their own people?" She turned to stare at the four shaauri. "And what do you get out of this, *Sh'eivali*?" she asked, in the blunt, simplified Shaurii pidgin that only Kinsmen, and a very few other humans, could speak. She didn't bother with courtesy beyond the general shaauri address; her rudeness was deliberate, forcing them to acknowledge her and recognize her lack of fear.

Anger and contempt came from the minds of the shaauri, impossible to mistake. Jonas shifted in his chair and halfway rose. The shaaurin nearest him twitched an ear in his direction and spoke in the fluid, half-audible shaauri tongue, showing the tips of his sharpened front teeth.

"Dakiro Aarys says," Constano translated, "that his Line will be glad to see that no other humans walk among shaauri. His Line will do whatever is necessary to end these negotiations."

Kori wasn't used to reading shaauri as Kinsmen were trained to do, but she thought Constano spoke the truth. Except . . .

"That isn't entirely accurate," Jonas said, settling back in his chair. "Dakiro Aarys also said that if it were up to his Line, all humans would be cast out of shaauri space forever. He includes Kinsman." He gave Constano a half-smile. "The Aarys Line is notorious for hating anything human. They've no Kinsman adoptees among their families. They even refuse to learn our language. I'm surprised they would work with us."

"The lesser of two evils," Constano said. But his face was rigid, as if Jonas had reminded him of something he would rather have forgotten. "They can be trusted to handle any information leaks on the shaauri side."

"And where is this shaaurin I'm supposed to kill?" Kori demanded.

Constano spoke to the aliens in fluent pidgin. They pushed at the centermost shaaurin until he rose from his seat. His slight build, paler color, and lack of bars suggested that he was young, not yet a full adult.

"May I introduce you to Haiimo Evalan, youngest son of the chief negotiator to the Throne of Persephone," Constano said. "Our allies arranged his capture, and an appropriate story to mask his absence, though it's hardly rare for youths on walkabout to disappear for some time during their years of wandering. His family wouldn't be concerned about him in any case—until they find evidence of his death at human hands."

Kori met the young shaaurin's gaze. Perhaps it was only a projection of human qualities, but she could have sworn she saw fear in his bright eyes. He kept his ears pointed straight forward, a gesture of defiance.

"If we hadn't found you," Constano said, "we'd have arranged his death to appear to be caused by other anti-shaauri humans. But you've made our task so much simpler."

"You're very sure of yourself," Kori said. "But you underestimate Thetis Challinor—and I think you misjudge the shaauri."

Constano chose not to answer. "We already have the *Eurydice* prepared. Within twenty-four hours, the *A'amia* and young Haiimo's vessel will be suitably altered to show the damage inflicted by these tragic conflicts. And now that Jonas has joined us, we have someone to carry word of the theft of his ship, and your hunt for vengeance against Haiimo, back to human space. Once, of course, we've verified his loyalty."

Kori held her breath and let it out silently. It was too much to hope for that they would accept Jonas's apparent shift in allegiance so easily. She could think of only one obvious way for Constano to test him.

A way Jonas would hate. A way that would strip him to the soul.

Constano would force his way into Jonas's mind, humiliate him, and then kill him.

"Jonas Kane VelArhan," Constano said with a sudden show of formality. "You know what we must ask of you. You will prove that our path is also yours. You will let down all your barriers and open your mind to me."

Jonas rose from his chair. "I'm ready," he said. His gaze flickered to Kori, and in that instant she saw in his eyes what he hadn't allowed to show before: his absolute promise of loyalty, his pride—in her—and his stubborn courage. He was going to let them do their worst. He was going to attempt to deceive them in spite of the risks and his own powerful inhibitions, lie to them even as they entered his mind. Make them trust him, so he could find Kori and Miklos and the others a way out of this deadly trap.

It wouldn't work. Even if his mind was healing, he surely hadn't the strength or skill to hold them at bay indefinitely—not these ruthless telepaths who would stop at nothing short of destruction. But he saw it as their only chance.

All Kori had ever learned of the shaauri tumbled through her mind. A solution came to her: a crazy one, rife with pitfalls. She wasn't even sure she had the details right. All she could do was pray.

Pray that Jonas wouldn't stop her.

She moved away from the table so quickly that her guards were left behind. Her long strides carried her face-to-face with Constano.

"Artur Constano VelRauthi," she said. "I challenge you. I challenge you to single combat, by the shaauri's honored and ancient custom, for the lives of my people."

Constano stared at her. He laughed. He gestured for the guards to take her away.

"Stop." The command in Jonas's voice was so strong that the guards halted in their tracks. He faced the shaauri and began to speak, rapidly, in a language that bore as much resemblance to Constano's pidgin as a baby's babble did to the speech of a great orator. His voice reached pitches that no ordinary human could create; all he lacked was the ears and whiskers.

If ever Kori had needed her telepathic abilities, it was now. She opened her mind, gathered all her concentration, and let Jonas's meaningless sounds flow through her. She became a Kinsman. And she understood.

"Sh'eivali!" he said. "I am Jonas Kane VelArhan. You know my Line. You know that I have lived among the shaauri for seven years. I speak as interpreter for the Lady Kori Challinor of Persephone, the woman you name enemy." He angled his body so that his back was to Constano. "Constano VelRauthi names himself your ally. He claims he is worthy of shaauri honor. I tell you now what Constano VelRauthi is afraid to tell you."

"Kane—" Constano snarled. His hand went to his sidearm.

The shaaurin farthest to the left leaped up in a motion almost too swift to follow and silenced Constano with a hiss that hurt Kori's ears. Constano went very still.

Kori heard the shaaurin's thoughts, so disorientingly alien, more clearly than the half-audible words he spoke.

"I hear you, VelArhan," he said. "Speak."

"The Lady Kori, daughter of Lord Georg Challinor, granddaughter of Thetis Challinor, has invoked the shaauri law of challenge in single battle to Constano VelRauthi. She claims the right to fight for the existence of her Line against the one who would destroy it."

The shaauri looked at each other, ears and whiskers atwitch in some silent communication. The leader made a sweeping gesture with one clawed finger.

"So?"

"Constano VelRauthi has not heard her challenge, because he is afraid of facing this small female. He denies her the right due even the least of shaauri, because he is a coward."

It was an insult of the highest magnitude. Shaauri ears pressed flat. Constano surged forward and stopped himself.

You're dead, Kane, he said in his mind, the thought as

loud as a shout. "*Sh'eivali,* it is true that I have not heard this female. She is human. She is not even of Kinsman blood. She has no right to invoke challenge."

"VelRauthi speaks truth," the shaaurin said to Jonas. "This female has no right."

"Perhaps not by shaauri law," Jonas said. "But what of daring and courage? Once it was considered an art in itself, worthy of admiration: *neeal-damera,* courage-beyond-hope. This female is of high status in her Line and deserves a chance of honorable death. Shaauri have not ceased to honor bravery in their enemies. Is it only you who have abandoned the heart of your people?"

The shaauri leader bared sharpened teeth, and the black-tipped fur on his shoulders bristled. No unarmed human could long stand against such a creature if he chose to attack.

But Jonas stared into the shaaurin's eyes, unbending. "You have been quick to trust one who holds no true loyalty. He is not adopted of *your* Line. Where are the Rauthi? They are not here. He hides from other Kinsmen. He breaks with his own Lines, shaauri and human." He made a scornful gesture with a sweep of one hand. "What did Constano promise you when this is done? An end to invading humans for all time? You know only what he wishes you to know, see what he wishes you to see." He pointed at Constano in blatant accusation. "I am human, but I am also Arhan. I know this man. I name him liar, and coward. He took the life of his sibling because of his own ambition. He desires wealth and power only for himself and those loyal to him; he cares nothing for shaauri or even his own race. He, and each of those who follows him, stands alone, like a mad outcast. Soon you will be like him, dragged down in his madness."

The slightly elongated pupils of the shaaurin's eyes expanded to black ovals that eclipsed the red-gold. "All of Line Aarys stands with us."

"Yet only *you* are here. As you fight for the purity of shaauri culture, you yourself have been tainted by what you most despise. You have learned to lie like humans. True shaauri would never ally themselves to a coward for the sake of expedience. You have adopted human ways and dishonored your own."

Kori thought he'd gone too far. But the shaauri leader did

not fling himself on Jonas. His ears cocked sideways, the tiny fringe of hairs rippling in agitation.

"We are not human," he said at last.

"You still honor shaauri law and custom?"

"We honor it."

"Then let there be challenge. Let Constano prove he is worthy of the trust you give so easily."

The shaaurin swiveled his ears to take in the sibilant whispers of his companions behind him. Only the young prisoner was silent, his attention fixed raptly on the exchange.

Abruptly the leader turned on Constano. "Do you fear this female, VelRauthi?"

His question was a challenge in itself, a test. Kori felt how much rested on Constano's answer. With all their contempt of humans, these shaauri were deeply stung by Jonas's words. Constano and his rebels had made a serious mistake somewhere in their plans.

Constano hesitated, but not out of fear. He was twice Kori's size. He must be calculating the risk of losing the respect of his shaauri allies, of his scheme unraveling bit by bit should anything at all go wrong. . . .

"We have nothing to fear from this female," the shaaurin said. "If you do not fear her, you will fight her. Now."

"No," Jonas said suddenly. "He will fight *me*. The Lady Kori Challinor is my lifemate, and under shaauri law I have the right to fight in her place."

Jonas was well aware of what he had done.

The shaauri were unsettled, hostile and dangerous, Constano looked ready to shoot him, and Kori . . . Kori gazed at him in consternation, her thoughts torn between incongruous joy and anger.

He knew she had offered the challenge to prevent Constano from exposing his deception, and he had sabotaged her plan. He admired her, profoundly, for her courageous act. But there was no time for explanations now, no going back.

"You are lifemated?" the head shaaurin asked. "I thought this was rare among humans."

"He's lying," Constano said. "All he says is lies."

"It is true," Kori said, her voice firm and clear. "We shared a bond of the mind that few can know. But I was the one who challenged—"

"*I* will fight for the lady," Jonas interrupted. "Or are you afraid of me as well, Constano?"

The rebel Kinsman cast a glance about the room, taking in the shaauri and his watching followers, from ranking telepaths to the least of the security guards. They were all watching him. Waiting.

He tossed his sidearm on the table. "I accept your challenge, Kane."

Jonas spoke again to the shaauri. "I hold you as witnesses, *Sh'eivali.* I, Jonas Kane VelArhan, have challenged Artur Constano VelRauthi to single battle, in the name of my lifemate, Lady Kori Galatéa Challinor. My challenge has been accepted. If I am victorious, I claim the lives and freedom of myself, my lifemate, her sibling Miklos Challinor, the crew of the *Eurydice*—and that of young Haiimo Evalan."

"And if I am victorious," Constano said through bared teeth, "You'll still die for our cause . . . but much less pleasantly." He stepped away from the table and drew a knife from a sheath tucked at the small of his back—his adoption-gift, like the one Jonas wore. He held out his hand, palm up, and drew the blade across his skin, leaving a thin line of red. Jonas faced him and repeated the action with his own weapon.

"It is witnessed," the lead shaaurin said. "Let it be done. Let none interfere."

With a mien of implacable gravity, the four shaauri, and their young captive, ranged themselves at one end of the open space between table and wall. Constano's Kinsmen formed a loose circle, exchanging glances and keeping hands conspicuously away from their weapons.

"You heard him," Constano said. "No interference."

The room went silent save for the perpetual hum of life support and station systems. Jonas loosened the fastenings at the top of his uniform and pulled off his boots, letting his bare feet test the deck. Kori's thoughts pushed against his mental barriers, demanding attention.

You hear *me,* she said. *Jonas—*

You can't stop this, he answered, refusing to turn. *It's our only—*

Her hand reached for his shoulder, pulled him around with angry strength. Her eyes burned with passion and promise. She drew his head down to hers and kissed him as she'd never kissed him before. He cupped the back of her neck in his hand, heedless of the blood, and held her close even as he denied her further entrance to his mind.

His mind, that she had miraculously begun to heal in the midst of their greatest passion. She didn't even know how much she'd done. But he couldn't lose himself in her now— not even if it was to be the last closeness they shared.

"Go," he said gruffly. "Don't interfere, Kori."

She went, but not before she gave him the one thing he did not expect.

Her love. Her love for *him*.

"Kane!" Constano shouted.

Once a shaauri challenge was witnessed, there were very few rules. He knew Constano would try to kill him. But he'd practiced shaauri martial arts with Hraan many times at Arhan Holding.

And he had so much more at stake.

He put Kori out of his thoughts—Kori, and her brother, the watching Kinsmen, all the humans he had ever known. He became shaauri, living in the moment, for *this* moment poised between life and death.

The hilt of his knife was warm and alive in his hand. He half crouched, balancing his weight on his right leg, knife held close to his body. Constano was the first to attack.

Jonas danced out of the way of his strike. He watched for Constano's brief hesitation and lunged forward, his own knife thrusting at Constano's arm. A red streak appeared on Constano's uniform.

Constano cursed and wasted no time in attacking again. He telegraphed his intentions with each motion. His downward cut missed Jonas's knife hand by several centimeters. Jonas was ready with a counterstrike, circling his opponent with trained speed and thrusting from an angle Constano didn't expect.

He nicked Constano's shoulder and grabbed the Kinsman's knife wrist with his free hand. Constano used sheer strength to break free and made a clumsy inner slash at Jonas's neck. He lost his balance and fell. Stumbling to his knees, he wasn't prepared when Jonas kicked the knife from his hand.

A lethal stroke would take a matter of seconds, swift and sure. Jonas's shaauri thoughts burned with desire for vengeance—for Jennara, for himself, for lost Kinsman honor.

But he hesitated. And Constano, lying at his feet, struck again—not with his blade, but with his mind.

He did what Kinsmen were trained from birth to despise, what Jonas had never truly believed possible, so smoothly and efficiently that Jonas's defenses crumbled before they were fully engaged. Constano used his own mind to tear through Jonas's as if it were so much tissue. He found the reopened neural pathways and twisted them into hopeless knots, bent only on destruction of the crudest kind.

Jonas was too newly healed, too vulnerable. He staggered away from the attack, covered his head with his hands as if such a futile gesture could protect what lay within. Second by second, he lost more of his ability to think, to hear, to see. Constano might deal him a lethal blow and he wouldn't know it until the last spark of life left his body.

Kori would die. Kori would die, because he couldn't leave Kinsman "honor" behind.

Kori.

All at once she was with him—*with* him, in his mind, lifting him up, bridging the rifts that Constano's violence had wrought. She wove strong, glowing fibers made of her own thoughts and will, creating a gossamer web as strong as love itself. The web meshed around and about him until he could feel no difference between his mind and hers.

They were one. Together they gathered their strength and rose to face Constano. Together they drove him from their minds and pushed, hard, until his will buckled and his face contorted in fear. But they did not do as he had done. They hadn't yet become what he was. They used their body, strong and lithe, to renew the attack. Constano fell. They straddled him, their blade at the pulse beating hard in his neck.

And Kori left him. Left him whole, and lucid, and victorious. His senses were his own. Constano stared up at him, waiting for the death blow that was his to give.

They all waited: Kinsmen, shaauri . . . and Kori. She had fallen to her knees, her eyes filled with hope. The oneness had passed, leaving in its wake the certainty that neither one of them would ever be alone again.

Jonas lifted his knife from his enemy's neck. He grabbed Constano by the collar and hauled him to his feet.

"*Sh'eivali*," he said to the shaauri, "I call upon you to witness my victory. I claim the rights I have won with my body. The Lady Kori Challinor, her brother, and the other prisoners must go free."

"We witness," the head shaaurin answered. Not even a twitch of his whiskers revealed a reaction to his own defeat. He turned to Haiimo, released his bonds, and pushed him away.

But it wasn't over yet. Constano's Kinsmen had tightened their circle about the combatants, and most of them had weapons out and ready. Jonas knew he couldn't kill Constano, not even now. And Constano's honor was nonexistent. He would have to be held prisoner until all the captives were off the station and aboard the *Eurydice*.

"Constano," he said, "tell your people to drop their weapons."

Constano laughed. "You haven't won. Killing me won't make any difference."

As if to prove the truth of his words, the Kinswoman nearest Kori stepped forward and neatly placed the muzzle of her disruptor against Kori's back. The shaauri shifted, ears and whiskers revealing their agitation.

"You keep assuming that the rest of us are like you," Constano said. "Soft. Obsessed with rules we imposed on ourselves to protect inferior humans. Bound by shaauri codes of honor." He shook his head. "No, Kane. We make our own rules from now on. Kinsmen will rule human space, as we were meant to."

"Orders, sir?" the Kinswoman asked.

"Carry on as planned. If the shaauri object, kill them, and dispose of them in a manner that reinforces our objectives. They'll simply be more unfortunate casualties of the new human-shaauri hostilities." He smiled at Jonas. "Your 'lifemate' is quite an interesting woman, Kane. It's a pity we must lose her genetic contribution to our ranks. I can make her death quick, or most unpleasant. Release me, and I may—"

The door to the room hissed open, and a frantic young Kinsman rushed in. "Sir!" he said. He skidded to a stop, staring at Constano and Jonas. "Sir? Three shaauri ships are approaching from Basterra wormhole. They've hailed us, demanding to speak to Jonas Kane VelArhan." He swallowed. "They're Arhan ships, sir. What are your orders?"

Jonas felt Constano go rigid in his grip. "Arhan? But no one else knows our location—"

"I'm afraid they do," Jonas said. "Before you captured the *A'amia,* I recorded a message for my shaauri Line recounting my suspicions about a possible conspiracy, as well as my actions to that point, in case something should happen to Kori and me. When you boarded, I sent a message capsule out by remote, routed directly to the Arhan Line Holding. It was admittedly a desperate act, but your delay in returning to the station allowed enough time for the message to be received. I suspect that someone in your faction leaked your base's coordinates . . . the Administrator on KS13, perhaps?"

Constano's face went blank. "Only three ships—"

"Only three, and you have more firepower than they do. But if you attack them, you'll have to destroy them. That's not going to be so easy to disguise. A single survivor, even a rumor, and all Arhan will be after you. It's part of those shaauri codes of honor you seem to despise."

"It's over, Constano," Kori said. She glanced at her guard, who lowered her weapon. The other Kinsmen slowly did the same. Kori met Jonas's gaze, and in less than a heartbeat their minds met and came to perfect agreement. "Give up now, and we'll use our influence to see that you aren't handed over to the shaauri for punishment." She swept the room with her glance. "I think you'd all rather face your fellow Kinsmen . . . wouldn't you?"

The last of the Kinsmen let their weapons fall. Their former shaauri allies moved quickly for the door, leaving the bewildered young Haiimo staring after them.

"So," Constano said with a twisted smile, "you've won after all. Take your shaauri vengeance."

Jonas released him. "No," he said. "I think you'll suffer enough when you're stripped of power and Kinsman privilege. Once all shaauri and humans know what you've done, it may actually facilitate the Persephonean negotiations—and alter Kinsman life forever."

"No," Constano whispered. But Jonas wasn't listening. He dropped his enemy in a heap at his feet and went to claim the woman he loved, just as the first of his Arhan brethren came gliding through the door.

As unlikely *as it seemed, the passenger seats on the* A'amia *converted to a remarkably comfortable bed, just big enough for two.*

Kori lay beside Jonas, her fingers and thoughts intertwined with his. At last they had privacy—*after* the Arhani had taken custody of the rebel Kinsmen, Jonas had compiled and sent a full report to Kinsman Prime, Haiimo was returned under Arhan protection to his own Family, and Miklos and crew were safely aboard the patched-up *Eurydice.*

The royal ship was already on its way back to human space with a personal Arhan shaauri escort . . . and what a story they would have to tell Archon Thetis Challinor.

Kori's grandmother was going to have to change her way of thinking about the shaauri, especially after they turned up on her doorstep with Miklos in tow. But shaauri and Kinsmen were going to have to change as well. The old ways of suspicion and resentment were coming to an end.

And so is everything we know, she thought. Jonas heard, and pulled her close.

It's not all endings. Not unless you want it to be.

Suddenly, irrationally afraid, she rolled away and sat on the edge of the bed, shielding her mind from him. It felt like cutting off a part of herself.

"At the rebel station," she said slowly, "why did you take the challenge from me? Did you think I couldn't handle it?"

She felt him move behind her, begin to reach out and stop. "I knew that Constano's shaauri allies had to be shamed into recognizing a challenge by a human, and I thought I could manage that better than you could."

"But you *did* convince them to accept my challenge— before you claimed the privilege of fighting in my place."

"As your lifemate."

Was that why she was afraid, now, of all times in the past

few days, when all physical threats were at an end? Because he might be lying—Jonas, who had never lied except to his enemies—or because he might be telling the truth?

"Wasn't that just part of your ploy, to protect me? It was very noble of you, but—"

He cupped her shoulder in his hand. "It wasn't a ploy." He pulled her around, forcing her to face him. "It happened that first night on the station. I didn't want you to realize it, then. I'd been trying to hide my . . . handicap . . . but you discovered it. You did more than discover it, Kori. You began to heal my mind without even knowing what you did."

"*I* . . . healed you?"

"No one else could have done it—only a woman whose mind was a perfect match for my own. That was when I knew. I knew we had what very few people, human or shaauri, ever come close to touching."

"That explains what I sensed when Constano first came aboard the ship. Your mind felt different, even though you wouldn't let me in."

"For the first time in years, I was able to pick up more than vague feelings from another human being. I tested it on Constano. It was from his surface thoughts that I discovered the role Jennara played in the accident, how she'd decided not to go through with her part in the conspiracy, and how Constano himself made certain the courier ship was destroyed with all aboard. Except for me. Constano knew I'd survived, but he didn't think I suspected anything until I recited his own thoughts back to him."

"You *lied* to him—to another telepath. And he didn't know it."

"I guess I'm better at deception than we both presumed—almost as good as you are." He traced his finger over her lower lip. "I wasn't sure it would work."

"And you hated doing it, even with Constano."

"It was necessary. But I still wasn't a complete match for Constano. He attacked my mind, and I didn't have strength enough to defend myself. You felt what was happening, and you gave me your strength. You didn't even think about it, did you?"

"No," she said, remembering. "I just understood what I had to do."

"And you saved me. We became one person. Lifemates."

The wonder and terror of that joining was something she would never forget. She had become Jonas, and he had become her. Yet, in the end, they had not lost themselves. They had only become stronger.

To be lifemated meant that the mental sharing would never go away. It would always be there between them, whenever they wanted it. No more loneliness—and no more complete independence. A life of commitment . . . and . . .

"Love," she said. "Is that part of it?"

"Can you doubt it?" he said, cupping her face in his hands. "Open your mind to me, Kori."

She did, and his love for her poured in like the breath of life itself. When her heart was full to bursting, she poured it back into him. All her love, her hope, her joy.

He kissed her. She kissed him. After a while, she pulled free and spread her fingers across his chest.

"Are you sure this isn't just a way to get me to keep my end of the bargain?"

Surprised darkened his eyes. "You mean the children?" His mouth curved slyly. "Wouldn't you keep your word?"

"I would. I do. I will." She closed her eyes. "I want our children, Jonas. Whatever they are."

"You'd leave Persephone, Kori? Forget your rank and duty, come with me to Kinsman Prime and try to heal the damage Constano did, as you healed my mind? Help us all find a new way?"

"A new way." She smoothed back his hair. "What will become of the Kinsmen now?"

"I don't know. I do believe that the Persephonean negotiations will be successful and the Kinsman trade monopoly will end. We won't be needed to guide and guard every human ship through shaauri space. We'll have to find a new occupation." He smiled crookedly. "We'll have to learn to be ordinary humans again."

"Not ordinary. Never that." She touched her forehead to his. "Think about it, Jonas. Your telepathy enabled you to understand and communicate with the shaauri. Why couldn't you do the same with all the other intelligent beings we haven't yet discovered? Think of it. A whole galaxy is waiting. The Kinsmen could become a new Corps of Explorers, perhaps under royal Persephonean charter—"

Jonas laughed. "I see you already have our future planned. Far be it from me to get in Lady Kori Challinor's way." He grasped her arms and fell back, pulling her atop him. Fastenings came undone, and breath quickened.

A warning chime sounded. Kori had just enough time to close her tunic before a large shaaurin walked through the hatch. The symbols on his vest identified him as Arhan, and the warmth from his mind was that of family, an individual Jonas knew well. Kori was only beginning to recognize the differences between one alien and another.

"Hraan!" Jonas said, half sitting up. "Kori," he said in Concordat, "you've already met my adopted brother, Hraan Arhan."

Kori carefully pronounced the formal shaauri greeting. Hraan twitched his whiskers and made a rumble almost below the threshold of Kori's hearing.

"He says not to be so formal," Jonas said. "You are family, after all." *You can understand him, Kori. Listen with your mind.*

The big shaaurin looked them over. His ears flickered sideways. "I wanted to become better acquainted with your lifemate, Jo-naas," he said in Shaaurii. "But since you are mating, I will return later."

Kori flushed, and Jonas laughed. "You may have to wait some time, brother."

Turn the page for an excerpt from
Susan Krinard's exciting new novel,

SECRET OF THE WOLF

coming in October from Berkley Books!

He knew exactly which room was hers.

As he watched from the ill-lit street across from the Frisby House, he could smell her scent, carried by the cool, wet winds from the strait and the ocean thirty miles to the west. He'd memorized the smell instantly when he went to work on that cowardly piece of filth among the dockside shacks.

He knew the boy was with her—but now that the whelp was safe, he was of no further interest. The woman was. He could not have said why, for she wasn't the kind of female he sought when sexual hunger came upon him. She wasn't beautiful, though her figure, full of hip and breast, was enough to rouse him.

Maybe it was because she'd stood there, so calm, when the scum attacked her. Remained calm when *he* appeared. He wasn't used to such composure when he was around. He preferred to provoke different emotions.

Maybe he was curious. She was a doctor. A female doctor. Because of her, the bastard would live . . . at least for today. She'd robbed him of his vengeance. She owed him for that.

But it wasn't his way to ponder what could not be explained. He existed by instinct, and emotion, and whim. Now his whim said that he wanted this woman, in a way no weak human soul could understand.

He could go after her, of course. He moved like the fog itself, all but invisible to human senses. He could steal her from that room with no one the wiser. Satisfy himself with her, and be done with it.

No one would stop him, least of all the Other. The one he wouldn't name, because to name the Other gave him power. And he wasn't ready to surrender himself.

Someday, he would keep what was his, and damn the Other to darkness and silence forever.

He dug his bare toes into the earth of the street, indifferent to the loss of his shoes. He didn't need them. He shifted from foot to foot, staring at the darkened window.

A bellow of raucous laughter burst from the nearest saloon, distracting him. The smell of liquor and beer drowned out the woman's scent. His mouth felt dry, ready for another drink. *That* took far less effort than climbing into the woman's room. It was the swiftest escape from the memories, the burden the Other had given him.

And in the saloon there were men who would cross him. Ruffians who would see only a lean, oddly dressed tenderfoot with too much money, ripe for the plucking.

He loped to the entrance of the saloon, whose doors spilled light like pale blood into the street, and went in. The room was full of carousers, with a couple of whores for good measure. He sat at the bar, pulled a handful of coins from his pocket and ordered a whiskey straight. Ten drinks later, even the bartender was staring in amazement. Still it wasn't enough. Not enough to drown the memories.

Someone kicked at his bare foot. He ignored the first blow. The second came harder, accompanied by a loud guffaw.

"Hey, boy. Someone steal yer shoes?"

Still he waited, taking another sip of his whiskey.

"You hear me, you scrawny li'l pissant? I'm talkin' to you." A blunt, dirty hand snatched at the coins. "Where'dja get all that chickenfeed, eh? You gotta share it with the rest of us. Right, boys?"

He ordered another drink and downed it in one swallow.

"Wha' 'r' you . . . some kind o' freak? Or is that water y'er drinkin'?" The glass was plucked from his hand.

He turned slowly to the man leaning on the nicked wooden bar beside him. Another drunk, of the belligerent variety. A brute, no longer young but massive from hard physical labor, the kind who found a little extra incentive for a quarrel in the contents of a bottle. Just like the one who'd been beating on the boy.

Just what he'd been waiting for.

He smiled with deliberate mockery. "What's it to you, you ugly son of a bitch?"

The drunk let fly after a moment's disbelieving pause. It was pathetically easy to dodge the blow and slip around behind.

He kicked the drunk's feet out from under him. The audience laughed and snickered as the brute went sprawling . . . until the man pulled a pistol from his trousers. His shot went wild and crashed into the stained mirror behind the bar.

Several onlookers jumped the shooter, disarmed him, and tossed him into the street. The bartender cursed over his shattered mirror, and the rest returned to their drinking and whoring.

But the "freak" wasn't satisfied. He stuffed the money back into his pockets and went in pursuit of his prey. He found the drunk on his knees in the street, swearing a blue streak and wiping hands on muddy trousers. Bloodshot eyes lifted to his, narrowed in hate.

"D'you really want to see a freak?" he asked pleasantly. When he had the drunk's full attention, he stripped and Changed. It hurt, the way it always did, but he didn't care. He reveled in the pain. He finished, every muscle and bone screaming in protest, and waited for his prey to realize what he saw.

The drunk's eyes nearly popped from their sockets. He tried to scream. He wet himself and fell into a dead faint.

Laughing with his wolf's grin, he raked his sharp foreclaws along the slack, pockmarked face. Let the drunk remember this encounter, as the previous bully would. Let him scare his fellows with mad tales of men who turned into beasts. No one would believe. They never believed.

He bent back his head and howled. The sound bounced off alley walls and floated on the fog like a banshee's wail. All noise from the saloon stopped; he could almost see the faces turned toward the door, the hasty gulping of whiskey, the furtive gestures made to appease God or the devil.

He belonged to neither. Let them listen and be afraid.

He Changed back, dressed quickly, and turned for the hotel . . . and the woman. But a vast weariness overtook him; curse it though he might, he knew what it portended. The more he fought, the greater the chance the Other would seize control.

He must rest. Find some quiet place where he wouldn't be disturbed, and he might wake still in possession of this body.

With the last of his strength, he began to search for a sleeping place. In the end, he found he could not leave the vicinity of the hotel, where *she* lay. He discovered an abandoned, fire-damaged cottage two blocks away, tore through the boards nailed across the door, and lay down close to a window, where he could still catch the merest whiff of her scent over the smell of burned wood and mouse droppings.

She's mine, he told the Other. *No matter how often you drive me out, I'll come back. I will have her in the end.*

And you will have nothing.

Immortality

Maggie Shayne

Prologue

For the first time in four thousand years I was ready to die. And it looked as if I would get my wish. For the flames surrounded me, searing my flesh, and every breath I drew burned in my throat and lungs. And yet I could see them. Beyond the smoke and dancing tongues of ravenous fire, I could see them. My husband, the man I had loved, and his mistress wrapped up tight in his arms, safe, outside, bathed in the cool night air while I roasted. Through the window glass I watched them, beyond the flaming draperies and through the thickening smoke—and then the window exploded, and the fire filled the open space. Even my preternatural eyesight couldn't pierce the wall of flames then.

It was over. He'd left me for dead, likely relieved to be rid of me. He would probably celebrate my demise.

The hell he would.

Something rose up in me. I was tired, tired of living, tired of fighting to stay alive, and tired of hating. I told myself to just close my eyes. Just lie there and let the hungry fire do its work. But something inside me fought back. It made me struggle to my feet, that insistent something. It forced me to drag myself through the inferno, toward what I sensed was the rear of the house. My dress caught fire. My hair smoldered and smoked, and my skin blistered. I would have screamed in anguish had I a voice, or even a breath left in me. But I didn't. If I'd been an ordinary woman, I'd have been dead at that point. But I wasn't ordinary. I wasn't mortal. So I stumbled onward, a living torch, and I tasted hell. Finally I fell, unable to go any farther.

But it was cool, damp ground beneath my body. It was blessed icy rain that pelted down on me from above. Life-giving rain.

And still that something inside, whatever it was, pushed me onward. Urged me irresistibly onward. I tried to get to my feet but couldn't rise even as far as my knees. So I dragged myself forward. I clawed my fingers into the wet soil, and I pulled myself inch by agonizing inch, onward. I suppose I couldn't bear the thought of *them* coming upon me this way. Seeing me with my skin charred black and my life force ebbing low. They would finish me off, if they found me.

Natum had taken everything from me. *Everything.* I wouldn't let his be the hand that took my life as well. No, I would die on my own terms.

And so I crawled . . . inched, toward the cliffs. "To hell with him," I whispered when at last I reached ahead of me to find there was no more ground to grasp. I opened my eyes and saw yawning darkness and far, far below, the boiling white froth of the sea. "To hell with both of them. And to hell with the world."

With one last effort, I, Queen Puabi, the darkest of the Dark Witches, pulled myself over the edge and into oblivion. And as I plummeted I wondered how many times I would drown and revive and drown again before my power ran out. And what would become of me then?

Could there be peace for one as purely evil as I? Or would I remain trapped in some semblance of awareness even while the sea creatures fed on my flesh? I didn't know. I didn't care.

I didn't care.

Anything was better than the anguish I left behind.

Or so I thought until I smashed through the surface of the sea, like smashing through concrete, and into its briny depths, which burned far more than the flames had done.

1

He thought his heart stopped cold when he saw the dead woman floating in the sea. At first he'd glimpsed only color and shape. Something white and oval hovering beneath the jewel-blue ripples of the ocean. He'd stopped rowing then and leaned over for a closer look. Her pale, lifeless face bobbed up, broke the surface.

"Jesus!" Matthew jerked away so fast he stumbled and fell, nearly tipping the small boat over. Then he sat there on the floor of his rowboat, stunned and gaping like the fish in his pail. His heart hammered. Squaring his shoulders, he got up onto the seat, slid to the side, and looked again.

She was still there, still dead, and she still looked startlingly like Gabriella. Dark, dark lashes rested eternally against her sculpted cheeks. Her lips were tinted blue and full, her nose, straight and small. Her arms were unclothed, hands delicate and lily white.

Water lapped over her face. Tiny waves, flinging themselves onto her lips, her eyes, as if in an effort to claim her.

Hell, he couldn't just leave her there.

Matthew told himself to buck up and do the right thing. If he had come to one conclusion during his temporary retreat from the world, it was that from now on, he would make an effort to do the right thing. So he would haul the dead beauty to his island, keep her there until the impending storm passed, and radio the authorities.

Sighing deeply, he knelt in the bottom of the small boat, leaned over, and managed to get hold of one of her arms. Then he frowned. She wasn't cold. Cool, yes. But not cold. He drew the woman closer, until he could get his hands beneath her shoulders, and then he pulled her up and inward. Her head cleared the boat's side and lolled backward. Her neck and shoulders were above the water level, and he bent to get a better grip, putting her face directly below his, upside down and void of expression. He did not like being this close to a dead person. He'd been spending far too much time contemplating death lately.

Suddenly the pale lips opened wide, and the dead woman sucked in a desperate, strangled breath. Her body arched backward so forcefully that he almost lost her to the sea. He was so startled by her sudden animation that he damn near let her go.

He rapidly regained his hold on her, tugging harder now that he realized he wasn't recovering a body but saving a life. God, he'd been so certain her chances were nil. Her eyes flew open, looking wild and dangerous, electric-blue— too vivid to be real, and flecked with gold—and she began to twist and struggle.

"No!" he barked. "Settle down, woman, or you'll drown yourself. I'm trying to save your life here."

She stilled instantly, maybe startled by his tone. It had startled him, too. He hadn't barked at anyone that way in almost three months. Hell, he'd probably scared her half to death, he thought. She seemed totally disoriented. He pulled her mostly nude body out of the water, into the boat, and she let him. Then she just lay there between the seats, water sluicing off her skin and her short, dark hair soaking his sneakers, his feet. Her clothes, what remained of them, were in tatters. Rags that might once have been a skirt clung to her from the waist down. From the waist up she was completely naked, and apparently unconcerned by it. She didn't try to cover herself. Then again, she'd nearly drowned. Having a stranger see her breasts was probably the least of her worries. And yet he did see, and he did notice. She was very cold. So it was tough not to notice.

She shivered, and he dragged his gaze away from her breasts.

"What do you want of me?" she whispered.

He narrowed his eyes on her, gave his head a shake, and started to peel his sweater off. As he pulled the sweater over his head, he caught the glint of sunlight on steel. Looking up fast, he saw her dainty, waterlogged hand clutching a deadly-looking blade—and bringing it down fast. He flung up an arm just in time to deflect hers. Then he caught her wrist in his hand, exerted pressure, and eyed the double-edged dagger she'd damn near plunged into his chest just now.

"Drop the knife, dammit!"

She shook her head, her eyes flashing with life, with anger, with violence, though only moments ago they'd been lifeless and dull. They were like lapis stones, her eyes.

"Crush my wrist," she all but growled. "Go ahead, mortal, and see how fast it heals again."

He stared at her, and wondered how someone could look so much like Gabriella and yet be so completely different. This woman personified rage. "You're delirious. Put the knife down before you make me hurt you."

She shook her head. Matthew squeezed her slender wrist in his hand until she cried out in pain and the blade clattered to the bottom of the boat. He eased his grip, set her down again. She slumped against the side of the rowboat, looking at her wrist as if confused.

"I'm weak," she muttered. Then she closed her eyes tiredly. "You should have left me in the sea."

"You try anything like that again, I'll throw you right back in."

Those blue eyes opened, and she glared up at him.

He glared back. Then he bent to pick up her blade, looked it over. It was a nice piece. If the stones embedded in the handle were real, it was worth some money, too. "I'll just hang on to this for you," he told her, tucking it into his belt. Then he retrieved his sweater from the seat where he'd dropped it and handed it to her. "Put this on."

She looked at him with fury in her eyes. But she took the sweater and pulled it over her head, thrust her arms into the sleeves. "Where are you taking me?"

He nodded at the tiny island in the distance. "There."

"And what is there?"

"Nothing much, besides my villa. It's a private island. *My* private island." He sat facing her and bent to the oars. He saw the way she looked toward the west. On a clear day, the ghostly shape of St. John's would be visible in the distance. Saba was closer, and you could almost always see its distinctive volcano-shaped cone, but not today. It was far from clear in the distance today. "There's not time to go any farther," he told her, and nodded toward the darkness far in the distance. "Storm coming."

She narrowed her eyes on him in suspicion.

"What, you think I'm lying? That I *want* a psychopathic drowned rat in my only haven? Trust me, lady, I'd take you to one of the big islands if I could. But I can't, so unless you think you can swim that far in a storm, you're stuck with me."

He thought those laser-blue eyes would burn him, they grew so fiery. "If you think I am *stuck* anywhere, you are sadly mistaken." Then she leaned back in the boat, closed her eyes, and there was not another sound from her.

He wasn't sure if she'd passed out, died, or was just ignoring him. He rowed faster. It didn't take long before he was out of the boat, tugging its nose up onto the sandy shore of the small island. Then he scooped her up and saw with relief that she was still breathing. She was light in his arms, limp in them, her body leaning into his chest as he carried her inland, over the sand to harder ground and then along the barely discernible path through the palms and tropical plants, to his home away from home. It wasn't much, his island villa. Not compared to his seaside mansion back home. But it served him well when he needed to escape. And he had needed that. Badly.

It was as if the fates didn't *want* him to escape, though. How else could he explain what had happened here just now? Finding this woman—a woman who, aside from her vivid blue eyes, could have been his wife's evil twin.

What the hell did it all mean? Who was she? And why would she want to drive her pretty dagger into her rescuer's heart?

* * *

Puabi woke to softness and a surrounding warmth that had worked its way into her body. She opened her eyes with a start, her fingers curling, clawlike, into the surface on which she lay. She'd expected water. Water had been her entire world for so long . . .

But that man had pulled her from the sea.

Sighing, she eased her grip on the mattress beneath her, tried to focus her vision, and took stock. She was alive. But far from strong. Her head still pounded. Her lungs ached. Her skin and eyes burned and felt raw. This tiredness clung to her, and her vision wasn't good even by mortal standards. It was blurred and dull.

The room around her seemed bright, sunny. She made out windows, and rich dark wood furnishings. A fire danced warmly in a freestanding fireplace. And the bed in which she lay was huge and soft. Fit for a queen, she thought, almost smiling at the irony.

"Awake, are you?"

She turned her head slowly and saw the man sitting in a rocking chair near the bed. He set aside the book he'd been reading and leaned forward, elbows resting on his knees. He was a big man. Broad-shouldered. Very dark. His skin bronzed by the sun, and his hair as black as her own. He had the thick, dark brows of a Sumerian, but aside from that she could make out little of his face.

"How are you feeling?"

"Why do you want to know?" Her voice emerged rusty with disuse.

He got to his feet, poured water into a glass, and offered it to her.

Puabi blinked at the large, blurred hand that held the glass.

"You're dehydrated," he said. "You should drink all you can stand."

She had never liked being told what to do. She liked it even less when the man doing the telling was correct. Sitting up with no small effort, she accepted the glass, tipped it to her lips and drank. She drained it, despite his protests, which began halfway through, then set the glass down. The cool water hit her stomach like a brick. For a moment she thought the liquid might come back up, but she quelled the sick feeling with a hand to her belly and slowly lay back onto the pillows.

"Probably a little at a time would have been better," he said. "Your stomach's been empty for a long time."

"How would you know that?" she asked, her eyes falling closed.

"Your hair is like straw, your skin is burned from the sun and chapped from the salt water. Your eyes are so bloodshot I'd be surprised if you could see straight."

"I can't."

He sighed and set the glass aside. "How long were you in the water?"

There was something about his voice. Its deep timbre had a controlled quality to it. As if he were keeping it level only with great effort. And there was something else, something that tickled her nerve endings with a static charge.

"I don't know," she answered.

"How did you get there?"

She opened her eyes to look at him, but as before, he was unclear. Dark hair, longer than was fashionable in men of consequence today. And he was one of those, she knew that much. He'd called this his island. He spoke with an air of authority and command. And something else. Pain.

He was waiting for her answer, she realized. She didn't give him one.

"There must have been a fire," he said. "What remained of your clothes had been burned."

"I don't want to talk about that."

He blinked slowly. She couldn't make out his eyes, but she knew they were focused on her face, and she felt their intensity. "Then you do remember."

"I remember. I wish I didn't. Either way, it's no concern of yours."

"You're right, it's not." He shrugged as if he could care less about her trauma. "There's a lukewarm bath waiting for you in the next room. Soak in it for a while. It'll soothe your skin."

Puabi tilted her head to one side and frowned at him. "I don't . . . understand."

"A little oatmeal in the water," he said. "An old trick my

father taught me. Good for everything from sunburn to poison ivy." She thought he might have smiled slightly, but sensed it wasn't a real smile. "Go ahead," he said. "Take your time." He started toward the door, then paused, turning back. "Uh . . . there's a bell on the nightstand to your left. Take it with you into the bathroom, just in case."

She blinked through her swimming vision as he left her alone. What was he up to, she wondered. Why was he bothering with her comfort? Bringing her water, running her bath? She got to her feet, but her head swam with dizziness. Gods, things were not right. Not with her—and even more clearly, not with the mortal. He was up to something. She felt it right to her bones.

2

Puabi lay in the cool, soothing water, head tipped back, eyes closed. The mortal had been right—though his actions were suspect. In her experience no man was this kind without some hidden motive. Still, whatever he'd put into the water did ease her burned skin. But her eyes . . .

She lifted a soft washcloth, dripping wet, and laid it gently over her closed eyes. No doubt the salty seawater had done some harm. But her body ought to have healed itself by now. It was taking an unreasonably long time. Ah, but then again, she had died and revived countless times at the whim of the sea. Her power must be waning very low indeed. And there was only one way to restore it, to prolong this hideous existence. To find another Immortal High Witch—one of the Light Ones—and kill her.

The idea held little appeal, oddly enough. And the mortal had taken her dagger. That did not bode well, and only added to her suspicions about him.

Sighing, she dunked her head beneath the water to rinse away the conditioner that had been soaking in her hair for several minutes now. She'd had all she could bear of lying up to her neck in water, after so many days surrounded by the stuff. Tiredly, her muscles protesting in pain, she got to her feet, stepped out of the tub, and used a thick soft towel to gently dab herself dry. Then she rubbed her hair down as well.

Her vision was still blurred, but it was slightly clearer than before. She could see more of the room's details. The tub was freestanding and claw-footed. The walls and ceiling were white, and bamboo mats were scattered around on the floor. Large, arching windows let sunlight flood the place, and she glanced through one of them for a moment. She glimpsed palm trees, blue sky, a sandy beach with waves lapping at it. Then the brilliance hurt too much, and she had to look away.

Hadn't the mortal claimed there was some horrendous storm looming? That yellow sunlight didn't look stormy to her.

So she'd caught him in a lie already. That confirmed her opinion that he was up to no good.

Sighing, she continued her inspection of the room. Aside from the porcelain fixtures, everything in the room was rattan—from the cabinets on the walls to the towel racks to the frame around the full-length mirror. She paused there and squinted at her hazy reflection. Her skin was still an angry red color. Tender to the touch, and warm. Her hair stuck up like black feathers, but it felt softer than before. Slinging the towel over her shoulder, she found a comb lying on a stand and pulled it through the short black layers.

"Everything all right?" His voice came from beyond the door, and again the sound of it made her skin prickle with some kind of awareness.

Looking toward the door, she noticed a large white article of clothing hanging from a hook there. "Fine. I'll only be a moment." She dropped the towel to the floor and went to retrieve the white clothing, which turned out to be a large cotton robe. Its touch was cool and delicious on her skin as she pulled it over her arms, around her waist, and tied the sash. It hung well below her knees. From what she could tell, she was decently covered—not that she particularly cared, but she was in no shape to gut the mortal should he try to assault her, driven to violent lust by a glimpse of her flesh. It wouldn't be the first time, she mused. She opened the door and stepped back into the bedroom.

And she smelled food. Her stomach growled loudly even

as her eyes sought the source. There, beside the bed, was a tray that emitted aromatic steam. The man stood near it. She sent him a suspicious look. "Why are you being kind to me?" she asked him.

"This isn't kindness," he said slowly. "It's decency. I'd do as much for a stray dog."

"And likely get your hand bit off for your trouble," she snapped, even as she walked quickly forward and climbed onto the bed, curling her legs beneath her and reaching for the tray of food. Drawing it into her lap, she leaned over it and sniffed. She smelled meat, vegetables, seasoning, toasted bread, melted butter, cheeses.

"How are the eyes?"

"Fine," she lied as she moved her hands around on the tray trying to identify the items. There was a bowl, and hot liquid. Soup. And a small plate held some kind of a sandwich. And a cup . . .

"Careful, the tea's hot," he warned.

She ignored him, picking up the sandwich and bringing it to her mouth. Grilled cheese. It was far from the finest meal she'd eaten in her lifetime, but she thought she enjoyed it as if it were. The soup turned out to be chicken broth with noodles, vegetables, and hunks of meat. She devoured the entire sandwich and drained every last drop of the soup. Then as she lifted the mug of tea, the man took the tray from her lap.

She looked up quickly, having nearly forgotten his presence. It was unusual for her to let her guard down with a stranger—especially one who had taken her dagger and lied to her in order to keep her here.

He set the tray aside. "I have some eyedrops here. They might help."

She shook her head, not trusting him. "I don't need them." Instead she sipped the tea.

"All right." He sighed and took a seat in the chair beside the bed. "So why don't you tell me who you are?"

"I am Puabi."

She could see well enough to know when he tipped his head to one side. "Just Puabi?"

"No, not *just* Puabi. Queen Puabi. I am of royal blood."

The flash of white told her he smiled. "Queen, eh? And what are you queen of?"

She averted her poorly functioning eyes. "A land that no longer exists. A world that is no more." Slowly, she closed her eyes. "You think I'm insane, no doubt."

"I didn't say that."

She took a fortifying sip of tea, but truly her head was feeling heavy on her shoulders. "Where am I?" she asked him, suddenly overwhelmed with the urge to go home, even though she knew there was no such place. She wouldn't recognize Sumer now. It was buried beneath the sands of four thousand years. New civilizations had covered over her own. They called it Iraq now, and it was peopled by children of Muhammad, not of Inanna.

"You're near the Virgin Islands. Roughly between St. John's and St. Kitts. The nearest inhabited island to us is called Saba. It's just five square miles—but it has a small airfield and a medical clinic."

She swallowed the lump that had formed in her throat. "I went into the Atlantic off the coast of Maine. I emerged in the Caribbean, in the tropics. Gods, how long must such a journey have taken?"

He was silent for a moment. When he spoke, he spoke softly. "I think you're still a little . . . disoriented."

"I came through the Triangle, didn't I?"

"The Bermuda Triangle? Yes . . . I suppose you could have."

"Perhaps that's got something to do with the way I feel."

"And how do you feel?"

She shook her head, searching for words. "I don't know. Odd. Different." She lifted her chin. "I want to leave here," she demanded. "I want to go to the mainland. The States. Now, today." She set the teacup on the nightstand, but it landed so near the edge that it toppled to the floor. She ignored the sound of the porcelain shattering, turned in the bed, and swung her legs to the floor.

"You can't leave yet," he told her.

"I can, and I will." She surged to her feet. Dizziness welled up like a tidal wave in her head, and her knees dissolved. Arms came around her, strong, fast, and firm. And there was something—some moment of déjà vu. A sense of odd, niggling familiarity about the man, even as he held her against his powerful body.

"Gods," she whispered. "Something is wrong with me. I feel . . . so strange."

"A few days in the sea will have that effect on a person," he said, and he lowered her carefully to the bed again.

"It's not that. It's more than that." She squinted up at his face, hovering over hers. "I know you," she whispered, the words dripping with accusation. "Who are you?" Why the hell wouldn't her eyes focus and allow her to see his face? She would know it. She was certain she would.

"Easy, Puabi. Come on, take it easy." His hand still cradled the back of her head, lowering it to the pillow before moving away.

"I want to leave," she said, but the words came weakly, softly.

"You can't. Not until the storm passes."

"There is no storm. You lie."

"I don't lie. There's a tropical storm stalled a hundred miles out to sea," he said. "The longer it sits there, the stronger it becomes. It could start moving in at any time, and I don't intend to be caught out there in a small boat when it does."

She let her eyes fall closed. It made her head hurt to strain them so hard in the effort to see him. "Then tell me your name. For I know we've met before."

"My name is Matthew. And we've never met. You're not the kind of woman a man would forget."

And that was all. She was out cold.

Matthew stared down at her, shaking his head in complete bewilderment. Who the hell was she? And just how much brain damage had she suffered? He sat on the edge of the bed, threaded his fingers into her hair, and probed her scalp. He took his time, felt every bit of it, but found no sign of head injury. That didn't mean much, though. The sun, the heat, the dehydration—she could have suffered a stroke or some kind of mental breakdown. Any number of things could be causing her delusions.

First she'd tried to kill him. Then she'd claimed to be a queen. And now she thought she knew him.

Hell, she certainly played the part of royalty well. She hadn't so much as thanked him for the food. Or for saving her life, for that matter. And a glance at the condition of the bathroom—towels on the floor amid puddles of water, tub still full—suggested she expected to be waited on.

But that wasn't fair, was it? She wasn't exactly in peak condition right now.

Asleep, it was stunning how much she looked like Gabriella. Awake, she couldn't have been more different. And the last thing he needed here was her face reminding him of his wife. Sweet, shy, lonely little Gabriella. She'd been lost. She'd foolishly thought he was her salvation. She said she loved him. And died because of it.

Hell. He closed his eyes, fought the regret that rose up. Gabriella was gone. The woman in the bed had nothing to do with his young wife. The resemblance was a coincidence. And she, Puabi, was a mystery. One he didn't need or want to solve.

Sighing, he reached for the bottle of eyedrops and leaned over her. With his thumb, he pulled one eyelid upward. "Trust me on this, your highness." He squeezed a few drops into her eye, then repeated the process on the other side. "I want you off my island just as badly you do."

Her eyes flew open and rolled back into her head. She thrashed, her arms flailing wildly. The lamp on the nightstand flew. Then she hit the stand itself, toppling it. She twisted and arched on the bed as he tried to catch hold of her, keep her still. God, she was burning up with fever. It had come out of nowhere. She kicked, then sat up, and though he tried, he couldn't hold her to the bed. How the hell could she be that strong? When she flung herself backward again, she slammed her head into the headboard. One hand slashed across his face and then raked her own chest. Trails of bright red blood beaded on her pale skin in the wake of her clawlike nails and trickled downward.

My God, she was strong! And she was hurting herself. She was like a wildcat, lashing out, convulsing, and he was damned if he knew what to do to keep her from harming them both. He caught one flying arm, then the other, and held on while she thrashed. He could only pray that she would wear herself out soon.

3

When Puabi woke again, she moaned softly and arched her back in pleasure even before she opened her eyes. She was lying facedown in the warm, downy-soft bed, and something cool and wonderful was stroking her back. Over and over, it moved soothingly, leaving blessed relief in its wake.

Then her mind cleared, her memory returned. She tried to roll over, even while reaching for a blanket to cover herself as she realized she was naked and fully exposed. But her hands didn't move. Frowning, she lifted her head, and tugged at the soft strips of cloth that bound her wrists to the headboard above her.

"You *dare* . . ."

"What, now you're complaining?" he said in that rich, velvet tone that stroked every nerve ending to life.

She couldn't see him. Could only hear his voice, and feel his hands smoothing something creamy and cool over her flesh. "A few seconds ago you were damn near purring."

"Take your hands off me," she commanded, and even to her own ears, the order lacked any real power.

"In a minute. Your skin is so burned it's blistered in places. This stuff will help."

"I don't want your help."

"You're not exactly in any condition to know *what* you

want. Much less what's good for you, so I've taken the decision out of your hands."

His hands smoothed a path over her buttocks. Cool, clinical, so soothing she wanted to sigh in relief. She twisted away from his touch, but she couldn't go far. "I knew you couldn't be trusted," she seethed. "I knew you were up to something."

"The only thing I'm up to is keeping you from killing yourself, or me, or both of us."

His hands moved down the backs of her thighs, spreading that coolness to the creases behind her knees, and lower, over her calves.

She relaxed in spite of herself. "I reacted the way I did when you pulled me from the sea out of sheer instinct. If you'd lived the life I have, you'd have done the same. And it's moot, anyway, because you took my dagger from me. I'm no threat to you now."

"Somehow I doubt that." He was massaging her feet, gently working the salve, or whatever it was, into them. But he stopped, and moved into her line of vision, and then he knelt beside the bed, looked her in the eye, and pointed to his face. Red scratches marred it. "You did this without any help from your fancy knife."

She flinched when he said it. She hadn't meant to. Her vision was significantly clearer than it had been earlier, and suddenly she wished it wasn't. "I did that?" she whispered hoarsely.

"Is that remorse I see in those strange eyes of yours, Puabi?"

She frowned at him, but she was no longer looking at his neck. Instead she'd turned her vision inward, searching her mind, her self, for the source of this uncommon emotion. "Yes," she said. "I think it may be. Incredible."

Blinking, she focused on his face, seeing it more clearly now than before. Brown eyes, hard eyes. Lines at the corners, small ones, frown lines. Wide jaw. Lips and nose both full. Sensual. By the Gods, he was handsome.

"You sound incredulous that you're capable of feeling sorry for having attacked me."

She nodded. "I am. Why should I be sorry? Your injuries

are minor, so why should even the slightest remorse plague me?"

His brows rose as one. "Maybe . . . because I saved your life?"

"You underestimate me. I was still a long way from dead when you found me. Though I suppose I might have expired, eventually, had you not."

He studied her, shaking his head. "Here I thought the big question was why you'd want to kill me after I took you in, fed you, tried to help you . . ."

"I told you, instinct. I've had to fight to stay alive for a very long time. It's my nature to attack before the attacker has the chance. Strike fast, strike first, live to strike again."

"That's a pretty brutal philosophy." Then he tilted his head. "Actually, it sounds a lot like my own."

"Really?"

He nodded. "Yes. Really. Until recently."

"Then you've changed your mind? Why?"

He averted his eyes as she searched them, and she knew she had hit on something sensitive—some tender spot. He was vulnerable there. It was good to know a man's weakness early on.

"Roll over. The ointment's pretty well soaked in on this side."

Pursing her lips, she thought about refusing. She considered snapping the bonds that held her, which she was certain she could manage with minimal effort, even in her weakened state. The one thing she could be certain of, however, was that her back felt a great deal better than before, while the front of her still burned and stung as if she'd been dragged naked over sandpaper. The man hadn't tried anything inappropriate yet. If he did, she would kill him. Perhaps. Or perhaps not. It wasn't a complicated matter at all.

She rolled over, the strip of cloth that held her wrists twisting easily.

The man went still, his gaze sliding slowly down her body, lingering where it shouldn't, heating with desire.

"Look your fill and let's get on with this, shall we?"

He let his eyes slide up her, from her toes to her eyes. "Pretty full of yourself, aren't you?"

"You're the one who tied me up and stripped off my robe."

"*My* robe," he corrected. "And I only tied your hands because you went wild on me. Look at your chest."

She lifted her head from the pillows and saw the marks she'd dug across her own chest. "Point taken. But just why am I bound now, Matthew Fairchild?"

He frowned at her. "How did you know my last name?"

"I assume you told me."

"I didn't."

She frowned in thought, but quickly dismissed the question with a shake of her head. "I'm in significant pain, mortal. Would you apply your lotion already?"

He nodded, reached for the cloth that bound her wrists. She shook her head. "Leave it."

His eyes flew to hers, flaring slightly.

She met his gaze without blinking.

"I'm not into playing bondage games."

"Oh, come now. Have you ever tried?" She taunted him with her eyes. Then she shrugged. "Besides, I can pull free of your little knots easily. Remind me to show you sometime how to properly restrain a subject."

Matthew shook his head and kept his eyes averted. As if he thought she might not see the animal desire in them that way. Much less the guilt that came with it. She did, though. She saw it all. He might be an amusing distraction, this handsome mortal.

He sat on the edge of the bed, and dipped his fingers into the jar on the nightstand, and they came out dripping with a clear, gel-like substance. He moved his hand toward her, and she stiffened in anticipation. The cold stuff touched her heated skin, her shoulder, and slowly he smoothed it down her arm.

"What is it?" she asked.

"Aloe, mostly. It's working wonders on your back already."

"I'm a fast healer," she said softly, her eyes riveted on his hand as he dipped it into the jar, drew it out again, and spread more of the stuff over her neck, and then gently upward, following the line of her jaw, sliding over her chin. His fingers moved against her face, her cheeks. She closed her eyes, and he touched her forehead, her nose, the bit of skin above her lip. There was something in his touch . . .

His hand was trembling.

The moment she noticed it, he drew it away, and she opened her eyes to look at him. "What is it?"

He shook his head, but there was pain in his eyes. "You . . . remind me of someone," he said at last. Then the emotional look left him, and the more cynical one returned to his eyes. "At least you do when you aren't bitching at me or trying to kill me."

She tilted her head, ignoring his barb. "Who?"

"No one." He coated his fingers again and returned to his work, spreading the stuff over her other arm, all the way to her wrist, skipping only the part covered by the strip of cloth. He moved on to her hands, her fingertips, which he did one by one. Then he went to the foot of the bed, and started at her ankles, smearing ointment up her shins, over her knees, and along her thighs. He didn't shy away when he neared their juncture. He kept going, painting her pelvic bones, hips, lower abdomen. He only skipped the dark curls. Then he was at her waist, her belly. Her rib cage and sides. His hands worked some kind of magic, soothing away her pain and leaving a cold fire in their wake. His touch felt good. Like the caress of a lover. And she was too much a woman not to be aroused by it.

He took his hand away, gathered more aloe from the jar. Came back. She couldn't help it. As his hand neared her breast, she closed her eyes in anticipation. And then that coolness touched her, and she let her breath whisper out of her. As his fingers neared the center, she knew her nipples hardened expectantly. She didn't care. And then his fingers were there, softly, gently rubbing the cold gel over her nipple. Too soon they moved away. But he began again at the other breast, and she thought she would die if he didn't touch her more thoroughly. When he got to the nipple this time, a soft cry was wrenched from her. His hand stilled, fingers on her hard nipple. She arched her back to press herself against his touch, and he responded with gentle pressure. Too gentle. And then he swore softly and moved his hand away.

"Don't stop," she whispered. She opened her eyes, met his, and saw a flicker of desire in his velvet-brown gaze. "You may take me if you like."

His eyes flared wider, slid down her body again, and he licked his lips.

"It's been a very long time since a man's touch has felt the way yours does," she whispered. "We're both adults, Matthew."

He turned his head away from her, forcing his eyes elsewhere. "As I said before, you're in no condition to know what you want right now."

She set her jaw, and with a deep growl, tore free of the fabric that bound her wrists. "To hell with you, then."

He looked back quickly, eyes sharp on her. She thought he expected another attack. But what kind, she wondered. Was he afraid she would kill him or ravage him? Then she looked at his eyes, and she knew he wasn't afraid. Not at all. He stood there expectantly, watching her, and waiting. Fully ready to deal with whatever she might attempt to do.

She narrowed her eyes on him. "This woman I remind you of," she said softly. "She was your lover?"

"She was my wife."

"And you wronged her in some way?" she asked, certain that he had. It was the only explanation for his having shown any tendency at all toward kindness to her—the only reason he hadn't throttled her by now, or tossed her back into the sea where he'd found her. And the only reason he hadn't taken her up on her offer of sex. Guilt. She could smell it on him.

He was stone silent for a long moment, and then, his face stark, he said, "I killed her."

4

Night fell, and the strange woman slept. He sat in a chair beside the bed and wondered what the hell he was going to do with her. She didn't look *exactly* like Gabriella, he mused as he studied her face. In fact, the more time he spent with her, the more different she seemed. Gabriella had been fragile, and frail. She'd been clingy and dependent. She'd been hollow and empty inside. She'd been quiet and shy.

Puabi was the opposite in every way. She was fire to Gabriella's ice. She was technicolor to Gabriella's pastel. She was aggression, and sexuality and danger.

Hell, the two women looked less alike by the second.

She dreamed. She hadn't dreamed in so long, she couldn't even remember the last time. She'd thought once, that perhaps when one became immortal, one lost the ability to dream. But she'd never been sure.

The dream was not a good one. She was floating, tossed up and sucked down by the icy sea. Gods, she was so cold. It was as if she would never be warm again. And it was getting colder. She spun, caught as if in a whirlpool, sucked deeper and deeper into the frigid hubs of the sea. And then she was floating there, freely floating, not struggling to breathe. The water looked like sky. The fish, like stars, and she was no longer certain where she was. Around her, she saw other forms floating. Faint, misty shapes, some more distinct than others. And she wondered who they were.

Souls. The word whispered in her mind. *I'm in the Hall of Souls.*

Blinking, she tried to see them more closely, but this damn blurred vision wouldn't allow it. She realized she was in the Devil's Triangle. And somehow, she was seeing things that were not real.

But they are real, that voice said in her mind. And she realized suddenly it was not her own voice. Not some inner knowing. It was coming from without.

"It's not real," she cried aloud, but her words were only bubbles in the waters. "I don't have a soul."

You gave it up, Puabi. You gave it up when you made yourself into one of the Dark Ones. But now you'll have the chance to get it back again.

"How?" she asked, breathless, desperate, close to death.

You have a mission, Puabi. A job to do.

"What?"

Suddenly she was being pulled upward again, spiraling back to the surface before she'd received her answer. "No! No, not yet! Not yet! You have to tell me what I have to do! What am I supposed to do?"

"All right, all right, it's okay."

"No, no, no." She was shaking, freezing, shivering so hard her teeth chattered. And then he was beside her, around her, holding her to him. Gods, he was strong, and warm. His chest was firm and his arms powerful. He wouldn't let her fall into that cold sea again. He wouldn't.

Slowly his warmth seeped into her, and she stopped shivering. But his arms never eased their grip. "I loved you so much once. Why couldn't you love me?" she whispered, her voice weak, breaking. "All I ever wanted was for you to love me."

She felt him stiffen against her, and for a moment she wondered if she was speaking to Natum or to the stranger, Matthew. But it made no sense. She'd never loved Matthew. She snuggled closer and fell into a deep, dreamless sleep.

Once she heard him speak to her softly, but she couldn't respond. "Who the hell are you?" he whispered. "Where did you come from?"

*W*hen *Puabi woke, there was sienna-colored light in*fusing the place with a muted glow. She studied it, wondering why she felt there was something she had to do today. A . . . mission. Something . . . there had been a dream . . . or was it a memory?

Warmth, heaviness, against her and around her.

Matthew.

She rolled over carefully. The man, the stranger who had pulled her from the very mouth of death, was holding her close to him. He lay on his side, facing her now, his mouth only inches from hers. His legs were entwined with hers, and his arms held her close. It was as if she were his beloved.

She almost laughed, a bitterness welling up in her belly. To think that she could ever be that important to anyone. It had taken her more than forty lifetimes to finally figure it out. No one would ever love her. And why in hell would they? She closed her eyes as the memories of the things she had done came crashing in upon her like waves on the shore.

Why? What the hell was the matter with her? After all this time, had she suddenly developed a conscience? Gods, it made no sense! What was happening to her?

Lips touched her mouth. Lightly, very softly. A hand gently cupped her head, fingers sinking into her hair. His mouth was warm, and moist, and tender as it tasted hers. Oh, God, it felt good to be kissed by a man this way. She parted her lips and kissed him back. His arms tightened around her, and she slid hers around his waist, hands splayed on his muscular back. The kiss deepened then, as he came slowly awake. He moaned, and his tongue slid into her mouth to taste deeply, as if she were some luscious confection that he craved. He licked at her mouth, suckled her tongue, fed on her lips, and she relished every second of it.

And then he drew away and opened his eyes. Fiery eyes, passion-filled. His voice gruff, tense, he whispered, "Tell me your name."

"Puabi," she said. "I'm Puabi."

He nodded, closing his eyes slowly. Then he rolled over and sat up in the bed, lowering his feet to the floor, holding his head in his hands. "You said something last night. In your sleep. You said, 'Why couldn't you love me?' "

She closed her eyes. "I don't know why I even care."

His head came up slowly, but he didn't face her. "About who?"

Swallowing hard, sensing he had a reason for asking that went beyond anything obvious, she saw no harm in speaking of it, even though she recalled feeling confusion at the time—naturally there was only one man she could have been speaking to in her troubled sleep. "My husband. Natum—Nathan is the name he uses now. He never loved me. Every time I needed him, he was with his lover. When I lost our child, when I was left for dead in that burning house, when I was swept away by the sea. All he could think of was her."

Matthew turned slowly, a look of pain etched on his hard face. "You lost a child."

She lowered her head. "A son. Stillborn." Her heart constricted. "It destroyed me."

"I'm sorry. And . . . sorry about your husband, too."

"Don't be. I've wasted far too much time fighting for a man who never wanted me."

"You deserve better."

She closed her eyes. "I deserve exactly what I got. You don't know me, Matthew. I'm . . . evil."

He looked down at her, his eyes intense—she didn't have a clue as to why he always seemed so intense when he looked at her. But it wasn't the first time she had noticed it. "He did that to you, and you think you're the one who's evil?"

"You don't know the whole of it."

"I don't want to know the whole of it," he said, walking to a chair and picking up some clothes she hadn't seen before. A pair of shorts with a drawstring and an oversized tank top. He handed them to her. "Do you feel up to breakfast?" he asked, changing the subject.

She nodded, sitting up in the bed. "The more I eat, the faster I'll mend."

He let his eyes move down her body, and a frown darkened his brow. "You mend any faster and I'll wonder if you're even human."

She glanced down at her chest, where he was looking. The scratches she'd put there herself were completely healed. And her skin looked as smooth as a newborn's.

"Yesterday you were burned so badly you were blistered. Today your skin looks as if it's never even seen the sun."

Puabi shrugged. "Who knew aloe was so powerful?"

She felt his eyes on her, probing, so she forced herself to meet his steady gaze head-on. He knew she wasn't telling him something. And she knew he knew it. "Matthew—there are things about me that you are better off not knowing. For now, suffice it to say that I'm not like other women."

"I'd figured that much out, Poppy."

She lifted her eyes to his. "Why do you call me that?"

Matthew shrugged, getting to his feet. "Puabi is a mouthful. Poppy—suits you. Beautiful. Deadly. Mysterious. Occasionally mind-boggling and quite possibly addictive." He said it playfully, teasingly, but there was a serious undertone to his words.

He inclined his head and led the way out of the room. She quickly pulled on the makeshift clothing he'd brought to her and followed him, relieved that he didn't push her for any more information.

The living area of the villa was huge, and took up most of the front of the place. Wicker furniture was scattered sparsely in the high-ceilinged rooms beneath giant fans that spun in perpetual slow motion. The place was not all that large or fancy, but you could feel the money behind it all the same. It took wealth to make a place look this casual. This comfortable. This effortless.

"The kitchen's this way," he said. "What would you like for breakfast?"

"What do you have?"

"Everything," he said, leading her through to a smaller room equipped with spotless white appliances. Marble tiles lined the walls and the floor. "I had a full supply flown in so I wouldn't have to leave until I was ready."

She narrowed her eyes on him. "Just how long have you been out here?"

He looked away. "Two, almost three months."

"Alone? All this time?"

His shrug pretended to be careless. "For the most part."

"Why?"

He didn't answer her. "Bacon and eggs sound good?"

"Sounds fine."

He nodded and turned to the refrigerator. Left with nothing to do but wait, Puabi wandered back into the living room, and then she caught sight of something so surprising that she made some sound of alarm without meaning to.

Matthew came to her, asking what was wrong. Then he followed her gaze to the photograph that hung on the wall and swore softly. "I'm sorry. I forgot it was there," he said.

"My God, who is she?"

Drawing a breath, he sighed deeply. "Gabriella. My wife."

Puabi stepped closer, eyes riveted. "She could be my twin. No wonder you look at me the way you do." Turning to him, she saw the pain in his face, in his eyes. "You loved her very much."

"No," he said. "I should have loved her. But I didn't. And she died because of it."

Frowning, she tilted her head to one side. "She's the reason you're out here, hiding away from the world? Because you should have loved her, and didn't? How could that kill a person?" Then she blinked slowly. "Was it suicide, Matthew?"

He met her eyes and she knew she was right. "I'm not a good person, Poppy. I'll tell you that much. I'm a bastard, to be honest. A lot like your own husband, I imagine, which makes it even more ironic that you ended up here. Only in my case, it wasn't another woman I preferred over my own wife. It was my business, and my freedom."

She shook her head. "I don't believe you. My husband was relieved by my death—or, my presumed death. You . . . you've exiled yourself from life to come here and grieve for her. It's not the same at all."

"No? Well, she's just as dead, Poppy. And so is the child she was carrying." He spun on his heel and returned to the kitchen.

Puabi let him go, her knees trembling so much she had to sit down in a big wicker chair before she fell down. Her gaze was drawn irresistibly back to the photograph of the woman who was her mirror image except that her eyes were black as night. Ebony eyes that, for a moment, seemed to stare right back at her. "Gabriella," she whispered. "A child. Gods, a child." Her own pain, old, but so very sharp still, cut again into her heart and clutched tight in her barren womb. Nothing had ever hurt her so much as losing her baby, so long ago. Nothing ever would. It had been the end for her. Part of her had died with her tiny stillborn son.

Gabriella's face was softer than Puabi's. The lines of jaw and cheekbone, less harsh and drawn. And her eyes were jet, while Puabi's were blue with flecks of gold.

Puabi stared at her, anger rising up. "You're nothing like me," she whispered. "I'd have given anything to save my child. If you were anything like me you couldn't possibly have taken yours with you into death."

Pans banged in the kitchen, and Puabi looked that way. Matthew was hiding here, punishing himself for not loving his wife. How could he blame himself for that? You couldn't force yourself to feel something that simply wasn't there.

She lowered her head, bit her lip. By the Gods, neither could Natum.

Oh, what the hell is this? I'm feeling sorry for Natum now? I'm pitying him and understanding why he wronged me so? What the hell is this?

Why couldn't she have stayed the way she was? Hating, raging against everything and everyone, acting without conscience or consequence, despising her husband and his lover for betraying her. It had served her well for more than four thousand years. Why should it begin to change now?

One thing was sure. No matter how many deaths Matthew Fairchild claimed—he couldn't come close to the blood that stained her hands.

Smells reached her from the kitchen. Coffee. Bacon. They made her stomach growl. Then there was something else that distracted her from those smells. A sound, like a deep, droning buzz, that grew louder. She rushed to the window and looked out to see a small yellow airplane descending on the island.

5

"What the hell is she thinking?" Matthew hurried to the doorway when he heard the familiar sound of the pontoon plane's motors. Poppy was there ahead of him.

"Who is it?" She looked nervous.

He opened the door impatiently.

"Matthew, give me my dagger."

Frowning, he looked at her. "You expecting some kind of attack, Poppy?"

Licking her lips, she averted her eyes. "You never know."

He took her hand in his and started for the door. They were outside and halfway down the path by the time he realized he was still holding it. It had been an impulse, grabbing her hand that way. It had been automatic. And it still felt right, her small hand in his. He stopped walking, looked down at their joined hands, then at her face.

She met his eyes briefly. Something unspoken moved between them, some palpable, electrical charge. And he didn't know what the hell it was, but he decided not to let go. Then her eyes seemed to shutter themselves, as if in defense, and she tugged her hand free. "I'm not Gabriella," she told him.

"I know that."

"Do you?"

He felt his lips quirk upward at the corners. Not a smile,

but close to one. "If you'd ever met her, you wouldn't ask, Poppy."

"It's Puabi."

She was still damned bristly. Almost hostile. He had yet to figure out why, but then again, he hadn't figured out anything about her. How she managed to heal at the speed of sound being at the top of the list. And now was not the time. He turned and continued to lead the way. The path was a winding one, shaded by palms even on the brightest days. This was not one of those. It was damned ominous outside today. Still. Utterly still, with that odd heaviness to the brick-tinted atmosphere.

They emerged from the trees near the horseshoe-shaped inlet where the yellow pontoon plane was just now skiing to a halt. He stopped where he was and waited for the engines to shut down, the hatch to open. Finally, Murial hopped out onto the pontoon nearest her. She reached up to close the hatch, then turned and stepped off the floating ski and onto the sand.

Matthew waved and moved toward her, and when she caught sight of him she waved back, but then she froze, her hand in midair, her eyes fixed on a spot beyond him.

He glanced sideways, but Puabi wasn't there. She'd stopped walking a few steps back and stood now staring at Murial.

"What's wrong?" he asked. "Come on, it's all right. She's a friend of mine."

Poppy met his eyes. "A friend?"

He nodded. "Murial works for me. Has for years. I'd trust her with my life."

Her eyes narrowed on his. "And I suppose you think that means I ought to trust her with mine?"

"Come on, Poppy. Look at her." Murial was willowy, pale, and with her ready smile not at all menacing or frightening.

Puabi breathed slowly. She still seemed exceedingly wary. "All right, then. If you trust her."

"I do." He started forward again, and this time she came with him. When they reached the point where Murial stood, they found her gaping. Murial was tall and slender as a reed, with long, perfectly straight blond hair and the sun-kissed face of a girl half her age. Pale lashes and brows, light blue eyes, a killer smile. She wasn't smiling now, though. She looked stunned, and Matthew felt a twinge in his gut. He should've left Poppy behind at the villa, so he could have prepared Murial for her appearance.

"It's okay, Murial," he said softly. Waves lapped against the pontoons, making slapping sounds. Other than that there was dead silence.

"But . . . but how . . . how could she . . . ?"

He reached out and clasped Murial's hands in his. "This is Puabi," he said. "Not Gabriella. Although I understand your reaction. Mine was pretty much the same."

The woman frowned, her eyes dragging themselves away from Puabi to meet his. "My God, the resemblance is . . . but what's she doing here, Matthew?"

"I'm stranded here," Puabi answered. Matthew knew by her tone, regal and impatient, that she resented Murial's asking him instead of her. "Until the storm passes."

Murial looked at her, studied her, her gaze intense.

"Exactly," Matthew said. "And speaking of the storm, what the hell were you thinking coming out here today, Murial? Do you know what a risk you're taking?"

She seemed to shake herself out of her inspection of Puabi. "I come out with the weekly reports every Friday."

"But the storm could have kicked up while you were in the air."

"It didn't," she replied.

"It wasn't worth the risk."

She rolled her eyes. "You're as overprotective as always, I see." Then she slipped her arms around him, hugged him gently. "How are you, Matthew?"

"Better," he said. And he glanced at Poppy and realized he wasn't lying about it. He'd given Murial the same reply every Friday for more than two months now, and this was the first time it had actually been true.

Poppy had something to do with that. He wasn't sure what. Maybe she'd just given him something else to think about besides his own guilt. Right now, though, Poppy looked even bitchier than usual.

Murial released him, and he said, "Let's get you back to the house. We were just about to have some breakfast."

"Great. You know I never turn down a meal."

You wouldn't know it to look at her, he thought idly. "Murial is my executive assistant," he told Poppy as they headed back along the path to the villa. "But she's more than that, too. Frankly, I don't know how I'd have made it through the last few months without her." He shook his head slowly. "I couldn't have left the business to anyone else. I'd have had to stay myself."

"Are you sure that would have been a bad thing?" Puabi asked.

Her tone startled him, and he shot her a look. "I needed to get away, to grieve in private, and try to heal. It was Murial who made me see that, and by stepping in for me, she gave me the means to do it."

Puabi sent Murial a saccharine smile. "You must be a very kind and generous soul."

Murial's expression was just as sweet, though more genuine, Matthew thought. "I care a great deal about Matthew."

"And Gabriella, no doubt," Puabi put in.

Murial nodded. "I was her best friend."

Puabi glanced pointedly at Murial's hand, which was on Matthew's shoulder, and said, "I can see that."

Whoa, what the hell was up here? He could feel the tension emanating from Puabi, and she was definitely firing rounds at Murial, but he wasn't sure why. He picked up the pace, and the two women kept up.

"I apologize for staring at you back there," Murial said after a moment. "You look so much like her—I thought I was seeing a ghost at first."

"Real people are far more frightening than ghosts," Puabi replied, and the words had an undertone that was almost threatening.

Back at the villa, the moment Murial went into the bathroom to wash up, Matthew took Puabi by the arm and drew her into the kitchen, closing the door behind them.

"You don't like her," he said. "Why?"

"I don't like anyone," she responded.

"You like me."

Her gaze raked him. "You're confused, Matthew. I have a compelling urge to have every imaginable form of sex with you. Repeatedly. That does not mean I like you."

His throat was suddenly very dry. To have her put it so bluntly . . . hell.

Poppy smiled wickedly at him. "I've rendered you speechless?"

He shook his head and tried not to visualize her words quite so clearly in his mind. But for a moment all he could see was a vision of tangled, sweaty limbs, and moist lips, and . . . hell. "I just want to know why you took such an instant dislike to Murial." He frowned then as a thought occurred to him. "Is it . . . jealousy?"

She tipped her head to one side. "I suppose it could be some form of that. But if it is, it's based on simple animal instincts. I haven't had my fill of you yet, so I resent the competition of another female." She seemed to mull that over for a moment. "Yes, that could be it."

He closed his eyes. "Murial is not interested in me in that way. Gabriella was never the least bit threatened by her."

"Gabriella was a naive, trusting, needy little girl."

He frowned, hard. "How do you know that?"

Blinking, Puabi looked at the floor and shook her head. "I'm not sure. I just do. I knew it as soon as I saw her photo." Lifting her eyes, she said, "Am I right?"

"Yes. About Gabriella, at least."

"About Murial, too. I don't know what she wants from you, Matthew. Whether it's the same thing I do or not. But regardless, she wants something. And whatever it is, she's not telling you. I dislike games and hidden motivations. I prefer people who say what they mean and mean what they say. Even an honest enemy is preferable to a dishonest ally."

He turned away from her, faced the food that was even now cooling in its pans on the stove. "You're honest, I'll give you that." He reached to the cupboard over his head, and took three plates down, then turned and handed them to her. "Here, put these on the table, will you?"

She lifted her brows, looking down at the plates with disdain.

"Oh, come on, don't give me the royalty routine. You're obviously feeling better. So pull your weight." He put the plates in her hands, and as she carried them out of the room, he tried very hard to erase the images she had painted in his mind. She wasn't delirious anymore. She wasn't sick or fe-

verish or in shock. And she openly admitted to wanting to—
how had she put it?—have every imaginable form of sex
with him. Repeatedly. But she didn't like him.

Hell, did he really care? He didn't like her all that much
either.

The lovely, lithe Murial spent most of the morning en-
sconced in a sitting room with Matthew, on the pretense of
discussing business. Puabi listened at the door a few times,
and each time she did, that was precisely what they were
doing. Discussing business.

Maybe she'd been wrong about the woman. Murial
seemed kind, concerned. She spoke softly, smiled easily.

But how was she, Puabi, to believe she could be mistaken
about the woman? She'd been the ruler of Ur, most powerful
city-state of Sumer. She did not make mistakes.

She used the time when she was left alone to snoop
through Matthew's villa, where he had come to lick his
wounds after his young wife's death. At Murial's urging,
Puabi reminded herself. Interesting. It wasn't a large house,
but every inch was spotless, neat, organized. No television
or radio anywhere to be found, other than the shortwave radio she located in a small room in the back. She couldn't
have operated the thing if she'd wanted to, and had no interest in it anyway. What did interest her were the items she
found in the bottommost drawer of the stand on which the
radio rested.

Inside were things she knew instinctively had belonged to
the dead Gabriella. Photographs of her with Matthew on their
wedding day. Clippings announcing the marriage. A dark,
blurry ultrasound printout, showing the tiny pollywog-shaped
fetus she had carried.

Something hot stabbed at Puabi's belly.

At the very bottom of the drawer there was a diary.

Puabi reached for it, then hesitated, her hand hovering a
hairsbreadth from the tiny book. She glanced behind her, into
the hallway, but no sounds reached her. Matthew was still
occupied with Murial. She would have time.

She picked the diary up, opened it, and began to read. And
very soon, she was engrossed. All sense of time deserted her

as she fell into the pages, because the story that unfolded on those pages could easily have been her own. The only difference was that Gabriella had grieved while Puabi had raged. Gabriella had given up where Puabi had fought. Gabriella, in the end, turned her pain inward. Puabi had turned hers outward, unleashing it on everyone she encountered.

As she closed the book, Puabi was stunned to feel dampness flooding her eyes. She lifted a hand, touched her fingertip to her cheek, and drew them away staring in disbelief at the teardrop she had caught. She was even more stunned to hear Matthew's deep voice from the doorway, saying softly, sadly, "So now you know."

6

She looked up quickly, no doubt startled to have been caught red-handed with his most private possessions. No matter. It seemed perfectly logical to Matthew that Puabi would find and read Gabriella's diary. He felt almost as if he'd expected it.

What he hadn't expected was to see tears on her face.

She dashed them away with an angry swipe of her hand and got to her feet. "I'm sorry. I . . . couldn't help myself."

He nodded. "I didn't think any sad story would be enough to melt that hard, practical heart of yours, Poppy. But it looks like Gabriella's did."

She shook her head slowly, then turned and tucked the book back into the drawer. "Not her story. Mine."

"Yours?"

She faced him again, sliding the drawer closed. "Almost word for word."

He glanced behind him, into the hallway. He'd left Murial in the study, where she'd been making notes of his instructions for the coming week. She would be busy for a moment. And this was a side of the mysterious Puabi that he hadn't yet seen. He wanted to probe it—in private. He closed the door softly, then turned to face her again, and he said, "Tell me."

She shook her head slowly.

"Come on, Poppy, you owe me. You violated my privacy. You read my dead wife's most intimate thoughts. You know my worst secrets. Now tell me yours."

He saw her face change, saw the capitulation there. He hadn't expected that either, not without more persuasion than he had yet applied. Maybe . . . maybe she needed to talk it out as much as he needed to hear it.

He watched her sink back into the chair where she'd been sitting. Her eyes focused not on his, but on some spot beyond the wall. "You already know most of it," she said, her tone gruff. "My story is Gabriella's. I married a man as a matter of convenience. Although in my case, unlike Gabriella's, it wasn't a one-night stand or an accidental pregnancy. It was a treaty between nations. But the results were the same. I fell in love. He didn't. Not with me, at least. And it wasn't enough for me."

He nodded, not moving from his spot, afraid to jar her out of this revealing mood. "He was a fool, then. As much a fool as I was."

"No, Matthew. He couldn't force himself to feel something he didn't. No more than you could. I see that now. I just . . . I don't know why I didn't see it then." She drew her focus back in, from wherever it had been. She looked at him now. And her eyes were clear and sharp. "I think what pushed me beyond the edge of my endurance was the day I lost our son. He was stillborn while my husband was out searching for his mistress. I just couldn't forgive him. After that, hating came easily to me. I made it my life's work, in fact."

Sighing deeply, Matthew moved toward her, unable to stop himself. He reached down to brush a tear from her cheek with his thumb. "I'm sorry, Poppy. Losing a child—that's a hurt no one should ever have to know."

"On that we agree."

"Obviously the outcome was different for you than for Gabriella. You're still alive."

She nodded. "For now."

"What's that supposed to mean?" He tried to search her face, but she lowered her head. Matthew dropped to one knee and pushed her hair aside, trying to read her.

She refused to look at him, and changed the subject. "Gabriella's response to rejection was despair. Mine was rage. I lashed out against them—my husband, his lover. In the end, they escaped unscathed and my rage rebounded like a boomerang, coming back to harm only me. The house burned. I was trapped inside, and they left me there, left me for dead."

"How did you manage to escape?" he asked, his gut churning because he sensed that every word she spoke was true.

She shook her head. "I don't know. Something in me made me keep fighting. I dragged myself out of the fire, to the cliffs, and fell into the sea. I honestly didn't expect I'd ever emerge again. Not alive." Looking deeply into his eyes, she said, "And the rest you know."

He nodded slowly. Then he swallowed hard and decided to say what he was thinking. She'd been bluntly honest with him, after all. "It . . . has crossed my mind that you didn't end up here by accident. That maybe you're . . . some kind of chance at redemption for me."

"*Me?* Your *redemption*?" She smiled bitterly. "No, Matthew."

"I couldn't save Gabriella. But I could save you."

She shook her head again. "By saving my life, you cursed humankind to suffer my existence a bit longer."

"Don't say that, Poppy. It's bullshit and you know it. You're no more evil than I am."

She looked as if she were about to argue, but stopped herself. "Tell me what happened to Gabriella. I feel . . . I feel as if I know her, somehow."

Drawing a breath, he sighed deeply, rose to his feet. He couldn't get through this if he had to look her in the face. Instead, he paced a few steps away as he spoke. "It was a one-night stand. She worked in the mail room, and she caught my eye. I had too much to drink one night and . . ." He sighed. "She got pregnant. I married her. I said it was because of a takeover in progress with a Christian book publisher whose owners placed a high value on morality. But, hell, it wasn't that. There was something about her that just— I don't know—drew me." Looking at the floor, he paused for a moment. "I didn't intend to, but I became . . . fond of her. She was such a tender thing. So needy. She took my kindness for more than it was and began to imagine a happy ending for us. We'd agreed to a quiet divorce once the child was born. I'd promised her a generous settlement. She knew I would provide for her and the baby. I thought it would be enough."

"And it wasn't," Puabi said.

Having reached the far end of the room, he turned. "No. It wasn't enough. She confessed her love for me one night, told me she didn't want to go through with the plan. I was shocked . . . I reacted badly. Reminded her she'd signed an agreement."

Puabi closed her eyes, gave a little sigh.

"I know, I know. She was furious. We argued, and she took the car and left. I was going to go after her, but Murial called with a business emergency. She convinced me to give Gabriella time to calm down, and talk to her later, when we were both more settled."

"But later never came."

He met Poppy's eyes. "No. She drove the car off the road and over an embankment. It plunged eighty feet to the ground. The gas tank exploded and . . ." He looked at the floor as the memory of what had remained of his naive little wife floated through his mind.

Puabi came to him, and her hands curled over his shoulders. Her breath fanned his face when she spoke. "I'm sorry, Matthew."

"So am I. Sorry I wasted so much time. I could have had a devoted wife who loved me unconditionally. I could have had my child, safe and healthy and wonderful. Instead, I have my precious freedom and my all-important business." Lifting his head, he met her eyes. "And I don't give a damn about either of them anymore."

Their gazes locked. He saw the pain in hers, and recognized it. Knowing its source made it even more powerful to him. And she drew him suddenly, like a magnet. He leaned nearer. Her eyes fell closed, those thick lashes caressing her cheeks. And her lips parted expectantly. He closed his hands on her waist and bent his head. His mouth brushed over hers, and he could feel her breath on his lips.

"Matthew?" a voice called.

Jerking his head up quickly, he glanced toward the door. Then he looked at Poppy. She lowered her head and turned her back on him. One hand was pressed to her forehead, the other, braced on the nearby table.

"Are you all right?"

She nodded, but didn't face him.

"Poppy, what is it?" He clasped her shoulders from behind, felt them trembling just slightly. Was this a reaction to that almost kiss? It seemed like far more.

She stiffened her spine and turned to face him with a smile painted on her face. "I'm fine."

The door opened. Murial stood there, looking from one of them to the other with innocently curious blue eyes.

"I'm ready to head back," Murial said. "See you next Friday?"

Matthew turned, forced his attention on his friend. "Oh, no, you're not."

Murial frowned at him. "What do you—"

"You're staying right here, Murial. It's already late enough that you'd be flying in the dark, and that storm could easily hit before morning. I'm going to have to insist that you stay. And when you do go back . . . Poppy and I will be hitching a ride."

Murial's eyes flared wider. "You . . . but, Matthew, you aren't ready."

"I wasn't." He looked at Poppy and she met his eyes. "I think maybe I am now. Either way, it's time."

$\mathcal{P}$uabi wasn't sure what brought on the rush of weakness that nearly put her on her knees when Matthew had been about to kiss her. Or what brought on the other feelings. Feelings that were utterly foreign to her. Her heart had twisted for Gabriella. And she'd felt Matthew's pain as well. Why? How could she feel for him when he'd treated his wife almost exactly the way her own husband had treated her? And when she'd anticipated his kiss, it hadn't been animal hunger alone burning in her. It had been something more. Something she . . . and her kind . . . did not feel. Were incapable of feeling—or so she had always believed.

The rush of dizziness that had followed, though, that was physical. Her legs had turned to water, her stomach had knotted up, and she would have fallen if she hadn't had the table for support.

Whatever it was, it passed quickly enough. But it left her weak and shaken. And wondering just how much life remained in her. If she suffered another mortal death—would she revive again? Or had she used every life she had ever stolen, during her endless months at sea?

They sat outside that night. Despite the storm so nearby, the sky was clear, and stars dotted it everywhere. Matthew had suggested a walk along the beach, since Puabi hadn't seen much of the island yet, and so the three of them walked barefoot in the sand between the shore and the villa. It honestly was beautiful here, Puabi thought. Like a small, lush oasis in a vast desert. Only the desert was sea.

"What's that?" she asked, pointing to a charred circle in the sand.

"They used to build bonfires there, I think."

"They?"

"The people I bought the island from."

"But you never have?" Puabi asked.

Murial clapped a hand over her own mouth to stifle a bark of laughter, but it escaped anyway. Matthew looked at her. "What?"

"Just the image of you, Mr. Tycoon, building a bonfire . . ." She shrugged. "Then again, I wouldn't have pictured you walking barefoot in the sand, either."

"No. Neither would I a short while ago."

Murial's smile turned softer. "This place is good for you, Matthew. It's healing you, I can see it."

"And I have you to thank for that."

A twinge of something that might have been jealousy nipped at Puabi's gut when Matthew reached out a hand to touch Murial's face. But it was brief. He dropped his hand to his side again quickly and said, "Let's build a fire."

"You're kidding," Murial said, and she shot Puabi a smiling look of disbelief. "He's kidding, isn't he?"

"Sit, both of you. I'll do the honors."

Puabi shrugged and looked around, spotting a hollow log that looked as if it had served as a bench in times past. She walked to it and sat, surprised when Murial sat on the other end. Matthew hurried into the woods, and came back moments later with an armload of twigs, dried leaves, and other debris. Then he vanished again, and returned with more sticks, larger ones. He arranged the kindling as carefully as if he were building a bridge, then headed back for more wood.

"A few weeks ago, I was afraid he would never bounce back," Murial said softly.

"It's like you said—the island is good for him."

Murial tilted her head to one side. "Maybe you're what's good for him."

Blinking in surprise, Puabi searched the woman's face. "I'm surprised to hear you say that."

"Why?"

A soft breeze kicked in from the sea, and Murial's blond locks danced in its touch. Puabi studied her face and saw nothing sinister there. "I guess I thought . . . you might have some romantic interest in him yourself."

"No, Puabi. I don't. I work for him. And I care for him, but only as a friend. Obviously, though, things are different between the two of you."

Puabi shook her head. "They can't be."

"Why not?" Murial asked.

Looking out toward the sea, Puabi was silent for a moment. The moon was just rising now, far out over the distant edge of the water. It sent silver ripples toward them. "There are reasons," she said at last.

Murial sighed, nodding to herself. "Puabi, you care about him. I can see that much." Puabi met the woman's eyes, but didn't reply. "Try to talk him into spending just a little more time out here. You don't know what he was like before. I was afraid for his life, I truly was. He'll listen to you. He needs more time. He's not ready to face those memories— not yet."

Before she could reply, Matthew was back, carrying logs this time. He arranged them near the fire and finally searched his pockets for a match. Murial got to her feet and offered him a lighter.

"Always prepared for anything," he said. "Aren't you?"

"I try to be," she told him.

Matthew knelt down and lit the fire.

7

$\mathcal{P}$*uabi was in Matthew's bed. She'd realized that only* today. It was where he'd put her that first night, and where she'd been ever since, despite the fact that there was a guest room in the house. She knew there was, because that was where Murial was spending the night. Matthew had taken the sofa. She wondered about that. His putting her in his own room that first night, rather than the guest room. What did it mean? Or did it mean anything at all?

Better question, she thought, suddenly scowling into the darkness, *why the hell do I care?* She was not the sort of woman who spent her time musing over a man's motivations. Then again, she wasn't an empathic sort, either, most of the time. But there was no question she was feeling empathy for Matthew's suffering, and for that of the ill-fated Gabriella. Gods, Gabriella. She couldn't seem to go five minutes without thinking of the woman, seeing her in her mind's eye, like a younger, sweeter, innocent version of herself. Like a little sister.

"Sickening," she muttered, rolling over and punching the pillow into a more comfortable shape. And her mind was so occupied with all of these new and inexplicable feelings, that she was sure she was missing something else. Something vital. Her powers were weak, yes, but not gone. She sensed something afoot here. Unseen forces were stirring in the astral. Magick was at work. She could feel it, almost taste it in the air. But she couldn't identify it or pinpoint its source, much less its intent or nature. It was more an inkling on her part. A static charge and a whisper she couldn't quite hear.

What did it all mean?

She tossed and turned for hours, and when she finally did begin to drift off, it was only to be shaken awake again by that ghostly memory—or was it a vision? She was in the water, and the water turned to sky, and someone had spoken to her in a voice that sounded like her own—told her she had a mission, a job to do.

Sitting up in bed, shivering and sweating at once, she pressed her hand to her forehead, closed her eyes on hot tears. "What is it?" she whispered. Gods, her stomach was churning, her head awash in questions. "What the hell am I supposed to be doing?"

But no answer came. She listened, looked for signs, and heard only the soft whisper of the wind on palm fronds outside, and the occasional cry of a night bird.

Sighing, she flung the covers aside, and rose from the bed naked, warm, welcoming the kiss of that dark breeze coming in through the open windows. A walk, she thought idly. To clear her head. She pulled on Matthew's white cotton robe, cinched the sash at her waist, and padded quietly out of the bedroom and through the villa. She tiptoed through the living room, careful not to disturb Matthew, who she assumed was curled beneath the mound of blankets on the sofa. The door didn't squeak when she pulled it open, thank goodness. And then she was outside.

Closing her eyes, she hurried away from the house, along the path through the lush growth. Most of the plants were foreign to her. She heard scurrying in the brush and wondered what sorts of animals dwelled here. And then she didn't care. She emerged on the beach and stood there for a long time where the waves washed in, lapping around her ankles, covering her feet, muddying the sand that oozed between her toes. The breeze here was stiffer, cooler, invigorating somehow. She found herself closing her eyes, opening her arms to it. As if in response it blew harder, buffeting her body, tousling her hair. It was damp, that wind. It kissed her face with moisture, tasted of salt and seawater.

"What am I doing here?" she whispered. Opening her eyes, she searched the distance, the dark sea, and the black velvet sky. Its starry face was streaked with dark, clawlike fingers of cloud. "I don't understand."

"Maybe you're not supposed to."

The voice, soft and deep, came from very close to her, and she didn't need to turn to recognize it. Matthew's hands curled around her waist, and he drew her backward until her body pressed to his. "Maybe it doesn't matter."

Her head tipped back against his shoulder, and he bent his, so his lips touched her neck lightly, softly, then lingered there.

"There's some reason, Matthew," she whispered. "You were right about that. None of this is coincidence, and I should know . . ."

His whiskers rasped over her sensitive skin, and she sucked in a breath.

"Right now," he said. "There's only right now. This moment. What came before, what comes later, those things don't exist."

"But they do—"

"Not if we say they don't. Try, Poppy. We deserve this moment. We need it."

She did try. She felt the waves wash over her feet, and as they retreated, she imagined them taking time itself away with them. Her past, her crimes, the blood that stained her hands, all washed out to sea. Yes. Gods, yes, to be free of all of it.

She broke away from Matthew, running forward until the depth stopped her. The white robe dragged, wet and heavy, and still she moved forward, dragging her legs through the cooling water, deeper and deeper. The water reached her chest, and a wave broke over her head, soaking her and driving her to her knees. Then it surged back, lifting her, tugging her into its embrace.

But there were other hands. Human hands. Matthew's hands and his arms locked around her. His body melded tight to hers, and his mouth claimed hers. The tide washed back out to sea without her. She was anchored to him. And he was carrying her toward the shore, carrying her in his arms,

kissing her, and there was nothing else. There was only here
and now. This moment, just as he had said.

She clung to him, tasted the seawater in his kiss, and more.
Her fingers tangled in his wet hair as he dropped to his knees
in the sand. Still kissing her, he laid her down, and stared
down at her hungrily, eyes blazing, as he untied the sash and
flung the robe open wide. Then he bent over her and drank
every drop of seawater from her skin, kissing her dry. It
seemed to Puabi that his lips left fire in their wake, heating
her flesh beyond endurance.

Then rising above her, he looked deeply into her eyes.
"Don't love me," he said. "I don't deserve to be loved. I
destroy what loves me."

"Don't love me," she told him in return. "I destroy all that
I touch. And I will break your heart in the end if you let
me."

He held her eyes for a long moment, and when he kissed
her again, any hint of restraint washed away in with the
waves that ebbed and flowed around them. Puabi pushed at
his jeans, until he helped her to strip them away. And then
he bent over her, nursing at her breasts, one, then the other.
She arched toward him as his mouth moved over her body,
in a useless effort to quench the fires he'd ignited in her skin,
her belly, her thighs. And when he tasted more of her, she
twisted her fingers into his hair and held on. The wet sand
was cool beneath her back. The water washed over them in
an ever more urgent rush. His hot mouth, demanding and
hungry, fed at her. Pressing her wider, he delved inside with
his tongue, sucking at her as if she were a ripe fruit oozing
juices he craved. He pinched gently, deliciously, with his
teeth, as if he could squeeze out more, then lapped up every
drop, and demanded more.

She screamed aloud when she came, and her entire body
shuddered with the force of her climax. And even then, he
was sliding his wet, warm body up over hers, higher, covering her, spreading her, filling her.

It had been so long since she'd held a man inside her. So
long. And her orgasm never stopped. It eased only slightly
before beginning to build again as he moved deeper, drew
back, and thrust into her again and again. Her nails raked his
back. She whispered words of old, in a tongue long forgotten.

Again the peak burst upon her, and shattered her very being. This time he was there with her, grating his teeth, moaning her name—the name he'd given her. Poppy.

Slowly, their bodies uncoiled. Matthew rolled to the side, pulling her into his arms, holding her against him. She felt his heart pounding in his chest. Powerful and strong. Her own beat rapidly, too. But it wasn't as strong. She could feel, more than ever, the flaws in its imperfect rhythm. The weakness in its most powerful beat.

He stroked her hair. "What language was it that you were speaking to me, Poppy?"

She lay against him, loving the feel of strong male arms around her, no matter what else was wrong in her world. "Sumerian," she told him. "It was spoken four thousand years ago, in my homeland."

He nodded. She felt the movement of his head. "Oh, I get it now. That's where I've heard that name of yours before, isn't it? You're named for some ancient queen, aren't you?"

She shook her head slowly. "No, Matthew. I'm not named for anyone."

Rising up on his elbows, he studied her face, a hint of humor in his eyes. "You mean you actually are some ancient queen."

"Of course I am."

He bent and kissed her shoulder. "And what were you saying, my sexy, crazy, Sumerian queen?"

"It was a bit of ancient poetry, part of a song they say the goddess Inanna sang to her husband. 'Your kiss is like honey. Touch me and I tremble, my strong, powerful lion. Your kiss is like honey sweet. Kiss me again.'"

He lifted her chin and kissed her lips, as if in response to her request. But when he lifted his head away again, his eyes were serious. "It wasn't a mistake, what just happened, between us."

She shook her head. "No. It can't have been."

He nodded. "I don't want to hurt you the way I've hurt others in my life, Poppy. Don't let me."

She let her gaze roam his face, his stubbled chin, strong jaw, full lips. "I'm not the one in danger of getting hurt here." She lowered her lashes. "Don't get attached to me, Matthew. I don't have that much more time."

"You've said that before. I'm going to have to insist you tell me what the hell you mean by it this time. Because if you're thinking about—about—"

"Suicide?" she asked. "No. I just . . ." She looked at his face, at the sudden intensity in his eyes, and she couldn't tell him the truth—that she probably wouldn't live very much longer. She knew it, though. Sensed it with every breath she drew. Better to spare him that knowledge. "When we get back to civilization, Matthew, I'm going to leave. You need to know that. Be aware of it. And prepare yourself."

He stared at her. But finally he licked his lips and nodded. "All right. If that's what you have to do, then . . ." Lowering his head, he shook it slowly. "I don't want to think about it, to tell you the truth. Here and now, remember? That's all I want to think about."

She smiled very slightly. "That's good, Matthew. Because here and now is all we have."

He frowned, searching her face, but she said no more. Instead she rolled to her feet, ran into the waves, then dove into the water.

8

Something was wrong with her, he knew it with the same uncanny clarity with which he knew other things about her. He knew, for example, that she was not an ordinary woman. There was something otherworldly about her. Something older than time. He knew, too, that she hadn't come here by accident. That it had been predestined. That he was supposed to help her in some way. To save her—from what, he wasn't sure. Maybe from whatever it was he sensed was wearing her down.

She wasn't getting stronger here, as he'd expected, but weaker. Day by day, weaker. Sure, she'd recovered somewhat from her ordeal at sea. But this was something else. Something he felt, more than saw. It did show, physically. It showed in how easily she could become breathless. A short walk would do it. It showed in how she grew paler all the time, no matter how much sunlight she got. It showed in her eyes, which revealed pain she wouldn't admit to feeling. But he sensed it even more powerfully. He sensed something in her slowly fading. Like a bright light growing gradually dimmer as its fuel burned away.

They made love, and slept, and woke and made love again, until finally Poppy fell into a deep, heavy sleep. Sensing she wouldn't wake again until morning, he wrapped her in the nearly dry robe, and carried her back to the villa. She never stirred. And maybe it was his imagination, but she seemed lighter than before. Frail and light and cool in his arms. Less substantial than the last time he'd carried her over the same path.

He tucked her into his bed and brushed her hair away from her face. Her skin was cool, and he thought he detected the bare beginnings of shadows beneath her eyes. She was sick. He would lay odds that she'd been sick long before her time in the ocean. She might even be dying.

And she seemed to have accepted it. But she hadn't counted on him. She had no clue as to what the kinds of things a man with his power, his wealth, and his connections, could accomplish. He hadn't been able to save Gabriella. But he would damn well pull out all the stops to save her dark sister.

Her dark sister. When had he begun to think of Poppy that way?

Smiling very slightly, he bent to press a kiss to her forehead. "Don't you worry, Poppy. I'm going to fight this thing. And you're going to fight it with me. I'm not giving you any choice in the matter."

Dawn broke in neon. Blazing orange and glowing yellow painted her eyelids from beyond the windows and burned through them until she awoke. The light made her head ache, and she immediately turned away from it and groaned.

Then she realized she was in bed. She'd expected to wake up on the beach. In Matthew's arms.

Gods, last night . . . She closed her eyes, remembering. She'd never felt that way before. Not even with Natum. How was that possible? Natum had been the love of her life . . . hadn't he?

She heard voices then and, frowning, got to her feet. Her legs were oddly watery and her head heavy. Still, she moved closer to the door, listening as the voices outside rose.

"It's too soon, I tell you! Why are you so damned stubborn, anyway?"

"I have my reasons, Murial. And since when are you my keeper?"

"Dammit, Matthew, that hurts. I'm your friend. You know that."

His tone was softer when he replied. "I know that. I'm sorry. But I don't want to argue about this anymore. The Weather Service says there's still time. So we're going back—this morning."

There was a long pause. Poppy opened the door a crack and peeked out. She could see down the hall, into the living room where the two stood facing each other. Matthew had a cup of coffee in his hand. Murial looked close to tears.

Backing inside, Poppy gathered her strength and quickly showered and dressed in some of the too-large clothes Matthew had found for her. By the time she joined them, Matthew was putting plates of food on the table and refilling his coffee cup.

He smiled when she came in, pulled out a chair for her. "Morning, Poppy," he said. Gods, if she went by the look in his eyes, she might think he was speaking to someone he cherished. "How are you feeling?"

Odd question, she thought with a frown. "Fine. I'm feeling fine." She slid a glance toward Murial as she sat down. "In fact, I think this island air is good for me. A few more days out here and I'll be as good as new." She forced a bright smile as she spoke the lie.

Matthew set a plate of food in front of her that could have fed three grown men. "I wish I could agree with you, there, but as I've already told Murial, I think we need to get back."

She lifted her gaze to his. "But why? I thought we were going to wait out the storm here."

He shook his head, then took his own seat. "No, that's impossible. For one thing, the Weather Service says the storm is close to hurricane force now. It's moving in, but slowly. They expect it to hit us by nightfall, and it's just not going to be safe here."

She nodded, sliding a surreptitiously apologetic glance at Murial, who was so deep in thought that she didn't even notice. "So it would be too dangerous to stay," she said, looking at Matthew again. "I'm confused, Matthew. Just yesterday, you thought it would be too dangerous to leave."

"We have better information today. There's plenty of time to make the flight back to Miami. We'll be flying away from the storm, and, as I said, it's moving slowly. At this point, it would be far more risky to stay than to go."

Again she nodded. "And what's the other reason?"

"Other reason?" He leaned over to fill her cup with coffee. She hadn't asked. She'd barely glanced at the cup, thought of coffee, and he'd acted. It was as if he could read her thoughts. Or maybe he was just watching her that closely.

"You said, 'for one thing' before you mentioned the storm. That implies some other thing."

He averted his eyes, gave his head a shake. "I'm just ready to go back. I think it's the best thing."

He was keeping something from her. She could barely believe it. She sighed impatiently and ate a few bites of the food, but her stomach didn't receive it well. "You're just going to leave the place to the storm, then?"

"This place isn't that hard to button up," he said, looking relieved at the change of subject. "It's not as if hurricanes are a rarity out here. I'll have the barriers on the windows and doors inside an hour. So finish up your breakfast and grab what you want to take with you." He glanced at his watch. "We'll leave at nine. All right?"

It seemed there was no talking him out of it. And who was she to try, if this was what he felt he needed to do? Maybe it would be good for him to go back, to face his past and deal with his ghosts, despite what Murial thought.

Something twisted into a tight, hard little knot inside her, and she hated to admit that the idea of leaving him, as she knew she would have to do when they arrived back in the States, was painful. Almost unbearable.

She hadn't arrived on the island with much. Her dagger and her tattered clothes. So there wasn't much for her to throw into the small bag that Matthew gave her, but she managed to find a few things. The toothbrush and hairbrush he'd given her. The white robe—she'd grown rather attached to the silly oversized thing. And Gabriella's diary. She didn't intend to keep it, of course. But she couldn't bear the thought of leaving it here to be washed away by the storm. She would give it to Matthew before she went on her way to face an uncertain future alone.

Murial climbed into the plane first. She started its engines, and the whir of the propellers sent sea spray flying in a fine mist that dampened anyone who came near. Matthew stood near the front end of the pontoons, untying the rope that held the plane to the island. "Go on, Poppy, climb aboard." He had to shout to make himself heard above the roar of the engines. "I'll have to give this baby a push to get her into the water and turned around."

Nodding, Poppy went to the open door, gripped a handle, and put her foot on a step. She looked up, met Murial's eyes, and returned her ready smile. Then she reached out a hand.

Murial clasped it.

The jolt that rocked through her at that touch would have knocked her down to the sand, if the other woman hadn't held on so tight. Murial tugged, and Puabi found herself pulled right into the plane's cockpit, shoved through a doorway into the rear section, then down into a seat.

She blinked up at Murial, her heart racing. That jolt of contact could only mean one thing. "You . . . you're an Immortal High Witch!"

"A Dark One," she whispered. "Just like you. It took you long enough, Puabi. I was beginning to think you'd never figure it out."

"But . . . but I don't understand. What do you want with Matthew? He's a mortal. He's just an ordinary man."

"Oh, I think we both know there's nothing ordinary about Matthew Fairchild," she said with a slow, wicked smile. "But it isn't him I want. And I'm afraid you aren't going to live long enough to learn any more than that. Neither of you is."

Puabi reached for her dagger, her hand shooting automatically to her thigh. Years of battle had made the reaction a reflex. But her dagger wasn't at her thigh—it was packed in her bag. She'd thought she wouldn't need it at hand at least until they reached the mainland. Gods, when had she become so complacent?

"What's the matter, Puabi? Do you think I want your heart? You know perfectly well that the hearts of the Dark Ones are weak trophies at best, and yours is all but used up. Tell me, Puabi, why haven't you killed one of the Light Ones to rejuvenate yourself? I just can't figure that out."

Puabi surged to her feet, balled up a fist, and swung at her, but Murial ducked the blow and easily shoved Puabi down on the seat again. "I don't want to fight you, Puabi. I just want you out of my way."

She brought her hand around, and Puabi glimpsed the object in it. Large, metallic, red. She ducked fast, then drove her head toward Murial's belly. But the other woman was faster and stronger—in peak condition, while Puabi was running on empty. Murial simply dodged the attack and swung again. The small fire extinguisher smashed down on Puabi's head, and lights exploded in her eyes. Then one by one, they blinked out. The last thing she heard was Murial's voice, cruel and deep. "You're going to die, Puabi. For keeps this time, if you ask me."

Matthew waded into the surf, tugging the plane easily around to face away from the island. Then he used the pontoon as a step, climbed in, and pulled the hatch shut behind him. "All set," he said, turning to Murial.

She sat at the controls, smiling at him, her light blue eyes sparkling. "Great. We're on our way. Go on, now, go buckle up." Even as she spoke, she set the thing in motion. Matthew turned toward the rear and made his way back, through the small doorway toward the set of passenger seats, smiling as he caught sight of Poppy relaxing there. The warmth that moved through him whenever he saw her was amazing. He wasn't a fool. He knew damn well that part of the attraction was her resemblance to Gabriella—the woman he'd taken for granted and lost. But it wasn't only that. There was something more to Poppy.

Moving nearer, he felt his smile freeze in place and then slowly change into a frown. "Poppy? Hey, what's wrong?" She was slumped against one side of the plane, eyes closed, body limp. He knelt in front of her, gripping her hands, touching her face. "What is it? Poppy?"

"Anything wrong?" Murial called. "What's going on back there?" The plane was banging against the incoming waves now, shuddering a little, but then it lifted off and left the choppy waters behind.

"It's Poppy. She's out cold." He checked for a pulse, watched her chest, and held his breath until he felt hers whispering from her lips to bathe his face. Finally, he detected the soft thrum of the blood rushing through her veins. "She's alive," he said, as much to confirm it to himself and the universe—to make it so—as to inform Murial. "What the hell happened in here? She seemed fine . . ."

"Damned if I know." The plane was banking now, settling into flight. "She was okay when I helped her aboard. Gee, maybe she's sicker than I realized. I mean, I sensed she wasn't quite well, but I had no idea she was seriously ill."

He sank into the seat beside Poppy, pulling her into a more comfortable position with care. "She is, I'm afraid. That's why I wanted to get back today, Murial. I want her to see the top specialists in the country. The world, if necessary."

"You know what's wrong with her, then?"

"No. I think it may be her heart, but she hasn't told me." He frowned then, as the clouds parted briefly, and the sun slanted through the window. It reflected on something shining or wet in Poppy's hair. Bending closer, he probed with his fingers, and then found the small cut, and felt a knob the size of a goose egg forming around it. "For the love of . . ." He got to his feet and laid her on the seat, then pried back one eyelid with his thumb, trying to check her pupils. "She has a head injury!" he shouted. "Jesus, Murial, something must have happened in here!"

"Oh, no!" Murial said. "You know, I heard her fall, when she was getting into her seat, but she said she was fine. I should have checked."

Matthew grimaced, then went for the first aid kit mounted to the wall nearby. He took out a cold pack and crushed it to activate it, then laid it on Poppy's head. "Hard to believe she could have fallen hard enough to do this much damage," he muttered.

"Look, I'll have you in Miami in under two hours. Just hang in there, okay? She'll be fine."

He nodded. And he sat with Poppy for a time, holding her, speaking softly to her.

It kept getting darker by degrees. It didn't register right away, but when it did, Matthew feared the storm may have picked up its pace. Maybe it was coming in faster than predicted. Hell, that was all they needed.

"Better get a weather update," he called to Murial. "I don't like the looks of this." She didn't answer, and he turned to shout toward the front. "Murial, did you hear me? I said you ought to get a storm advisory in case . . ." As he spoke he glanced out the window, and he was briefly disoriented because the storm clouds were on the wrong side of the plane. "Jesus, Murial, where the hell are you taking us?"

Still no answer, and his stomach clenched. "Dammit, Murial, answer me!" A rush of air and sound came then. Matthew made his way forward, only to see Murial vanish through the open hatch. He reached for her but grabbed only air, and he watched her plummet with a sense of horror before he realized that she was wearing a parachute. It bloomed far below, and beyond it he saw the familiar shape of Saba. Then he yanked the hatch closed, his mind racing with questions.

"She's trying to kill us, Matthew. Both of us."

He turned to see Poppy, clinging to the walls to hold herself up, leaning into the cockpit. She looked so weak. "But I don't understand. Why?"

"There's no time now," she whispered. "Look."

He looked out the windshield, and what he saw made his heart flip over. The whirling, swirling black sky. Murial had pointed them directly into the hurricane before bailing.

"Do you know how to fly this thing?" Poppy asked weakly.

He met her eyes, his own grim. "No."

9

The engines coughed as if to punctuate his answer, and he scanned the panel to try to figure out why. It wasn't a difficult puzzle. The needle of the fuel gauge pointed to Empty. "She must have dumped the fuel. She wasn't taking any chances." One last sputter, a cough, and the craft began to descend.

"I won't give up without a fight, dammit." Matthew got himself into the seat, took the controls. He'd been in the plane with Murial often enough to have picked up a few things. He found the lever that would lower flaps and, he hoped, slow their airspeed. He used the stick to keep the nose from dipping too low as the plane's engines died all at once. And then they drifted on the air, and he could hear the wind all around them. It was damned eerie.

"Where did she go?" Poppy asked. "How could she jump into all that ocean?"

"Island," he said, his attention on the controls, on the plane, on the water rushing up at them. "Saba. Back there." Faster and faster the sea rose toward him. "Sit down, Poppy! Brace yourself!"

He didn't know if she did or not. They hit, a wing dipped, and the plane cartwheeled. Matthew was tossed around vio-

lently as water rushed on him from all directions and his
body smashed into hard objects.

And then there was only water. Stillness, and water, all
around. He didn't know which way was up or down. So he
struggled toward the light. It was all he had to go by.

His head broke the surface. He sucked in a breath, and a
wave slapped his face and crawled down his throat. Choking,
gasping, and spitting, he tread water, sought air.

Poppy! Jesus, where was she? "Poppy! Poppy, where are
you?"

He couldn't see her. God, he couldn't see her! "Poppy!"
More water down his throat, in his lungs. Hell, where was
she? The sky was black, the wind picking up. A huge wave
broke over his head and drove him under. When he tried to
struggle to the surface, something bumped his leg.

Shark. The word whispered through his mind like a razor-
edged blade.

Then the thing bumped him again, its body hitting his.
And the next thing he knew he was on the surface, sucking
in air.

The animal circled him, arched out of the water, and vanished again. Not a shark. A dolphin.

The clouds burst, and rain fell in a deluge, powerful drops
driving into him like icy pellets. He searched for Poppy,
screamed her name until he was so hoarse he could barely
speak. The waves increased, and he was thrown under again,
and again, but each time the dolphin pushed him back up.
He was barely conscious the last time it happened, and his
hand closed around the dorsal fin.

And suddenly the animal shot forward, cutting through the
waves like a knife through butter. He held on for dear life—
that was all he could do.

Matthew coughed, rolled onto his side, choked and
gagged. Water trickled out of his mouth, and he rose up onto
all fours, arching his back as his lungs expelled more salt
water.

When the spasm ended, he rose to his knees in the black
sand, wiping his mouth with the back of his hand. "Poppy,"
he whispered, staring out to sea. "God, did you make it?"

Something moved in his peripheral vision, and he swung his head around. There, farther along the beach, tangled in seaweed was . . . something. The dolphin?

The tail rose and lowered again. The woman moaned softly. He blinked, and rubbed his eyes. And there was no tail. No mermaid lying there in the sand. There was only Poppy.

He ran forward, fell to his knees beside her, and lifted her slowly. "Baby, Poppy, are you all right?"

Opening her eyes very slowly, she nodded. "I have . . . to tell you . . ."

He pressed a finger to her lips. "No. No, you're too weak. I need to get you to a doctor." He looked around him, frantic. "Wait a minute, this is a black sand beach. And there, there's the crater. See it?"

She looked where he pointed. The peak of the tiny volcano island rose into the storm clouds.

"This is Saba," he told her, scanning the place to get his bearings. "Yes, there's a road off this way. And there's a town a mile farther. God, I hope they haven't evacuated the entire island."

He scooped her up into his arms and carried her. "How did you get to shore, Poppy? God, I was so afraid. I couldn't find you. How did you do it?"

She opened her eyes and stared up at him, her vision unfocused. "I swam. And I pulled you with me."

He frowned, wondering if her fever was back. She'd been through so much. "No, baby. A dolphin towed me in. But it's okay, I understand—"

"It was me. I only made you think I was a dolphin. It was easier than answering all the questions you would have . . ." she turned her head to the side, and coughed.

"But, Poppy, that's impossible."

"No. It's a spell. The *glamourie*. It's only a trick of the mind."

He kept walking, kept carrying her. "Even if you could make me think you were a dolphin, you couldn't swim that fast," he said.

"Yes, I could. Faster, if I were at full strength. But I used up almost every bit of power left in me, Matthew. And I won't last much longer now."

"Yes, you will, dammit. I'll find a doctor. I'll save you, somehow, I swear."

She smiled weakly. "We haven't much time. I must tell you now, what I am. I'm a witch, Matthew. Not an ordinary witch. I am an Immortal High Witch. I've been alive for more than four thousand years. I survive by taking the lives of others like me. Taking their hearts—"

"No."

"Yes, it's true. Just listen to me, I beg of you!"

He swallowed hard, tried to walk faster. The village he sought was in sight now. The road was muddy and slick, the rain coming down in sheets. "If you're immortal, then you can't die. Yet you keep telling me you're not going to live much longer."

"We die. And we revive again. Over and over, but only so long as our stolen power holds out. At least that's how it is for the Dark Ones, like me. I could make myself strong again by killing another. But . . . something has changed, Matthew. I can't do it anymore."

He closed his eyes briefly. It was insanity, she was talking insanity!

"Murial is what I am. She's the same. And she wants something from you. I don't know what. I cannot even guess, but there's something. You have to kill her, Matthew. You have to kill her, and there are very few ways you can do that."

His jaw was clenched, rain streaming down his face. Her hair was plastered to her head, her clothes to her body.

"You need to cut out her heart. And when that's done, you must burn her body, and her heart as well. That will release her spirit. And Matthew . . . you must do the same to me."

"This is ridiculous! You're talking crazy. You aren't going to die, Poppy, you—"

"Please," she whispered. "Promise me you'll see to it that my wishes are carried out."

He stared down at her as he trudged onward, through the rain. "All right. If . . . if the worst should happen, I'll see to it."

She nodded slowly, relaxing in his arms, and he figured it was worth it, making that ridiculous promise, if it eased her mind. He'd be damned before he would do it, though.

"You were right, you know," she murmured. "I did wash up on your island for a reason. I think it was to save you from drowning, and now that I've done that, I probably won't live much longer. It doesn't seem like enough—to redeem me, I mean. But it's something, anyway."

She closed her eyes then.

Matthew stopped walking. Her head tipped back and hung limply. He shook her. "Poppy? Poppy, dammit, don't you go! Not yet, not like this. I love you, do you hear me? I don't give a shit what you did in the past, or what kind of monster you think you are. I love you. Dammit, Poppy, I love you!"

No response. He looked up, and saw a miracle standing in front of him, in the form of a sign carved in wood, with an arrow pointing to the right. The sign read, SABA MEDICAL CLINIC.

10

The clinic was in a large house in the middle of a banana plantation, and he guessed the doctor who ran it likely lived in it as well. He hoped desperately that someone was home, as he carried Poppy to the door and pounded on it.

A light came on within. Footsteps. Then a tall, almost regal-looking dark-skinned woman opened it. She wore white, and her name tag called her Aliyah. "Please," he said. "She needs help."

"Of course! Come in! What's happened to her?" She barely glanced at Poppy as she led them quickly into a room and pointed to a bed. "There, lay her down there. I'll call Dr. Sloane."

Matthew laid Poppy in the bed, noticing that she wasn't the only patient. There was another bed in the room, a curtain drawn around it, in typical hospital-room fashion, to block it from view, but he could hear the steady beep of some kind of monitor. The nurse had depressed a button on the wall and was now leaning over Poppy, one hand to her cheek.

But then she sucked in a breath and jerked backward, her eyes widening. "I don't . . . I don't understand . . ."

Poppy drew a shuddering breath and opened her eyes. "I'm so cold," she whispered.

Shaking herself, the nurse pointed at the closet. "There are dry nightgowns in there. And blankets. Get them. Go!"

He did, and by the time he came back with the requested items, she had efficiently stripped Poppy of her soaking-wet clothes and dried her with towels. She dressed her quickly in a white flannel nightgown, then had Matthew lift her up so she could strip away the wet bedding and briskly put warm, dry sheets on the bed. Then he laid her down again and tucked blankets around her.

The nurse stuck a thermometer into her mouth and was taking Poppy's pulse when the sound of shuffling steps alerted him, and he turned to see an aging man with skin so tanned it stood in shocking contrast to his snow-white hair. He was in his seventies, easily. "Well, now, what have we here? A couple of refugees from the storm? Should have evacuated with the others, son."

"We were in a small plane that veered off course and went down," Matthew explained. "We were lucky to make it to the shore."

The old man arched his brows in surprise. "My God, you're lucky to be alive!" He nodded to the nurse. "Go on and find this fellow some dry clothes. I'll see to the girl."

"A moment, please, Dr. Sloane?"

He glanced up at the nurse, who stood beside Poppy's bed, leaning over her. She sent him a look filled with meaning, and he frowned and went closer. Aliyah nodded at Poppy, and the old man looked down. Then he blinked, and his brows drew close. "How in the . . ."

"Why do you both keep looking at me so strangely?" Poppy asked, a hint of her former haughty attitude making its way into her tone. It did Matthew a world of good to hear it.

"I . . . well, I . . . you look very much like . . . someone."

"Yes, she does," Matthew said, coming closer. "She looks like my late wife, Gabriella."

"Gabriella," the nurse whispered, and she crossed herself. "Jesus, Joseph, and Mary."

"What the hell is the matter with the two of you?" Matthew demanded.

"Go on, Aliyah," the doctor said. "Get those dry things for the young man." She left, and the doctor seemed to square his frail shoulders as he faced Matthew. "I'm Alan Sloane," he said.

"Matthew. Matthew Fairchild. Now, can we skip the part where we discuss the weather and get to the point here? I can see something isn't right."

Dr. Sloane nodded slowly. "You're quite right about that. You see, about three months ago a patient—a young woman who looked remarkably like this one," he said with a nod at Puabi, "was transferred here to this clinic. Brain-dead, but on full life support. Her sister paid us a generous amount—enough to keep the clinic running for years—to keep her here, and care for her until—"

Matthew turned slowly, his eyes moving from the doctor's to that closed curtain that surrounded the other bed. Another patient. She looked like Poppy. And she'd been here for three months. His knees jelled, and Poppy reached out from her bed to clasp his hand.

More clearly than before, now, he heard the steady beeps and the pumping and hissing of the machines that kept someone alive according to some warped definition of the word. He pulled free of Poppy's hand and walked toward the curtains.

"There's more," the doctor began.

But he tugged the white curtains open. There, in the bed, lay Gabriella, her skin pale and waxy. Her hair neat and short. They'd cut it, probably to make it easier to care for her. It was as short as Poppy's now. But the biggest difference in his young wife, was the swollen mound that was her belly, expanded to the size of a beach ball underneath the sheets. And even as he stared at it in utter shock and total disbelief, the child inside her moved. He saw it.

"Sweet Jesus," Matthew whispered as he dropped to his knees, unable to hold his emotions in check any longer.

Puabi ignored the sudden skipping of her heart, like a motor working to keep from stalling. She couldn't focus on herself now. Not with Matthew on his knees, his entire body shaking with the force of his emotions. She glanced at the doctor. "Give us just a moment, will you?"

"No, not yet. You need medical attention, and I need answers." He moved toward Matthew, clasped his shoulder from behind. "As no doubt, you do as well. Is this woman your wife?"

"Yes." The word was stark, and Puabi felt the pain in it. She struggled to sit up in the bed.

"And what happened to her, so far as you knew, I mean?"

Swallowing hard, Matthew lifted his head, but his eyes never left the body of that small woman in the bed. Puabi understood that, because she couldn't take her eyes off the woman either. So like her. And yet, softer somehow. And the fact that her belly was swollen with a child she would never know seemed like a twist of fate too cruel to bear. Why? "She could be my sister," Puabi heard herself whisper. "My small, frail little sister . . ."

"She was in a car accident. Her body—someone's body—was burned beyond recognition. We . . . we thought she was dead. I buried her, I—God, Gabriella . . ."

"And her sister? The one who brought her here to us, made these arrangements for us to keep her on life support until the baby was born—she never told you?"

He finally looked away from his wife, his head turning slowly to face the doctor. "She doesn't have a sister."

"Murial," Puabi whispered. "It had to be Murial." Her heart shuddered, and she tried to catch her breath without letting on that she was in distress. Short, shallow, open-mouthed breaths were all she could manage. She got to her feet, somehow, moved until she was at Gabriella's bedside. And once there, she reached out and touched the face of the woman in the bed, the woman who looked so very much like her.

"You really could be my little sister."

Matthew lifted his gaze to the doctor's. "The baby? It's . . . all right?"

Puabi glanced downward at the swollen belly and lowered her hand gently to it. She could feel the life force inside, powerful and strong. "Fine. The baby's fine," she said, a little louder now, a smile pulling at her lips.

Dr. Sloane clasped Matthew's hand and helped him to his feet as they both looked at Puabi. The doctor seemed puzzled, but he nodded. "Yes, you're right. The baby appears to be perfectly healthy in every way. In fact, we'd originally scheduled the C-section for tomorrow. Though we may very well have to put it off another day if this storm hits the way they're predicting it will."

Matthew's eyes turned bleak. "What about that, Dr. Sloane? The storm, I mean. If the power goes out—"

"We're prepared for that. We have a backup generator. It kicks on automatically, son. The baby will be safe until its birth, we'll see to that."

Matthew nodded, seeming relieved, but only for a moment. Then he looked grim again. "And then what?" he asked.

Puabi returned her hand to the woman's face and stroked her hair, feeling an odd ripple of emotion that she had never felt before. *Never.*

Dr. Sloane looked at Gabriella, his expression sad. "She's not going to come out of the coma. She's brain-dead, son, she has been for months. The kind thing to do, the only decent thing to do, would be to take her off the life support. Let her go."

As had happened before, Puabi's heart seemed to skip, leaving her short of breath. Then it contracted—as if being slowly squeezed by a large, powerful hand.

The steady, monotonous pattern of the beeps emanating from the machine behind her suddenly changed. Rapid-fire, then slowing.

Matthew looked up sharply, and Dr. Sloane literally lunged toward the bed. Puabi stepped away to give him room as he put his stethoscope into his ears and pressed it to Gabriella's chest.

"What was that, Doctor? What happened?" Matthew asked.

The doctor held up a hand, frowning, listening. He shook his head. "Her heartbeat is fine. Must have been a glitch in the monitor." But he still looked puzzled.

Puabi was too dizzy by now to stand up without giving herself away, so she sat down in a chair in the corner. The nurse had gone to get those dry clothes the doctor had requested for Matthew. And the two men seemed too busy fussing over Gabriella to notice her.

The nurse returned, her arms full of clothes for Matthew. She handed them over, then frowned at Poppy. "You ought to be in bed. We haven't even examined you yet."

"I'm fine," she said. "Really, I'm feeling much better." She couldn't lie down. Not yet. She was too tired, and she was afraid—so afraid—that if she rested, she might slip away. She might die, for the final time. And now—now she sensed that her mission, her reason for washing up into Matthew's life—was not yet complete. There was more. It had to do with Gabriella. And her child.

Dr. Sloane said, "I'll leave you alone for a minute or two now. But not long. I want to examine you, young lady." He nodded to Matthew. "I'll be nearby. Call if you need me."

Matthew nodded, never opening his eyes until the doctor left them and closed the door. Then, he went to Poppy in the chair, knelt in front of her, clasped her hands. "Are you all right?"

She smiled through moist eyes. "Me? Matthew, how can you think of me when you're going through so much?"

"Because I care about you, as much as you detest hearing sappy emotional garbage like that. And I can see you're feeling like hell right now. And because I know what a shock all of this is to you, walking in here, seeing her for the first time. The baby . . ." He looked toward the bed.

"It's a boy, you know," she whispered. "A son, like the son I carried, and bore. Only yours is strong and healthy."

He sighed deeply, shaking his head. "Why is fate so damned cruel, Poppy? Why did a healthy, loving mother like you have to lose her child? Why does a strong, healthy baby have to lose his mother?"

She shook her head slowly. "I don't know. I only know that you need to grab on to whatever joy you find in life. And you've just found some, Matthew. You have a son on the way. You won't be left alone. You'll be a father. That's what you need to focus on here. Not losing Gabriella. Not even losing me. But the joy of this gift. This miracle." Her eyes seemed too heavy to keep open. She was so tired all of a sudden.

She expected him to look toward the woman in the bed again, as she did, but instead he frowned. "Poppy?" His palm pressed to her cheek. "Poppy, what is it? Dammit, you're in trouble, aren't you? Poppy?"

But she only smiled weakly at him and slipped into sleep as Matthew shouted for the doctor.

*There was chaos. Dr. Sloane, Matthew, and Aliyah sur-*rounded Poppy's hospital bed.

"I called for more help, Doctor," Aliyah said. "They're on the way."

"We're losing her," the doctor yelled.

Aliyah raced into the hall, and when she came back three other strangers followed, two women and a young man. Aliyah pushed a large box with ominous paddles attached.

"Oh, God, no . . . no, please." Matthew's heart was breaking. Jesus, this couldn't be happening.

"What the . . . what the *hell*?" The nurse beside him exclaimed.

He glanced at her, saw her gaze riveted on Gabriella's monitor. And when he followed that gaze, he saw erratic spikes and valleys in the lines on the screen, heard its frenzied beeping, totally out of rhythm.

"Doctor!" the nurse shouted as she rushed to Gabriella's side.

"Not now," the doctor yelled. Then he shouted, "Clear!" and Matthew saw Poppy's body arch off the bed.

"No good," someone said. "Hit her again."

"For the love of God, Dr. Sloane!" the nurse near Gabriella said.

The doctor looked up, started to say something, then stopped as his eyes raked over Gabriella's monitor. Frowning, he handed the paddles over to a nearby set of hands. "Keep working on her, Sally. I'll only be a sec."

Sally took the paddles. "Let's try again," she said. She nodded to the woman who was slowly squeezing air into Poppy's lungs, even as Dr. Sloane crossed the room to Gabriella.

"Clear!" Sally yelled.

This time, Matthew was looking at Gabriella. And he saw *her* body arch off the bed in response to the electric shock jolting through *Poppy's* heart.

Dr. Sloane froze in his tracks and crossed himself.

Sally said, "Wait a minute, wait a minute—"

"We have sinus rhythm, Doctor," a nurse said from near Poppy's side. "She's back."

Dr. Sloane turned to Gabriella's monitor, and Matthew saw it was again bleeping in normal time, with regular patterns in the lines on the screen. "My God, I've never . . . my God!" Sloane looked from one monitor to the other.

So did everyone else.

What they saw, Matthew realized, was two women who looked damn near identical to one another, and two hearts beating out an identical pattern. The beeping of the machines sounded like one louder beep. The patterns on the monitors were a perfect match.

Dr. Sloane said to a nurse, "I want printouts of both EKGs over the past"—he glanced at his watch—"ten minutes." Then he turned to Matthew. "You said Gabriella didn't have a sister. Are you sure? Could these two be sisters—twins?"

"I don't know."

"Hell, even if they were, it wouldn't explain . . ." He looked at the nurse who had first alerted him to Gabriella's condition. The one he'd called Sally.

"Yes, Dr. Sloane," she said. "I saw it, too."

"So did I," Aliyah said.

Dr. Sloane shook his head slowly. "Let's just see to it that they stay stable until we can figure this out." He looked at Matthew. "Son, do you know anything at all about your . . . Poppy, you call her?"

"Her name is Puabi. Poppy's . . . just a nickname."

"Do you know anything about her medical condition?"

He shook his head. "I think she believes she's dying. That her heart is wearing out and that nothing can be done."

"Do you know where she's from? A family doctor? Anything?"

"No. No, I'm sorry. She came here from Maine, but that's not where she's from. She . . . told me once that she was born in the desert. I think it's Iraq nowadays, but . . ." He stopped, unsure of whether to continue. She'd also said she was four thousand years old, an ancient queen, a witch, and some kind of shape-shifter. Was he supposed to tell the old doc all of that, too?

Frowning, Dr. Sloane squeezed his shoulder.

"The baby's still fine," Sally announced, removing her

stethoscope and smoothing the blankets gently back over Gabriella.

"Thank goodness," Aliyah said, as she ever so carefully taped Poppy's IV in place, her eyes tender and caring.

"Good. That's something to cling to, then, isn't it?" Sloane said. "I've got tests to run. Calls to make while we still have phone lines. We may need more expertise than I have to figure this out, young man, but I promise you, I'm going to give it my best shot. For now . . . well, you need to get into those dry clothes. Get warm, and get some rest."

"I'm not leaving them."

Sloane sighed. "I figured you'd say something like that. Stay in here, then, but the rest still goes. I'm going to have nurses watching them both round the clock. Once we get through this damned storm, we'll bring in cardiologists to examine . . . Puabi. Okay?"

Matthew looked at Poppy in the bed, nodded slowly. "Okay."

Dr. Sloane turned to leave. Then he turned back. "Puabi. Wasn't that the name of some ancient queen of . . . Babylon or something?"

"Sumer," Matthew said vaguely. "Four thousand years ago."

"Right. Sumer." He clapped Matthew on the shoulder. "Let's just get them through the storm, okay? Let's just focus on that, and we'll move on from there. All right, Matthew?"

Matthew nodded. But somehow he didn't think there was going to be an aftermath to the storm that approached outside. He felt certain it would sweep down and swallow up his entire world.

11

Hours later, Matthew sat in a chair against the rear wall, with his dead—or was she only partly dead?—wife on his right side and the woman he loved on his left. His child's life seemed to hang in the balance. No matter how often Dr. Sloane assured him that his son would be fine whatever else might happen, Matthew found himself doubting it. How could anything be fine? The two women he'd cared for more than anything else in his life were dying, as if in some twisted brand of cosmic synchronicity. God, it was as if the two were connected somehow, the way their hearts seemed to beat almost as one.

No. Not almost. Not almost at all. He was freaking trapped in some esoteric *Twilight Zone* episode, with no script and no control. Jesus, it was maddening!

Outside, the storm unleashed its full might on the tiny island. It raged. It clawed at the windows and pounded on the walls as if determined to get inside. It didn't take much imagination to think of the storm as some dark-robed angel of death, storming the gates—on its way here to collect a soul or two.

Or three?

"You're not taking them," Matthew whispered. "I'm not gonna let you take them, dammit."

But the storm raged even harder. Something smashed against the windows—a limb, or perhaps a sign ripped from some nearby business. The safety glass shattered but didn't break apart. A corner of something wooden stabbed through, then the wind tore it free, and the rain and wind sluiced in through the hole. Matthew was on his feet instantly, even as one of the nurses rushed in to help. He balled up a spare blanket from the foot of Poppy's bed and crammed it into the hole. The wind stopped rushing in. The rain was blocked out. He lowered his head in a bone-deep sigh of relief . . .

. . . and then the lights went out. The steady beats of the heart monitors stopped, and their screens went dark. The machine that had been pumping air into Gabriella's lungs stopped its hissing.

"Gabriella! God, the baby!"

Immediately, even before Matthew finished shouting in alarm, the lights came back on, as the backup generator kicked in. So did the monitors. But their tones were long and steady, and the lines on their screens, flat.

The life-support machine did not come back on. The nurse, Aliyah, started hitting its buttons, her eyes growing more and more desperate as she tried to make the machine work. Then suddenly the control panel popped and sent a shower of sparks out from it like a fireworks display. Aliyah backed away, shielding her face with her arms.

"Dammit, do something!" Matthew cried. He turned to Poppy, fell to his knees beside the bed, and gripped her cool hand. Her monitor was flat-lined as well, he realized in horror, droning its steady death tone. "Don't go! For the love of God, don't do this, Poppy, please . . ."

"Start CPR!" Sloane shouted. Sally, one other nurse, and a young man crowded around Poppy and followed his instructions. Pumping her chest. Forcing air into her lungs by squeezing a bag. The doctor turned back to Aliyah, who was doing likewise to Gabriella. "Keep her oxygenated or we'll lose the baby!" he shouted toward the door. "Get a surgical tray in here!"

Matthew didn't know whom he was shouting to. The old guy must have rounded up a few more volunteers, or he'd had others here that Matthew hadn't yet encountered. Within seconds an older, white-haired woman was wheeling a tray into the room. She might even have been Mrs. Sloane.

"What the hell is wrong with the machine?" Matthew demanded, still clinging to Poppy's hand, his own tears streaming freely now as he watched Aliyah and Dr. Sloane working frantically on Gabriella. "Why isn't it working?"

The older woman bared Gabriella's belly and was swabbing it with horrible-looking reddish-brown disinfectant. The others still worked over Poppy, stopping every few seconds to try to find a pulse—only to go right back to pumping her chest again.

"Try to stay calm, Matthew," Dr. Sloane said, his voice loud to overcome the noise in the room and the storm raging outside. "We have to take the baby now, and a C-section is a remarkably fast procedure." Sloane looked across the room. "How's Poppy doing?"

They paused in working on her and checked again. "We have a heartbeat, Doctor," Sally reported, with a sigh of relief. "Weak but steady."

"Thank God," Matthew muttered, his head falling forward, his neck like water.

The curtain around Gabriella was pulled shut, and Matthew had no choice but to let them be. Let them work to save his child. He focused his attention on Poppy, sitting close to her, right on the edge of her bed, holding her hand, stroking her hair. "If you can just get through the storm, Poppy. Things will be better then. We're going to find you the best specialists there are. You're going to be . . ."

"We're losing the fetal heartbeat, Doctor!"

The voice from beyond the curtain made Matthew's own heart stand still. Then suddenly Poppy's hand tightened on his. He looked at her, saw her eyes open and clear. She smiled gently at him. "Don't worry about the baby, Matthew. I'm not finished yet."

"God, Poppy," he whispered. "Honey, it's all right. You're going to be all right."

She shook her head slowly. "I'm done, either way. What power I have left . . ." She stopped talking and stared past him, her gaze turning more intense than he'd yet seen it. He followed her gaze and saw the slight gap in the curtains, and Gabriella's lifeless face visible there.

"Scalpel," the doctor said from beyond the curtain. "Hurry, dammit!"

"The baby's back," Aliyah said. She sighed and even laughed slightly. "Must have been a glitch in the monitor."

Poppy's hand on Matthew's went slack. He turned back to her. Her eyes were still open. But she was gone. He knew it in that single glance. The life was gone, the light in her eyes extinguished. Matthew heard her heart monitor's tone turn to a steady drone once more. "No," he cried. "Oh, Poppy, no."

"Keep the oxygen coming," the doctor said. "Stop CPR so I can make the incision."

"Doctor . . . wait. Don't make that cut!" Aliyah said.

"Why the hell not, Nurse?"

"I . . . I'm getting a pulse."

Minutes ticked by, and the storm raged.

Sally and the others at Poppy's bedside worked on her as before, pumping her chest, but it was different this time. Matthew was holding her hand, and he felt the truth with gut-wrenching clarity. This wasn't Poppy anymore. It was as if she'd pulled her tender hand away and left him holding an empty glove. It was just like that. She was gone. God in heaven, she was gone.

Kneeling on the floor beside the bed, he tipped his head skyward. "Why? For the love of God, will somebody please tell me why? Poppy, Poppy . . ." He lowered his head, sobbing now, unashamed. He loved her. And she was gone.

Behind him, the nurse put her hand on his shoulder, and he heard her breath hitch in her throat, as the others who were crowded around Poppy seemed to realize the futility of their desperate attempts to revive her. "I'm so sorry," someone said.

Brushing the tears from his cheeks, he managed to pull himself to his feet again. Leaning over Poppy, he kissed her gently, and then with hands that trembled he closed her lapis-blue eyes.

His stomach in knots, he turned, wondering if he would come away from this night with anything but loss and heartache. His entire body ached with the loss of the only woman he'd ever loved. He parted the curtain, and no one tried to stop him. He looked at Gabriella on the table. At the others standing around her, just staring at her, and at the heart monitor, which was beeping, showing spiked lines instead of a flat one, even though no one was doing CPR, and the life-support system was a smoking, burned-out wreck.

"What's . . . going on?" he asked, unable to speak above a whisper. And then, suddenly, Gabriella opened her mouth and sucked in a harsh, desperately sharp breath, as her body arched itself off the bed.

Then she relaxed again, falling against the pillows.

"Normal sinus rhythm, Doctor." Aliyah said the words, but they were a bare whisper, and her eyes registered sheer disbelief.

"My God," Sloane said, "she's breathing on her own." He turned to the others. "She's *breathing on her own*."

Matthew stared at Gabriella's face, rubbed his eyes, and stared some more. He didn't understand what was happening.

"The heartbeat is getting stronger, Doctor," another nurse said.

Sloane said, "I can't believe this."

Then the impossible happened. Gabriella opened her eyes.

But they were not Gabriella's eyes. They were not ebony. They were a startlingly bright blue, flecked with gold, like lapis stones. "Matthew?" she whispered, and her voice was harsh with disuse.

There was stunned silence in the room. Then a burst of activity as they all bent toward her, whipping out penlights and stethoscopes. Matthew shoved them all away. "Please, please, just . . . just for a second."

They backed away mere inches, Dr. Sloane never taking his eyes off the monitors. Matthew bent toward her, frowning as he searched her face, not seeing Gabriella—seeing Poppy instead. He didn't know how, he didn't know why, he didn't even believe it fully. He glanced toward the bed on the other side of the room, but he could make no sense of it.

He turned back to the woman in the bed, fixed his gaze on her eyes once again. "Tell me your name," he whispered.

She frowned at him. "You know my name. It's Puabi. Even if you do refuse to use it." And her smile was weak. "To be honest, I like when you call me Poppy." Her gaze slid lower, then suddenly widened when she saw the shape of her belly under the blankets. "What—Matthew, what's happening? Why am I . . . where is . . . ?"

She lifted her head from the pillows, glancing across the room to the body in the other bed. "Gabriella?" she whispered. Then she looked up at Matthew again, her eyes round and confused. "Why did we change beds?" she asked. Then she frowned. "Why did we change *clothes*?"

Then slowly, her brows lifted and she met Matthew's eyes. "Oh, by the Gods, Matthew . . . I think I'm in Gabriella's . . ." But she didn't finish the sentence. Instead she grimaced and grabbed her belly.

"What is it? What's wrong?"

Poppy looked back at him. No doubt about it. It was Poppy, not Gabriella. And she said, "I think I'm in labor."

The labor hit hard and fast, and Puabi was already dizzy with confusion. It was as if she were trapped in some kind of dream where everything she had known was changed. Altered. Her senses seemed dulled, as if she were seeing and hearing everything through a filter. Gone were the sharply honed senses of four thousand years of living as an immortal. Gone.

And her heart . . . it beat in her chest powerfully. She'd become adept over the centuries at feeling her heart, knowing its condition. Moments ago, she'd known it was weak, winding down like an old clock, and probably beating its last. She'd known she had very little power or magick left in her, and she had willed every ounce of it to Gabriella's unborn child. Whatever strength she had, she'd consciously sent to him, realizing at last that saving Matthew's son was the mission she'd been meant to accomplish. And that it would be her last deed on Earth.

Now, though, she felt a strong, steady beat in her chest. A healthy heart.

A healthy *mortal* heart.

And with it, an iron manacle of pain, tightening around her belly and lower back. She gritted her teeth and came upright in the bed, and Matthew held her hand and stared at her in shock and wonder. Gods, he must be as confused as she was by all this!

The doctor and his nurses swarmed, and argued. She was too weak for a natural birth. It was too risky. She was too weak for surgery, it could kill her. And the contractions came hard and fast, and one of the nurses nurse said, "Doctor, this baby is coming. Now!"

Matthew leaned closer, his hand fisted around hers, his face close to hers. He couldn't seem to take his eyes off her, kept checking and rechecking to be sure she was who she was. Hell, *she* wasn't even sure who she was anymore. He stroked her hair, bathed her face with cool water. Talked to her as she struggled to give birth, while the storm outside raged on and on. And mingled with the pain were memories, images, and sounds floating through her mind of a past that was not her own. She remembered the day she had told Matthew she was pregnant. She remembered the day they'd been married.

How could that be? She wasn't Gabriella!

Then she was pushing, and all her attention was focused on the task. Nothing else dared distract her.

Finally, what seemed like hours later, she felt the pressure ease in a rush. She fell backward onto the pillows, her hair damp with sweat, her new heart pounding fiercely in her chest, breath rushing in and out of her lungs.

And then a sound, soft and congested, rose up like the most fragile bleat of a newborn lamb. A sound she had longed to hear for longer than any woman ever had. Her newborn child's first cry.

Puabi blinked and met Matthew's eyes. They were wet and locked on hers. And he tore them away only when Aliyah came between them to lower the baby, wet and slick and wrapped in a tiny blanket, into her arms. The nurse said, "I've seen a lot of things. But tonight, I've witnessed my first honest-to-goodness miracle." She smiled, tears rolling down both cheeks. "Welcome back, Gabriella."

Puabi frowned at the name. "But I'm not . . ." she began, but Matthew shook his head at her. She licked her lips. "Thank you."

The nurse backed away, and Matthew leaned close to her, bent to kiss her forehead, and then the baby's. "Our son," he said.

"Our . . . but . . . ohhh," she whispered, losing track of her confusion when she looked at the tiny face, the wrinkled little nose and hazy blue eyes. "Oh, how can this be real?" she whispered. "How can this be real?" Her own tears flooded, and though she tried to contain them, they overpowered her. Her entire body shook with the force of the emotional storm raging inside her every bit as powerfully as the one outside. Sobs bent her over her child, and her tears rained down on his beautiful face.

Aliyah reappeared, easing the baby from her arms. "It's overwhelming, I know. It's all right, honey. We'll take the baby just for a few minutes. The doctor needs to be sure he's a hundred percent. I'll bring him back all clean and dry for you soon. You rest with your husband now. You two have so much to talk about."

Puabi nodded, still sobbing, and Matthew put his arms around her, pulled her close to him, and just held her while she cried.

12

Everyone left the room, though she doubted they had left the clinic, since the storm still threw its temper tantrum outside.

"Matthew," a voice said from the doorway. "My God, I can't believe you survived it."

Poppy looked up and saw her. Murial, standing there, wet from the rain, and vicious. "I see your girlfriend wasn't so lucky," she added with a nod toward the body on the other side of the room. The body that had housed Puabi.

"Think again, Murial," Poppy said. She pushed back the covers, darting a quick glance around the room and seeing the stainless-steel surgical tray, which had been pushed aside but not yet removed.

Murial frowned at her. "Gabriella? But you were braindead."

"You made sure of that, didn't you!"

Matthew rose, standing between Poppy and Murial. "What do you mean by that?"

"Oh, it was no accident that night, Matthew. And it wasn't a suicide attempt, either. This bitch ran me off the road. She pulled me out of the wreckage and bashed my head in with a tire iron. She had a life-support unit in the back of a van, ready and waiting. This was all planned."

"Honey," he whispered. He was facing Murial but darting odd, worried glances at her. "How can you know this?"

"I don't know. But I do. I remember it very clearly. Just as clearly as I remember my days on the throne of Sumer and my time on that island with you." She fought the confusion and went on, letting the words come as they would. "She tossed some other body into the car, torched it, and brought me here, claiming to be my sister. She asked them to keep my body functioning until I could deliver the baby—and then to pull the plug."

"Very good," Murial murmured, stepping forward. Matthew moved toward her, but Poppy got to her feet and stepped around him.

"This is my fight, my love."

"You're weak," he said.

Murial smiled. "Not to mention mortal. Don't bother sacrificing yourself, Gabriella." Then she frowned and looked more closely. "Or is it Puabi?"

"I have a feeling it's both," Poppy replied. "And we'd both die happily before we'd let you touch our child."

Murial looked confused, but only briefly. She kept glancing toward the other bed, with the sheet-draped body, then back at Poppy again.

"What do you want with my son, Murial?" Matthew asked. "What the hell can you possibly want with him?"

She lifted her brows. "I'm sure by now you know what I am," she said. And when he nodded, she continued. "Every witch has a certain gift. It's enhanced to incredible degrees in Immortal ones. Hers used to be the *glamourie*," she said, with a nod toward the bed. "Oh, yes, she could make you see her any way she wished. Mine was the gift of prophecy. I see into the future. Not everything, but certain things. I knew your son would be born with a very special power—one I want to make my own. And there's only one way to do that."

"Over my dead body," Poppy said, and she reached out and snatched the scalpel from the tray. She lunged past Matthew as Murial crouched and whipped out her own dagger.

Footsteps came from the hallway. Poppy saw Aliyah step into view, the baby in her arms.

Murial laughed aloud, the sound long and low and evil.

"Ahh, my delivery is here." She clutched the dagger in her fist, lifting it high, and turned toward the baby.

Poppy screamed and launched herself, even as Matthew did the same.

But at that very instant a horrendous crack and a terrible roar split the air. The entire ceiling came down on them all, leaving a cloud of dust and water. Rain flooded in, and the wind whipped, roared, tore through the place. Curtains flew, objects went sailing around the room, crashing into walls.

She pushed the debris off her. She hurt everywhere, but nothing seemed broken. She got to her feet. Matthew was beside her, his arms around her. And Murial? Poppy glimpsed one pale, bloody hand, sticking out from beneath a massive beam.

She didn't even spare the woman a moment's attention as she climbed over the rubble in search of her child.

Aliyah was still standing, several feet away. She'd turned her back to the storm and was hunched over the baby protectively, and the others were even now rushing to her. Matthew took his son gently and held him very close. He held Poppy to his side with his other arm. "We need to get out of here."

Dr. Sloane gestured them toward the exit. "My truck is right out front. We can make it into town, to the shelter. It'll be safe there."

Matthew nodded, and they all started toward the front door.

Poppy stopped herself. Then she turned back toward the rubble, beneath which Murial lay. "Go on, take the baby," she shouted above the wind and rain. "I need to finish this."

"I'm not going anywhere without you, Poppy. Your son needs you now."

"But—"

"You're finished with that, Poppy. That part of your life is over. Now, come on."

She blinked, and swallowed hard. Could it be true? Would she never have to kill another being again? Never have to carve out a heart to ensure her own survival? Was it even possible?

She didn't have time to find out. More of the roof came down, and Murial was buried under so much rubble that

Puabi realized heavy equipment would be needed to dig her
out. The house shuddered under the force of the storm, and
Matthew pulled her outside. He held her tightly as they raced
for the doctor's SUV. Then they all crowded into it, and Dr.
Sloane drove them over the muddy, rutted roads and through
the fury of the storm toward town.

$\mathcal{D}$*awn broke, and Poppy stood in the warm sunshine*
and the slight tropical breeze, surveying the rubble that had
been the Saba Medical Clinic. She held her son in her arms,
and Matthew stood beside her.

She'd slept like a rock last night, her husband and child
snuggled close. But so far she hadn't so much as changed
the darling baby's diaper. Too many willing volunteers at the
shelter were loathe to see her lift a finger after her ordeal.
She had become a local celebrity—the comatose woman who
had given birth during a storm and somehow returned to life.

"She's gone," Poppy said softly, staring at the collapsed
house, knowing that Murial was no longer trapped beneath
the rubble.

"How can you be so sure?"

"I don't know. I feel it."

"I thought you weren't a witch anymore, Poppy."

She smiled up at him. "I'm not an immortal anymore.
There's a difference."

He led her to a large rock and helped her to sit down on
it. Soon the boat he had sent for would be arriving to carry
them back to Miami, and Poppy would begin her new life—
as a mortal woman, wife, and mother. It would be odd. And
yet, she thought, it was a dream come true.

"Why did she want the baby?" Matthew asked. "I just
can't understand why she would think he would have any
kind of . . . power she might be able to steal."

"I don't know. I don't understand it." The baby whimpered, and Poppy unfastened the front of the borrowed blouse
she wore, held him to her breast, and watched him suckle
with a sense of wondrous ecstasy enveloping her entire body.

Close by her side, Matthew stroked her hair and watched
his child take nourishment. "Poppy, what do you think happened here last night?"

She sighed deeply. "It goes back a lot further than last night," she whispered. "Matthew, when I lost my first child, I think a part of me died with him. The good part. I went mad. I turned into . . . something else. Something dark, without any light at all in me. It was something I was never meant to be. By using the foulest black magic, the darkest of the dark arts, I kept myself alive. For four thousand years I lived on, at the expense of the lives of others. But in all that time, part of me was gone. Part of me, the good part, had moved on without me."

She ran her fingertips over the baby's face. Gods, but it was so soft.

"It was Gabriella," he said softly. "It was her, wasn't it?"

"I think so. I think she was the part of me that moved on. You said yourself that she never seemed whole. That she craved something she couldn't seem to identify, much less obtain. And that resonated so well with me, because I'd always felt the same. She was lightness without dark. I was darkness without light. I think we were reunited last night—somehow, we melded."

He nodded, staring into her eyes. "Two halves . . . of the same soul? The dark and the light?"

She nodded slowly. "Somehow we were put back together. I have my memories now, but I also have hers. I feel complete—for the first time in, in forever."

"But how did it happen?" he asked.

"I don't know. I knew I was dying. I lay there, trying to will my remaining strength and life force into her, to help save your son. I didn't realize it was possible to will my soul to heal and to rejoin its other half as well."

"This is all just . . . it's so . . ."

"Far-fetched. I know. But it's true. I feel it, Matthew, it's all true. I felt it when I set eyes on her. In a way, she truly was my sister. And a part of me."

She could sense him trying to deal with this knowledge. "So are you Gabriella or are you Puabi?"

She shook her head slowly. "I like to think I was reborn last night. You named me, when you pulled me from the sea. Poppy. That's who I am now."

He smiled gently, stroked her hair and kissed her mouth. "I love you. I love you by any name. Whole and well. You're my wife, you know. Legally, you're my wife. Gabriella Fair-child. And the mother of our son." He looked down quickly. "We need a name for him."

"Gabriel," she said. "After the best part of his mother."

He nodded. "I like it."

The baby released his hold on her breast, and Poppy turned him toward her, resting him against her shoulder and patting his back so he would burp. As she did, he squirmed and the blanket fell away.

Poppy looked down—and went still.

On the baby's right hip, clear as day, was a small, berry-colored birthmark in the shape of a crescent moon. The right side. Not the left, but the right. She had given birth to one of the Light Ones. An Immortal High Witch. Not a Dark One, as she had been. He would never need to kill to sustain his life. He'd received immortality as a gift. And suddenly she knew why Murial had wanted him. His heart must be a powerful one, indeed. He was special. And destined for great things.

"It's a miracle we've been given, Poppy," Matthew said, leaning close, replacing the blanket around the baby.

"Oh, Matthew," she whispered. "It's only just the beginning."

Turn the page for an excerpt from
Maggie Shayne's new romantic suspense novel,

THE GINGERBREAD MAN

coming in October from Jove Books!

Holly left the party. She had never done that before in the five consecutive years she and her mother had lived here. It wasn't a part of the detailed plans she'd made for tonight. She'd had it all worked out. After all, annual events weren't as easily controlled as daily ones. You could get into a habit, a routine, of doing certain things in a certain order every day, until it became second nature. But events that only happened once a year took more time. More effort. She was supposed to have spent a half hour catching up with Uncle Marty and Aunt Jen. She was supposed to have taken a minute to talk with Doc Graycloud. And she had planned to have some one on one time with Bethany, too, to start planning that Halloween costume, so she could go in search of a pattern on her Sunday shopping trip with Mom.

But no. No, her well-laid plan was destroyed, her carefully calculated outline of the evening's activities, torn to bits. All because of Vince O'Mally.

What interest could he possibly have in her past?

She walked away from the lake, from the cars in the lot, from the cabins. She walked until the fire's glow no longer reached her. The road was dark. No streetlights, not here. And no stars tonight, either. It was as if the sky matched her mood. Dark.

That cop was up to something. Something involving her, and her past, and that book. That damned book. That damn, damn, damn book. It had triggered something, when she'd heard the title of the missing book. It had set things into motion in her mind, things she'd locked away and managed to keep still for a long, long time.

A little girl voice starting singing in her mind. *Run, run, run, fast as you can—*

"No," Holly whispered. But it came again. *You can't catch me—*

She pressed her hands to her ears, closed her eyes. "No, no, dammit, no!" She wasn't going to think about it, she wasn't. It was in the past, and that was where it belonged. But then she was gone, sinking into an abyss of memory, and suddenly, she was small, and carrying a backpack as she walked. The gravel was replaced by a sidewalk, the night sky, by daylight. And a little girl with dimples and blue eyes and golden blond hair in braids skipped along beside her, clutching a copy of her favorite book in her hands . . . and she was singing . . .

"Run, run, run, fast as you can, can't catch me, I'm the Gingerbread Man."

Ivy sang the words she'd memorized from her favorite story as they walked home from school together. Holly used to walk home alone, but now that Ivy was in kindergarten, she had to walk with her. She was supposed to hold her little sister's hand all the way, but she rarely did so until they got within sight of the house.

"I can't believe you brought that book home, Ivy. It was supposed to be returned to the library before we came back from the lake!"

"I wanted to keep it."

Holly rolled her eyes. "Yeah, but it was on my library card. I only just got it this year. If you don't return your books on time, they don't let you take out any more."

Ivy looked up at her sister, her huge eyes wide. "I didn't mean to get you in trouble, Holly."

Holly softened. The kid looked near tears. "Never mind. I guess it'll be okay so long as we take it back next time we go down to the lake."

"Yeah!" Ivy smiled, her worry gone, and continued walk-

ing with her big sister, until Holly turned left instead of going straight at the end of the block.

"Holly?"

"It's okay, sweetie. I just want to take the long way home this time."

"Why?"

Licking her lips, Holly looked around. "Cause that new boy lives over this way, and I want to go past his house."

Ivy's smile spread wider. "Oooh. You like him, don't you?" she said in a sing song little girl voice. "Ivy and Johnny, sittin' in a tree—"

"Don't even," Holly threatened. "And if you tell a soul, I'll never get you another library book ever again. You hear?"

Ivy giggled, and skipped ahead. "I won't tell." Then she sang. "Holly's got a boyfriend, Holly's got a boyfriend.

They walked down the street they didn't usually take. And then the van came around the corner . . .

"No, no, no, no, no . . ."

"Holly!" Hands gripped her shoulders, shook her. "Holly!"

A sob welled up, she bit her lips, fighting the nightmare of her past, telling herself to pull out of it, but the words burst free anyway. "Mom told us to come straight home!"

"Holly, open your eyes and look at me. Right now." His tone was firm, and level and strong. She opened her eyes. Vince O'Mally was kneeling on the gravel road in front of her, looking at her as if he thought she might be dying. She was sitting down on the side of the road with her hands pressed to her ears. Her face was wet. Really wet. So wet that tears were dripping off her chin onto her blouse.

"What the hell happened to you? Was someone out here? Did they—?"

She held up a hand. He stopped speaking. "I'm okay. I'm okay now." Her hand decided to grip the front of his shirt. She'd been crying so hard her chest kept heaving with spasms, even though she'd forced the floodgates closed. His arms came around her, and she let them. She remained stiff, holding herself together by sheer will. He'd seen her out of control—twice now—but only briefly. It was not pretty. He wouldn't see it again. No one would.

He picked her up, carried her to his car.

She closed her eyes. "What's happening to me?" she asked aloud. More of herself than of him, though. "Why now?"

He opened a car door, set her on the seat, then hurried around to get in the other side. "I'd like to tell you it's all right, Holly, but I'm damned if I can do that until you tell me what the hell is the matter. Did someone—?"

"No." She curled her legs beside her, and turned her face into the soft fabric of the seat. "No one was out on that road but me. Me and my ghosts."

"Look," he said. She felt his eyes on her, sensed his hesitation. Then she felt his hand lower to her hair, very gently. She thought maybe it was shaking just a little. "Look," he said again, more softly this time, "if you tell me about it . . . then maybe I can help." He said it as if the words were being pried out of him.

"No one can help me, but me." She forced her voice level, refused to let it waver. It was broken by the occasional sob hiccuping through her diaphragm but that couldn't be helped. "I thought I was past all this. Apparently I have more work to do. And that's really all you need to know."

Seconds ticked by. She felt him watching her, felt the car moving after a while, took comfort in the darkness. She wished she could curl into it and never emerge. But she couldn't do that. She had beaten the past into submission once. She would simply have to do it again.

And she would do it on her own.

"I need to know a hell of a lot more than that," he said as he drove her to her house. "And I'm afraid I can't take no for an answer, Red."

Magic Like Heat Across My Skin

Laurell K. Hamilton

1

June had come in like its usual hot, sweaty self, but a freak cold front had moved in during the night and the car radio had been full of the record low temperatures. It was only in the low sixties, not that cold, but after weeks of eighty- and ninety-plus, it felt downright frigid. My best friend, Ronnie Sims, and I were sitting in my Jeep with the windows down, letting the unseasonably cool air drift in on us. Ronnie had turned thirty tonight. We were talking about how she felt about the big 3–0, and other girl talk. Considering that she's a private detective and I raise the dead for a living it was pretty ordinary talk. Sex, guys, turning thirty, vampires, werewolves. You know, the usual.

We could have gone inside the house, but there is something about the intimacy of a car after dark that makes you want to linger. Or maybe it was the sweet smell of spring-like air coming through the windows like the caress of some half-remembered lover.

"Okay, so he's a werewolf. No one's perfect," Ronnie said. "Date him, sleep with him, marry him. My vote's for Richard."

"I know you don't like Jean-Claude."

"Don't like him!" Her hands gripped the passenger side

door handle, squeezing it until I could see the tension in her shoulders. I think she was counting to ten.

"If I killed as easily as you do, I'd have killed that son of a bitch two years ago and your life would be a lot less complicated now."

That last was an understatement. But . . . "I don't want him dead, Ronnie."

"He's a vampire, Anita. He *is* dead." She turned and looked at me in the dark. Her soft gray eyes and yellow hair had turned to silver and near white in the cold light of the stars. The shadows and bright reflected light left her face in bold relief, like some modern painting. But the look on her face was almost frightening. There was a fearful determination there.

If it had been me with that look on my face, I'd have warned me not to do anything stupid, like kill Jean-Claude. But Ronnie wasn't a shooter. She'd killed twice, both times to save my life. I owed her. But she wasn't a person who could hunt someone down in cold blood and kill him. Not even a vampire. I knew this about her, so I didn't have to caution her. "I used to think I knew what dead was or wasn't, Ronnie." I shook my head. "The line isn't so clear-cut."

"He seduced you," she said.

I looked away from her angry face and stared at the foil-wrapped swan in my lap. Deirdorfs and Hart, where we'd had dinner, got creative on their doggy bags: foil-wrapped animals. I couldn't argue with Ronnie, and I was getting tired of trying.

Finally, I said, "Every lover seduces you, Ronnie, that's the way it works."

She slammed her hands so hard into the dashboard it startled me and must have hurt her. "Damn it, Anita, it's not the same."

I was starting to get angry, and I didn't want to be angry, not with Ronnie. I had taken her out to dinner to make her feel better, not to fight. Louis Fane, her steady boyfriend, was out of town at a conference, and she was bummed about that, and about turning thirty. So I'd tried to make her feel better, and she seemed determined to make me feel worse.

"Look, I haven't seen either Jean-Claude or Richard for

six months. I'm not dating either of them, so we can skip the lecture on vampire ethics."

"Now that's an oxymoron," she said.

"What is?" I asked.

"Vampire ethics," she said.

I frowned at her. "That's not fair, Ronnie."

"You are a vampire executioner, Anita. You are the one who taught me that they aren't just people with fangs. They are monsters."

I'd had enough. I opened the car door and slid to the edge of the seat. Ronnie grabbed my shoulder. "Anita, I'm sorry. I'm sorry. Please don't be mad."

I didn't turn around. I sat there with my feet hanging out the door, the cool air creeping into the closer warmth of the car.

"Then drop it, Ronnie. I mean drop it."

She leaned over and gave me a quick hug from behind. "I'm sorry. It's none of my business who you sleep with."

I leaned into the hug for a moment. "That's right, it's not." Then I pulled away and got out of the car. My high heels crunched on the gravel of my driveway. Ronnie had wanted us to dress up, so we had. It was her birthday. It wasn't until after dinner that I'd realized her diabolical scheme. She'd had me wear heels and a nice little black skirt outfit. The top was actually, gasp, a well-fitted halter top. Or would that be backless evening wear? However pricey it was, it was still a very short skirt and a halter top. Ronnie had helped me pick the outfit out about a week ago. I should have known her innocent, "oh, let's just both dress up," was a ruse. There had been other dresses that covered more skin and had longer hem lines, but none that camouflaged the belly-band holster that cut across my lower waist. I'd actually taken the holster along with us on the shopping trip, just to be sure. Ronnie thought I was being paranoid, but I don't go anywhere after dark unarmed. Period.

The skirt was just roomy enough and black enough to hide the fact that I wore the belly band and a Firestar 9 mm. The top was heavy enough material, what there was of it, that you really couldn't see the handle of the gun under the cloth. All I had to do was lift the bottom of the top and the gun was right there, ready to be drawn. It was the most user-friendly dressy outfit I'd ever owned. Made me wish they made it in a different color so I could have two of them.

Ronnie's plan had been to go to a club on her birthday. A dance club. Eek. I never went to clubs. I did not dance. But I went in with her. Yes, she got me out on the floor, mainly because her dancing alone was attracting too much unwanted male attention. At least with both of us dancing together the would-be Casanovas stayed at a distance. Though saying I danced was inacurrate. I stood there and sort of swayed. Ronnie danced. She danced like it was her last night on earth and she had to put every muscle to good use. It was spectacular, and a little frightening. There was something almost desperate to it, as if Ronnie felt the cold hand of time creeping up faster and faster. Or maybe that was just me projecting my own insecurities. I'd turned twenty-six early in the year, and, frankly, at the rate I was going, I probably wouldn't have to worry about hitting thirty. Death cures all ills. Well, most of them.

There had been one man who had attached himself to me instead of Ronnie. I didn't understand why. She was a tall leggy blond, dancing like she was having sex with the music. But he offered me drinks. I don't drink. He tried to slow dance. I refused. I finally had to be rude. Ronnie told me to dance with him, at least he was human. I told her that birthday guilt only went so far, and she'd used hers up.

The last thing on God's green earth that I needed was another man in my life. I didn't have a clue what to do with the two I had already. The fact that they were, respectively, a Master Vampire and an Ulfric, werewolf king, was only part of the problem. That fact alone should let you know just how deep a hole I was digging. Or would that be, already have dug? Yeah, already dug. I was about halfway to China and still throwing dirt up in the air.

I'd been celibate for six months. So, as far as I knew, had they. Everyone was waiting for me to make up my mind. Waiting for me to choose, or decide, something, anything.

I'd been a rock for half a year, because I'd stayed away from them. I hadn't seen them, in the flesh anyway. I had returned no phone calls. I had run for the hills at the first hint of cologne. Why such drastic measures? Frankly, because almost every time I saw them, I fell off the chastity wagon. They both had my libido, but I was trying to decide who had my heart. I still didn't know. The only thing I had decided was that it was time to stop hiding. I had to see them and figure out what we were all going to do. I'd decided two weeks ago that I needed to see them. It was the day that I refilled my birth-control pill prescription, and started taking it again. The very last thing I needed was a surprise pregnancy. That the first thing I thought of when I thought of Richard and Jean-Claude was to go back on birth control tells you something about the effect they had on me.

You needed to be on the pill for at least a month to be safe, or as safe as you ever got. Four more weeks, five to be sure, then I'd call. Maybe.

I heard Ronnie's heels running on the gravel. "Anita, Anita, wait, don't be angry."

The thing was, I wasn't angry with her. I was angry with me. Angry that after all these months I still couldn't decide between the two men. I stopped walking and waited for her, huddled in my little black skirt outfit, the little foil swan in my hands. The night had turned cool enough to make me wish I'd worn a jacket. When Ronnie caught up with me I started walking again.

"I'm not mad, Ronnie, just tired. Tired of you, my family, Dolph, Zerbrowski, everyone, being so damned judgmental." My heels hit the sidewalk with a sharp *clack*. Jean-Claude had once said he could tell if I was angry just by the sound of my heels on the floor. "Watch your step. You're wearing higher heels than I am." Ronnie was five feet eight, which meant with heels she was nearly six feet.

I was wearing two-inch heels, which put me at five five. I get a much better workout when Ronnie and I jog together than she does.

The phone was ringing as I juggled the key and the foil-wrapped leftovers. Ronnie took the leftovers, and I shoved the door open with my shoulder. I was running across the floor in my high heels before I remembered that I was on vacation. Which meant whatever emergency was calling at 2:05 in the morning was not my problem, not for another two weeks at least. But old habits die hard, and I was at the phone before I remembered. I actually let the machine pick up while I stood there, heart pounding. I was planning on ignoring it, but . . . but I still stood ready to grab the receiver just in case.

Loud, booming music, and a man's voice. I didn't recognize the music, but I recognized the voice. "Anita, it's Gregory. Nathaniel's in trouble."

Gregory was one of the wereleopards that I'd inherited when I killed their alpha, their leader. As a human, I wasn't really up to the job, but until I found a replacement, even I was better than nothing. Wereanimals without a dominant to protect them were anyone's meat, and if someone moved in and slaughtered them, it would sort of be my fault. So I acted as their protector, but the job was more complicated than I'd ever dreamed. Nathaniel was the problem. All the others were rebuilding their lives since their old leader had been killed, but not Nathaniel. He'd had a hard life: abused, raped, pimped out, and topped. Topped meant he'd been someone's slave—as in sex and pain. He was one of the few true submissives I'd ever met, though, admittedly, my pool of acquaintance was limited.

I cursed softly and picked up the phone. "I'm here, Gregory, what's happened now?" Even to me, my voice sounded tired and half-angry.

"If I had anyone else to call, Anita, I'd call them, but you're it." He sounded tired and angry, too. Great.

"Where's Elizabeth? She was supposed to be riding herd on Nathaniel tonight." I'd finally agreed that Nathaniel could start going out to the dominance and submission clubs if he was accompanied by Elizabeth and at least one other wereleopard. Tonight it had been Gregory riding shotgun, but without Elizabeth, Gregory wasn't dominant enough to keep Nathaniel safe. A normal submissive would have been safe in one of the clubs with someone there to simply say, no thanks, we'll pass. But Nathaniel was one of those rare subs who are almost incapable of saying no, and there had been hints made that his idea of pain and sex could be very extreme. Which meant that he might say yes to things that were very, very bad for him. Wereanimals can take a lot of injury and not be permanently damaged, but there is a limit. A healthy bottom will say *stop* when he's had too much or he feels something bad happening, but Nathaniel wasn't that healthy. So he had keepers with him to make sure no one really bad got hold of him. But it was more than that. A good dominant trusts his sub to say *when* before the damage is too great. The dom trusts the sub to know his own body and have enough self-preservation to call out before he is in past what his body can take. Nathaniel did not come with that safety feature, which meant a dominant with the best of intentions could end up hurting him badly before realizing Nathaniel wouldn't help himself.

I actually had accompanied Nathaniel a few times. As his Nimir-ra it was sort of my job to interview prospective . . . keepers. I'd gone prepared for the clubs to be one of the lower circles of hell and had been pleasantly shocked. I'd had more trouble with sexual propositions in a normal bar on a Saturday night. In the clubs everyone was very careful not to impose on you or to be seen as pushy. It was a small community, and if you got a reputation for being obnoxious, you could find yourself blacklisted, with no one to play with. I'd found the people in the scene were polite, and once you made it clear you were not there to play, no one bothered you, except tourists. Tourists were posers, people not really into the scene, who liked to dress up and frequent the clubs. They didn't know the rules and hadn't bothered to ask. They probably thought a woman who would come to a place like this would do anything. I'd persuaded them differently. But I'd had to stop going with Nathaniel. The other wereleopards said I gave off so much dominant vibe that no dominant would ever approach Nathaniel while I was with him. Though we'd had offers for ménage à trois of every description. I felt like I needed a button that said, "No, I don't want to have a bondage three-way with you, thanks for asking, though."

Elizabeth had supposedly been dominant, but not too much to take Nathaniel out and try to pick him up a . . . date.

"Elizabeth left," Gregory said.

"Without Nathaniel?" I made it a question.

"Yes."

"Well, that just fries my bacon," I said.

"What?" he asked.

"I'm angry with Elizabeth."

"It gets better," he said.

"How much better can it be, Gregory? You all assured me

that these clubs were safe. A little bondage, a little light slap and tickle. You all convinced me that I couldn't keep Nathaniel away from it indefinitely. You said that they had ways to monitor the area so no one could possibly get hurt. That's what you and Zane and Cherry told me. Hell, I've seen it myself. There are safety monitors everywhere, it's safer than some dates I've had, so what could have possibly gone wrong?"

"We couldn't have anticipated this," he said.

"Just get to the end of the story, Gregory, the foreplay is getting tedious."

There was silence for longer than there should have been, just the overly loud music. "Gregory, are you still there?"

"Gregory is indisposed," a man's voice said.

"Who is this?"

"I am Marco, if that helps you, though I doubt that it does." His voice was cultured—American, but upper crusty.

"New in town, are you?" I asked.

"Something like that," he said.

"Welcome to town. Make sure you go up in the Arch while you're here, it's a nice view. But what has your recent arrival in St. Louis got to do with me and mine?"

"We didn't realize it was your pet we had at first. He wasn't the one we were hunting for, but now that we have him, we're keeping him."

"You can't 'keep' him," I said.

"Come down and take him away from us, if you can." That strangely smooth voice made the threat all the more effective. There was no anger, nothing personal. It sounded like business, and I had no clue what it was about.

"Put Gregory back on," I said.

"I don't think so. He's enjoying some personal time with my friends right now."

"How do I know he's still alive?" My voice was as unemotional as his. I wasn't feeling anything yet; it was too sudden, too unexpected, like coming in on the middle of a movie.

"No one's dead, yet," the man said.

"How do I know that?"

He was quiet for a second, then, "What sort of people are

you used to dealing with, that you would ask if we've killed him first thing?"

"It's been a rough year. Now put Gregory on the phone, because until I know he's alive, and he tells me the others are, this negotiation is stalled."

"How do you know we are negotiating?" Marco asked.

"Call it a hunch."

"My, you are direct."

"You have no idea how direct I can be, Marco. Put Gregory on the phone."

There was the music-filled silence, and more music; but no voices. "Gregory, Gregory, are you there? Is anyone there?" Shit, I thought.

"I'm afraid that your kitty-cat won't squawl for us. A point of pride, I think."

"Put the reciever to his ear and let me talk to him."

"As you wish."

More of the loud music. I spoke as if I was sure that Gregory was listening. "Gregory, I need to know you're alive. I need to know that Nathaniel and everyone else is alive. Talk to me, Gregory."

His voice came squeezed tight, as if he were gritting his teeth. "Yesss."

"Yes, what, they're all alive?"

"Yess."

"What are they doing to you?"

He screamed into the phone, and the sound raised the hairs on my neck and danced down my arms in goose bumps. The sound stopped abruptly. "Gregory, Gregory!" I was yelling against the techno-beat of the music, but no one was answering.

Marco came back on the line. "They are all alive, if not quite well. The one they call Nathaniel is a lovely young man, all that long auburn hair and the most extraordinary violet eyes. So pretty, it would be a shame to spoil all that beauty. Of course, this one is lovely too, blond, blue-eyed. Someone told me that they both work as strippers? Is that true?"

I wasn't numb anymore, I was scared, and angry, and I still had not a clue to why this was happening. My voice came out almost even, almost calm. "Yeah, it's true. You're new in town, Marco, so you don't know me. But trust me, you don't want to do this."

"Perhaps not, but my alpha does."

Ah, shapeshifter politics. I hated shapeshifter politics. "Why? The wereleopards are no threat to anyone."

"Ours is not to reason why, ours is but to do and die."

A literate kidnapper, refreshing. "What do you want, Marco?"

"My alpha wants you to come down and rescue your cats, if you can."

"What club are you at?"

"Narcissus in Chains." And he hung up.

2

"Damn it!"

"What's happened?" Ronnie asked. I'd almost forgotten her. She didn't belong in this part of my life, but there she was, leaning against the kitchen cabinets, searching my face, looking worried.

"I'll take care of it."

She gripped my arm. "You gave me this speech about wanting your friends back, about not wanting to push us all away. Did you mean it, or was it just talk?"

I took a deep breath and let it out. I told her what the other side of the conversation had been.

"And you don't have any clue what this is about?" she asked.

"No, I don't."

"That's odd. Usually stuff like this builds up, it doesn't just drop out of the blue."

I nodded. "I know."

"Star 69 will ring back whatever number just called you."

"What good will that do?"

"It will let you know if they're really at this club, or whether it's just a trap for you."

"Not just another pretty face, are you?" I said.

She smiled. "I'm a trained detective. We know about these

things." The humor didn't quite reach her eyes, but she was trying.

I dialed, and the phone rang for what seemed forever, then another male voice answered, "Yeah."

"Is this Narcissus in Chains?"

"Yeah, who's this?"

"I need to speak with Gregory?"

"Don't know any Gregory," he said.

"Who is this?" I asked.

"This is a freaking pay phone, lady, I just picked up." Then he hung up, too. It seemed to be my night for it.

"They called from a pay phone at the club," I said.

"Well, at least you know where they are," Ronnie said.

"Do you know where the the club is?" I asked.

Ronnie shook her head. "Not my kind of scene."

"Mine either." In fact the only card-carrying dominance and submission players that I knew personally were all at the club waiting to be saved.

Who did I know that might know where the club was, and something about its reputation? I couldn't trust what the wereleopards had told me about it being a safe place. Obviously, they'd been wrong.

One name sprang to mind. The only one I knew to call that might know where Narcissus in Chains was, and what kind of trouble I'd be in if I went inside. Jean-Claude. Since I was dealing with shapeshifter politics, it might have made sense to call Richard, with him being a werewolf and all. But the shapeshifters were a very clannish lot. One type of animal rarely crossed boundaries to help another. Frustrating, but true. The exception was the treaty between the werewolves and the wererats, but everyone else was left to fend, and squabble, and bleed, among themselves. Oh, if some small group got out of hand and attracted too much unwanted police attention, the wolves and rats would discipline them, but short of that, no one seemed to want to interfere with each other. That was one of the reasons I was still stuck baby-sitting the wereleopards.

Also, Richard didn't know any more about the D and S subculture than I did, maybe less. If you're wanting to ask questions about the sexual fringe, Jean-Claude is definitely your guy. He may not participate, but he seems to know who's doing what, and to whom, and where. Or I hoped he did. If it had just been my life at stake, I probably wouldn't have called either of the boys, but if I got killed doing this, that left no one to rescue Nathaniel and the rest. Unacceptable.

Ronnie had kicked off her high heels. "I didn't bring my gun, but I'm sure you have a spare."

I shook my head. "You're not going."

Anger makes her gray eyes the color of storm clouds. "The hell I'm not."

"Ronnie, these are shapeshifters, and you're human."

"So are you," she said.

"Because of Jean-Claude's vampire marks, I'm a little more than that. I can take damage that would kill you."

"You can't go in there alone," she said. Her arms were crossed under her breasts, her face set in angry, stubborn lines.

"I don't plan on going in alone."

"It's because I'm not a shooter, isn't it?"

"You don't kill easily, Ronnie, no shame in that, but I can't take you into a gang of shapeshifters unless I know that you'll shoot to kill if you have to." I gripped her upper arms. She stayed stiff and angry under my touch. "It would kill a piece of me to lose you, Ronnie. It would kill a bigger piece to know that you died because of some shit of mine. You can't hesitate with these people. You can't treat them like they're human. If you do, you die."

She was shaking her head. "Call the police."

I stepped away from her. "No."

"Damn it, Anita, damn it!"

"Ronnie, there are rules, and one of those rules is you don't take pack or pard business to the police." The main reason for that rule was that the police tended to frown on fights for dominance that ended with dead bodies on the ground, but no need to tell Ronnie that.

"It's a stupid rule," she said.

"Maybe, but it's still the way business is done with the shifters, no matter what flavor they are."

She sat down at the small two-seater breakfast table, on its little raised platform. "Who's going to be your backup then? Richard doesn't kill any easier than I do."

That was half true, but I let it slide. "No, I want someone at my back tonight who will do what needs doing, no flinching."

Her eyes were dark, dark with anger. "Jean-Claude." She made his name a curse.

I nodded.

"Are you sure he didn't plan this to get you back into his life, excuse me, death?"

"He knows me too well to screw with my people. He knows what I'd do if he hurt them."

Puzzlement flowed through the anger, softening her eyes, her face. "I hate him, but I know you love him. Could you really kill him? Could you really stare down the barrel of a gun and pull the trigger on him?"

I just looked at her, and I knew without a mirror that my eyes had grown distant, cold. It's hard for brown eyes to be cold, but I'd been managing it lately.

Something very like fear slid behind her eyes. I don't know if she was afraid for me, or of me. I preferred the first to the last. "You could do it. Jesus, Anita. You've known Jean-Claude longer than I've known Louie. I could never hurt Louie, no matter what he did."

I shrugged. "It would destroy me to do it, I think. It's not like I'd live happily ever after, if I survived at all. There's a very real chance that the vampire marks would drag me down to the grave with him."

"Another good reason not to kill him," she said.

"If he's behind the scream that Gregory gave over the phone, then he'll need better reasons to keep breathing than love, or lust, or my possible death."

"I don't understand that, Anita. I don't understand that at all."

"I know," I said. And I thought to myself it was one of the reasons Ronnie and I hadn't been seeing as much of each other as we once had. I got tired of explaining myself to her. No, of justifying myself to her.

You're my friend, my best friend, I thought. But I don't understand you anymore.

"Ronnie, I can't arm wrestle shapeshifters and vampires. I will lose a fair fight. The only way I survive, the only way my leopards survive, is because the other shifters fear me.

They fear my threat. I'm only as good as my threat, Ronnie."

"So you'll go down there and kill them."

"I didn't say that."

"But you will."

"I'll try to avoid it," I said.

She tucked her knees up, wrapping her arms around those long legs. She'd managed to get a tiny pick in one of the hose; the hole was shiny with clear nail polish. She'd carried the polish in her purse for just such emergencies. I'd carried a gun and hadn't even taken a purse.

"If you get arrested, call, and I'll bail you out."

I shook my head. "If I get caught wasting three or more people in a public area, there won't be any bail tonight. The police probably won't even finish questioning me until long past dawn."

"How can you be so calm about this?" she asked.

I was beginning to remember why Ronnie and I had started drifting apart. I'd had almost the exact conversation with Richard once when an assassin had come to town to kill me. I gave the same answer. "Having hysterics won't help anything, Ronnie."

"But you're not angry about it."

"Oh, I am angry," I said.

She shook her head. "No, I mean you're not outraged that this is happening. You don't seem surprised, not like . . ." She shrugged. ". . . not like you should be."

"You mean not like you would be." I held up a hand before she could answer. "I don't have time to debate moral philosophy, Ronnie." I picked up the phone. "I'm going to call Jean-Claude."

"I keep urging you to dump the vampire and marry Richard, but maybe there's more than one reason why you can't let him go."

I dialed the number for Circus of the Damned from memory, and Ronnie just kept talking to my back. "Maybe you're not willing to give up a lover who's colder than you are."

The phone was ringing. "There are clean sheets on the guest bed, Ronnie. Sorry I won't be able to share girl talk tonight." I kept my back to her.

I heard her stand in a crinkle of skirts and knew when she walked out. I kept my back facing the room until I knew she was gone. It wouldn't do either of us any good to let her see me cry.

3

Jean-Claude wasn't at the Circus of the Damned. The voice on the other end of the phone at the Circus didn't recognize me and wouldn't believe I was Anita Blake, Jean-Claude's sometimes sweetie. So I'd been reduced to calling his other businesses. I'd tried Guilty Pleasures, his strip club, but he wasn't there. I tried Danse Macabre, his newest enterprise, but I was beginning to wonder if Jean-Claude had simply told everyone that he wasn't in if I called.

The thought bothered me a lot. I'd worried that after so long Richard might finally tell me to go to hell, that he'd had enough of my indecision. It had never occurred to me that Jean-Claude might not wait. If I was so unsure how I felt about him, why was my stomach squeezed tight with a growing sense of loss? The feeling had nothing to do with the wereleopards and their problems. It had everything to do with me and the fact that I suddenly felt lost. But it turned out he was at Danse Macabre, and he took my call. I had a moment for my stomach to unclench and my breath to ease out, then he was on the phone, and I was struggling to keep my metaphysical shields in place.

I hated metaphysics. Preternatural biology is still biology, metaphysics is magic, and I'm still not comfortable with it. For six months when I wasn't working, I was meditating, studying with a very wise psychic named Marianne, learning ritual magic, so I could control my God-given abilities. And so I could block the marks that bound me to Richard and Jean-Claude. An aura is like your personal protection, your personal energy. When it's healthy it keeps you safe like skin, but you get a hole in it, and infection can get inside. My aura had two holes in it, one for each of the men. I suspected that their auras had holes in them, too. Which put us all at risk. I'd blocked up my holes. Then only a few weeks ago, I'd come up against a nasty creature, a would-be god, a new category, even for me. It had been powerful enough to strip all my careful work away, leaving me raw and open again. Only the intervention of a local witch had saved me from being eaten from the aura down. I didn't have six more months of celibacy, meditation, and patience in me. The holes were there, and the only way to fill them was with Jean-Claude and Richard. That's what Marianne said, and I trusted her in a way that I trusted few others.

Jean-Claude's voice hit me over the phone like a velvet slap. My breath caught in my throat, and I could do nothing but feel the flow of his voice, the presence of him, like something alive, flowing over my skin. His voice has always been one of Jean-Claude's best things, but this was ridiculous. This was over the phone, how could I possibly see him in person and maintain my shields, let alone my composure?

"I know you are there, *ma petite*. Did you call merely to hear the sound of my voice?"

That was closer to the truth than was comfortable. "No, no." I still couldn't gather my thoughts. I was like an athlete who had let her training go. I just couldn't lift the same amount of weight, and there was weight to wading through Jean-Claude's power.

When I still didn't say anything, he spoke again. "*Ma petite,* to what do I owe this honor? Why have you deigned to call me?" His voice was bland, but there was a hint of something in it. Reproach perhaps.

I guess I had it coming. I rallied the troops and tried to sound like an intelligent human being, not always one of my best things. "It's been six months . . ."

"I am aware of that, *ma petite*."

He was being condescending. I hated that. It made me a

little angry. The anger helped clear my head a little. "If you'll stop interrupting, I'll tell you why I called."

"My heart is all aflutter with anticipation."

I wanted to hang up. He was being an asshole, and part of me thought I might deserve the treatment, which made me even angrier. I'm always angriest when I think I'm in the wrong. I'd been a coward for months, and I was still a coward. I was afraid to be close to him, afraid of what I'd do. Damn it, Anita, get ahold of yourself. "Sarcasm is my department," I said.

"And what is my department?"

"I'm about to ask you for a favor," I said.

"Really?" He said it as if he might not grant it.

"Please, Jean-Claude, I'm asking for help. I don't do that often."

"That is certainly true. What would you have of me, *ma petite*? You know that you have but to ask, and it will be yours. No matter how angry I may be with you."

I let that comment go, because I didn't know what to do about it. "Do you know a club called Narcissus in Chains?"

He was quiet for a second or two. *"Oui."*

"Can you give me directions and meet me there?"

"Do you know what sort of a club this place is?"

"Yeah."

"Are you sure?"

"It's a bondage club, I know."

"Unless the last six months has changed you greatly, *ma petite,* that is not one of your preferences."

"Not mine, no."

"Your wereleopards are misbehaving again?"

"Something like that." I told him what had happened.

"I do not know this Marco."

"I didn't figure you did."

"But you did think that I knew where the club was?"

"I was hoping."

"I will meet you there with some of my people. Or will you allow only me to ride to your rescue?" He sounded amused now, which was better than angry, I guess.

"Bring who you need."

"You trust my judgment?"

"In this, yeah."

"But not in all things," he said softly.

"I don't trust anyone in all things, Jean-Claude."

He sighed. "So young to be so . . . jaded."

"I'm cynical, not jaded."

"And the difference is what, *ma petite*?"

"You're jaded."

He laughed then, the sound caressing me like the brush of a hand. It made things low in my body clench. "Ah," he said, "that explains all the differences."

"Just give me directions, please." I added the please to speed things along.

"They will not harm your wereleopards too greatly, I think. The club is run by shapeshifters, and they will smell too much blood and take matters into their own hands. It is one of the reasons Narcissus in Chains is no-man's-land, a neutral place for the fringe of our groups. Your leopards were right, it is usually a very safe place."

"Well, Gregory wasn't screaming because he felt safe."

"Perhaps not, but I know the owner. Narcissus would be very angry if someone became overzealous in his club."

"Narcissus, I don't know the name. Well, I know the Greek mythology stuff, but I don't recognize it as local."

"I would not expect you to, he does not often leave his club. But I will call him, and he will patrol your cats for you. He will not rescue them, but he will make sure no further damage is done."

"You trust Narcissus to do this?"

"Oui."

Jean-Claude had his faults, but if he trusted someone, he was usually right. "Okay. And thank you."

"You are most welcome." He drew a breath then said quietly, "Would you have called if you had not needed my help? Would you ever have called?"

I'd been dreading this question from either Jean-Claude or Richard. But I finally had an answer, "I'll answer your question as best I can, but call it a hunch, it may be a long conversation. I need to know my people are safe before we start dissecting our relationship."

"Relationship? Is that what we have?" His voice was very dry.

"Jean-Claude."

"No, no, *ma petite,* I will call Narcissus now and save your cats but only if you promise that when I call back we will finish this conversation."

"Promise."

"Your word," he said.

"Yes."

"Very well, *ma petite,* until we speak again." He hung up.

I hung up the phone and stood there. Was it cowardly to want to call someone else, anyone else, so the phone would be busy and we wouldn't have to have our little talk? Yeah, it was cowardly, but tempting. I hated talking about my personal life, especially to the people most intimately involved in it. I had just about enough time to change out of the skirt outfit when the phone rang. I jumped and answered it with my pulse in my throat. I was really dreading this conversation.

"Hello," I said.

"Narcissus will see to your cats' safety. Now, where were we?" He was silent for a heartbeat. "Oh, yes, would you ever have called if you had not needed my help?"

"The woman I'm studying with . . ."

"Marianne," he said.

"Yes, Marianne. Anyway, she says that I can't keep blocking the holes in my aura. That the only way to be safe from preternatural creepy-crawlies is to fill the holes with what they were meant to hold."

Silence on the other end of the phone. Silence for so long that I said, "Jean-Claude, you still there?"

"I am here."

"You don't sound happy about this."

"Do you know what you are saying, Anita?" It was always a bad sign when he used my real name.

"I think so."

"I want this very clear between us, *ma petite.* I do not want you coming back to me later, crying that you did not understand how tightly this would bind us. If you allow Richard and me to truly fill the marks upon your . . . body, we will share our auras. Our energy. Our magic."

"We're already doing that, Jean-Claude."

"In part, *ma petite,* but those are side effects of the marks. This will be a willing, knowledgeable joining. Once done, I do not think it can be undone without great damage to all of us."

It was my turn to sigh. "How many vampire challenges to your authority have there been while I've been off meditating?"

"A few," he said, voice cautious.

"More than a few I'd bet, because they sensed that your defenses are not complete. You had trouble backing them down without killing them, didn't you?"

"Let us say that I am glad that there were no serious challengers over the last year."

"You'd have lost without Richard and me to back you up, and you couldn't shield yourself without us there to touch. That worked when I was in town with you. Touching, being with each other helped us plug in to each other's power. It offset the problem."

"*Oui,*" he said, softly.

"I didn't know, Jean-Claude. I'm not sure it would have made a difference, but I didn't know. God, Richard must be desperate, he doesn't kill like we do. His bluff is all that keeps the werewolves from tearing each other apart, and with two gaping holes in his most intimate defenses . . ." I let my voice trail off, but I still remembered the cold horror I'd felt when I realized how much I'd endangered all of us.

"Richard has had difficulties, *ma petite*. But we each have only one chink in our armor, the one that only you can heal. He was driven to merge his energies with mine. As you say, his bluff is very important to him."

"I didn't know, and I'm sorry for that. All I've been thinking about was how scared I was of being overwhelmed by the two of you. Marianne told me the truth when she thought I was ready to hear it."

"And are you done being frightened of us, *ma petite*?" His voice was careful when he asked, as if he were carrying a very full cup of very hot liquid up a long and narrow staircase.

I shook my head, realized he couldn't see it, and said, "I'm not brave. I'm pretty much terrified. Terrified that if I do this, there is no going back, that maybe I'm fooling myself about a choice. Maybe there is no choice and hasn't been for a long time. But however we end up arranging the bedrooms,

I can't let us all go around with gaping metaphysical wounds. Too many things will sense the weakness and exploit it."

"Like the creature you met in New Mexico," he said, voice still as cautious as I'd ever heard it.

"Yeah," I said.

"Are you saying that tonight you will agree to letting us merge the marks, that we will at last close these, as you so colorfully put it, wounds?"

"If it doesn't endanger my leopards, yeah. We need to do it as soon as possible. I'd hate to make the big decision and then have one of us get killed before we could batten down the hatches."

I heard him sigh, as if some great tension had left him. "You do not know how long I have waited for you to understand all this."

"You could have told me."

"You would not have believed me. You would have thought it was another trick to bind you closer to me."

"You're right, I wouldn't have believed you."

"Will Richard be meeting us at the club, as well?"

I was quiet for a heartbeat. "No, I'm not going to call him."

"Why ever not? It is a shapeshifter difficulty more than a vampire one."

"You know why not."

"You fear he will be too squeamish to allow you to do what needs doing to save your leopards."

"Yeah."

"Perhaps," Jean-Claude said.

"You aren't going to tell me to call him?"

"Why would I ask you to invite my chief rival for your affections to this little tête-à-tête? That would be foolish. I am many things, but foolish is not one of them."

That was certainly true. "Okay, give me directions, and I'll meet you and your people at the club."

"First, *ma petite,* what are you wearing?"

"Excuse me?"

"Clothes, *ma petite,* what clothes are you wearing?"

"Is this a joke? Because I don't have time . . ."

"It is not an idle question, *ma petite.* The sooner you answer, the sooner we can all leave."

I wanted to argue, but if Jean-Claude said he had a point he probably did. I told him what I was wearing.

"You surprise me, *ma petite*. With a little effort it should do nicely."

"What effort?"

"I suggest you add boots to your ensembles. The ones I purchased for you would do very well."

"I am not wearing five-inch spikes anywhere, Jean-Claude. I'd break an ankle."

"I planned on you wearing those boots just for me, *ma petite*. I was thinking of the other boots with the milder heels that I bought when you were so very angry about the others."

Oh. "Why do I have to change shoes?"

"Because, delicate flower that you are, you have the eyes of a policeman, and so it would be better if you wore leather boots instead of high heels. It would be better if you remember that you are trying to move through the club as quickly and smoothly as possible. No one will help you find your leopards if they think you are an outsider, especially a policeman."

"Nobody ever mistakes me for a cop."

"No, but they begin to mistake you for something that smells of guns and death. Look harmless tonight, *ma petite*, until it is time to be dangerous."

"I thought this friend of yours, this Narcissus, would just escort us in."

"He is not my friend, and I told you the club is neutral ground. Narcissus will see that no great harm comes to your cats, but that is all. He will not let you come barging in to his world like the proverbial bull in the china shop. That, he will not allow, nor will he allow us to bring in a small army of our own. He is the leader of the werehyenas, and they are the only army allowed inside the club. There is no Ulfric, or Master of the City, within its walls. You have only the dominance you bring with you and your body to see you through."

"I'll have a gun," I said.

"But a gun will not get you into the upper rooms."

"What will?"

"Trust me, I will find a way."

I didn't like the sound of that at all. "Why is it that most of the time whenever I ask you for help, it's never a case where we can just run in and start shooting?"

"And why is it, *ma petite,* that when you do not invite me that it is almost always a case where you run in and shoot everything that moves?"

"Point taken," I said.

"What are your priorities for the night?" he asked.

I knew what he meant. "I want the wereleopards safe."

"And if they have been harmed?"

"I want vengeance."

"More than their safety?"

"No, safety first, vengeance is a luxury."

"Good. And if one, or more, is dead?"

"I don't want any of us going to jail, but eventually if not tonight, another night, they die." I listened to myself say it, and knew that I meant it.

"There is no mercy in you, *ma petite.*"

"You say that like it's a bad thing."

"No, it is merely an observation."

I stood there, holding the phone, waiting to be shocked at what I was proposing. But I wasn't. I said, "I don't want to kill anyone if I don't have to."

"That is not true, *ma petite.*"

"Fine, if they've killed my people, I want them dead. But I decided in New Mexico that I didn't want to be a sociopath, so I'm trying to act as if I'm not. So let's try to keep the body count low tonight, okay?"

"As you wish," he said, then he added, "Do you really think that you can change the nature of what you are merely by wishing it?"

"Are you asking if I can stop being a sociopath, since I already am one?"

A moment of silence, then, "I think that is what I'm asking."

"I don't know, but if I don't pull myself back from the brink soon, Jean-Claude, there won't be any going back."

"I hear fear in your voice, *ma petite.*"

"Yeah, you do."

"What do you fear?"

"I fear that by giving in to you and Richard that I'll lose myself. I fear that by not giving in to you and Richard I'll lose one of you. I fear that I'll get us killed because I'm thinking too much. I fear that I'm already a sociopath and there *is* no going back. Ronnie said that one of the reasons that I can't give you up and just settle down with Richard is that I can't give up a boyfriend that's colder than I am."

"I am sorry, *ma petite*." I wasn't sure exactly what he was apologizing for, but I accepted it anyway.

"Me, too. Give me directions to the club, I'll meet you there."

He gave me directions, and I read them back to him. We hung up. Neither of us said good-bye. Once upon a time we'd have ended the conversation with *je t'aime*, I love you. Once upon a time.

4

The club was over the river on the Illinois side, along with most of the other questionable clubs. Vampire-run businesses got a grandfather clause to operate in St. Louis proper, but the rest of the human-run clubs—and lycanthropes still counted legally as human—had to go into Illinois to avoid pesky zoning problems. Some of the zoning problems weren't even on the books, weren't even laws at all. But it was strange how many problems the bureaucrats could find when they didn't want a club in their fair city. If the vampires weren't such a big draw for tourists, the bureaucrats'd have probably found a way to get rid of them, too.

I finally found parking about two blocks from the club. It meant a walk to the club in an area of town that most women wouldn't want to be alone in after dark. Of course, most women wouldn't be armed. A gun doesn't cure all ills, but it's a start. I also had a knife sheath around each calf, very high up, so that the hilts came up on the side of my knees. I wasn't really comfortable that way, but I couldn't think of any other place to put knives so I could get to them easily. There was a very good chance I'd have bruises on my knees after tonight. Oh, well. I also had a black belt in Judo, and was making progress in Kenpo, a type of karate, one with fewer power moves and more moves using balance. I was as prepared as I could get for the wilds of the big city.

Of course, I usually don't walk around looking like bait. My skirt was so short that even with boots that came up to mid-thigh there was a good inch between the hem and the top of the boots. I'd put a jacket on for the drive, but had left it in the car because I didn't want to be carrying it around all night. I'd been in just enough clubs, whatever flavor they were, to know that inside it would be hot. So the goose bumps that traveled over my bare back and arms weren't from fear, but from the damp, chill air. I forced myself not to rub my arms as I walked and to at least look like I wasn't cold or uncomfortable. Actually the boots only had two-inch heels, and they were comfortable to walk in. Not as comfortable as my Nikes, but then, what is? But for dress shoes, the boots weren't bad. If I could have left the knives home, they'd have been peachy.

There was one other bit of protection that I'd added. Metaphysical shields come in different varieties. You can shield yourself with almost anything; metal, rock, plants, fire, water, wind, earth, etc. . . . Everyone has different shields because it's a very individual choice. It has to work for your own personal mind-set. You can have two psychics both using stone, but the shields won't be the same. Some people simply visualize rock, the thought of it, its essence, and that's sufficient. If something tries to attack them, they are safe behind the thought of rock. Another psychic might see a stone wall, like a garden wall around an old house, and that would do the same thing. For me, the shield had to be a tower. All shields are like bubbles that surround you completely, just like circles of power. I'd always understood this when I raised the dead, but for shielding I needed to see it in my head. So I imagined a stone tower, completely enclosed, no windows, no chinks, smooth and dark inside with only what I allowed in or out. Talking about shielding always made me feel like I was having a psychotic break and sharing my delusions. But it worked, and when I didn't shield, things tried to hurt me. It had only been in the last two weeks that Marianne had discovered that I hadn't really understood shielding at all. I'd thought it was just a matter of how powerful your aura was and how you could reinforce it. She said the only reason I'd been able to get by with that for as long as I had was that I was simply that powerful. But the shielding goes *outside* the aura like a wall around a castle, an extra defense. The innermost defense is a healthy aura. Hopefully by the end of the night I'd have one of those.

I turned the corner and found a line of people that stretched down the block. Great, just what I needed. I didn't stop at the end of the line, I kept walking toward the door, hoping I'd think of something to tell the doorperson when I got there. I didn't have time to wait through all this. I was about halfway up the line when a figure pushed out of the crowd and called my name.

It took me a second to recognize Jason. First, he'd cut his baby-fine blond hair short, businessman short. Second, he was wearing a sheer silver mesh shirt and a pair of pants that seemed mostly made of the same stuff. Only a thin line of solid silver ran over his groin. The outfit was so eye-catching that it took me a moment to realize just how sheer the cloth was. What I was really seeing wasn't the silver, but Jason's skin through a veil of glitter. The outfit, which left precious little to the imagination, ended in calf-high gray boots.

I had to make myself look at his face, because I was still shaking my head over the outfit. The outfit didn't look comfortable, but of course, Jason rarely complained about his clothes. He was like Jean-Claude's little dress-up werewolf, as well as morning snack. Sometimes bodyguard and sometimes a fetch-and-carry boy. Who else could Jean-Claude get to stand out in the cold, nearly naked?

Jason's eyes looked bigger, bluer somehow, without all the hair to distract your eye. His face looked older with the shorter hair, the bone structure cleaner, and I realized that Jason was perilously close to that line between cute and handsome. He'd been nineteen when we met. Twenty-two looked better on him. But the outfit—there was nothing to do but grin at the outfit.

He was grinning at me, too. I think we were both happy to see each other. In leaving Richard and Jean-Claude I'd left their people behind, too. Jason was Richard's pack member, and Jean-Claude's lap wolf.

"You look like a pornographic space man. If you were wearing street clothes, you might have gotten a hug," I said.

His smile flashed even wider. "I guess I'm dressed for

punishment. Jean-Claude told me to wait for you and take you in. My hand's already got a stamp on it so we can just go straight inside."

"A little cold for the clothes, isn't it?"

"Why do you think I was standing deep in the crowd?" He offered me his arm. "May I escort you inside, my lady?"

I took his arm with my left hand. Jason put his free hand on top of mine, doing a double hold. If that was the worst teasing he did tonight, then he'd grown up some. The silver cloth was rougher than it looked, scratchy where it rubbed against my arm.

As Jason led me up the steps, I had to look behind him. The cloth that covered his groin was only a thin thong at the back, leaving nothing but a fine glitter over his butt. The shirt was not attached to the pants, so as he moved I got glimpses of his stomach. In fact the shirt was loose enough through the shoulders that when he took my arm the shirt pulled to one side, revealing his smooth, pale shoulder.

The music hit me at the door like a giant's slap. It was almost a wall we had to move through. I hadn't expected Narcissus in Chains to be a dance club. But except for the patrons' clothing being more exotic and running high to leather, it looked like a lot of other clubs. The place was large, dimly lit, dark in the corners, with too many people pushed into too small a space, moving their bodies frantically to music that was way too loud.

My hand tightened just a touch on Jason's arm, because truthfully I always feel a little overwhelmed by places like this. At least for the first few minutes. It's like I need a depth chamber between the outside world and the inside world, a moment to breathe deep and adjust. But these clubs are not designed to give you time. They just bombard you with sensory overload and figure you'll survive.

Speaking of sensory overload, Jean-Claude was standing near the wall just to one side of the dance floor. His long black hair fell in soft curls around his shoulders, nearly to his waist. I didn't remember his hair being that long. He had his head turned away from me, watching the dancers, so I couldn't really see his face, but it gave me time to look at the rest of him. He was dressed in a black vinyl shirt that looked poured on. It left his arms bare, and I realized I'd never seen him in anything that bared his arms before. His skin looked unbelievably white against the shiny black vinyl, almost as if it glowed with some inner light. I knew it didn't, though it could. Jean-Claude would never be so déclassé as to show such power in a public place. His pants were made of the same shiny vinyl, making the long lines of his body look like they had been dipped into liquid patent leather. Vinyl boots came up just over his knees, gleaming as if they'd been spit polished. Everything about him gleamed, the dark glow of his clothes, the shining whiteness of his skin. Then abruptly he turned as if he felt me gazing at him.

Staring full into his face, even from across a room, made me catch my breath. He was beautiful. That heartrending beauty that was masculine but treaded the line between what was male and what was female. Not exactly androgynous, but close to it.

But as he moved toward me, the movement was utterly male, graceful as if he heard music in his head that he quietly danced to. But the walk, the movement of his shoulders—women did not move like that.

Jason patted my hand.

I jumped, staring at him.

He put his mouth close enough to my ear to whisper-shout above the music, "Breathe, Anita, remember to breathe."

I blushed, because that was how Jean-Claude affected me—like I was fourteen and was having the crush of my life. Jason tightened his grip on me, as if he thought I might make a run for it. Not a bad idea. I looked back and saw that Jean-Claude was very near. The first time I saw the blue-green roil of the Caribbean, I cried, because it was so beautiful. Jean-Claude made me feel like that, like I should weep at his beauty. It was like being offered an original da Vinci, not just to hang on your wall and admire, but to roll around on top of. It seemed wrong. Yet I stood there, clutching Jason's arm, my heart hammering so hard I almost couldn't hear the music. I was scared, but it wasn't knife-in-the-dark scared, it was rabbit-in-the-headlights scared. I was caught, as I usually was with Jean-Claude, between two disparate instincts. Part of me wanted to run to him, to close the distance and climb his body and pull it around me. The other part wanted to run screaming into the night and pray he didn't follow.

He stood in front of me, but made no move to touch me, to close that last small space. He seemed as unwilling to touch me as I was to touch him. Was he afraid of me? Or did he sense my own fear and was afraid he might scare me off? We stood there simply staring at each other. His eyes were still the same dark, dark blue, with a wealth of black lashes lacing them.

Jason kissed my cheek, lightly, like you'd kiss your sister. It still made me jump. "I'm feeling like a third wheel, you two play nice." And he pulled away from me, leaving Jean-Claude and me staring at each other.

I don't know what we would have said, because three men joined us before we could decide. The shortest of the three was only about five feet seven, and he was wearing more makeup on his pale triangular face than I was. The makeup was well done, but he wasn't trying to look like a woman. His black hair was cut very short, though you could tell that it would be curly if it was long. He was wearing a black lace dress, long-sleeved, fitted at the waist, showing a slender but muscular chest. The skirt spilled out around him, almost June Cleaverish, and his stockings were black, with a very delicate spiderweb pattern. He wore open-toed sandals with spike heels, and both his toenails and his fingernails were painted black. He looked . . . lovely. But what made the outfit was the sense of power in him. It hung around him like an expensive perfume, and I knew he was an alpha something.

Jean-Claude spoke first, "This is Narcissus, owner of this establishment."

Narcissus held out his hand. I was momentarily confused about whether I was supposed to shake the hand or kiss it. If he'd been trying to pass for a woman, I'd have known the kiss would have been appropriate, but he wasn't. He wasn't so much cross-dressing as just dressing the way he wanted to. I shook his hand. The grip was strong, but not too strong. He didn't try and test my strength, which some lycanthropes will do. He was secure, was Narcissus.

The two men behind him loomed over all of us, each well over six feet. One had a wide, muscular chest that was left mostly bare through a complicated criss-cross of black leather straps. He had blond hair, cut very short on the sides and gelled into short spikes on top. His eyes were pale, and the look in them was not friendly. The second man was slimmer, built more like a professional basketball player than a weight lifter. But the arms that showed from the leather vest were corded with muscle all the same. His skin was almost as dark as the leather he was wearing. All these two needed were a couple of tattoos apiece, and they would have screamed badass.

Narcissus said, "This is Ulysses and Ajax." Ajax was the blond, and Ulysses was the oh-so brunette.

"Greek myths, nice naming convention," I said.

Narcissus blinked large, dark eyes at me. Either he didn't think I was funny, or he simply didn't care. The music stopped abruptly. We were suddenly standing in a great roaring silence, and it was shocking. Narcissus spoke at a level where I could hear him, but people nearby couldn't. He'd known the music would stop. "I know your reputation, Ms. Blake. I must have the gun."

I glanced at Jean-Claude.

"I did not tell him."

"Come, Ms. Blake, I can smell the gun, even over . . ." he sniffed the air, head tilted back just a little, "your Oscar de la Renta."

"I went to a different oil for cleaning, one with less odor," I said.

"It's not the oil. The gun is new, I can smell the . . . metal, like you would smell a new car."

Oh. "Did Jean-Claude explain the situation to you?"

Narcissus nodded. "Yes, but we do not play favorites in dominance struggles between different groups. We are neutral territory, and if we are to remain so, then no guns. If it is any comfort, we didn't let the ones who have your cats bring guns into the club either."

I widened my eyes at that. "Most shapeshifters don't carry guns."

"No, they do not." Narcissus's handsome face told me nothing. He was neither upset nor concerned. It was all just business to him—like Marco's voice on the phone.

I turned back to Jean-Claude. "I'm not getting into the club with my gun, am I?"

"I fear not, *ma petite.*"

I sighed and turned back to the waiting—what had Jean-

Claude called them—werehyenas. They were the first I'd met, as far as I knew. There was no clue from looking at them what they became when the moon was full. "I'll give it up, but I'm not happy about this."

"That is not my problem," Narcissus said.

I met his eyes and felt my face slip into that look that could make a good cop flinch—my monster peeking out. Ulysses and Ajax started to move in front of Narcissus, but he waved them back. "Ms. Blake will behave herself. Won't you, Ms. Blake?"

I nodded, but said, "If my people get hurt because I don't have a gun, I can make it your problem."

"Ma petite," Jean-Claude said, his voice warning me.

I shook my head. "I know, I know, they're like Switzerland, neutral. Personally, I think neutral is just another way of saving your own ass at the expense of someone else's."

Narcissus took a step closer, until only a few inches separated us. His otherworldly energy danced along my skin, and as had happened in New Mexico with a very different wereanimal, it called that piece of Richard's beast that seemed to live inside me. It brought that power in a rush down my skin, to jump the distance between us, and mingle with Narcissus's power. It startled me. I hadn't thought it could happen with shields in place. Marianne had said that my abilities lay with the dead, and that was why I couldn't control Richard's power as easily as I could Jean-Claude's. But I should have been able to shield against a stranger. It scared me a little that I couldn't.

It had been wereleopards and werejaguars in New Mexico. They had mistaken me for another lycanthrope. Narcissus made the same mistake. I saw his eyes widen, then narrow. He glanced at Jean-Claude, and he laughed. "Everyone says you're human, Anita." He raised a hand and caressed the air just above my face, touching the swirl of energy. "I think you should come out of the closet before someone gets hurt."

"I never said I was human, Narcissus. But I'm not a shape-shifter either."

He rubbed his hand along the front of his dress, as if trying to get the feeling of my power off his skin. "Then what are you?"

"If things go badly tonight, you'll find out."

His eyes narrowed again. "If you cannot protect your people without guns, then you should step down as their Nimir-Ra and let someone else have the job."

"I've got an interview set up day after tomorrow with a potential Nimir-Raj."

He looked genuinely surprised. "You know that you don't have the power to rule them?"

I nodded. "Oh, yeah, I'm only temporary until I can find someone else. If the rest of you weren't so damn species-conscious, I'd have farmed them out to another group. But no one wants to play with an animal that isn't the same as them."

"It is our way, it has always been our way."

And I knew the "our" didn't mean just werehyenas but all the shifters. "Yeah, well it sucks."

He smiled then. "I don't know whether I like you, Anita, but you are different, and I always appreciate that. Now give up the gun like a good little girl, and you can enter my territory." He held his hand out.

I stared at the hand. I didn't want to give up my gun. What I'd told Ronnie was true. I couldn't arm wrestle them, and I would lose a fair fight. The gun was my equalizer. I had the two knives, but frankly, they were for emergencies.

"It is your choice, *ma petite.*"

"If it will help you make the choice," Narcissus said, "I have put two of my own personal guards in the room with your leopards. I have forbidden the others from causing further harm to your people until you arrive. Until you enter the upper room where they're waiting, nothing more will happen that they don't want to happen." Knowing Nathaniel, that wasn't as comforting as it could have been.

If anyone would understand the problem, it would be someone who ran a club like this. "Nathaniel is one of those bottoms that will ask for more punishment than he can survive. He has no stopping point, no ability to keep himself safe. Do you understand?"

Narcissus's eyes widened just a touch. "Then what was he doing here without a top of his own?"

"I sent him out with one that was supposed to watch over him tonight. But Gregory said that Elizabeth deserted Nathaniel early in the evening."

"Is she one of your leopards, too?"

I nodded.

"She's defying you."

"I know. The fact that Nathaniel suffers for it doesn't seem to bother her."

He studied my face. "I don't see anger in you about this."

"If I was angry at everything Elizabeth did to piss me off, I'd never be anything else." Truthfully, I was just tired. Tired of having to rescue the pack from one emergency after another. Tired of Elizabeth being up in my face and not taking care of the others, even though she was supposedly dominant to them. I'd avoided punishing her, because I couldn't beat her up, which was what she needed. The only thing I could do was shoot her. I'd been trying to avoid that, but she just may have pushed me far enough that I was out of options. I'd see what actual damage had been done. If anyone died because of her, then she would follow. I hated the fact that I didn't care whether I killed her. I'd known her off and on for over a year. I should have cared, but I didn't. I didn't like her, and she'd been asking for it for as long as I'd known her. My life would be simpler if she were dead. But there had to be a better reason to kill someone than that. Didn't there?

"Some advice," Narcissus said, "all dominance challenges, especially from your own people, must be handled quickly, or the problem will spread."

"Thanks. Actually I knew that."

"Still she defies you."

"I've been trying to avoid killing her."

We looked at each other very quietly, and he gave a small nod. "Your gun, please."

I sighed and raised the front of my shirt, though the material was stiff enough that I had to roll it back to expose the butt of the gun. I lifted the gun out and checked the safety out of habit, though I knew it was on.

Narcissus took the gun. The two bodyguards had moved, blocking the crowd's view of us. I doubted most people knew what we'd just done. Narcissus smiled as I rolled my shirt back into place over the now-empty holster. "Truthfully, if I didn't know who you were and what your reputation was, I wouldn't have smelled the gun, because I wouldn't have been trying to. Your outfit doesn't look like it could hide a gun this big."

"Paranoia is the mother of invention," I said.

He gave a small bow of his head. "Now enter and enjoy the delights, and the terrors, of my world." With that rather cryptic phrase, he and his bodyguards moved through the crowd, taking my gun with them.

Jean-Claude trailed his fingers down my arm, and that one small movement turned me toward him, my skin shivering. Tonight was complicated enough without this level of sexual tension.

"Your cats are well until you enter the upper room. I suggest we do the mark now, first."

"Why?" I asked, my pulse suddenly in my throat.

"Let us go to our table, and I will explain." He moved off through the crowd, without touching me further. I followed and couldn't stop myself from watching the way the vinyl fit him from behind. I loved watching him walk, whether he was coming or going—a double threat.

The tables were small, and there weren't many of them crowded against the walls. But they'd cleared the dance floor so they could set up for some sort of show or demonstration. Men and women dressed in leather were setting up a framework of metal with lots of leather straps. I was reeeally hoping to be elsewhere before the show started.

Jean-Claude took me to one side before we got to the table that Jason and three complete strangers were gathered around. He stepped in so close to me that a hard thought would have made our bodies touch. I pressed myself against the wall and tried not to breathe. He put his mouth against my ear and spoke so low what came out was merely the soft sound of his breath against my skin. "We will all be safer when the marks are married, but there are other . . . benefits to it. I have many lesser vampires that I have brought into my territory in the last few months, *ma petite*. Without you at my side, I dared not bring in greater powers, for fear that I could not hold them. Once the marks are married between us, you will be able to sense those vampires that are mine. The exception, as always, is a Master Vampire. They can hide their allegiances better than the rest. The marriage of marks will also let my people know who you are, and what will happen to them if they overstep their bounds with you."

I spoke, lips barely moving, lower than he had spoken, because he could still hear me. "You've had to be very careful, haven't you?"

He rested his cheek against my face for a moment. "It has been a delicate dance to choreograph."

I had gone into this evening with my metaphysical shield tight in place. Marianne had taught me that with my aura ruptured, the other shielding was of paramount importance. I shielded with stone tonight, perfect, seamless stone. Nothing could get in, or out, without my permission. Except Narcissus's power had already danced inside my shields. I was afraid that touching Jean-Claude would be enough to shatter the stone, but it wasn't. I wasn't even aware of the shielding, unless I really concentrated. It could stay in place even when I slept. Only when you were attacked did you have to concentrate, if you were good at shielding. I'd spent a week at the beginning of the month in Tennessee with Marianne, working on nothing but this. I wasn't great at it, but I wasn't bad either.

My shields were in place. My emotions were drowning in Jean-Claude, but my psyche wasn't, which meant that Marianne was right. I could hold the dead outside my shield easier than the living. This gave me the courage to do a little more. I leaned my face against Jean-Claude's, and nothing happened. Oh, the feel of his skin against mine sent a thrill through my body, but my shields never wavered. I felt some tension that I hadn't even known was there ease out of me. I wanted him to hold me. It wasn't just sex. If that was all it was, I could have been rid of him long ago. He must have felt it, too, because his hands rested lightly on my bare arms. When I didn't protest, his hands caressed my skin, and that small movement brought my breath to a sigh.

I leaned into him, wrapping my arms around his waist, pressing the lines of our bodies together. I rested my head on his chest, and I could hear his heart beating. It didn't always beat, but tonight it did. We held each other, and it was nearly chaste, just a renewal of the fact that we were touching again. I'd worked on the metaphysical stuff, so I could do this and not lose myself. It had been worth the effort.

He pulled back first, enough to look into my face. "We can marry the marks here, or find somewhere more private." He wasn't whispering as much as before. Apparently he didn't care now if others knew what we were doing.

"I'm not clear on what marrying the marks means."

"I thought your Marianne had explained it to you."

"She said we'll fit together like puzzle pieces and there'll be a release of power when it happens. But she also said that the manner in which it is done is individual to the participants."

"You sound as if you are quoting."

"I am."

He frowned, and even that small movement was somehow fascinating. "I do not want you to be unpleasantly surprised, *ma petite*. I am striving for honesty, since you value it so highly. I have never done this with anyone, but most things are sexual between us, whether we will, or no, so it is likely this will be, too."

"I can't leave the leopards here long enough to grab a hotel room, Jean-Claude."

"They will not be harmed. Until you go upstairs. They will be safe."

I shook my head and pulled away from him. "I'm sorry, but I am not leaving here without them. If you want to do this afterwards, that's fine with me, but the leopards are priority. They're waiting for me to rescue them, I can't go off and have what amounts to metaphysical sex while they're afraid and bleeding somewhere."

"No, it cannot wait. I want us to have this done before the fight begins. I do not like that your gun is gone."

"Will this marriage of the marks give me more . . . abilities?"

"Yes."

"And you, what do you get out of it?" I was standing against the wall now, not touching him.

"My own defenses will be strong once more, and I will gain power, as well. You know that."

"Are there any surprises connected with this that I should know about?"

"As I said, I have never done this with anyone, nor have I seen it done. It will be as much a surprise to me as to you."

I stared up into his lovely eyes and wished I believed that.

"I see the distrust in your eyes, *ma petite*. But it is not me that you do not trust. It is your power. Nothing ever goes as it should with you, *ma petite*, because you are like no power come before you. You are wild magic, untamed. You throw the best of plans to the wind."

"I've been learning control, Jean-Claude."

"I hope it is enough."

"You're scaring me."

He sighed. "And that was the last thing I wished to do."

I shook my head. "Look, Jean-Claude, I know everyone keeps saying my people are fine, but I want to see for myself, so let's just get this done."

"This should be something special and mystical, *ma petite*."

I looked around the club. "Then we need a different setting."

"I agree, but the setting was your choosing, not mine."

"But you're the one insisting on it having to be right now before all the fireworks start."

"True." He sighed and held out his hand to me. "Come, let us at least go to our table."

I actually thought about refusing his hand. Funny how quickly I could go from wanting to jump his bones to wanting to be rid of him. Of course, it wasn't exactly him, but more the complications that came with him. The mystical stuff between us was never simple. He said that was my fault, and maybe it was. Jean-Claude was a pretty standard Master Vampire, and Richard, a pretty standard Ulfric. They were both wonderfully powerful, but there was nothing too terribly extraordinary in that power. Well, there was one thing about Jean-Claude. He could gain power by feeding off sexual energy. In another century he'd have been called an incubus. It's rare even for a Master Vamp to have a secondary way to gain power outside of blood. So it was impressive, sort of. The only other masters I'd met who could feed off something other than blood had fed on terror. And of the two, I preferred lust. At least no one had to bleed for it. Usually. But I was the wild card, the one whose powers seemed to fit nothing but legends of necromancers long dead.

Legends so old that no one believed they could be true, until I came along. Sad, but true.

The table had cleared out while we were whispering. Now just Jason and one other man were there. The man was dressed in brown leather, from what I could see of his pants to the zipped-front, sleeveless shirt he was wearing. He was also wearing one of those hoods that left your mouth, part of your nose, and your eyes bare, but covered the rest of your face. Frankly, I found the hoods creepy, but hey, it wasn't my bread that was being buttered. As long as he didn't try anything with me, we were cool. It wasn't until he looked up into my face that I recognized those pale, pale blue eyes—the startling ice blue eyes of a Siberian Husky. No human I'd ever met had eyes like that.

"Asher," I said.

He smiled then, and I recognized the curve of his lips. I knew why he'd worn the hood. It wasn't sexual preference, or at least I didn't think so. It was to hide the scars. Once, about two hundred years ago, some well-meaning church officials had tried to burn the devil out of Asher. They'd done it with holy water. Holy water is like acid on vampire flesh. He'd once been, in his own way, as breathtaking as Jean-Claude. Now half his face was a melted ruin, half his chest, most of the one thigh I'd seen. What I'd seen of the rest of him was perfect, as perfect as the day he died. And the parts I hadn't seen, I wasn't sure I wanted to know about. Through Jean-Claude's marks I had memories of Asher before. I knew what his body looked like in smooth perfection—every inch of it. Asher and his human servant, Julianna, had been part of a ménage à trois with Jean-Claude for about twenty years. She'd been burned as a witch, and Jean-Claude had only been able to save Asher after the damage had been done.

The events were over two hundred years old yet they both still mourned Julianna, and each other. Asher was now Jean-Claude's second in command, but they were not lovers. And they were uneasy friends, because there was still too much left unspoken between them. Asher still blamed Jean-Claude for failing them, and Jean-Claude had a hard time arguing with that, because deep down he still blamed himself, too.

I leaned down and gave Asher a quick kiss on the leather

cheek. "What did you do with all your long hair? Please tell me you haven't cut it."

He raised my hand to his mouth and laid a gentle kiss on it. "It is braided, and longer than ever."

"I can hardly wait to see it," I said. "Thanks for coming."

"I would move all of hell to reach your side, you know that."

"You French guys do talk pretty," I said.

He laughed, softly.

Jason interrupted, "I think the show is about to start."

I turned and watched a woman being led toward the framework that had been erected. She was wearing a robe, and I really didn't want to see what was under it.

"Whatever we're going to do, let's do it and go get the leopards."

"You don't want to see the show?" Jason asked. His eyes were all innocent, but his smile was teasing.

I just frowned at him. But his eyes looked behind me, and I knew someone Jason didn't like was coming toward us. I turned to find Ajax standing there. He ignored me and spoke to Jean-Claude. "You have fifteen minutes, then the show starts."

Jean-Claude nodded. "Tell Narcissus I appreciate the notice."

Ajax gave a small head bow, much like his master had done before, then walked off through the tables.

"What was all that about?" I asked.

"It would be considered rude to do something magical during someone else's performance. I told Narcissus that we would be calling some . . . power."

I must have looked as suspicious as I felt. "You are beginning to piss me off with this cloak-and-dagger magic act."

"You are a necromancer, and I am the Master Vampire of this city. Do you really believe that we can merge our powers and not have every undead in this room, and more, notice it? I do not know if the shapeshifters will be able to feel it, but it is likely, since we are also both bound to a werewolf. Everything nonhuman in this club will feel something. I don't know how much, or exactly what, but *something, ma petite.* Narcissus would have taken it as a grave insult if we had interrupted this performance without warning him."

"I don't mean to rush you," Asher said, "but you will use up your time in talking if you are not quick about it."

Jean-Claude looked at him, and the look was not entirely friendly. What was happening between them that Jean-Claude would give such a look to Asher?

Jean-Claude held his hand out to me. I hesitated a second, then slid my hand in his and he led me to the wall near the table. "Now what?" I asked.

"Now you must drop your shields, *ma petite,* that so-strong barrier you have erected between me and your aura."

I just stared at him. "I don't want to do that."

"I would not ask if it were not necessary, *ma petite.* But even if I were able to do it, neither of us would enjoy me breaking down your shielding. We cannot merge our auras if my aura cannot touch yours."

I was suddenly scared. Really seriously scared. I didn't know what would happen if I dropped the shields with him right there. In times of crisis our auras flared together forming a unique whole. I didn't want to do this. I am a control freak, and everything about Jean-Claude ate at that part of me that most needed control.

"I'm not sure I can do this."

He sighed. "It is your choice. I will not force it, but I fear the consequences, *ma petite.* I do fear them."

Marianne had given me the lecture, and it was really too late to get cold feet. I could either move forward with this, or eventually one of us would die. Probably me. Part of my job was going up against preternatural monsters—things with enough magic to sense a hole in my defenses. Before I'd ever been able to sense auras, or at least before I knew that I was doing it, my aura had been intact. With my own natural talent, that had been enough. But lately I seemed to be running up against bigger, badder monsters. Eventually, I would lose. That, I might have been able to live with, sort of. But costing Jean-Claude or Richard their lives? That I couldn't handle. I knew all the reasons I should do this, and still I stood there gazing up at Jean-Claude, my heart beating in my throat, my shields tight in place. The front part of my brain knew this needed doing. The back part of my brain wasn't so sure.

"Once I drop my shield, then what?"

"We touch," he said.

I took a deep breath in and blew it out as if I were about to run a race. Then I dropped my shields. It wasn't like tearing down the stone walls. It was like absorbing them back into my psyche. The tower was just suddenly not there, and Jean-Claude's power crashed over me. It wasn't only that I felt the sexual attraction full force, I could feel his heartbeat in my head. I could taste his skin in my mouth. I knew he'd fed tonight, though intellectually I'd known that when I heard his heart beating. Now, I could feel that he was well fed and full of someone else's blood.

His hand moved toward me, and I flattened against the wall. The hand kept moving, and I pulled away from it. I moved away because more than anything in the world at that moment I wanted him to touch me. I wanted to feel his hand against my bare skin. I wanted to rip the vinyl from his body and watch him, pale and perfect above me. The image was so clear that I closed my eyes against it, as if that would help.

I felt him in front of me, knew he was leaning close. I ducked under his arm and was suddenly standing by the table, leaving him near the wall. I kept backing up, and he kept watching me. Someone touched me, and I screamed.

Asher was holding my arm, gazing up at me with those pale eyes of his. I could feel him, too, feel the weight of his age, the heft of his power in my head. That was my power, but I realized in shielding so strongly from Jean-Claude I'd also cut myself off from some of my own powers. Shielding was a tricky thing. I guess I still didn't have the hang of it.

Jean-Claude moved away from the wall, holding one slender hand out to me. I backed up, Asher's hand sliding over my arm as I pulled away. I was shaking my head back and forth, back and forth.

Jean-Claude walked slowly toward me. His eyes had gone drowning blue, the pupil swallowed by his own power. I knew with a sudden clarity that it wasn't his power or lust that had called his eyes, it was mine. He could feel how my body tightened, moistened, as he moved toward me. It wasn't him I didn't trust. It was me.

I took one step backwards and fell on the small step leading down to the dance floor. Someone caught me before I hit the floor, strong arms around my waist, pressing me against the bare skin of a very masculine chest. I could feel that without looking. I was held, feet dangling, held effortlessly, and I knew those arms, the feel of that chest, the smell of his skin this close. I craned my head backwards and found myself staring at Richard.

5

I stopped breathing. To be suddenly inches away from him after all this time was too much. He leaned that painfully handsome face over mine, and the thick waves of his brown hair fell against my skin. His mouth hovered over mine, and I think I would have said, *no,* or moved, but two things happened at once. He tightened his one-armed hold around my waist, a movement that was almost painful. Then his newly free hand gripped my chin, held my face. The touch of his hands, the strength in them made me hesitate. One moment I was staring into his deep brown eyes, the next, his face was too close and he was kissing me.

I don't know what I expected, a chaste kiss, I think. It wasn't chaste. He kissed me hard enough to bruise, hard enough to force my mouth open, then he crawled inside, and I could feel the muscles in his mouth, his jaw, his neck working as he held me, explored me, possessed me. I should have been angry, pissed, but I wasn't. If he hadn't held me immobile I'd have turned in his arms, pressed the front of my body against his. But all I could do was taste his mouth, feel his lips, try to drink him down my throat, as if he were the finest of wines and I was dying of thirst.

He finally drew back from me, enough for me to see his face. I stared breathlessly at him, as if my eyes were hungry for the sight of those perfect cheekbones, the dimple that softened an utterly masculine face. There was nothing feminine about Richard. He was the ultimate male in so many ways. The electric lights caught strands of gold and copper, like metallic wire through the deep brown of his hair.

He lowered me slowly to the ground from his height of six one. His shoulders were broad, chest deep, waist tight and narrow, stomach flat, with a fine line of dark hair running down the middle of it and vanishing into the black vinyl pants he was wearing. More black vinyl! I was sensing a theme here, but my gaze traveled down his body just the same. Tracing the narrow hips, lingering where I shouldn't have been, noticing things I wished I hadn't, because we were in public, and I wasn't planning on seeing him naked tonight. Knee-high leather boots completed his outfit. The only things he was wearing on his upper body were leather and metal-studded "bracelets" and a matching collar.

A hand touched my back, and I jumped and whirled around, turning so I could face them both, because I knew who was behind me. Jean-Claude stood there, eyes having bled back to normal.

I finally found my voice. "You called him."

"We had an arrangement that whoever you called first would contact the other."

"You should have told me," I said.

Jean-Claude put his hands on his hips. "I am not taking the blame for this. He wished to be a surprise, against *my* wishes."

I looked at Richard. "Is that true?"

Richard nodded. "Yes."

"Why?"

"Because if I'd played fair I still wouldn't have gotten a kiss. I couldn't stand the thought of seeing you tonight and not touching you."

It wasn't so much his words as the look in his eyes, the heat in his face, that made me blush.

"I have played you fair tonight, *ma petite,* and yet I am punished, rather than rewarded." Jean-Claude held out his hand to me. "Shall we begin with a kiss?"

I was suddenly aware that we were standing on the dance floor near the metal framework and the waiting "actors." We had the audience's attention, and I didn't want that. I realized something I hadn't with the stone shield in place. Almost everyone in the room was a shapeshifter. I could feel their energy like the brush of warm electric fur, and they could feel ours.

I nodded. I suddenly wanted the privacy that Jean-Claude had offered earlier. But staring from Jean-Claude to Richard, I realized I didn't trust myself alone with them. If we had a room to ourselves I couldn't guarantee that the sex was merely metaphysical. Admitting that even to myself was embarrassing. As uncomfortable as it was to do what we had to do in public, it was still better than in private. Here I knew I'd say *stop,* anywhere else I just wasn't sure. I wasn't thinking about the wereleopards. I was thinking about how large and bare my skin felt. Shit.

"A kiss, why not?"

"We can get a room," Richard said, voice low.

I shook my head. "No, no rooms."

He reached out as if to touch me, and one look was enough to make his hand drop. "You don't trust us."

"Or me," I said, softly.

Jean-Claude held out his hand to me. "Come, *ma petite,* we delay their show."

I stared at his hand for a space of heartbeats, then took it. I expected him to pull me in against his body, but he didn't. He stopped with the width of a handspan between us. I looked a question at him, and he touched my face, gently, tentatively, fingers hovering on either side of my face, like hesitant butterflies, as if he were afraid to touch me. He lowered his face toward me, as his fingertips found my skin. His hands slid on either side of my face, cupping it like something delicate and breakable.

I'd never felt him so tentative around me, so unsure. Even as his lips hovered over mine I wondered if he was doing it this way on purpose to contrast with Richard's forcefulness. Then his lips touched mine, and I stopped thinking. It was the barest of brushes, his mouth over mine. Then softly, he kissed me. I kissed him back, being as tenative as he, my hands raising, covering his hands as they cradled my face. He'd thrown that surprisingly long black hair over one shoulder so that the right side of his face was bare to the lights and the hair didn't get in the way of the kiss. I ran one hand down the side of his jaw, tracing the shape of his face, ever so gently, as we kissed. He shuddered under that light brush of my hand, and the feel of him trembling under my hand brought a soft sound from low in my throat. Jean-Claude's mouth pressed against mine hard enough that I could feel the press of his fangs against my lip. I opened my mouth and let him inside me, ran my tongue between the delicate points. I'd learned how to French kiss a vampire, but it was a hazardous pleasure, one to be done with care, and I was out of practice.

In slipping my tongue between his fangs, I nicked myself. It was a quick, sharp pain, and Jean-Claude made a soft guttural sound, a heartbeat before I tasted blood.

His hands were suddenly at my back, pulling me against his body. The kiss never stopped, and the urgency of it grew, until it was as if he were feeding from my mouth, trying to drink me down.

I might have pulled away, I might not have, but the moment the front of our bodies touched, it was too late. There was no going back, no saying no, nothing but sensation. I felt that cool, shimmering wind that was his aura touch mine. For one trembling moment we were pressed together, our energy breathing against each other like the sides of two great beasts. Then the boundaries that held our auras in place gave way. Think of it as if you were making love and suddenly your skin slid away, spilling you against your partner, into your partner, giving you an intimacy that was never imagined, never planned, never wanted.

I screamed, and he echoed me. I felt us begin to fall to the floor, but Richard caught us, cradled us against his body, laid us gently on the floor. The power did not leap across to him, and I didn't know why.

Jean-Claude's body was on top of mine, pinning me to the floor, his groin pressed over mine. He drove his hips in against me, forcing my legs apart around the slick covering of his legs. I wanted him inside me, wanted him to ride me while the power rode us.

He struggled up on his arms, leaning up and away from me, forcing his lower body tighter against mine. And the power built in a skin-tingling rush, building, building, like that shining edge of orgasm when you can feel it growing large and overwhelming but can't quite reach it.

I saw Richard leaning over me like a dark shadow against the haze of the lights. I think I tried to say, *no, don't,* but no sound came. He kissed me, and the power flared, but still he wasn't part of it. He kissed my cheek, my chin, my neck, working lower, and I suddenly knew what he was doing. He was kissing his way down to the hole over my heart chakra, my energy center. Jean-Claude had already covered the one at my base, my groin. Richard's chest stretched above me, smooth, firm, so temptingly close, and I raised my mouth to his skin, so that as he kissed down my body he drew his naked chest across my tongue. I licked a wet line down his body. His mouth buried inside the halter top and touched over my heart, and my mouth found his heart at the same moment.

The power didn't just build, it exploded. It was like lying at ground zero of a nuclear explosion, the shock waves shooting out, out, out into the room, while we melted together in the center. For one shining moment I felt both of them inside me, through me, as if they were wind, pure power, pouring through me, through us. Richard's electric warmth buzzed over us; Jean-Claude's cool power poured over and through like a chill wind; and I was something large and growing, holding the warmth of the living and the cold of the dead. I was both and neither. We were all and none.

I don't know if I passed out or if I just lost time for some metaphysical reason. All I remembered was that I was suddenly lying on the floor with Richard collapsed beside me, pinning one of my arms, his body curled around my chest and head, his legs touching down the other side of my body. Jean-Claude was collapsed on top of me, his body pressing the length of mine, with his head to one side resting on Richard's leg. They both had their eyes closed, their breath coming in ragged pants, just like mine.

It took me two tries to say a breathless, "Get off me."

Jean-Claude rolled to one side without ever opening his eyes. The fall of his body forced Richard's legs to move a little farther out, so that Jean-Claude and I both lay in the semicircle of Richard's body.

The room was so quiet I thought we were the only ones

left in it. As if all the others had fled in terror of what we'd done. Then the room thundered in applause and howling and other animal noises that I didn't have words for. The noise was deafening, beating against my body in waves as if I had nerves in places where I'd never had nerves before.

Asher was suddenly standing over us. He knelt beside me, touching the pulse in my neck. "Blink if you can you hear me, Anita."

I blinked.

"Can you speak?"

"Yes."

He nodded and touched Jean-Claude next, stroking a hand down his cheek. Jean-Claude opened his eyes at the touch. He gave a smile that seemed to mean more to Asher than to me, because it made Asher laugh. The laugh was a very masculine one, as if they'd shared some dirty joke that I didn't understand. Asher crawled around me until he was kneeling by Richard's head. He lifted a handful of thick hair so he could see Richard's face clearly. Richard blinked at him, but didn't seem to be focusing.

Asher bent low over Richard, and I heard him say, "Can you hear me, *mon ami*?"

Richard swallowed, coughed, and said, "Yes."

"Bon, bon."

It took me two tries but I had a smart-aleck comment, and I was going to make it. "Now, everyone who can stand, raise their hands." None of us moved. I felt distant, floating, my body too heavy to move. Or maybe my mind was too over-whelmed to make it move.

"Have no fears, *ma cherie,* we will attend you." Asher stood, and it was as if it were a signal. Figures moved out of the crowd. I recognized three of them. Jamil's waist-length cornrows looked right at home with his black leather outfit. He was Richard's lead enforcer, or sköll. Shang-Da didn't look comfortable in black leather, but the six-foot-plus Chinese never looked comfortable outside of nice dress clothes with polished wing tips. Shang-Da was the other enforcer for the pack, the Hati. Sylvie knelt beside me, looking splendid in vinyl, her short brown hair touched with burgundy high-lights. Though it looked good, I knew she was conservative enough that it was probably a temporary color. She sold insurance when she wasn't being Richard's second in command, his Freki, and insurance salespeople didn't have hair the color of a good red wine.

She smiled at me, wearing more makeup than I'd ever seen her in. It looked great, but it didn't really look like Sylvie. For the first time I thought how pretty she was, and that she was almost as delicate-looking as me.

"I owed you a rescue," she said. Once upon a time a bunch of nasty vampires had come to town to teach Jean-Claude, Richard, and me a lesson. They'd taken prisoners along the way. Sylvie had been one of them. I'd gotten her out, and I'd kept my promise to see everyone who touched her dead. She did the actual killing, but I delivered them up to her for punishment. She kept a few bones as souvenirs. Sylvie would never complain that I was too violent. Maybe she could be my new best friend.

The werewolves took up positions around us, facing outward like good bodyguards. None of them were as physically imposing as Narcissus's bodyguards had been, but I'd seen the wolves fight, and muscles aren't everything. Skill counts, and a certain level of ruthlessness.

Two vampires came to stand with Asher and the wolves. I didn't recognize either of them. The woman was Asian, with shining black hair that fell barely to her shoulders. The hair was nearly the same color and brilliance as the vinyl cat suit that clung to nearly every inch of her body. The suit made sure you were aware of her high, tight breasts, her tiny waist, the swell of her shapely hips. She gave me an unfriendly look with her dark eyes, before she turned her back on me and stood, hands at her side, waiting. Waiting for what, I wasn't sure.

The second vampire was male, not much taller than the woman, with thick brown hair that had been shaved close to his head, except for a layer left on top that came about halfway to his eyes, shining and straight. He gazed down on me with a smile, eyes the color of new pennies, as if his brown eyes held just a trace of blood in them.

He turned his attention outward, arms crossed over the black leather of his chest. They too faced outward like good bodyguards, letting the crowd know that even though we couldn't stand up, we weren't helpless. Comforting, I guess.

Jason crawled in between their legs, head hanging down, as if he were almost too tired to move. He raised his blue eyes to me, and the look was almost as unfocused as I felt.

He gave a pale version of his usual grin and said, "Was it good for you?"

I was feeling better enough to try and sit up, but failed. Jean-Claude said, "Lie a little longer, *ma petite.*"

Since I had no choice, I did what he suggested. I lay staring up at the dark, distant ceiling with its rows of lights. They'd turned off most of them, so that the club was nearly dark. Like the soft gloom that comes when you close the drapes during the day.

I felt Jason lay down on the other side of me, head resting on my thigh. Not long ago I'd have made him move, but I'd spent my time away learning how to be comfortable being close with the wereleopards. It had made me more tolerant of everyone, apparently. "Why are *you* tired?"

He rolled his head up to look at me without raising it from my leg, one hand curving over my calf as if to keep his balance. "You spill sex and magic through the whole club and you ask why I'm tired? You are such a tease."

I frowned at him. "One more comment like that and you'll have to move."

He snuggled his head on my hose. "I can see that your underwear matches."

"Get off of me, Jason."

He slid to the floor without being told twice. He could never leave well enough alone, our Jason. He always had to get the last joke, the last comment, that one bit too many. I worried that someday with someone else that little quirk might get him hurt, or worse.

Richard propped himself up on one elbow, moving slowly as if he wasn't sure everything was working. "I don't know if that felt better than anything else we've ever done, or worse."

"It feels like a combination of a hangover and mild flu to me," I said.

"And yet it feels good," Jean-Claude said.

I finally got upright and found that they both had a hand at my back to support me, as if their movements had been simultaneous.

I actually leaned in against their hands, rather than telling them to move. One, I was still shaky, two, I just didn't find the physical contact unpleasant. All these months of trying to forge the wereleopards into a cohesive, friendly unit, and it was me that had learned to be cohesive and friendly. Me that had learned that not every helping hand is a threat to my independence. Me that had learned that not every offer of physical closeness is a trap or a lie.

Richard sat up first, slowly, keeping his hand on my back. Then Jean-Claude sat up, keeping his hand very still against me. I felt them exchange glances. This was the moment that I usually pulled away. We'd have some fantastic sex, metaphysical or otherwise, and that was my cue to close down, hide. We were in public, all the more reason to do it.

I didn't pull away. Richard's arm slid cautiously up my back, over my shoulders. Jean-Claude's arm moved lower around my waist. They both pulled me into the curve of their bodies as if they were some huge, warm vinyl-covered chair with a pulse.

Some say that that moment during sex when you both have an orgasm your auras drop, you blend your energies, yourselves together. You share so much more than just your body during sex, it's one of the reasons you should be careful who you do it with. Just sitting there on the floor with them was like that. I could feel their energies moving through me, like a low-level current, a distant hum. In time I was pretty sure it would become white noise—something you can ignore, like psychic shielding when you no longer have to concentrate on it. But now it was like we would always walk, move, through that dreamy afterglow where you were still connected, still not quite back in your own skin. I didn't push them away, because I didn't want to. Pushing them away would have been redundant. We didn't need to touch to breach the barriers anymore. And that should have scared me more than anything else, but it didn't.

Narcissus walked out into the middle of the floor and a soft light fell upon him, growing ever so gradually brighter. "Well, my friends, we have had a treat tonight, have we not?"

More applause, screams, and animal noises filled the dimness. Narcissus held up his hands until the crowd fell quiet. "I think we have had our climax for the night." A smattering of laughter at that. "We will save our show until tomorrow, for to do less would be to dishonor what we have been offered here tonight."

The woman, who was still standing to the back of the dance floor in her robe, said, "I can't compete with that."

Narcissus blew her a kiss. "It is not a competition, sweet Miranda, it is that we all have our gifts. Some are merely more rare than others." He turned and stared at us as he said the last. His eyes were pale and oddly colored, and it took me a second or two to realize that Narcissus's eyes had bled to his beast. Hyena eyes, I guess, though truthfully, I didn't know what hyena eyes looked like. I just knew they weren't human eyes.

He knelt beside us, smoothing his dress down in an automatic and strangely odd gesture that I'd never seen a man make before. Of course, he was also the first man I'd ever seen in a dress. There was probably a cause and effect.

Narcissus lowered his voice, "I would love to speak with you in private about this."

"Of course," Jean-Claude said, "but first we have other business."

Narcissus leaned in close, lowering his voice until it was necessary to lean forward to hear him. "As I have two of my guards waiting with her leopards so no harm will come, there is time to talk. Or should I say, *your* leopards, for surely now, what belongs to one, belongs to all." He had leaned so far over that his cheek nearly touched Jean-Claude on one side and my face on the other.

"No," I said, "the leopards are mine."

"Really," Narcissus said. He turned his face that fraction of an inch and brushed his lips against mine. It might have been an accident, but I doubted it. "You don't share everything, then?"

I moved my face just far enough away so we weren't touching. "No."

"So good to know," he whispered. He leaned forward and pressed his mouth to Jean-Claude's lips. I was startled, frozen for a second wondering exactly what to do.

Jean-Claude knew exactly what to do. He put one finger in the man's chest and pushed, not with muscle, but with power. The power of the marks, the power that we had all just moments before solidified. Jean-Claude drew on it as if he'd done it a thousand times before, effortlessly, gracefully, commandingly.

Narcissus was pushed back from him by a rush of invisible power that I could feel tugging on my body. And I knew that most of the people in the room could feel it, as well. Narcissus stayed crouched on the floor, staring at Jean-Claude, staring at all of us. The look on his face was angry, but there was more hunger in it than rage, a hunger denied.

"We need to talk in private," Narcissus insisted.

Jean-Claude nodded. "That would be best, I think."

There was a weight of things left unsaid in that short exchange. I felt Richard's puzzlement mirror my own, before I turned my head to glance back at him. The movement put our faces close enough so that we could almost have kissed. I could tell just by the expression in his eyes that he didn't know what was going on. And he seemed to know that I could tell, because he didn't bother to shrug or make any outward acknowledgment. It wasn't telepathy, though to an outsider it might look that way. It was more extreme empathy, as if I could read every nuance on his face, the smallest change, and know what it meant.

I was still pressed in the circle of Richard's and Jean-Claude's arms, a strange amount of bare skin touching all of us—my back, Richard's chest and stomach, Jean-Claude's arm. There was something incredibly right about the touching, the closeness. I felt Jean-Claude's attention turn, before I moved my head to meet his eyes.

The look in those drowning eyes held worlds of things unsaid, unasked, all so tremblingly close. Because for once he didn't see in my eyes the barriers that kept all those words trapped. It had to be the marriage of the marks affecting me, but that night I think he could have asked me anything, anything, and I wasn't sure I'd say no.

What he finally said was, "Shall we retire to privacy to discuss business with Narcissus?" His voice had its usual smoothness. Only his eyes held uncertainty and a need so large he almost had no words for it. We'd all waited so long for my surrender. I knew that the phrasing wasn't mine. It sounded more like something Jean-Claude would think, but with Richard also pressed against my body I wasn't really sure who was thinking it. I only knew it hadn't been me.

Even before the marks had merged I'd had moments like this. Moments when their thoughts invaded mine, overrode mine. The images had been the worst—nightmare flashes of feeding on the warm bodies of animals, of drinking blood from people I didn't know. It had been this mingling, this loss of self, that had terrified me, sent me running for anything that would keep me whole—keep me myself. Tonight that just didn't seem important. Definitely an aftereffect of the metaphysical union of marks. But knowing what it was didn't make it go away. It was a dangerous night.

Jean-Claude said, "*Ma petite,* are you well? I am feeling much better, energized in fact. Are you still ill?"

I shook my head. "No, I feel fine." *Fine* didn't really cover it. *Energized* was a good word for it, but there were others. How long could it take to rescue the wereleopards from yet another disaster? The night wasn't young, dawn would come, and I wanted to be alone with them before that. I realized with a jolt that ran all the way down my body, that tonight was it. If we could get some privacy and not be interrupted, all things would suddenly be possible.

Richard and Jean-Claude both stood up, in a boneless movement of grace for the vampire and pure energy for the werewolf. I gazed at them as they stood above me, and I was suddenly eager to have the other business done with. I wasn't as worried about the leopards as I should have been, and that did bother me. Whatever this effect was, it was distracting me from more important things. Saving the leopards was why I'd come. It was the first time I'd really thought of them in a while.

I shook my head trying to clear it of sex and magic and the weight of possibilities in Richard's eyes. Jean-Claude's eyes were more cautious, but I'd taught him caution where I was concerned.

I held my hands up to both of them. I never asked for help to stand unless I was bleeding or something was broken. The two of them exchanged glances, then they held their hands out to me, again in perfect unison, like choreographed dancers that knew what the other would do.

They could feel my desire, but that had always been there, it told them nothing. I took their hands and let them lift me up. They were both still looking unsure, almost suspicious, as if they were waiting for me to recoil from them and run screaming from the intimacy of it all. I had to smile. "If we can get everyone all tucked in safe and sound before dawn, all things will be possible."

They exchanged another look between them. Jean-Claude made a small movement, as if encouraging Richard. It was a tiny, almost-push with his head, as if to say, *go ahead, ask.* Normally seeing them plot behind my back pissed me off, but not that night.

"Do you mean . . ." Richard let the thought trail off.

I nodded, and Richard's hand tightened on mine. Jean-Claude's hand was strangely quiet in mine. "You do realize, *ma petite,* that this new . . ." he hesitated, "willingness, may be a by-product of joining the marks tonight. I don't wish you to later accuse us of trickery."

"I know what it is, and I don't care." I should have, but I didn't. It was like being drunk, or drugged, and even thinking that made no difference.

I was looking at Jean-Claude, and I saw him let out the breath he'd been holding. I felt Richard do the same. It was as if a great weight had been taken from both of them. And I knew that I was that burden. I'd try not to be a burden from now on. "Let's go get the leopards," I said.

Jean-Claude raised my hand to his mouth, brushing the knuckles across his lips. "And be gone from this place."

I nodded. "And be gone from this place," I said.

6

I'd been complaining to Jean-Claude for years that his decorating scheme was too monochromatic, but one look at Narcissus's bedroom and I knew I owed Jean-Claude an apology. The room was done in black, and I mean *black*. The walls, the hardwood floor, the drawn drapes against one wall, the bed. The only color in the room was the silver chains and the silver-colored implements hanging from the wall. The color of the steel seemed to accentuate the blackness rather than relieve it. Chains dangled from the ceiling above the huge bed. It was bigger than king-sized. The only term that came to mind was *orgy-sized*. The bed was four-postered, with the largest, heaviest, darkest wood I'd ever seen. More chains dangled from the four posts, set in heavy permanent rings. If I'd been on a date, I'd have turned and run for it. But this wasn't a date, and in we all trooped.

My understanding about most people who were into D and S was that their bedrooms were separate from their "dungeons." Nearby perhaps, but not the same room. You needed somewhere to go to actually sleep. Maybe Narcissus just never rested from the fun and games.

There was a door in the opposite wall, and the drapes were drawn over the middle of one wall. Maybe his real bed was behind door number two or the drapes. I hoped so.

The only chair in the room had straps attached to it, so Narcissus offered us the bed to sit on. I don't know if I would have sat down or not, but first Jean-Claude, then Richard did. Jean-Claude settled against the black bedspread as he did everything, with grace, settling his body against the pillows as if he felt utterly comfortable. But it was Richard who surprised me. I expected to see in him some of the discomfort I felt about the room, but he didn't seem in the least uncomfortable. In fact, I realized for the first time, that the heavy leather cuffs at his wrists and the collar at his throat had metal hooks in them, so they could be attached to chains or a leash. He'd probably worn them so he could blend into the club scene, as I'd worn the boots. But . . . but I could feel that he was calm about the room and everything in it. I wasn't.

I looked at Jean-Claude and Richard and knew I'd decided to sleep with both of them tonight, however we arranged it. But seeing them on the bed in the middle of all this, watching them at home in it, made me wonder about my decision. It made me think that maybe, after all this time, I still didn't know what I was getting myself into.

Asher was wandering the room looking at the things on the wall. I couldn't read him like I could read the others, but he, too, seemed unruffled, and I didn't think it was an act. Narcissus had swept into the room with Ajax at his back. He'd agreed to leave everyone else in the hallway, or downstairs, in exchange for us leaving our extra wolves outside the room. I guess for true privacy you did need less than a double-digit worth of people in a room.

Richard held his hand out to me. "It's okay, Anita. Nothing in this room can hurt you without your permission, and you're not going to give that." That wasn't exactly the comforting comment I'd wanted, but I guess it was the truth. I used to believe that truth was good, but I'd begun to realize that it is neither good, nor bad. It's just the truth. Life had been simpler when I believed in black and white absolutes.

I took his hand and let him draw me to the bed, between Jean-Claude and himself. Well, Narcissus had already made a play for Jean-Claude, so I guess we needed to make the hands-off point. But it still bothered me that Richard put me between them, not simply beside him. The warm, fuzzy feel-

ing I'd had from the marriage of the marks seemed to be
receding at an alarming rate. Magic does that sometimes.

I felt stiff and uncomfortable on the black bed between
my two men. "What is wrong, *ma petite*? You are suddenly
very tense."

I looked at Jean-Claude, raising my eyebrows. "Am I the
only one here that doesn't like this room?"

"Jean-Claude liked this room very much, once," Narcissus
said.

I turned and looked at the werehyena as he paced the room
in his stocking feet. "What do you mean?" I asked.

Jean-Claude answered, "Once, I submitted to unwanted
advances because I was told to do so. But those days are
past."

I stared at him, and he wouldn't meet my gaze. His eyes
were all for Narcissus, as the other man paced around the
bed.

"I don't remember you being unwilling," Narcissus said.
He leaned against the far post of the bed.

"I learned long ago to make a virtue of necessity," Jean-
Claude said. "Besides, Nikolaos, the old Master of the City,
sent me to you. You remember how she was, Narcissus. Refusal of an order was not allowed."

I'd had the horror of meeting Nikolaos personally. She had
been very, very scary.

"So I was an unpleasant duty." He sounded angry.

Jean-Claude shook his head. "Your body is pleasant, Narcissus. What you like doing with your lovers, if they can take
the damage, is not . . ." Jean-Claude looked down as if
searching for the right word, then raised his midnight blue
eyes to Narcissus, and I saw the effect that his gaze had on
the shapeshifter. Narcissus looked like he'd been hit between
the eyes with a hammer—a handsome, charming hammer.

"Is not *what*?" Narcissus asked, his voice hoarse.

"Is not to my taste," Jean-Claude said. "Besides, I must
not have pleased you very much, for you did not do what
my late master wished you to do."

I was the reason that Nikolaos was the *late* Master of the
City. She'd been trying to kill me, and I'd gotten lucky. She
was dead, I wasn't. And now Jean-Claude got to be Master
of the City. I hadn't planned that. How much of it Jean-

Claude had planned was still up for debate. It is not just prejudice on my part that makes me trust him less than Richard.

Narcissus put one knee on the bed, one hand still around the bedpost. "You pleased me very much." The look on his face was too intimate. They should have been alone for this conversation. But, then again, watching the way Narcissus looked at Jean-Claude, maybe that wouldn't have been such a great idea. From Jean-Claude all I sensed was a desire to sooth any injured feelings. But I was betting if I could peek inside Narcissus's head I'd find a different kind of desire.

"Nikolaos thought I failed her and punished me for it."

"I could not ally myself with her—not even for you as my permanent toy."

Jean-Claude raised an eyebrow at that. "I do not remember that being part of the deal."

"When I first told her *no,* she sweetened the offer." Narcissus crawled onto the bed. He stayed crouched on all fours, as if he were expecting someone to come up behind him.

"In what way did she sweeten the offer?"

Narcissus started to crawl across the bed, slowly, his knees catching on the hem of his dress as he moved. "She offered you to me for always, to do with as I wished."

A thrill of terror ran through me from my toes to the top of my head. It took me a second to realize it wasn't my fear. Richard and I both turned to Jean-Claude. His face showed nothing. It was his usual polite, attractive, almost bored mask. But we could both feel the cold, screaming terror in his mind at the thought of how close he'd come to being Narcissus's permanent . . . guest.

It filled him with a fear that was larger than the shapeshifter. Images flashed through my mind, memories. Chained on my stomach on rough wood, the sound of a whip going back, the shock of it biting into my skin, and the knowledge that it was only the first blow. The wave of utter despair that followed that memory left me blinking back tears. I had a confused image of being tied to a wall, with a hand rotted to green pus caressing my body. Then the images stopped abruptly, like someone had thrown a switch. But the body the hand had been traveling down had been male. They were Jean-Claude's memories, not mine. He'd been projecting his memories on me and when he realized it, he'd blocked it.

I looked at him and couldn't keep the horror out of my
eyes. My hair hid my face from Narcissus, and I was glad
because I couldn't be blasé about what I'd just seen. Jean-
Claude didn't look at me but kept his eyes on Narcissus. I
was trying not to cry, and Jean-Claude's face betrayed nothing.

Jean-Claude hadn't been remembering Narcissus's abuse,
but others, many, countless others. It wasn't the pain I carried
away from the memories, but the despair. The thought that
I . . . no, he. He had not owned his own body. He had never
been a prostitute, or rather, he had never traded sex for
money. But for power, the whim of whoever was his current
master, and strangely for safety, he had traded sex for centuries. I'd known that, but I'd pictured him as the seducer.
What I'd just seen had nothing to do with seduction.

A small sound came from Richard, and I turned to him.
His eyes were shiny with unshed tears, and he had the same
look of numb horror that I felt on my own face. We looked
at each other for a long frozen moment, then a tear trickled
down his face a second before a hot line of tears eased down
my own.

He reached for my hand and I took it. And we both turned
to Jean-Claude. He was still watching, even talking, though
I hadn't heard any of it, with Narcissus. The other man had
crawled all the way across that huge bed to be within touching distance of us all. But it wasn't *us all* that he wanted to
touch.

"Sweet, sweet, Jean-Claude, I thought I had forgotten you,
but seeing you tonight on the floor with the two of them
made me remember." He reached out toward Jean-Claude,
and Richard grabbed his wrist.

"Don't touch him. Don't ever touch him again."

Narcissus looked from Jean-Claude to Richard and finally
back to Richard. "Such possessiveness, it must be true love."
I had a ringside seat and watched the muscles in Richard's
hands and forearm tense as he squeezed that dainty wrist.

Narcissus laughed, voice shaky, but not with pain. "Such
strength, such passion, would he crush my wrist just for trying to touch your hair?" His voice held amusement and what
I finally realized was excitement. Richard touching him,

threatening him, hurting him. . . . He was enjoying it.

I felt Richard realize it, too, but he didn't let go. Instead he jerked the other man off balance until he fell against his body. Narcissus made a small surprised sound. Richard kept one hand on his wrist, and he put the other to the man's neck. Not squeezing, just there, large and dark against Narcissus's pale skin.

The bodyguard, Ajax, had moved away from the wall, and Asher had moved to meet him. Things could go very bad, very quickly here. It was usually me that lost my temper and made things worse, not Richard.

Narcissus had to sense rather than see the movement, because Richard had him facing away from the rest of the room. "It's alright, Ajax, it's alright. Richard is not hurting me." Then Richard did something that made Narcissus's breath stop in his throat and come out harsh. "You may crush my wrist, if it's foreplay, but if it's not, then my people will kill you, all of you." His words were reasonable, his tone was not. You could hear the pain in his voice, but there was also anticipation, as if whichever way Richard answered, it would excite him.

Jean-Claude spoke, "Do not give him an excuse to have us at his mercy, *mon ami.* We are in his territory tonight, his guests. We owe him a guest's duty to his host, as long as he does not forfeit that right."

I wasn't a hundred percent sure what a guest's duties to his host were, but I was willing to bet that crushing their limbs wasn't among them. I touched Richard's shoulder, and he jumped. Narcissus made a small protesting sound, as if Richard had involuntarily tightened his grip.

"Jean-Claude's right, Richard."

"Anita councils you to temperance, Richard, and she is one of the least temperate people I have ever known." Jean-Claude moved forward, laying his hand on Richard's other shoulder, so we both touched him. "Besides, *mon ami,* hurting this one will not undo the harm already done. No drop of blood less will have been spilt; no pound of flesh less will have been lost; no humiliation will have been stopped. It is over, memories cannot harm us."

For the first time I wondered if Richard and I had gotten the same memories in that flash of shared insight. What I'd

seen had been horrible, but it hadn't affected me like it had
him. Maybe it was a guy thing. Maybe a white, Anglo-Saxon,
upper-middle-class male like Richard would take memories
of being abused and raped harder than I would. I was a
woman. I knew things like that could happen to me. Maybe
he had never thought they could happen to him.

Richard spoke low, his voice fallen to a rolling growl, as
if his beast lurked just behind that handsome throat. "Never
touch him again, Narcissus, or we'll finish this." Then Richard slowly, carefully, slid his hands away from Narcissus. I
expected him to scoot away, clutching his injured wrist, but
I underestimated him, or maybe overestimated him.

Narcissus did cradle his wrist, but he stayed pressed
against Richard's body. "You've torn ligaments in my wrist.
They take longer to heal than bone."

"I know," Richard said softly. The level of anger in those
two words made me flinch.

"With a thought I can tell my men to leave her wereleopards to the mercy of their captors."

Richard glanced at Jean-Claude, who nodded. "Narcissus
can contact his . . . men mind-to-mind."

Richard put his hands on Narcissus's shoulders, I think to
push him away, but Narcissus said, "You've revoked your
safe conduct by injuring me against my will."

Richard froze, and I could see the tension in his back, feel
the sudden uncertainty.

"What is he talking about?" I asked. I wasn't even sure
who I was asking.

"Narcissus has a small army of werehyenas within this
building and on the surrounding buildings as guards," Jean-
Claude said.

"If the werehyenas are so powerful, then why doesn't
everyone talk about them in the same breath with the wolves
and the rats?" I asked.

"Because Narcissus prefers to be the power behind the
throne, *ma petite*. It means that the other shapeshifters are
constantly currying his favor with gifts."

"Like Nikoloas used you," I said.

He nodded.

I looked at Richard. "What have you been giving him?"

Richard eased away from Narcissus. "Nothing."

Narcissus turned on the bed, still cradling his wrist. "That's about to change."

"I don't think so," Richard said.

"Marcus and Raina had an arrangement with me. They and the rats dictated that my hyenas could never rise above fifty in number. To make this happen they used gifts, not threats."

"The threat was always there," Richard said. "War between you, us, and the rats, with you on the losing side."

Narcissus shrugged. "Perhaps, but have you not wondered what I've been doing since Marcus died and you took over? I wondered when the gifts would start arriving, but instead all gifts stopped, even the ones I'd begun to count on." He looked at me, then. "Some of those gifts were yours to give, Nimir-Ra."

I must have looked as confused as I felt, because Jean-Claude said, "The wereleopards."

"Yes, Gabriel, their old alpha, was a dear, dear friend of mine," Narcissus said.

Since I'd killed Gabriel, I didn't like the way the conversation was going. "You mean that Gabriel gave some of the wereleopards to you?"

Narcissus's smile made me shiver. "All of them have spent time in my care, except Nathaniel." His smile faded. "I assumed Gabriel kept Nathaniel to himself because he was his personal favorite, but now that you've told me what Nathaniel is, I know that wasn't it." Narcissus leaned forward on his knees. "Gabriel was afraid to give me Nathaniel, afraid of what we might do together."

I swallowed hard. "You covered your reaction really well when I told you."

"I'm an accomplished liar, Anita. Best remember that." He looked up at Richard. "How long has it been since Marcus's death, a little over a year? When the gifts stopped coming, I assumed the pact was at an end."

"What are you saying?" Richard asked.

"There are over four hundred werehyenas now; some new, some recruited from out of state. But we rival the wererats and werewolves now. You will have to negotiate with us as equals instead of peons."

Richard started to say, "What do you . . ."

Jean-Claude interrupted, "Let us come to terms." I felt the

fear that was behind his calm words, and so did Richard.
You did not ask a sexual sadist what he wanted. You offered
what you were willing to give up.

Narcissus looked at Richard. "Are they Jean-Claude's
wolves now, Richard? Do you share your kingship?" The
tone was mocking.

"I am Ulfric, and I will set the terms, no one else." But his
voice was cautious, the temper slowed. I'd never seen Richard
like this, and I wasn't sure I liked the change. He was reacting
more like me. As I thought of it, I wondered . . . I channeled
some of his beast, some of Jean-Claude's hunger, what did
they gain from me?

"You know what I want," Narcissus said.

"You would be wise not to ask for it," Jean-Claude said.

"If I cannot have you, Jean-Claude, then perhaps to watch
the three of you make love on my bed would be enough to
wash this insult clean between us."

Richard and I said together, "No."

He looked at us, and there was something unpleasant in
his eyes. "Then give me Nathaniel."

"No," I said.

"For one evening."

"No."

"For an hour," he said.

I shook my head.

"One of the other leopards?"

"I won't give you any of my people."

He looked at Richard. "And you, Ulfric, will you give me
one of your wolves?"

"You know the answer, Narcissus," Richard said.

"Then what would you offer me, Ulfric?"

"Name something I'm willing to give."

Narcissus smiled, and I had a sense of Ajax and Asher
circling each other as they felt the tension rising. "I want to
be included in the conferences that run the shapeshifter community in this town."

Richard nodded. "Fine. Rafael and I thought you had no
interest in politics, or you would already have been asked."

"The Rat King does not know my heart, nor do the
wolves."

Richard stood. "Anita needs to go to her people."

Narcissus smiled and shook his head. "Oh, no, Ulfric, it is not that easy."

Richard frowned. "You're to be included in decision making. That's what you wanted."

"But I still want gifts."

"No gifts pass between the rats and the wolves. We are allies. If you wish to be an ally then there will be no gifts, except that we will come to your aid when you need us."

Narcissus shook his head again. "I do not wish to be allies, to be dragged into every squabble between animals that do not concern me. No, Ulfric, you mistake me. I wish to be included in the conferences that set policy. But I do not wish to tie myself to anyone and be dragged into a war that is not of my own making."

"Then what are you asking?" Richard said.

"Gifts."

"Bribes, you mean," Richard said.

Narcissus shrugged. "Call it what you will."

"No," Richard said.

I felt Jean-Claude tense a moment before Richard said it. *"Mon ami . . ."*

"No," Richard said and turned to Jean-Claude. "Even if he could kill us all, which I doubt, my wolves, your vampires, they would rain down on this club and take it apart brick by brick. He won't risk that. Narcissus is a cautious leader. I learned from watching him deal with Marcus. He puts his own safety and comfort above all else."

"The comfort and safety of my people above all else," Narcissus said. He looked at me. "What of you, Nimir-Ra, how confident do you feel? Do you think if I had my people kill your kittens that the werewolves and vampires would lift a finger to avenge them?"

"You forget, Narcissus, she's also my lupa, my mate. The wolves will defend who she tells them to defend."

"Ah, yes, the human lupa, the human leopard queen. But not really human, is she?"

I met his gaze and said, "I need to go collect my leopards. Thanks for the hospitality." I pushed to my feet and stood beside Richard.

Narcissus looked at Jean-Claude, who still lounged on the bed. "Are they really such children?" he asked him.

Jean-Claude gave a graceful shrug. "They are not like us, Narcissus. They still believe in right and wrong. And rules."

"Then let me teach them a new rule." He stared up at us, still kneeling on the bed, still wearing the black lace dress, and suddenly his power burst out before him in lines of heat. It slammed into my body like a giant hand, nearly staggering me. Richard reached out to steady me, and the moment we touched, his beast jumped between us, in a rush of warmth that raced through my body in goose bumps and shivers. Richard's body shuddered, and I felt his breath, our breath, catch. That otherworldly power curled between us, and for the first time I realized that the power came both ways. I'd thought what was inside me was an echo of Richard's beast, but it was more than that. Maybe it would have been different if I hadn't separated myself from him for so long. But now the power that had once been his was mine. The warmth spilled between us like two streams converging into a river, two scalding streams that spilled into a river that boiled over my skin. It was so hot that I half expected my skin to peel away and reveal the beast underneath.

"If she shifts, then my men are free to enter this fight." Narcissus's voice was shocking. I think I'd forgotten he was there, forgotten everything but the hot, hot power flowing between Richard and me. Narcissus's face began to grow longer. It was like watching sticks move behind clay.

Richard ran his hand just in front of my body, caressing the power that flowed off of my skin. There was a look of soft wonderment on his face. "She won't shift. You have my word," Richard said.

"Good enough. You always keep your word. I may be a sadist and a masochist, but I am still Oba of this clan." His voice had become a strange high-pitched growl. "You have insulted me and, through me, all that is mine." Claws slid out from his small fingers until he raised curved paws, not hands at all.

Jean-Claude came to stand beside us. "Come, *ma petite*, let them have room to maneuver." He touched my hand, and that scalding power poured from my skin to his. He collapsed to his knees, hand still pressed against my skin, as if the heat had welded it in place.

I knelt by him, and his eyes raised, drowning blue, the

pupil lost in a rush of power, but not his power. He opened his mouth to speak, but no sound came out. He stared at me, and, judging by the look on his face, he felt lost, over-whelmed.

"What's wrong?" Asher asked from across the room, still facing Ajax.

"I'm not sure," I said.

"He seems in pain," Narcissus said. It made me glance up at him. Except for his face and hands, he was still in human form. The really powerful alphas could do that, partial changes.

"The power spills over him," Richard said, and his voice held that edge of growl. His throat was hidden behind the leather collar, but I knew if I could see it, that the skin would be smooth and perfect. His voice could howl from his mouth like a dog's without any change in his appearance.

"But he is a vampire," Narcissus said. "The power of the wolves should be closed to him."

"The wolf is his animal to call," Richard said.

I looked into Jean-Claude's face from inches away, watched him struggle through the hot, scalding power and knew why he wasn't dealing well with it. This was primal energy, the life and beat of the earth under our feet, the rush of wind in the trees, the stuff of life. And Jean-Claude for all that he walked and talked and flirted wasn't alive.

Richard knelt beside us, and Jean-Claude let out a low moan, half-collapsing against me. "Jean-Claude!"

Richard rolled him over into his arms, and Jean-Claude's spine bowed, his breath coming in ragged gasps.

Narcissus was above us on the bed. "What's wrong with him?"

"I don't know," Richard said.

I put a hand on Jean-Claude's throat. The pulse wasn't just racing, it was beating like a caged thing. I tried to use the ability I had to sense vampires, but all I could feel was the heat of the beast. There was nothing cold or dead in the circle of our arms.

"Lay him on the floor, Richard."

He looked at me.

"Do it!"

He laid Jean-Claude gently on the floor, hand still touching his shoulder.

"Move away from him." I did what I asked of Richard, standing and moving around the vampire, pushing Richard back with my body until Jean-Claude lay alone beside the bed.

Narcissus's body had re-formed, until he was the graceful man we'd met downstairs. He'd moved off the bed without being told, but moved around so he could still watch.

Jean-Claude rolled slowly onto his side, and moved his head to stare at us. He licked his lips and tried twice before he could speak. "What have you done to me?"

Richard and I still stood in a cocoon of heat. His hands brushed my arms, and I shuddered against him. His arms locked around my waist, and the more of our bodies that touched the more heat rose around us, until I thought the very air should tremble like the heat of a summer's day off a tar road.

"Shared Richard's power with you," I said.

"No," Jean-Claude said, and he rose slowly to sit, propped heavily on his arms. "Not just Richard, but you, *ma petite,* you. Richard and I have shared much, but it never did this. You are the bridge between the two worlds."

Asher spoke, "She bridges life and death."

Jean-Claude looked up at him sharply, a harsh look on his face. *"Exactement."*

Narcissus spoke, "I knew Marcus and Raina could share their power, their beasts, but Anita is not a werewolf. You should not be able to share your beast with each other, wolf to leopard."

"I'm not a wereleopard," I said.

"Me thinks the lady doth protest too much," Narcissus said.

"Or wereanimal to vampire," Asher said.

I looked at Asher. "Don't *you* start."

He smiled at me. "I know that you are not a true shapeshifter, but your . . . magic has changed because of the addition of Richard. There is something about you, that if I did not know better, I would say you were indeed one of them."

"Richard said the wolf is Jean-Claude's animal to call," Narcissus said.

"That doesn't explain this," Asher said. He knelt by Jean-Claude, reaching toward him.

Jean-Claude caught his hand before it could touch his face, and Asher jerked back. "You're hot to the touch. Not just warm, hot."

"It is like the rush after we feed, but more . . . more alive." He gazed up at us, and his eyes were still drowning blue. "Go save your leopards, *ma petite,* and let us retire before dawn. I want to see how hot," he took a deep breath, and I knew he was drawing in the scent of us, "this power will grow."

"It is all very impressive," Narcissus said, "but I will have my pound of flesh."

"You're beginning to get on my nerves," I said.

He smiled. "Be that as it may, I still have a right to ask for the insult to be avenged."

I looked at Richard. He nodded. I sighed. "You know it's usually me that gets us into this kind of trouble."

"We're not in trouble yet," Richard said. "Narcissus is grandstanding. Why do you think I didn't change?" He stared at the smaller man.

Narcissus smiled. "And here I thought you were just decorative muscle standing behind Marcus."

"You won't fight unless you run out of options, Narcissus, so no more games." There was a coldness in Richard's voice, a firmness that could not be crossed or reasoned with. Again it echoed me more than him. Just how tough had the last few months been on him and his wolves? There's only a few things that will harden you this fast. Death of those close to you; police work; or combat where people are actually dying around you. In civilian life, Richard was a junior high science teacher, so it wasn't police work. I think someone would have mentioned if he'd lost family members. That left combat. How many challengers had he fought? How many had he killed? Who had died?

I shook my head to clear away the thoughts. One problem at a time. "You can't have any of us, or our people, Narcissus. You're not going to start a war over the refusal, so where does that leave us?"

"I will take my men out of the room with your cats, Anita. I will do that." He came to stand in front of me, his back to the bedpost, one hand playing with the chains attached to it, making the metal jingle. "The . . . people that have them are not terribly creative, but they have a certain raw talent for pain." He stared at me with human eyes again.

"What do you want, Narcissus?" Richard said.

He wrapped the chain around one wrist over and over. "Something worth having, Richard, *someone* worth having."

Asher said, "Do you merely want someone to dominate, or are you interested in being dominated?"

Narcissus looked back at him. "Why?"

"Answer the question truthfully, Narcissus," Jean-Claude said. "You may find it worthwhile."

Narcissus looked from one vampire to the other, then back to Asher, standing there in his brown leather outfit. "I prefer to dominate, but with the right person I'll allow myself to be topped."

Asher walked toward us, making his tall, slender body sway. "I'll top you."

"You do not have to do this," Jean-Claude said.

"Don't do it, Asher," I said.

"We'll find another way," Richard said.

Asher looked at us with those pale, pale blue eyes. "I thought you'd be happy, Jean-Claude. I've finally agreed to take a lover. Isn't that what you wanted me to do?" His voice was mild, but the mockery came through just the same, the bitterness.

"I have offered you nearly all in my power, and you have refused all. Why him? Why now?" Jean-Claude got to his knees, and I offered him a hand up, not a hundred percent sure that I should.

He looked at the offered hand.

"If you think it's safe," I said.

He wrapped his hand around mine, and the power flowed in a burning rush down my hand over his, down his arm, and I felt it hit his heart like a blow. He closed his eyes, swayed for a second, then looked at me. "It was unexpected the first time." He started to stand, and Richard went to his other side, so that we held him between us.

"I don't know if this is good for you, or not," I said.

"You fill me with life, *ma petite*. You and Richard. How can it be bad?"

I didn't say the obvious, but I thought it really hard. If you could fill the walking dead with life, should you? And if you did, what would happen to that walking dead? So much of what we were doing between us magically had never been done before, or only once before. Unfortunately we'd had to kill the other triumvirate that consisted of a vamp, a werewolf, and a necromancer. They'd been trying to kill us, but still, they might have been able to answer questions that no one else could have answered. Now we were just swinging in the dark, hoping we didn't hurt each other.

"Look at you, Jean-Claude, between them like a candle with two wicks. You will burn yourself up," Asher said.

"That is my concern."

"Yes, and what I do is mine. You ask, why him? why now? First, you need me. Which of the three of you would be willing to do this?" Asher moved around Narcissus as if he weren't there, eyes on Jean-Claude, on us. "Oh, I know that you could have topped him. You can do it when you want, and make a virtue of necessity, but he's had you beneath him, and nothing less will satisfy him now." He stood close enough that the energy swirled outward, over him like a lip of hot ocean water. His breath came out in a shuddering sigh. *"Mon Dieu!"* He stepped back until his legs touched the bed, then he sat down on the black sheets. His brown leather didn't match as well as the rest of us had.

"Such power, Jean-Claude, and yet none of you wishes to pay the price for Richard's temper tantrum. But I will pay that price."

"You know my rule, Asher. I never ask of others what I'm not willing to do myself," I said.

He looked at me curiously, face unreadable behind the mask, except for his eyes. "Are you volunteering?"

I shook my head. "No. But you don't have to do this. We will find another way."

"And what if I want to do it?" he asked.

I looked at him for a second, then shrugged. "I don't know what to say to that."

"It disturbs you that I might want to do this, doesn't it?" His eyes were intense.

"Yes," I said.

That intense gaze moved past me to Jean-Claude. "It bothers him, too. He wonders if I am ruined and all that is left for me is pain."

"You once told me that everything worked. That you were scarred, but . . . functional," I said.

He blinked and looked at me. "Did I? Well, a man does not like to admit such things to a pretty woman. Or to a handsome man." He looked up at us, but the only person he was really looking at was Jean-Claude. "I will pay the toll for our handsome Monsieur Zeeman's display of strength. But I will not be the whipping boy. Not this time."

Not ever again, hung heavy in the air, unsaid, but there all the same. Asher had had two hundred years of being at the mercy of the people who had given Jean-Claude the memories that Richard and I had flashed on. Two centuries more of that kind of care and torment. When Asher had first come to us he'd been cruel occasionally. I thought we'd cured of him of it. But watching the look in his eyes now, I knew we hadn't.

"And do you know the best part of all?" Asher asked.

Jean-Claude just shook his head.

"It will cause you pain to think of me with Narcissus. And even after I am with him, he will still not answer the question you have been wanting, so desperately, to have answered."

Jean-Claude stiffened, hand tightening on mine. I felt him slam his own shields into place, keeping us out of what he was thinking, feeling, at that moment. The warm, roiling power between us began to dissipate. Jean-Claude had made himself part of our circuit. Now he was shutting us down, though I didn't think it was on purpose. He just couldn't shield himself from us and keep the flow going.

His voice came out calm, his usual bored, yet cultured, tone, "How can you be so sure that he will not talk?"

"I can be sure of what I do. And I will not give him the answer you want."

"What answer?" I asked. "What are you guys talking about?"

The two vampires looked at each other. "Ask Jean-Claude," Asher said.

I looked at Jean-Claude, but he was staring at Asher. In a way the rest of us were superfluous, an audience for a show that didn't need one.

"You're being petty, Asher," Richard said.

The vampire's gaze moved to the man on my other side, and the anger in those eyes made the blue spill across the pupils in a frosted gleam. He looked blind. "Have I not earned the right to be petty, Richard?"

Richard shook his head. "Just tell him the truth."

"There are three people in his power that I would strip for, that I would allow to touch me, and answer that so important question." He stood in one graceful movement, like a liquid puppet on strings. He stepped close enough for the power to spill around him, bringing his breath shuddering from his lips. The power recognized him, flared stronger, as if he could act as our third, if we weren't careful. Did the power just need a vampire, and not specifically Jean-Claude? Richard shut down his side of the power, clanging a shield in place that made me think of metal, strong and solid, uncompromising.

Asher caressed the air just above Richard's arm and had to step away, rubbing his hands on his arms. "The power fades." He shook himself like a dog coming out of water. "If you would say *yes,* his torment could end."

I frowned at them both, not sure I was following the conversation, not sure I wanted to.

Asher turned those pale, drowning eyes to me. "Or, our fair Anita." He was already shaking his head. "But no, I know better than to ask. I have enjoyed shocking our so heterosexual Richard by my overtures. But Anita is not so easily teased." He came to stand in front of Jean-Claude. "And of course, if he wanted the answer badly enough he could do it himself."

Jean-Claude's face was at its most arrogant. Its most hidden. "You know why I do not."

Asher moved back to stand in front of me. "He refuses my bed, because he fears that you would . . . what is the American word . . . dump him, if you knew he were sleeping with a man. Would you?"

I had to swallow before I could answer. "Yeah."

Asher smiled, but not like he was happy, more like it had been a predictable answer. "Then I will pleasure myself here with Narcissus, and Jean-Claude will still not know if I stay because I have become a lover of such things, or because this type of love is all that is left for me."

"I haven't agreed to this," Narcissus said. "Before I take second—no *fourth* choice—let me see what I'm buying."

Asher stood, turning so that his left side was toward the werehyena. He unzipped the mask and lifted it over his head. We were standing enough to one side so that I could see that perfect profile. His golden hair—and I mean golden—was braided along the back of his head so that nothing interfered with the view. I was used to looking at Asher through a film of hair. Without it, the lines of his face were like sculpture, something so smooth and lovely that you wanted to touch it, trace the movement of it with your hands, layer it with kisses. Even after the little show he'd put on, he was still beautiful. Nothing seemed to change that when I looked at Asher.

"Very nice," Narcissus said, "very, very nice, but I have many beautiful men at my beck and call. Perhaps not as beautiful, but still . . ."

Asher turned to face the man. Whatever Narcissus was about to say died in his throat. The right side of Asher's face looked like melted candle wax. The scars didn't start until well away from the midline of his face. It was as if his torturers all those centuries ago had wanted him to have enough left to remember the perfection he'd once been. His eyes were still golden-lashed, his nose perfect, his mouth full and kissable, but the rest. . . . The rest was scarred. Not ruined, not spoiled, but scarred.

I remembered Asher's smooth perfection, the feel of that perfect body rubbing against mine. Not my memories. I had never seen Asher nude. I had never touched him that way. But Jean-Claude had, about two hundred years ago. It made it impossible for me to look at Asher with unprejudiced eyes, because I remembered being in love with him, in fact, was still a little in love with him. Which meant that Jean-Claude was still a little in love with him. My personal life just can't get more complicated.

Narcissus drew a shuddering breath and said in a voice gone hoarse, eyes wide, "Oh, my."

Asher threw the hood on the bed and began to unzip the front of the leather shirt, very slowly. I'd seen his chest before and knew that it was much worse than his face. The right side of his chest was carved with deep runnels, the skin hard to the touch. The left side, like his face, still had that angelic beauty that had attracted the vampires to him long ago.

When the zipper was halfway down his body, baring his chest and upper stomach, Narcissus had to sit down on the bed as if his legs wouldn't hold him.

"I think, Narcissus," Jean-Claude said, "that after tonight you will owe us a favor." His voice was empty when he said it, devoid of anything. It was the voice he used when he was at his most careful, or his most pained.

Asher asked in a careful voice that didn't quite match the striptease he was doing, "What level of pain does Narcissus enjoy straight—how do you say—out of the box?"

"Rough," Jean-Claude said. "He can control his desire and not step outside the bounds of his submissive, but if he is to be topped, then rough, very rough. You do not need a warming up period for this one." Jean-Claude's voice was still empty.

Asher looked down at Narcissus. "Is that true? Do you like to start out with a . . . bang?" That last word was slow, seductive. One word, and it held worlds of promise within it.

Narcissus nodded slowly. "You can start with blood, if you've the balls for it."

"Most people have to work up to that for it to be pleasurable," Asher said.

"I don't," Narcissus said.

Asher finished unzipping and lowered the shirt off his arms, held it in his hands for a moment, then struck out with a movement so quick it was only an after-image blur. He slapped Narcissus across the face with the heavy zipper once, twice, three times, until blood showed at the corner of his mouth and his eyes looked unfocused.

I was so startled by all of it that I think I forgot to breathe. All I could do was stare. Jean-Claude had gone very still between Richard and me. It wasn't the utter stillness that he was capable of, that all the old masters were capable of, and I realized why. He couldn't sink into that black stillness of death with the lingering touch of the "life" we'd pumped through him.

Narcissus used the tip of his tongue to taste the blood on his mouth. "I am an accomplished liar, but I always give fair trade." He was suddenly more serious than he had been, as if the flippant tease was just a mask and underneath was a more solemn, thinking, person. When he looked up, there was a person in his eyes that I knew was dangerous. The flirt was real, too, but it was partially camouflage to make everyone underestimate him. Looking into his eyes, I knew that to underestimate him would be a very bad thing.

He turned those newly serious eyes to Asher. "For this, I will owe you a favor, but only one favor, not three."

Asher reached up and undid his hair, letting the heavy sparkling waves fall around his face. He stared down at the smaller man, and I couldn't see the look he gave, but whatever it was, it made Narcissus look like a drowning man. "I am only worth one favor?" Asher said, "I think not."

Narcissus had to swallow twice before he could speak. "Perhaps more." He turned and looked at us, and his eyes were still raw, real. "Go, save your wereleopards, whoever they belong to. But know this, the ones inside are new to our community. They do not know our rules, and their own rules seem harsh by comparison."

"You warn us, Narcissus, thank you," Jean-Claude said.

"I think that this one would not like it if you were hurt, no matter how angry he is with you, Jean-Claude. I am about to let him bind me to this bed, or the wall, and do to me whatever he wishes."

"Whatever I wish?" Asher asked.

Narcissus's gaze flicked back to him. "No, not whatever, but until I use the safety word, yes." There was something almost childlike in the way he said the last, as if he were already thinking of what was to come, and not really concentrating on us.

"Safety word?" I asked.

Narcissus gazed at me. "If the pain grows too much, or if something is proposed that the slave does not want to do, you use the word agreed upon. Once the word is spoken the master must stop."

"But you'll be tied up, you won't be able to make him stop."

Narcissus's eyes were drowning, drowning in things that

I didn't understand, and didn't want to. "It is both the trust and the element of uncertainty that makes the event, Anita."

"You trust that he'll stop when you say stop, but you like the thought that he might not stop, that he might just keep going," Richard said.

It made me stare at him, but I caught Narcissus's nod.

"Am I the only one in this room that doesn't understand how this game is played?"

"Remember, Anita," Richard said, "I was a virgin until Raina got me. She was my first lover, and her tastes ran . . . to the exotic."

Narcissus laughed then. "A virgin in Raina's hands, what a frightening image. Even I wouldn't let her top me, because you could see it in her eyes."

"See what?" I asked.

"That she had no stopping point."

Having almost been a star in one of her little bedroom dramas, saved only by the fact that I'd killed her first, I had to agree.

"Raina liked it better if you didn't want to do it," Richard said. "She was a sexual sadist, not a dominant. It took me a long time to realize how big a difference there was between the two."

I looked at his face, but he was safe behind his shields, I couldn't read him. He and Jean-Claude had more practice at shielding than I did. But, frankly, I didn't want to know what was behind the lost look on Richard's face. I realized with a start that I had Jean-Claude's memories but not Richard's. It had never occurred to me to ask why that was. But later, later. Right now I wanted to be out of this room. "I want out of here."

Jean-Claude pulled gently away from both of us to stand on his own. "Yes, the night is running out, and we have much to do."

I didn't look at him, or Richard. I'd pretty much promised that if dawn stayed at bay we'd have sex tonight. But somehow staring at Asher's naked back, with Narcissus gazing up at him with a look somewhere between adoration and terror, I just wasn't in the mood anymore.

Dear Reader,

If this is the first time you've met Anita and the boys, welcome. Hope you enjoyed your short visit. If you'd like a longer visit, at least an overnighter or maybe a weekend, pick up *Narcissus in Chains*, a Berkley hardcover coming in October 2001. Take the phone off the hook and tell your friends you're tied up—with at least two men. Maybe more.

I don't think you'll be disappointed.

See you then—

LAURELL K. HAMILTON

COMING SOON IN HARDCOVER

NORA ROBERTS

MIDNIGHT BAYOU

PUTNAM